"The Brothers Ashkenazi is a novel that pulsates with life—

the life of the Jews in Poland from the 1880s to the rise of independent Poland. I. J. Singer has fashioned a panoramic drama of the rise and fall of a family against the background of tumultuous industrial Lodz. His characters are driven by elemental passions—love and lust, ambition and greed, jealousy and envy. Their personal lives are framed by the turbulent history of their times—the rise of the industrial era in Poland, the Tsarist Empire, the rush of secularism and radicalism into traditional Jewish life, the recurrence of strikes and pogroms, the succession of wars and revolutions.

"THE BROTHERS ASHKENAZI is a wonderful read. It is also much more: a kaleidoscopic recreation of a world that no longer exists. I. J. Singer has painted that world with the brushstrokes of realistic truth and breathed into it a living spirit. . . . If you want to understand something of that world before it disappeared in the smoke of the Holocaust, read THE BROTHERS ASHKENAZI."

—Lucy S. Dawidowicz

I. J. SINGER

THE BROTHERS ASHKENAZI

*A new translation from the Yiddish
by Joseph Singer*

Introduction by Irving Howe

BANTAM BOOKS
TORONTO · NEW YORK · LONDON · SYDNEY

55128

🖅

THE BROTHERS ASHKENAZI
*A Bantam Book | published in association with
Atheneum Publishers*

PRINTING HISTORY
The original Yiddish title for this work was Di brider Ashkenazi.
*Atheneum edition published November 1980
A Selection of Book-of-the-Month Club, February 1981
Bantam edition | December 1981*

ISBN 0–553–20105–0

Published simultaneously in the United States and Canada

Bantam Books are published by Bantam Books, Inc. Its trademark, consisting of the words "Bantam Books" and the por-
trayal of a rooster, is Registered in U.S. Patent and Trademark
Office and in other countries. Marca Registrada. Bantam
Books, Inc., 666 Fifth Avenue, New York, New York 10103.

PRINTED IN THE UNITED STATES OF AMERICA

0 9 8 7 6 5 4 3 2 1

Dedicated to
the Memory of My Son
Y A S H A

———————

Introduction

———

IRVING HOWE

There are two Singers in Yiddish literature and while both are very good, they sing in different keys. The elder brother, Israel Joshua Singer (1893–1944), was one of the few genuine novelists to write in Yiddish. The younger brother, Isaac Bashevis Singer, who won the Nobel Prize for literature in 1978, has become a prominent figure in American literary life through the frequent translation of his work from Yiddish into English. The younger Singer is strongest as a writer of short stories and novellas blending folk and grotesque motifs, though he has also tried his hand, not very successfully, at the full-scale social or family novel.

Each of these talented brothers has won an American following, at different cultural moments and for strikingly different reasons. When I. J. Singer was first published here in English translation during the thirties, his books—notably *The Brothers Ashkenazi* (1936)—gained a large popular success, appealing as they did to readers of traditional tastes, those who enjoy the sort of thick and leisurely family chronicle that dominated European literature at the turn of the century. For Yiddish writers, it should be stressed, this kind of novel did not come easily. The pioneer Yiddish "classicists" of the late nineteenth century—Mendele, Sholom Aleichem, Peretz—turned spontaneously to short fictions, as if seeking a modest form to go together with the narrow social range of the *shtetl* life that was their usual setting. Only with later Yiddish writers, those coming to prominence during the first few decades of this century, did the large-scale, many-layered "polyphonic" novel begin to flourish. And this, of course, was partly due to the increasing urbanization of the East European Jews, which, in turn, brought about a more complex latticing of classes than had been possible in the _shtetl_. It also brought about a new exposure to contemporary European culture, with its large variety of literary forms. The family chronicle or social novel in Yiddish, as _The Brothers Ashkenazi_ vividly demonstrates, is both sign and cause of the increasing "Europeanization" of Jewish life in Poland and Russia.

Intent upon portraying the historical changes that had created heavy Jewish concentrations in cities like Warsaw and Lodz, I. J. Singer built his work upon spacious architectural principles. He sought to compose novels with a multitude of characters, interwoven strands of plot, and social groups depicted as active and coherent social forces: novels such as we associate with the early Thomas Mann, Arnold Bennett, Jules Romains, and Roger Martin du Gard. Tremendously popular during the early years of the century, this sort of family chronicle took as its assumption the relative stability and "thereness" of bourgeois society, though with some of its keener practitioners, such as Mann and Martin du Gard, there was also a gathering awareness of conflict, disintegration, unnerving change. By focusing on a family as its basic unit, by placing in this family representatives of both the official outlook of society and the emerging tendencies to call into question the values of that society, such writers were able to concentrate—which is to say, dramatize—in one sweeping narrative what they took to be the central problems of the day. Stability and crisis could be pitted against one another within the perimeter of a family, often through the device of a struggle between brothers.

I. J. Singer mastered, as few Yiddish writers have, the problems of construction peculiar to this kind of novel: how to link and contrast parallel plots, how to balance clusters of characters against one another, how to bring together a large span of novelistic time with at least some moments of intensely realized detail. It's hard to say, and probably not very important, whether he modeled himself consciously on the European masters of the family chronicle or, because he was subject to parallel pressures and needs, developed on his own parallel strategies of composition. But what strikes one as especially interesting here is that Singer submitted himself, rather like the European novelists of the early twentieth century, to the _idea_ of history, the persuasion that overwhelms Dickens and Zola, Flaubert and Tolstoy that men are caught up by vast, often incomprehensible historical forces which shape and break them. I. J. Singer learned to think, that is, in terms of historical momentum and sweep; learned to see his characters as representative of public energies, agents of public causes. Quite as if he had gone to school with the European masters, or had learned their lessons outside of school, he came to see modern society as a complex organism with "a life of its own," a destiny superseding and sometimes canceling out the will of its individual members. He even came to recognize the extent to which historical events can be deeply irrational, a mere onrush of destructive impulses neither understood nor controlled.

For a Yiddish writer of sixty or seventy years ago, all this was decidedly new. It meant a struggle to master both an ambitious mode of narrative and an underlying complexity of social relations that could not easily be acquired within the limits of traditional Yiddish culture. Yet I. J. Singer's intense self-awareness that he was a *Yiddish* writer, or a Jew who wrote novels, also meant that he had to make some modifications in the scheme of the family chronicle. The Jewish past enters *The Brothers Ashkenazi* in a series of evocations that seem to be in contrast with the idea of historical dynamism, for that past bears an aura of fixity, of unrelenting stasis. More striking, *The Brothers Ashkenazi* ends rather bitterly with a tacit repudiation of the very idea of history that has served as its organizing principle; finally, suggests I. J. Singer, the Jews cannot expect much (or anything) good from the uproar of industrialism, revolution, and other modes of gentile action—finally, they are left with the perennial problem, or possibility, of being Jews. It's as if I. J. Singer had hitched a ride on a European vehicle and at the end decided he had to jump off, or acknowledged that he had been pushed off.

When the fiction of I. J. Singer first became popular in America some forty years ago, the social novel seemed very attractive to readers, including those who thought of the novel as a serious art form and not just a passing entertainment. Today I. J. Singer's work may appear a little old-fashioned—mistakenly so, I would argue—to young people brought up on the postmodernist writers.

It is precisely such young people who form a significant portion of the public that has responded enthusiastically to the younger Singer. This is a public composed of third-generation and semiassimilated Jews, as well as gentile literary fellow travelers, whose nostalgia or curiosity about Jewishness has its visible limits but who find in the author of *Satan in Goray* and *Shosha* a congenial voice. They are not entirely mistaken. Isaac Bashevis Singer brings together touches of esoteric Judaica, mostly from the cabalistic and Sabbatian traditions, and a playful sophisticated tone: the first requires no serious commitment from the reader, only a frisson of response, and the second allows for immediate familiarity. It is a rather odd mixture, but it speaks to cultivated American readers as the work of no other Yiddish writer can—at least for the moment. These are readers who take for granted the necessity, perhaps even desirability, of the disintegration of the traditional nineteenth-century novel and assume it to be a literary sign of some larger social disintegration. They have become, or been taught to be, impatient with books like *Buddenbrooks* or *The Old Wives' Tale* or *The Thibaults*. A certain misunderstanding, I would argue, is at work here between American readers and Isaac Bashevis Singer, a misunderstanding which for obvious reasons neither takes pains to remove. For while the admirers of the younger Singer are right in feeling that he is closer to them than any other Yiddish writer they are likely to encounter—closer in quizzical tone, in fondness for extreme states of being, in spiritual restlessness—still, the truth is that he is not quite the delightfully perverse modern voice some of his admirers take him to be. Despite his canniness and charm, the younger Singer goes his own way, and it is not along paths his admirers are likely to go.

We have here another example of the notorious instability of literary taste. It would be convenient to foreclose the matter by saying that I. J. Singer, the elder brother, is a premodernist writer and that I. B. Singer, the younger brother, is a modernist, or that the first drew his acclaim from middlebrow and the second from highbrow audiences; but that would be rather glib, even if with a shred of truth. For both Singers are serious writers, and the varying responses to their work have less to do with their intrinsic merits or qualities than with their imaginative relation to the Jewish tradition. I. J. Singer writes within the orbit of, even as he begins a withdrawal from, the moral values of Yiddish secular culture: humanist, rationalist, socially concerned. I. B. Singer has taken a step his older brother could not take. Though a master of Yiddish prose, he has cut himself off from the norms and styles of Yiddish culture, simultaneously moving backward to a pre-Enlightenment sensibility and forward to modernism.

What the generation of Yiddish writers contemporaneous with I. J. Singer sought most of all was to break away from the introspective themes and winding rhythms of *shtetl* writers like Mendele and Sholom Aleichem, to bring into Yiddish literature the worldly concerns and narrative sweep of the European novel, to project Jewish figures no longer merely passive and pious but now aggressively on the historical stage: capitalists, revolutionists, political leaders. A now-aging or perhaps already-gone generation of Yiddish readers was inclined to praise a writer like I. J. Singer as *universal*. To such readers, starting to find their way into Western life and culture, there could be no higher praise; to us, some decades later, things are decidedly less clear.

Somehow, whether directly or not, I. J. Singer absorbed the lesson of Turgenev and Flaubert that the novelist must keep himself strictly out of the events he renders, as if in literature he were an invisible hand somewhat like the one projected by Adam Smith in economics.* This assumption was no more congenial to the earlier Yiddish writers, the generation of Mendele and Sholom Aleichem, than laissez-faire was to the *shtetl* economy in which they grew up, for in a sense not true in more sophisticated cultures, the Yiddish writers had to be present in their fictions as stage managers, *raissoneurs,* ethical monitors, stand-ins for characters, and prompters for readers. The idea of "esthetic distance" was, for most of the late-nineteenth-century Yiddish writers, neither possible nor desirable. It is an idea that simply made no sense to a culture constantly in peril of destruction.

In the fiction of I. J. Singer, nevertheless, one is strongly aware of the kind of detachment—a tactical employment of a subject or milieu rather than a cultural submission to it—which is entirely familiar to recent Western literature. This, in part, is obviously a sign of the gradual secularization of the East European Jewish world. Yiddish writers of I. J. Singer's

---

* In an interview published in *Encounter*, February 1979, Isaac Bashevis Singer says:

> When I began to write myself, my brother encouraged me and he gave me certain rules for writing. He said: when you write tell a story, and don't try to explain the story. If you say that a boy fell in love with a girl you don't have to explain to the reader why a boy falls in love, the reader knows just as much as you do or more so. You tell him the story, and the explanations and interpretations he will make himself, or critics will do it for him. He had two words which he used: *images* and *sayings*. Sayings were for him essays, interpretations. He called sayings, *zugerts*. It means you just talk, you just say things. You don't paint a picture, or bring out an image. He said, leave the *zugerts* to the others. You tell them a story. Because you may know stories which they don't know—but you don't know more about life than they do. Although these rules were very simple it took me years to understand what he meant by image, what he meant by *zugerts* or sayings.

generation tried consciously to find literary models outside their
own tradition; they were weary of *shtetl* woes and *shtetl*
charms; they wanted a richer, more worldly literature than
their immediate predecessors could manage or saw any need for.
But there is more to it with the older Singer. One suspects
that the coolness, the somewhat clenched distance that are his
characteristic stance had a deeply personal source, the con-
sequence of a temperament somewhat rare in Yiddish literature. A good many of the characters, especially the central
one, Max, in *The Brothers Ashkenazi*, are inflamed, driven,
compulsive; they go through their lives with a red-eyed submission to imperatives beyond their grasp or even naming,
but Singer himself writes with a deeply skeptical tone. Or so,
at least, I read him. The passion of his characters is evoked,
with frequent success, the passion of the historical traumas
through which they move is often brilliantly captured; but
Singer himself keeps at a distance. He was a deeply skeptical
writer, not merely with regard to the political and national
ideologies raging through the Jewish communities of Poland
and Russia during the last few decades of the nineteenth
century but also with regard to the whole human enterprise:
the possibility of happiness, the relevance of salvation.

Now in part this flows from the conventions of the social
novel as composed in Europe during the early twentieth
century—conventions of motivating attitude and narrative
point of view that indicate a deep uncertainty about the survival
of European civilization. In part the skepticism of the older
Singer may have emerged from the Haskalah (Enlightenment) line of Jewish opinion that was rationalistic, dubious
about invoked sublimities, and hostile to the sort of religio-
political ecstatics that the younger Singer has written about.
But beyond such possibilities, one feels in I. J. Singer's work
an ineradicable personal bias, that root of temperament which
yields the gray flowers of skepticism and perhaps even nihil-
ism.* Though sharing little of his younger brother's taste for
the bizarre and perverse, he is finally a writer more austere
and disenchanted, certainly less given to blurring the world
with charm. Whoever listens to the tone of *The Brothers
Ashkenazi* will, I think, hear the austerity and "toughness"
of which I speak. It is a tone also to be heard in *Yoshe Kalb*,

---

* The Yiddish literary critic B. Rivkin writes that I. J. Singer's early fiction, because of its "excessively sober" realism, had the effect of "frightening" David Bergelson, the distinguished Soviet Yiddish novelist. Some
withdrawal of affect, some clamming up or dryness of spirit, seems already
to have been evident to Singer's colleagues in the Yiddish literary world.

I. J. Singer's short, brilliant novel about the Hasidic milieu. And it can be heard most subtly of all in Singer's story "Repentance" (see *A Treasury of Yiddish Stories*, edited by Howe and Greenberg, or *The River Breaks Up*, by I. J. Singer), where the Hasidic obsession with joy is shown gradually turning into a kind of moral ruthlessness.

The narrative pattern of *The Brothers Ashkenazi*, as it seeks to encompass the historical novelties of East European Jewish life in the late nineteenth century, necessarily imposes limits on the author. Of inner psychic being, of the nuances of feeling and reflection that we have come to expect in the depiction of character, *The Brothers Ashkenazi* has rather little. When Singer turns to the more intimate spheres of human experience, the writing can seem embarrassed; the romantic scenes tend toward the slapdash, as if something to be gotten over with. We see Max Ashkenazi mainly from the outside and his brother, Jacob, from varying distances; mostly this is as it should be, for the inner lives of such men can be of only limited interest. What matters about them is what they do, not what they think.

Singer is dealing here with one of the great themes of the nineteenth-century European novel, a theme especially exciting to Yiddish readers of, say, forty or fifty years ago—the rise of capitalism in its "heroic" or adventuresome phase and the accompanying entry of the Jews onto the stage of historical action, whether through the accumulation of capital which obsesses Max Ashkenazi or through the gathering of rebellion which forms the goal of his socialist antagonists. If the objectives of these two contending forces are at polar opposites, Singer brilliantly shows how their outpourings of energy, their hungers to leave a mark move along parallel lines. From a traditional Jewish point of view, both styles of conduct must seem equally disturbing and ominous.

It is a virtue of this new translation of *The Brothers Ashkenazi*, undertaken by the author's son, that it succeeds in capturing something of the rush, the energy of the original Yiddish. This is not the kind of novel that calls attention to its language, elegant phrase by phrase or fine sentence by sentence; its strength lies in larger verbal units, whole paragraphs and indeed passages, where the power of denotation and accumulation can be registered. The translator has been especially sensitive to these larger rhythms of I. J. Singer's narrative, rhythms of sweep and surprise, turn and return, precisely the kind one has come to expect in fictions that deal primarily with man as social actor or victim.

Perhaps the most vivid pages in *The Brothers Ashkenazi* are those in which Singer evokes, in a tone of notable detachment, the mania for accumulation and the consequent loosening of moral constraints that mark the rise of the Jewish bourgeoisie in Lodz.

Lodz seethed in ferment as the city grew day by day, hour by hour. Strangers converged from all over: German engineers and master weavers; English chemists, designers, and patternmakers; Russian merchant princes in blue coats and wide trousers over short patent-leather boots; Jewish traveling salesmen and commission agents—gay, lusty young men who descended upon Lodz to make money and to have fun.

The youth of Lodz began to shave their beards and don worldly attire. Restaurants, cabarets, and gambling casinos opened and drew huge crowds. Hungarian dancers came to further their careers and fatten their purses. Circuses and carnivals arrived from Warsaw and Petersburg, from Berlin and Budapest. Russian functionaries and officers accepted bribes and kickbacks, which they squandered on wine, women, and cards. Lodz drank, sang, danced, attended theaters, caroused in brothels, gambled. Wealthy Hasidim were caught up in the mood of revelry. They lingered in kosher restaurants, where waiters in silk skullcaps brought fat goose thighs and plump waitresses served dried chick-peas and foamy beer. Wastrel Hasidic youths, living on the largess of their fathers-in-law, ceased studying the Torah and played cards in studyhouses.

It is here, in the breaking away from the traditional passivity of East European Jewish life and the new excitements of public will, that I. J. Singer finds his commanding subject. In reading *The Brothers Ashkenazi,* one is therefore likely to respond most of all to the larger rhythms of narrative and fate, the ferocity with which Jews like Max Ashkenazi—entirely a creature of will, set in contrast with the easy grace of his twin, Jacob—enter the dynamism of modern society. Max is fascinated by the accumulation of capital not so much because it brings him luxuries—which, in any case, he hardly knows how to enjoy—but because it means a chance to bear down upon the world, to show what a frail, unfavored little Jew can accomplish in shaping the life about him. One sometimes fancies, in reading this novel, that Max's frantic hunger to accumulate symbolizes a release of the blocked energies of whole generations.

In the end it becomes clear that Max cannot really do very much, even as he spins and turns, rushes and calculates. His empire collapses, his brother is murdered by a loutish anti-Semitic officer, and he himself, the great magnate, dies in helpless loneliness, just like everyone else. Jews may enter history, Jews may delude themselves with the excitements of wealth and the enticements of power, but finally, they are puny and helpless before the large brutal forces of the external world, puny and helpless before Polish hatreds and Russian revolutions and Western competition. Max Ashkenazi scribbles on any piece of paper within reach, always calculating risks. His obsessions are not so different from the obsessions of revolutionists who also scribble on pieces of paper, their calculations ideological rather than financial—especially if one regards them with a certain Jewish detachment. In the end, suggests Singer, it all comes to nothing: perhaps for everyone, certainly for Jews.

Singer is also very keen at depicting the Jewish milieu torn apart by the clashing impulses of old piety and new skepticism, traditional ways and burgeoning appetites. The half-religious or half-skeptical Jew, uncomfortable in his modernity, is one of his recurrent types, yet he quite escapes the sentimental nostalgia for pietistic traditionalism which has become fashionable in recent decades. (He is especially severe on the Hasidim, who often emerge in his pages as uncouth, even savage.) There is a striking passage early in the novel where Singer depicts a group of Jewish boys released from the disciplines of school who

for hours . . . wandered through the streets of Lodz. They raced down side streets and alleys, exulting in their freedom. They visited marketplaces where peasants milled among their wagons, horses, cattle, swine, poultry, sacks of grain. Jewish housewives in bonnets over shaved skulls wandered among the wagons. They tested the chickens by blowing into their behinds, even poked their fingers inside their cloacas to see if they were carrying eggs. Jews slapped gentile palms to seal bargains; haggled, chewed kernels of grain.

Where readers of Isaac Bashevis Singer yield themselves, conditionally, to fragments of a lost *shtetl* world, savoring the charms and values of traditionalism, the readers of Israel Joshua Singer are transported to the bracing vitality of the rising world of commerce, with all the energy and freedom it promises. *The Brothers Ashkenazi* gains much of its strength from Singer's authoritative handling of the Jewish bourgeoisie in Poland; his sketching of the radicals seems a bit less certain, perhaps because they are shown at an early stage of development, not yet fully formed or politically ripe.

Outwardly, then, Singer follows the familiar curve of the social novel: the rise and fall of a house, an infatuation with worldliness and subsequent disenchantments, everything, in short, that is familiar from reading novels like *Lost Illusions* and *Great Expectations* and *Buddenbrooks.* But the peculiar tone of Singer's novel derives first from his still-powerful ties to the East European Jewish culture and then from his own distancing sensibility. That sensibility is sharply at odds with the scheme of the novel. Passages of strong narrative, reflecting the rise of capitalism in the Polish cities, follow the rhythm of historical expansion, but only in part, never with full assent, does Singer yield himself to this narrative rhythm. His deepest persuasion emerges as a distrust of all classes and programs, a creeping suspicion of all worldly projects, a bleak skepticism about the very history he has brought into Yiddish literary consciousness. He is not at home in the world he writes about. He no longer possesses the faith of his fathers in its completeness or radiance, but he still keeps something of their critical judgment about the world. And it is this tension between the thrust of the story and the withholding of the author that gives the novel its bruising tone of inner conflict: an imagination fruitfully at war with itself.

I

BIRTH

ONE

———◆———

DOWN THE SANDY ROADS leading from Saxony and Silesia into Poland, through fields, forests, towns, and villages razed and ravaged by the Napoleonic Wars, rolled a strange procession of vehicles, people, animals, and objects.

Polish serfs stopped tilling the earth to shield pale eyes and gaze at the spectacle; women pushed back red headkerchiefs and leaned on hoes; flaxen-haired children raced with dogs out of mud huts and beyond thatched fences to point and stare.

Before Jewish country inns, boys with black earlocks and ritual garments dangling over ragged breeches gaped at the odd caravans rolling by and cried, "Come see, Mama. . . . Come see!"

Nothing like it had ever been seen in Poland. These weren't the splendid coaches of the gentry, the long latticed carts of peasants, the patched covered wagons with dangling buckets of Jewish draymen, the stagecoaches with teams of four and trumpets blaring. Even the harness was different—full of odd straps, bands, and traces.

Some of the wagons were wide with high heavy wheels and drawn by sturdy horses. Some were like houses on wheels with the roofs and sides of circus wagons. Some were ribbed and canopied like gypsy wagons. There were carts drawn by big dogs and even by man-and-woman teams while children pushed behind. And in each case, the occupants matched their conveyances.

The sturdier wagons contained fat, pipe-smoking men, clean-shaven in front but with blond beards dangling behind their chins and watchchains straining across their bellies. Their equally fleshy women wore bonnets and clogs over red woolen stockings. The wagons were loaded with bedding, clothes, copperplates of kings and battles, Bibles and prayer books, crates of squawking fowl and rabbits scurrying in the hay. Fat, heavy-uddered cows brought up the rear.

Nags as lean as their masters limped as they strained to
pull the poorer wagons, dragging their muzzles close to the
ground. Only the smallest children rode inside, while the
parents and older offspring trudged alongside, prodding a horse
or freeing a wheel from ruts. It there was a cow, she was all
alone and often emaciated and half dry.

The leanest, meanest lot were those with carts pulled by
themselves or by dogs. They had plenty of children but no other
animals, except for a rare goat. The women struggled alongside their men, heavy ropes cutting into their shoulders.

But prosperous or poor, they all shared one item—a polished
wooden loom strapped to their cart or wagon.

The peasants called out, "Blessed be the name of our Lord
Jesus Christ. Where are you headed, strangers?"

The only response was a *"Guten Tag. . . . Grüss Gott,"*
and the peasants spat and crossed themselves.

"Heathens! You can't make out a proper Christian word.
. . ."

The Jewish innkeepers made better contact with their
Yiddish. They invited the strangers to wash down the dust
from their throats with a pint of aquavit, but the travelers declined. They carried their own food, slept in their wagons,
and didn't spend a single groschen along the way.

They were weavers from Germany and Moravia coming
to settle in Poland since there were too many people and not
enough bread at home, while in Poland there was bread but
no goods. The Polish peasants wore coarse linen clothes they
wove of flax, but the city dwellers and the military had to
rely on foreign imports brought in by Jews and usually shipped
down the Vistula from Danzig. This created a drain of money
out of the country. Agents were sent to Germany to induce
German weavers to settle in Poland, where they were promised
free land, exemption from military service, deferment of taxes
in the initial years, and the freedom to follow their customs
and to worship in the Protestant faith.

The weavers, who were essentially farmers, brought all their
possessions with them, from livestock to household pets, from
spindles to concertinas, from cat-o'nine-tails to plows. Among
them were Lutheran pastors with their families who would
guard the Protestant faith in this hotbed of popery and assure
continued allegiance to the German God and to the kaiser.

The caravans headed for the lowland regions stretching from
Zyrardow to Kalisz, from Pabjanice to Zgierz to Piotrkow.
Some of the weavers settled around the town of Lodz, which
lay beside a stagnant body of water called Ludka. On the

outskirts of town, by a road leading to pine forests, they built houses, laid out gardens, dug wells, planted wheat and potatoes, and set up their wooden looms. The Poles called the community Wilki, Polish for wolves, which frequently roamed the area on cold days, and they forbade Jews from settling there.

The few dozen Jews who were permitted to live in Lodz were tailors whose services were essential to the gentile community. They had their own guild and a shack where they met to discuss the restrictions imposed upon them by their gentile neighbors. On a table inside this shack stood a plain wooden ark containing a scroll of Law, since the Jews also conducted their services there. They had no rabbi, ritual bath or cemetery. If a woman had to visit a ritual bath, she was taken to a stream outside town and protected against the depradations of gentile youths. In winter, a hole was chopped in the ice, and the women immersed themselves. Jewish corpses were transported by peasant cart to the community of Leczyca, of which the Jews of Lodz were officially a part.

The Jews of Lodz were at odds with the Jews of Leczyca, who were mostly impoverished tailors. While the Lodz Jews were kept busy the year round sewing for the gentiles, the Leczyca Jews starved between the seasons when Jews order new gabardines. The Leczyca tailors, therefore, smuggled themselves into Lodz and agreed to work for lower fees. To protect their livelihood, the Lodz Jews denounced the interlopers to the authorities as bunglers and botchers who undercut legitimate guild members and taxpayers. Their humble petition also pledged a donation of tallow for the church and a prayer for the continued well-being of that illustrious sire the prefect.

The prefect's subordinate, the subprefect, sent constables to round up the interlopers. They confiscated their shears and irons and ran them out of town. Those who tried to sneak back were hogtied and flogged.

The Leczyca Jews then refused to bury any more Lodz Jews until they received a ducat per corpse in tribute. The Lodz Jews responded by refusing to pay their communal levies. The Leczyca town elders struck back and persuaded the authorities to post a soldier in each Lodz Jewish household. The soldiers made themselves quite at home. They sliced their pork with kosher knives, talked smut, made free with the women and mocked the men at prayer. Passover, when it is forbidden for a gentile to be in a Jewish home lest he render it impure, was coming, and the Lodz Jews were forced to lay aside the work they had to finish for the gentiles' Easter and to beg the

Leczyca rabbi to have the soldiers removed from their homes.

The Leczyca elders forced the Lodz Jews to remove their boots and humble themselves before them in their stockinged feet. The Lodz Jews also paid an additional tribute and swore on the Torah never again to turn over a Leczyca citizen to gentile hands. The soldiers were duly withdrawn, and the Leczyca Jews began to settle unimpeded in Lodz.

But when a Jew occasionally stumbled into German Wilki, flaxen-haired youths pelted him with rocks and set their dogs on him with the ancient cry *"Hep, hep Jude . . . !"*

TWO

—————

THE LODZ MERCHANT AND COMMUNITY HEAD, Abraham Hersh Ashkenazi, known as Abraham Hersh Danziger for his frequent trips to Danzig, sat over a Tractate Zebahim, brooding and tugging at his long and thick black beard.

He wasn't worried about making a living. Even after decades of exclusion from Wilki and the Weavers' Guild a sizable Jewish community had managed to flourish in Lodz, complete with its own rabbi, assistant rabbis, ritual slaughterers, ritual bath, synagogues, and cemetery.

The reason the Jews prospered was that the German weavers produced a very inferior cloth that was disdained by the rich and the discriminating, who demanded the soft wools, fine silks, gleaming satins and velvets from abroad. To fill this need, the wealthier Jews took wagons and, later, the first trains to Danzig and Leipzig, while those less affluent conspired with border guards to smuggle in fabrics from Germany. At the same time barefoot Jewish peddlers and runners fanned out across sandy country lanes to buy wool from the peasants to sell to Lodz merchants, who in turn shipped it abroad to be spun into yarn. The peasants, who used to leave their sheep filthy and unshorn, now bathed them in streams to render the fleece white and clean. Speculators and leaseholders bought up entire future yields of flocks on landed estates.

The German master weavers of Lodz vilified the Jews for importing foreign goods from Germany at the expense of the local industry. They also resented the fact that Jewish merchants issued cotton to the poor German weavers, thus bringing down the price of the finished goods. These cotton merchants weren't able to obtain credit at the banks, as were their German competitors, and they lacked the cash with which to pay the weavers. They therefore issued their own scrip to the weavers when they delivered the finished goods on Friday evenings, and the Jewish tailors, cobblers, and shopkeepers accepted the scrip in lieu of money.

When the German master weavers complained, the authorities outlawed the practice. They also sent a representative to England to buy up cotton, thus pushing the Jews out of business. But the cotton ended up being stolen by government officials. The authorities generally found it easier to accept bribes from the Jews, who continued issuing the scrip and doing business as usual.

Among the most respectable and affluent citizens of Lodz was Abraham Hersh Ashkenazi, who traveled to Danzig on buying trips several times a year. He had just returned from such a journey which had proved even more profitable than usual. He had fine presents for his wife and daughters and a handsome silver cup that he was saving to present to the Rabbi of Warka, whose disciple he was.

Things at home were going along splendidly, and Abraham Hersh was delighted. But as a leader of the community, a position he held despite his youth and as the result of his wealth, scholarship, and piety, he was disturbed by a number of problems that had cropped up during his absence.

First, funds were needed to provide Passover products for the town's poor, not only the beggars but also those who worked but hadn't managed to save up enough from a year's toil to buy the necessary matzos, wine, eggs, meat, and cooking fat for the holiday. Upon his return, Abraham Hersh had taken his red kerchief and, accompanied by several other community leaders, had solicited the affluent households. It hadn't sufficed, and the poor had stormed the communal house, demanding their due.

Second, there were Jewish prisoners to be ransomed. Throughout Poland, the tsar's Cossacks were fighting the Polish gentry, who sought to restore a Polish king to the throne, and loyal Jewish leaseholders were engaged in smuggling gunpowder to their Polish masters hiding in the forests. Just recently, a group of Jews had been caught smuggling a quantity of gunpowder in barrels of apples. At first, the Cossacks had found nothing by poking their lances into the barrels, but as they started appropriating the apples, they found the powder. Some of the Jews were hanged on the spot; others were thrown into prison. Those who were executed had to be given decent Jewish burials. Those in prison had to be ransomed or at least provided with matzos for the holiday.

Third, a group of newly rich, enlightened Jews who were anxious to shed the yoke of Jewishness had petitioned the government to allow them to put up a modern school where their children could learn the ways of the gentile. There were rumors that they also planned to build a German type of temple with an organ and a cantor who chanted like a priest. Although the authorities were slow to respond to this request, the parvenu Jews were tossing money about freely, and everyone knew what money could accomplish. Abraham Hersh and the other traditionalists considered such a temple far worse than a church since only Christians and converts attended the latter, while the former was liable to entice the poorer Jews away from the path of righteousness, which was the first step toward apostasy.

Fourth, Jewish runners who roamed the countryside buying up wool, hides, and hog bristles learned that a wayward Lodz youth, Naftali the Convert, who more than once had been driven from the synagogue courtyard for flouting the laws of Jewishness, had apprenticed himself to a German weaver, for whom he worked on the Sabbath and with whom he ate pork.

Abraham Hersh sent for the youth and warned that he would turn him over to the authorities for conscription, but the fellow remained recalcitrant. The authorities refused to conscript him despite the community's pleas, and this helped encourage other Jewish youths to make overtures to the gentiles. One, Mendel Flederbaum, who employed several gentile weavers, learned the trade from his workers and applied to the gentile guild to accept him as a master weaver. He was helped in this by the authorities after he had shaved his beard, renounced the traditional garb, and learned to speak and write Russian.

Following this, several others of shaky faith got the urge to emulate the renegades. At this time an epidemic swept the town, and children died of the scarlet fever. This was seen as a clear sign of God's punishment upon Lodz for the sins of its heretics.

Another thorn in Abraham Hersh's side was his wife's objections to his visiting his rabbi on the holiday. He was accustomed to going to Warka not only on Rosh Hashanah, Yom Kippur, and Shevuot but also on Passover, despite his wife's annual complaints that she would be forced to celebrate the Seder at her father's, the assistant rabbi of Ozorkow, like some widow, God forbid.

Not that Abraham Hersh was one to be moved by female tears. A woman was only a woman, after all. But this time things were somewhat different. His wife was due at any time now, and since the child kicked on her right side she expected a boy.

"I'll kill myself if you're not here for the circumcision! I'll never endure the shame of it . . ." she bleated.

Nor were the roads to Warka safe, people warned him. The Cossacks were scouring the countryside and harassing travelers. Innocent people had been flogged and even hanged.

But Abraham Hersh had urgent reasons to go. On his last visit he had mentioned that his wife was pregnant, to which the rabbi had commented, "Your generations shall be men of wealth."

This had disturbed Abraham Hersh, and he had quickly said, "I would prefer them to be God-fearing men, Rabbi."

But the rabbi hadn't responded, and Abraham Hersh hadn't pressed the issue. Still, the remark had sounded ominous, and Abraham Hersh was anxious to resolve it before it was too late.

The dangers of the road didn't concern him at all—he was accustomed to dealing with such things. The only thing that held him back was leaving his wife alone during the labor and delivery, and later, at the circumcision if, with God's help, the baby turned out to be a boy.

But there were other considerations. A number of impoverished Warka Hasidim were looking forward to a trip at his expense, and they would jeer at him for letting a woman dissuade him. It wasn't fair to deprive Jews of a holiday at their rabbi's table. Besides, how would it look if he presented the rabbi the silver Elijah's cup on Shevuot instead of on Passover? . . .

Had his wife been a sensible person instead of a woman, she would have urged him to go and resolve the question of their child's future with the rabbi. But he, being a man, couldn't allow her tears to sway him.

He went to the closet, got down the large leather valise that he always took with him to Danzig, and packed his phylacteries, prayer shawl, a satin gabardine, some shirts, the silver cup, and some holy books to study along the way. Being a good Warka Hasid, he remembered to include several bottles of Passover aquavit and sent the maid, Sarah Leah, for the coachman.

Belly jutting, his wife erupted with her usual complaints, but Abraham Hersh didn't even blink an eye. He kissed the doorpost amulet, and as he already stood on the threshold, he wished her an easy delivery. He suddenly reminded himself.

"If, with God's help, it's a boy, he is to be named Simha Bunem after the Przysucha Rabbi, blessed be his memory. That's the way I want it, you hear?" he shouted into the room.

THREE

MISTRESS ASHKENAZI HADN'T BEEN WRONG—
the signs presaging the birth of a boy proved true. But instead
of one son there were two.

After a night of anguish which coincided with the first
Seder, a child was born at dawn. The neighbor women in attendance slapped the infant's rump to make it cry and held it
up to the lamp.

"Congratulations, it's a boy!" they announced to the mother.

But she didn't stop screaming. The women stroked her
sweating face. "Enough already. It's all over."

Sarah Leah, who was an experienced midwife, saw that it
was far from over. "Grab hold of the headboard, mistress darling," she advised. "It'll make things easier."

After a number of minutes another infant emerged, a big,
heavy baby that needed no slap to make it bawl.

Sarah Leah took it and held it to the light. "Another boy!
A real buster this time, the evil eye spare him."

The women found two different colored ribbons to tie around
the boys' wrists, but it wasn't necessary since only a fool could
have mistaken the two. The elder was slight, scrawny, with
sparse fair hair over a narrow skull, while the younger was
long and robust with a huge head of black curly hair. The
elder piped in a shrill wail, while the younger bellowed like
a bullock.

"One just like the mistress and the other a spitting image
of the master," Sarah Leah said, handing the cleansed, dressed
infants to their mother, who quickly clasped the elder twin to
her breast.

"Hush, don't carry on so," she chided the younger twin,
who howled as if out of jealousy.

She sprayed a few drops of milk into the mouths of the
boys to teach them how to suckle. The younger took to the

nipple without a sound, but the elder could only scream in frustration.

For the whole eight days preceding the circumcision the mother fretted against her mound of pillows about the problem of naming the babies. She had mentioned to her husband that if it turned out a boy, she would have liked to name it after her grandfather Jacob Meir, the Rabbi of Wodzislaw, but Abraham Hersh wouldn't hear of it. He insisted it be called Simha Bunem after the Przysucha Rabbi.

"You can name girls after whomever you want, but the boys belong to me," he told her.

Now that he was away, the responsibility lay upon her. Having had twins, she had the latitude of apportioning four names, but for all that, she was uneasy. She knew how unreasonable her husband could be, and she knew that whatever she decided would displease him—he wouldn't tolerate even one name from her side of the family.

Women advised her to send a messenger to her husband asking him to come home, but she wouldn't. She was furious with him. She hadn't enjoyed a happy moment since their wedding. He was either away on business or at his rabbi's. When he was home, he was either with his Hasidic cronies at the studyhouse or poring over the books in his study.

Not that she demanded much. She herself came from a Hasidic family, her own father behaved no differently, and she knew that a learned Jew had nothing to say to a female, who wasn't even allowed to make her presence known in her own home when strange men came to call. That was the woman's lot, and she accepted it. Each morning she thanked God for having created her a female according to His will. Still, she chafed under the conditions.

True, she was well-off and fecund, providing her husband with a child each year, and bright, healthy children at that, for which she was envied. He brought her gifts from Danzig—a Turkish shawl or a piece of jewelry—but he paid no attention to her. They couldn't even share a Sabbath meal together since he always brought some pauper home and she was forced to eat in the kitchen with the maid after a single sip of the benediction wine and a slice of the ceremonial Sabbath loaf.

Nor could they go anywhere together since neither was allowed to mix with the opposite sex. On the rare occasions when they visited relatives, he always walked in front while she followed a few paces behind. The moment they entered the house, they quickly parted, each to his own gender. On Sabbaths, he lingered so long at the services that she almost fainted from hunger until the meal could be served.

But what irked her most was the air of superiority he adopted toward her. He never asked her advice, never reported how his business affairs were going, never confided in her when he was troubled. He would open his heavy purse and dole out the money she needed for household expenses, and that was the extent of their relationship. He never even addressed her by name but called her "thou" in the manner of the fanatics. When he came home from a trip, he never told her about it but merely kissed the doorpost amulet and grunted, "How are things in the house?" while he held out her present. If she took it from his hand, it was a sign that she was available for marital relations. If not, he only glanced at her darkly and went off to his Hasidim to hear news of their rabbi.

She feared him, his brooding silences, his booming chant as he studied the Gemara, his burly masculinity, his grim face. She didn't ask much—a kind word or a loving smile as compensation for her empty existence that was little better than a servant's, but even this he denied her. If he loved her in his own fashion, he showed it only in their bed, as the Law prescribed. Otherwise, he was quite rigid about a woman's role in life. She was to bear children, rear them, observe the laws of Jewishness, run a household, and obey her husband blindly. If his friends chose to drop in for a late get-together, he expected her to serve them refreshments regardless of the hour. "Woman," he shouted into the kitchen, where she had to sit with the maid, "whip up a mess of groats for us men!" And she had to stay up preparing the food.

He was away on all holidays, even on Passover when the humblest Jewish women joined their husbands and families at the table, while she had to be alone like some widow, God forbid. All these indignities she had borne in silence, but this time he had gone too far. She had begged and pleaded with him to be with her for the birth, but as usual he had ignored her, and a sense of deep outrage, built up over years of gray, unfulfilled existence, consumed her. She disregarded the women's advice and determined not to send a messenger after him. Actually she wasn't all that sure that he would heed her plea.

All the female pride that her husband had so long trampled underfoot now emerged full-blown. She lay in her bed, cordoned off with sheets and draped with amulets to guard against the evil forces. Responding with firm "amens" to the traditional prayers recited by heder boys on the other side of the sheets, bolstered by a sense of pride in her maternal accomplishments, she took it upon herself to arrange for the circumcision. Issuing orders like any imperious male, she decided on the names she would give her sons in defiance of her husband's wishes. She didn't feel bold enough to cross him completely, and she effected a kind of compromise. She named the elder twin Simha after the Przysucha Rabbi, but added Meir after her grandfather, and gave the remaining two names to the younger—Jacob Bunem.

The moment Abraham Hersh returned from Warka, he asked to see his newborn son. He was amazed to learn that there were two, and he gazed in bewilderment at the tightly swaddled infants.

"Which is the older?" he asked brusquely.

"The smaller one," his wife said, lowering her eyes under his burning gaze.

"What's he called?"

"Simha."

"Just one name?"

"No. Meir, too. After my grandfather, the Wodzislaw Rabbi, blessed be his memory," she whispered, trembling at her audacity.

"Here, take him!" Abraham Hersh growled.

Sarah Leah brought the other infant.

"Go to your daddy, Jacob Bunem," she crooned with sly innocence.

Abraham Hersh glared at the infant, who looked back at him with open, shining eyes, and some of his anger dissipated. The knowledge that both of the Przysucha's Rabbi's names had been used mollified him somewhat, but the fact that they had been joined with that of some worthless nobody was hard to swallow.

"The image of the master . . . a shining light, may the evil eye spare him," Sarah Leah said.

"Pshaw! Take him away," the father growled in a fit of pique.

Eyes tearing, the mother clapped a son to each breast. "Suck, Meir darling," she urged the older, omitting the child's other name that her husband had forced upon her, but he only clamped his gums around her nipple and held it in a fierce grip.

She screamed in pain, and Sarah Leah came running. She plucked the infant from the breast and regarded him angrily. "Rascal, a baby mustn't pinch his mother's breast. Nurse like Jacob Bunem . . . so. . . ."

The baby emitted a howl of such indignation that Abraham Hersh shouted from his study, "Close the door! How can a man concentrate in all this tumult?"

He gathered scant joy from his sons' birth. He envisioned the time when he would present them to his rabbi and his shame would become public knowledge. He tried saying their names aloud, but they rang false to him. He wouldn't forgive his wife for defiling the rabbi's name, and he didn't go in to see her, even though she was still not fully recovered. To muffle the disgrace, he threw himself into his work. He no longer planned to go to Danzig since there was sufficient local business to keep him busy.

The town of Lodz grew from day to day. The first Jews to be granted the right to open weaving workshops had achieved this by adopting gentile ways and toadying to the authorities. But inevitably, ordinary observant Jews followed suit. The Russian officials who descended upon the country following the suppression of the Polish uprising were most eager for the bribes and gifts of Jews who sought permission to live and do business in prohibited areas, and soon Jewish looms clacked away in the old section of Lodz, even though the Germans still barred Jews from their guild.

At first, the Jews confined themselves to their own quarter. Seemingly overnight the houses already standing sprouted additional stories, annexes, wings, extensions, ells, attics, and garrets to accommodate the flow of newcomers converging upon Lodz from surrounding areas. Lacking legitimate sanction and permits, the construction was effected at night and proceeded helter-skelter, without order or plan. Buildings came down; buildings went up; buildings emerged slanted, top-heavy, leaning this way or that—all symmetry sacrificed to expediency. There was no time to do otherwise as the town grew by leaps and bounds.

Gradually the Jews began to spill out of their congested area into Wilki, which was officially closed to them. The first to stick a toe inside the restricted area were the more affluent, audacious Jews; presently the more timorous followed.

Then, like a torrent overflowing its banks, the Jews smashed down all barriers set up to exclude them. Thousands of rural leaseholders and innkeepers who had been dependent on the Polish nobility were now forced to seek their livelihoods in towns and cities. They opened dry goods stores by the hundred, but since the liberated serfs were starving, there were no customers, and the Jews turned to weaving. They set up their wooden handlooms wherever they could, but mostly they flocked to the city of Lodz. Having endured the irrational cruelty of their blueblooded former masters, they wouldn't be turned back by mere bans or decrees fashioned against them; they opened their workshops just as the German immigrants had done before them.

At first, they hired German weavers who couldn't afford to go out on their own and who preferred a Jewish master to a German, who would force them to kiss his hand twice a day. If a Jewish boss caught them with a snippet of wool in their pocket, he didn't beat them but merely reclaimed the wool and threw it back in the pile. As the Sabbath drew to a close, the German workers sat in their employers' kitchens, smoking pipes and conversing with their bosses' wives and daughters in flawless Yiddish.

"Hey, boss," they ragged their masters, who were reluctant to let go of the waning Sabbath, "let's have the few guldens already before the taverns close. . . ."

Gradually young Jewish men, both married and single, began to learn the trade. Down the sandy roads leading to Lodz, fathers accompanied by sons who had no heads for books walked barefoot and waved sticks to keep off the village dogs. On the outskirts of town they put on their boots and admonished their sons before apprenticing them for three years to Jewish master weavers.

"Act like an adult, obey your employer, be kind to God and man, be honest and respectful, and you will reap the benefits of this world and the world to come."

They dug down deep into the pockets of their sheepskins and took out purses, from which they drew the greasy, hard-earned bills with which to pay the master weavers for agreeing to feed and board their sons while they taught them their trade.

The skullcapped youths stood before the looms with ritual garments dangling over grimy trousers, lint clinging to curly thatches and sprouting beards, fingers deftly weaving wool and cotton cloth or ladies' kerchiefs from dawn to midnight. As they worked, they chanted cantorial pieces, trilling and quavering over selected passages. The bosses passed to and fro, making sure nothing was stolen, checking the output and prodding the worker who paused to wipe his brow or roll a cigarette.

The bosses' wives and daughters peeled potatoes, fried onions, and stirred soups in huge kettles while apprentices wound yarn onto spools, rocking cradles with their feet.

In the marketplaces Jews bought and sold piece goods and remnants. Ragpickers brought in all kinds of waste, which they sold to dealers, who reclaimed it into reusable material. Women and girls wound thread onto red wooden bobbins. Hosiers knitted coarse colorful stockings for women. Wherever one turned, machines clacked and clattered, accompanied by the tailors' cantorial chants and the seamstresses' love ballads.

Eventually the city grew too congested to contain its rapidly growing population. As the wealthy and enterprising lease-holder Solomon David Preiss, who had made his fortune importing wheat and rye to Prussia, lay awake one night, it suddenly struck him that a suburb might be built on the infertile flats of Baluty, the Kanarski brothers' estate just outside the city. The land was too sandy even to pasture livestock, and the only people living on it were the liberated serfs who had nowhere else to go.

The following morning after services, Preiss ordered his servant to hitch up the britska and drive him to the Kanarski estate. His ostensible reason for calling on the steward was to consider a purchase of rye. As he chewed on the kernels, allegedly to test the quality of the grain, he casually asked the steward how things were going. The Pole tugged his long mustache and spat out the expected tale of woe. The masters were in debt over their heads, but their solution was to go to Paris on sprees while the burden of maintaining the estate fell entirely upon him. Before leaving, Preiss hinted that he was examining sites where sand was plentiful for a possible glass plant. If he found such a property at a cheap enough price, he might consider its purchase.

Within days he was summoned to meet with the brothers at their manor. Forgetting the fact that a Polish nobleman was obliged to address a Jew by his first name only, the Kanarskis abjured protocol and were almost civil to their visitor.

"Mr. Solomon, there is enough sand in Baluty for ten glass plants, not one," they gushed, eyes glinting with greed.

Solomon David Preiss bargained shrewdly and eventually bought the huge expanse of land for a mere 20,000 rubles cash.

When the brothers, who had gone to Paris to squander their bonanza, learned from their steward that the Jew planned to build a suburb rather than a glass plant on their former property, they rushed back in an attempt to nullify the deal on the ground that they had been duped. The local judges and assessors, who were their friends, began to pore through the lawbooks, seeking some technicality that would void the sale.

Solomon David Preiss had no manor in which to entertain these gentlemen and their wives, but he had an even more persuasive argument—gold imperials of which the local functionaries were consummate connoisseurs. And it happened that instead of finding for their fellow Pole and social equal, the judges found for the Jew.

When the Kanarskis saw how things were going, they appealed to the higher powers for a strict enforcement of the prohibition against Jews residing outside their appointed areas.

Dignitary after dignitary arrived in splendid coaches at the
Kanarski manor house. They drank the brothers' wine, danced
with their daughters, hunted their game, and promised a swift
and fair resolution of the dispute. Briefs, precedents, writs,
arguments, and interpretations began to flow back and forth
between Lodz and Warsaw until no one could make sense of
anything anymore.

In the meantime, streets, alleys, and buildings sprouted on
the sandy flats like mushrooms after a rain. The construction
was chaotic, promiscuous, slapdash. Before the lime on the
walls had even dried, people moved in. Peasants brought in
bricks, dug ditches, uprooted stumps, slaked lime, sawed boards,
nailed roofs. Jewish carpenters, joiners, masons, tinsmiths, and
glaziers bustled, sweated, cursed. While the legal documents
gathered dust in the courts, there rose over the sandy flats a
city that no legal decision could abolish.

Before the municipality of Baluty, which the Jews promptly
shortened to Balut, could even consider official names for its
streets, the workers promptly named them after the surnames
or occupations of their inhabitants or after the synagogues or
studyhouses standing there. Thus, there soon appeared a Synagogue Street, a Feiffer Lane, a Jonah Feltmaker Place, a Gross-
man's Alley, and so forth.

On isolated corners there still remained a peasant hut or two,
complete with straw roof and livestock, but all vestiges of
rusticity vanished as the city engulfed the countryfolk and
transformed them into true cosmopolites who wore ready-made
clothes and earned and spent money. Their children learned
Yiddish, which enabled them to earn a groschen or a slice of
bread for lighting or dousing a candle in a Jewish home on
the Sabbath, heating an oven, and performing other such tasks
forbidden the Jew on the holy day. Poor German weavers
moved into abandoned peasant huts, and recruiters went out
into the country to hire peasants for the steam factories that
began to appear in Lodz, their tall chimneys poking up into
the murky skies.

In Wilki the German master weaver Heinz Huntze, who
had grown rich from handlooms, built a huge steam plant with
walls painted red and a bank of high windows. In the early
dawn its whistles shattered the stillness as they summoned the
men to work.

Soon after, Solomon David Preiss, who had realized a fortune
from his holdings in Balut, ordered a new rep gabardine, a
silk top hat, and an umbrella. Armed only with his Yiddish
and the roll of banknotes that he had sewn into the pocket of

his velvet vest and that he never removed even when he slept, he traveled to England. There he purchased machinery and hired an English engineer and a chemist, whom he brought back with him to Lodz.

On a huge lot that he bought for a song he built his own steam mill, the chimneys of which topped even Huntze's. Because his English assistants refused to take Saturdays off and work on Sundays, he hired no Jewish workers, and since it was a sin for a Jew to own a factory that operated on the Sabbath even with gentile help, Solomon David Preiss contrived a little subterfuge with his rabbi. He had him draw up a bill of sale in Hebrew and Aramaic and "sold" the factory to his Polish porter, Wojciech Smoliuch.

The terrified gentile stood trembling in the rabbi's study, his straw-colored mustache drooping, in dreadful fear of the fraud the Jews were perpetrating upon him. Even after it had all been explained to him, he still didn't understand it. "Sir, how can I buy your factory when I don't have a kopeck to my name?" he pleaded.

"Dummy! Do as you're told, and give me a ruble," Preiss insisted.

"But I don't have a ruble," the frightened Pole whined.

"Here is a ruble. Now give it back to me, and the sale is completed. When you have another ruble, you can pay back the loan."

Wojciech was sure that he was selling his soul to the devil or worse, but he was afraid to cross his boss, and he gingerly touched the tip of the red kerchief the rabbi extended to him to signify the sealing of a bargain. The rabbi then told him to sign the bill of sale, and the gentile made three crosses since he was illiterate.

Preiss and the rabbi grimaced at the sight of the despised symbols, but it was the only way. Preiss handed the bill of sale to Wojciech along with a ten-groschen tip, and the porter stuck the paper in his cap and dashed to the tavern for a badly needed drink.

Now Preiss could operate his factory on the Sabbaths with impunity and a clean conscience. Its machinery clattered away at full blast, shaking the red walls and belching black smoke into the skies. The poor German weavers gazed at the plant's towering chimneys that dehumanized them and rendered their skills meaningless. They looked down with despair at their veiny hands that would one day be obsolete.

The German master weavers incited their workers against Preiss's steam factory as a Jewish instrument of the devil. The workers grumbled into their beer and swore revenge.

One Saturday evening they gathered with torches, crowbars, and axes in front of the Jew's factory. Led by their masters, who displayed the standards of their guild, they smashed the machinery, doused the walls with kerosene, and set the factory on fire. Afterward, drunk and riotous, they raced through the Jewish quarter, and with skills honed by generations, they smashed, robbed, raped, and assaulted, shouting the ancient battle cry, *"Hep, hep Judel"*

The Cossacks herded them toward the Ludka Pond with swords bared and nagaikas flying.

But Solomon David Preiss's chimneys soon belched even denser smoke into the skies, and his whistles shrilled with unabated fury. Acknowledging the way the wind was blowing, the German master weavers, who were swamped with orders for goods, borrowed from Polish banks and put up steam factories of their own, and the wealthier Jews followed.

Like strange fruit, red brick steam factories sprouted in the fields around Lodz. They emitted slimy pools of sludge and poisoned the land, air, and water. Construction of residences, stores, workshops, and factories continued at a furious pace. Jewish artisans from all over Poland poured into Lodz. Peasants with too many children and too little land flocked in to take jobs in factories. Merchants from Russia arrived to snatch up goods for their own textile-starved country.

The end was nowhere in sight, and as Lodz flourished, so did the House of Abraham Hersh Ashkenazi.

FOUR

LONELY, WITHDRAWN, alienated from his parents, from other children and even from his sisters and his twin brother, little Simha Meir grew up in his father's house in Old City.

He had always gone his own way, never playing with children his own age. The courtyard of his father's house was like all those in the neighborhood—large, forbidding, closed off on all sides. From the section of it adjoining the smaller, poorer flats echoed a constant clatter of looms. Dust and lint issued from windows where waste was recycled. A roper twined cord the length of the yard. He and his three sons raced to and fro twisting the hemp, shouting harshly, "Pull, pull harder. Stop!"

The children loved the yard, no one more so than Jacob Bunem.

"Simha Meir," he would cry in a loud voice that expressed his lust for life, "come play tag."

"I don't want to," Simha Meir would say brusquely and turn away.

The twins didn't get along.

Jacob Bunem would have preferred it otherwise. He was bigger, stronger, full of laughter.

"Jacob Bunem, why do you always laugh?" others asked.

"'Cause I feel like it," he would say, and laugh again so that the others felt compelled to join it.

He put his whole heart and soul into the childish games. No one could run faster, or find better hiding places in the foundation when they played hide-and-seek, or catch the ends of the cord the roper dragged through the courtyard. He could excavate the biggest rocks and raise them overhead. He never grew tired of the games. Not only did he enjoy playing, but he wanted everyone, especially his brother, to do the same. But Simha Meir would have none of it.

He was very ambitious, little Simha Meir. He wanted always

to be the first, the best, the leader. But he wouldn't compete in the courtyard where he was clumsy and weak and helpless beside his brother. If he tried anything physical, he invariably tripped and bloodied his nose, and if there was one thing he feared, it was blood. He screamed in panic at the very sight of it.

In his own way, Jacob Bunem tried to help. He picked up a piece of glass, purposely cut his own hand, and laughed as the blood dripped out. "See, it's nothing," he said. The children, particularly the girls, oohed and ahed, and this irked Simha Meir even more. Jealousy and envy seethed within him.

When they were alone in the house, Simha Meir persuaded his brother to get down on all fours, and he mounted him like a horse. He kicked his ribs and whipped him with a whisk plucked from the broom as Jacob Bunem lumbered through the house.

Sarah Leah, who favored Jacob Bunem, grew annoyed. "Dummox, you'll tear your guts out!"

"I could carry two of him!" Jacob Bunem boasted, as Simha Meir laid on with a fury.

But Jacob Bunem was king of the courtyard. All the children, especially little Dinele, the daughter of the Ashkenazis' neighbor, Haim Alter, looked up to him. A plump, sweet, pretty child with curly chestnut hair tied in a big bow, she was infatuated with Jacob Bunem. He carried her piggyback and put her in the barrow the janitor used to collect refuse and pushed her around the yard.

Sarah Leah beamed each time she brought Jacob Bunem a slice of bread with honey. "Who would you like as your bridegroom?" she would ask the little girl.

"My daddy," the child said, bobbing her curls.

"And who else?"

Dinele pointed a chubby finger at Jacob Bunem. "Him!"

Sarah Leah sniffled into her apron from joy.

Simha Meir burned with rage and frustration, and he threw sand in the girls' hair. They came shrieking to Jacob Bunem for protection and then began a chant:

> Simha Meir is a liar,
> Watch him jump into the fire. . . .

The courtyard was a circus of wonders. Snatches of cantorial chants and ballads issued from open windows. Girls whose bowed heads were covered with lint and fluff sang of princes and princesses from storybooks, of star-crossed affairs between Jewish maidens and officers which inevitably ended in suicide, of female converts eloping with gentile lovers and ending up as drudges or prostitutes.

All this was fun to listen to, but the greatest attraction of all was the roper. A bruiser with tangled whiskers much like the hemp he worked with, with beetling brows and tufts of hair sprouting from nostrils and ears, legs bared to the knees and hairy as a bear's and hemp clinging to his dangling ritual garments, he worked with his sons who were every bit as bulky and powerful as their father. But big as they were, so jolly were they too. They didn't chase the children. If a boy asked to give the wheel a turn or run the length of the yard with a strand of rope, they didn't take the strap to him the way the other grownups did.

"Pull, pull," they urged the youngsters, hairy bodies shaking with laughter. "Don't let go of the rope or it'll grab you by your earlocks. . . ."

The children wouldn't leave the courtyard even to eat. The floor here wasn't completely cobbled; there were places where you could dig down deep enough to reach yellow sand and even water. The boys built pretty sand castles; the girls used tin box tops to make mud pies, mud cookies, cakes, breads. On the low roof of the janitor's shack there was a pigeon coop, and birds of all colors flew in and out, fluttered their wings, pecked crumbs, and cooed. Cats lurked within inches of them, but each time one seemed about to snare a pigeon, the bird would elude him indolently and land on the roof.

Jacob Bunem was enraptured with it all. "Simha Meir," he would cry, "let's feed the pigeons. They'll eat out of your hands, you'll see."

"Don't want," Simha Meir would say, and go off by himself.

He was slight, lightly freckled, with sharp features, very red, thin lips, and gray eyes that seemed to turn green when he became querulous. He always kept his hands inside the pockets of his black rep gabardine. His silk hat was shoved back on his head so that the high forehead fringed with thinly shorn hair and flaxen earlocks was exposed. His ears seemed forever cocked like a hare's, alert to every sound. His eyes seemed at first glance, mild, but a closer look revealed the mistrust with which they darted everywhere at once, suspicious and maybe a little mad. Nothing in the courtyard, no matter how trifling, escaped him. He saw and catalogued everything the children and even the adults did and said, as intently as the cats stalked the pigeons.

"Meirl," his mother urged from a window, "why don't you play with the other children, my precious?"

"Don't want," he replied curtly. "I don't like playing."

The pleasure of self-denial was stronger than the urge to join the others. This perversity even made him exult inwardly when one of them fell and skinned a knee.

He preferred being alone. He collected the colored tags that he tore off the bolts of goods in his father's storehouse, wound string onto bobbins, counted the coins he kept in a bank shaped like a rooster. The merchants who called on his father slipped him kopecks and even an occasional silver gulden, and he hid these in the clay rooster which had a slot in its tail. He loved to count his collection again and again. He would shake the clay rooster vigorously so that the other children would hear the coins clanging and be jealous. He would empty the bank, total the amount on the fingers of both hands, then refill it.

He couldn't relate to the others on an equal basis. He could only play with younger boys he could boss around or try to ingratiate himself with the older youths, who wouldn't have anything to do with him. If loneliness forced him to join the others, he demanded they appoint him their leader, their king. He then duped them out of their playthings, trampled their sand castles or mud pies, or grabbed things from their hands and ran away.

Most of all, he tormented his sisters and their friend Dinele. He loosened the bows in their pigtails; he heated a hairpin over the stove and held out the heated end to them so that they would burn their fingers; he tried to force flies and worms down their throats, knowing that they were terrified of insects. And if he bought himself candy, he wouldn't give anyone else a lick.

"Oh, it's so good," he teased, smacking his lips and watching their faces slyly.

Jacob Bunem, who had a sweet tooth and a longing for all of life's pleasures, succumbed. "Give us a lick, Simha Meir," he asked.

"Won't," Simha Meir said, and sucked even louder.

Jacob Bunem lost his temper. "How come I give you my candy and you don't give me any of yours?" he asked with feeling.

But Simha Meir didn't care and taunted some more. "You give me yours, but I don't give you mine. . . . Do me something!"

At this, Jacob Bunem snatched the candy from Simha Meir along with several flecks of skin. His sense of righteousness had been affronted. He wanted others to be as fair with him as he was with them, but he was ready to fight anyone of any size at any time when he felt he had been wronged.

Simha Meir rolled on the ground hurt and humiliated in front of the others. Since he couldn't retaliate against his younger brother with force, he vented his rage upon his sisters and tripped them up.

Jacob Bunem's rage passed as quickly as it came, and he held out his pinky to his brother to make up. He even extended a peace offering of two military buttons. When even this didn't work, he emptied his pockets of all his treasures in an effort to smooth things over.

But Simha Meir would have none of it, and ran to tattle to his father.

Abraham Hersh lived by one rule—children are always wrong, and a father is always right. He, therefore, used the strap on both his sons. Jacob Bunem took his punishment in stride as if it were something coming to him, but when it came Simha Meir's turn, he stretched out on the floor and kicked his feet as if in a fit. The mother came running, picked him up, fondled him, and put him to bed.

"Meirl, treasure of mine," she crooned, "may it be my life instead of your tiniest fingernail. . . ."

She gave him her gold watch to play with, all her diamond rings and earrings.

The father didn't whip him, but he was highly suspicious.

"How come he gets these fits only when I'm about to spank him?" he asked.

The mother fluffed up the boy's pillow and glared at her husband. "Brute," she whispered under her breath, "a heart of stone."

FIVE

———————▶———————

THE THICK WALLS of Heinz Huntze's luxurious office were covered with portraits, plaques, and decorations.

In a prominent position just above the massive oak desk hung the portraits of two emperors; on the right, that of Alexander II, Autocrat of All the Russias, King of Poland, Grand Duke of Finland, etc., etc.; on the left, that of Kaiser Wilhelm I. Centered just beneath the two portraits hung the one of the founder of the mighty Huntze dynasty himself.

His portrait was not as elaborate as those of the two monarchs. His breast didn't glitter with as many crosses and medals, nor was his face as smooth and sleek as those of the pampered rulers. His round bullet skull with its brush of closely cropped pig-bristle hair vividly recalled Huntze the weaver, who had arrived with two handlooms from Saxony, rather than Huntze the industrialist. The creases in his face, which the photographer had done his best to retouch, suggested years of effort, worry, and backbreaking toil. His black frock coat and starched linen, particularly the high, stiff collar, called to mind a common workman all dressed up for some fancy occasion. For all its majestic size, the portrait wasn't at all imposing, a factor emphasized by the two royal visages looming just above it. Still, the man with the common face wasn't without his marks of distinction.

True, his breast didn't glitter with many crosses and medals, but it wasn't totally bare either. First, an Order of St. Anne, wangled for him from Petersburg by the governor-general of Piotrkow in recognition of the huge flow of moneys he had brought into the country, draped his white vest. Not that this ribbon came cheaply—it cost Heinz's daughters a bundle in gifts for the governor-general and a string of pearls for his wife. But it was worth it. Huntze, who himself wouldn't have laid out a plug pfennig for this alleged honor, had to concede that his daughters hadn't been entirely wrong; the medal looked very handsome against the snow-white vest.

Since then his factory had earned a peck of gold, silver and bronze medals for its superior output and consistently high quality.

The factory attendant, the corpulent red-haired Melchior, fiercely mustached and side-whiskered, his vast bulk encased in forest green livery complete with stripes along the seams of his breeches, *fourragères*, brass buttons, and patent-leather boots with silver tassels dangling from the high-fitted tops, stood at ramrod attention just outside the door to respond to Huntze's every beck and call, just as if he, Huntze, were royalty.

The fact was that here, in his huge plant, Heinz Huntze *was* king of his domain. The fate of thousands—men, their wives, and children—rested in his hands. If he chose, he dismissed them early so that they could go to the taverns for a beer or stretch out on the grass beside the factory or go to their choral societies to harmonize their beloved old-country songs and church hymns. If a young man got a girl pregnant, it was within Huntze's province to decide whether or not they should marry. It was entirely up to him, too, to decide whether the mill kept going day and night so that the workers could earn a whole extra ruble a week and their wives could fatten their soup with lard instead of plain oil or whether it shut down until the workers walked about with tongues hanging and their wives had to sell their bodies for a loaf of bread.

It was to him that expectant mothers came, asking him to be godfather to their unborn children, and he was the only one with the power to grant raises to workers with growing families.

It was his alone—the plant, the workers' red cabins resembling barracks, the surrounding fields where his employees planted potatoes and cabbage, the forests where their wives gathered bark and fallen twigs for firewood, the church where they worshiped, the infirmary where they were taken when a machine lopped off their fingers, the cemetery where they were buried, the choral societies where they sang of home.

Here he was the absolute ruler, more despot than the emperors whose portraits dominated his. Toothless weavers recalled the days when he was one of them, when he gossiped with them and even joined them for a beer. Now his every step, gesture, and word was discussed in hushed, reverent tones.

Like every monarch, he despised those who dared be his equal. He seethed with rage at mention of Fritz Goetzke, a former employee who had erected a mill as imposing as his. Each new number or style Huntze produced, Goetzke imme-

diately pirated. What was worse, Goetzke wouldn't let himself
be intimidated. Huntze had already squandered a small fortune
trying to push him out. He had lowered his prices to where he
was selling below cost, but the bastard managed to hang on,
the devil take him. . . .

Huntze trembled with rage at the thought of it. "I'll beat
him to death!" he shouted in the Saxon dialect that his daughters had forbidden him to use. "Things can't go on this way!"

Sitting next to him, his sales representative, Abraham Hersh
Ashkenazi, shook his head. "Herr Huntze, enough," he
pleaded. "The most practical thing is to make up with him. It
is written that *sholom*, peace, is the foundation of the world."

Huntze nearly sprang from his chair.

"You want me to make *sholom* with that shithead, that
louse? I'd sooner croak, Reb Abraham Hersh. . . ."

Abraham Hersh was touched that the German had employed
the Hebrew word for peace and even more by the fact that he
had addressed him as Reb, which was a mark of respect among
Jews. But he disagreed with the old man's approach to the
problem, and he sat there stroking his beard and trying to
mollify his employer.

He fully understood why Huntze was so irked that some
upstart, a former employee, would dare compete with him, but
business was business. Money talks, and Goetzke had the money
to do lots of talking. Besides, he had backers ready to extend
him unlimited credit. He wouldn't be undersold, and a price
war would benefit only the buyers. The one result would be
that both factories would go broke. It would make much more
sense to get together, to form a partnership and join forces—
Huntze and Goetzke.

This time Huntze did spring from his chair. "I won't hear
of such crap!" he roared, pounding the table and switching
over to an earthy Lodz Yiddish. "Not another word, Reb
Abraham Hersh," he said, stopping up his employee's mouth.
"I'll never go partners with that swine. . . ."

Abraham Hersh smoothed his beard and went to the door.
He lingered for a moment. He wanted to quote yet another
parable to the German to the effect that rage spelled only de-
struction. He felt moved to tell him the story of Kamtza and
Bar Kamtza whose enmity caused the desolation of Jerusalem.
But he couldn't put these things into German, and he doubted
he could make the gentile understand in Yiddish. He shrugged
and merely uttered a few parting words in an intimate tone.
"Herr Huntze, when you have calmed down, think over what
I've said. Only this can save the business."

Old man Huntze was so aroused that he couldn't fill his own pipe. "You," he called to his attendant, "fill my pipe and make it quick, you snot!"

His rage had caused him to revert to expressions he had used in the days when he worked a handloom.

SIX

ABRAHAM HERSH ENROLLED his twin sons in separate Hebrew schools.

Although they were but minutes apart in age, they were
years apart in intellect. Jacob Bunem was normal for his age,
an average student who showed no exceptional promise. He
learned his lessons by sheer effort and by rote so that he could
display his progress when his father examined him after his
Sabbath nap.

"Well, so be it," Abraham Hersh grunted, not overly gratified by the boy's efforts. "Tell your mother to give you a piece
of fruit and try to do better next time."

Jacob Bunem saw that he had disappointed his father, and a
shadow fell over his merry face, but only for an instant. As
soon as his mother served him his cookies and prune stew, he
reverted to his normal self. He even felt like laughing for no
reason whatever.

It was different with Simha Meir. He was a prodigy, and
when his teacher failed to keep up with him, the father took
him out of heder, the elementary Hebrew school, and turned
him over to Baruch Wolf of Leczyca who taught boys of confirmation age and even older—youths already engaged to be
married.

Every Sabbath Baruch Wolf came to Abraham Hersh's house
to test his pupil. He drank gallons of blazing tea, poured from
a stone jug kept warm by a wrapping of rags, and tried to trip
up Simha Meir with tricky questions and pitfalls that the
youngster easily parried. Baruch Wolf sweated rivers from the
hot tea and from the boy's scholarship.

"Reb Abraham Hersh," he whispered in the father's ear in
a tone the youngster easily heard, "you're raising a genius, a
prodigy!"

Abraham Hersh was delighted, but he wouldn't allow himself to show it. "See to it he's God-fearing, Reb Baruch Wolf,"

he adjoined the teacher. "A decent Jew."

He never forgot what the Warka Rabbi had predicted, that his seed would be men of wealth, without adding that they would be God-fearing Jews as well. He was uneasy about this, more so about Simha Meir than Jacob Bunem. The very fact that the boy was such a genius frightened him. He showed traits that made the father apprehensive. He wanted to know everything; he stuck his nose in everywhere; he was inquisitive, demanding, restless. Abraham Hersh knew that all prodigies tended to be this way, but this didn't reassure him. He knew that it was more important to obey God than to be a good student, better to be dull but pious than learned and lax in one's faith

And he sent Simha Meir into the kitchen for his Sabbath treat while he had another word with the teacher. "Don't forget to make the benediction," he cautioned his son. "And don't rush through it—recite every word clearly!"

He turned to Baruch Wolf with a sigh. "Don't spare the rod with the boy; he needs a firm hand."

He had enrolled Simha Meir with Baruch Wolf of Leczyca for a reason. His wife had been strongly opposed to it since the teacher was known throughout Lodz as a martinet who maimed his pupils even as he pounded the learning into them. Also, he kept them at it for hours, from early dawn until late at night. On Thursdays they got no sleep at all but studied through the night until morning. Nor did he teach them the Gemara and exegesis alone, but commentaries as well—those of others and, even more important, his own.

But as usual, Abraham Hersh disregarded what a woman said. He was anxious that the boy be broken to the yoke of Jewishness, and no one was better at this than Baruch Wolf of Leczyca.

Although the teacher was nearly seventy, his powers were far from waning. He was lean, rangy; his fingers were like pincers, and his face was slightly twisted as a result of a chill suffered during a freezing journey on foot from Leczyca to his rabbi in Kotzk. This had caused the right side of his face to be somewhat elevated so that one pointed brow tilted up and the other down; one side of a mustache jutted up with abandon, while the other drooped angrily.

And Baruch Wolf's brain was as twisted as his face. He never taught his pupils the legends found in the Gemara since he considered these fit only for women. The Scriptures, the Pentateuch, and the lighthearted treatises dealing with customs and holidays he regarded as fluff. He preferred the more solemn treatises concerning business, promissory notes, reparations, contamination and purity, both in the land of Israel and outside it. That, and ritual slaughter, and questions dealing with the conduct of priests, the burnt offerings of cattle and sheep, and the rendering of fat and tallow constituted his curriculum.

His ever-present pipe emitted acrid smoke which permeated the pupils' eyes and throats and reminded them of the debate about burnt offerings that they were studying.

His method of teaching matched the dryness, spareness, and paucity of his person. He never approached a problem head-on as logic would dictate, but by some devious route. He never spelled out what he meant since he contended that a bright youngster should perceive his meaning from a hint, an insinuation. He mumbled half words that were further obscured by the tangle of smoke, beard, and mustache. He threw out snares, loaded questions, contradictions. He entangled himself so in his own webs that often he couldn't climb out of them. And he pounded the heavy pipestem on the table or on the boys' shoulders like a coachman straining to free his team from mud.

"Gentile-heads," he would shriek, grinding the few remaining yellow fangs in his mouth, "market peasants, Polacks, Esaus, may the plague consume you!"

He dealt out merciless punishment with the heavy pipestem. He didn't differentiate, as did other teachers, between boys of distinguished and commonplace families, between rich and poor students, didn't make allowances even if his victims were engaged young men already sporting gold watches presented by prospective fathers-in-law.

And the youths swayed over the books, rubbed their brows, and strained like exhausted horses trying to escape the coachman's whistling whip upon their scarred haunches.

But it was to no avail. For the umpteenth time they began anew: "The earth outside of Israel renders one impure. . . . Tosefot, therefore, asks—"

Baruch Wolf brandished his pipestem, but the "gentile-heads" still didn't catch on. It was then that he turned to Simha Meir, the prodigy who needed no whipping.

He squinted at him slyly with the elevated right eye and said, "Tell them, Simha Meir. Show the Polacks!"

Simha Meir was the youngest in the class. He was still three years short of his Bar Mitzvah, but he was the star pupil upon whom the teacher had placed all his hopes.

Simha Meir didn't even know the place in the text they were studying because he had been playing cards under the table. Swaying sanctimoniously over the great torn Gemara, his curly flaxen earlocks bobbing beneath his silk hat, he had been busy dealing the cards with swift, agile fingers and winning pot after pot from the other boys. Although he was the youngest and was known as a conniver, a cheat, and a liar, he dominated the game, and the others deferred to him, for reasons unknown to themselves. They knew that he cheated, but he was never caught at it. And just as he duped his classmates at cards, he duped the teacher and always emerged with his hide and reputation intact.

Baruch Wolf loved to catch a pupil who had lost his place. He would suddenly pounce, seize a youngster's shoulder, and demand ominously, "Where are we, eh?"

With joy supreme he would stretch his twisted face when the youth pointed to the wrong spot and would crack his finger with the pipestem. He was particularly anxious to catch Simha Meir, but he never could. No matter how much the boy was absorbed in the cards he somehow always kept one eye on the text, and one glance sufficed to orient him to the right word.

Baruch Wolf had a whole bag of tricks with which to trap the unwary student. He would lead him like a blind nag into a ditch and play the Good Samaritan.

"It therefore follows," he would chant guilelessly, "that Reuben is guil—"

"Guilty!" the boy would finish triumphantly, taking the bait.

"Wrong, gentile-head!" the teacher would shout, and crack the miscreant's hand. "The answer is not guilty, you numskull!"

The next time the boy would be prewarned to avoid the teacher's trap. But this time the teacher would hint at the *correct* answer, knowing full well that the youth would respond with the opposite and thus would be caught again.

But Simha Meir wouldn't be deceived. Without knowing a word of the text, he would fathom the teacher's devious intentions and, avoiding every pitfall, manage to slither out of the trap. When things looked especially ominous, he would go on the attack and at the same time raise his voice and create such a diversion that the old man grew confused.

Baruch Wolf's right eye then began to rise so high that it nearly vanished under the green velvet skullcap, and the stiffened side of his mustache bristled like that of a tomcat that has just lost his grip on a fat mouse. He was ashamed before his students that such a little snot as Simha Meir had made a fool of him; he tried to back off with his pride intact, but Simha Meir wouldn't let him.

Like a spider, the youngster wove his web tighter around his teacher. He toyed with him, tightened, then released the network of sophistry he had fashioned about him. He posed a series of questions that he answered himself, then challenged his own answers. He forced the old man to squirm, stammer, and clutch at straws like a drowning man, and finally he discredited him altogether.

The boys strained not to laugh at the old man's discomfiture.

For the next few days Simha Meir was free to play cards without even bothering to hide them from the teacher. "Fat and a whole offering shall be rendered—" he chanted from the text, then continued in the same singsong: "I got thirty-one. . . "

The other students were older, and they didn't like him. It was beneath them to associate with such a little punk, and they envied him his quick mind, about which their fathers were forever reproaching them. Nevertheless, every Thursday they came to him to be tutored in the weekly portion that they would need to recite at home.

He helped them, but he demanded payment. He didn't believe in free favors. So they bought him ice cream from the Russian who toted a barrel of the stuff balanced on his head like Melchizedek bringing the wine to Abraham. Whoever among them had a watch had to allow Simha Meir to open the lid and tinker with the works to learn what made it tick— something about which he was very curious. Poor youths who had nothing material to offer had to explain the ways of sex to him. He cocked his pointed ears when the boys described how their fathers, who shared their beds, crawled out at night while they, the sons, were feigning sleep.

Sometimes Simha Meir even played a trick on his classmates. He purposely gave a boy a false interpretation of a page of the Gemara and beamed with joy when the victim got soundly smacked for his error. Even then, the boys didn't retaliate. They strongly suspected that he had duped them, but they couldn't prove it. They bore all kinds of resentments against the little imp, but no one else could so befuddle the teacher, no one else could so skillfully deal the cards under the table, no one else could cause such spats between the teacher and his wife as could Simha Meir.

The teacher was married to his second wife, one much younger than he. She was clumsy, sloppy, and barren, the reason her first husband had divorced her. She didn't see or hear well; she spilled and dropped everything she touched and tripped over every straw. Baruch Wolf couldn't stand her. She didn't grasp his ironic subtleties, which annoyed him considerably, and whatever she said to him raised his hackles.

"Baruch Wolf," she whined in her singsong, drawing out each word as if it were rubber, "Baruch Wolf, will you come eat?"

"What then, you cow, the food will come to me?" he rejoined.

"Baruch Wolf, what would you like?"

"Chicken soup with noodles," he said.

"Where would I get chicken soup in the middle of the week?" she countered.

"Then why do you ask, jackass?" he raged.

"Baruch Wolf, will you wash up for dinner?"

"What then, ox, I'll wash the food instead?"

She didn't respond. She knew that he could never give a straight answer to anything. But when he really lost his temper at her, she burst into tears and dabbed her eyes with a corner of her apron, driving Baruch Wolf into a towering rage. Nothing irked him more than tears. Even his pupils dared not cry when he whipped them. He pounded his pipestem on the table, swept aside the Gemara, and dismissed the pupils.

"I don't want to be a teacher anymore!" he screamed. "Why should I break my back for you—so that you should drown me with your tears? I'll stay at the studyhouse, and Jews will feed me already. . . . Boys, go home!"

Before he could even get the words out, the boys were sliding down the banisters of the two-story winding staircase. They were anxious to get out before he changed his mind.

Even when Baruch Wolf's wife made every effort to avoid irritating her husband, Simha Meir helped things go wrong. When he was excused to go down to the water barrel in the courtyard to wash up and say a blessing after a bowel movement, he would first sneak into the kitchen and spill a pitcher of borscht or knock over the little iron cooking pot on the lopsided tripod.

The teacher's wife would be sitting absentmindedly darning a sock drawn over a glass and wouldn't notice the little rogue, who by then was already back in the courtyard piously intoning the words of the blessing. Hearing the crash, she would wring her hands and race into the kitchen to try to rescue the pot before her husband heard the commotion.

"Beat it, may an unnatural death befall you!" she would curse the cat, blaming it for the damage.

But the teacher, deep in some obtuse commentary, had already heard that his meal had been ruined, and he would launch a tirade. "A beggar you'll make of me yet, you booby! You'll drive me out of house and home!"

From fear and the urge to set things straight, she would smash a clay pot that shattered with a dull thud. The teacher would go completely berserk. Now she would no longer be able to contain her tears and would erupt in a wail. Baruch Wolf would pound the pipestem against the table and shriek, "Boys, go home! I'm no longer a teacher!"

For hours the youths wandered through the streets of Lodz. They raced down side streets and alleys, exulting in their freedom. They visited marketplaces where peasants milled among wagons, horses, cattle, swine, poultry, sacks of grain. Jewish housewives in bonnets over shaved skulls wandered among the wagons. They tested the chickens by blowing into their behinds, even poked their fingers inside their cloacas to see if they were carrying eggs. Jews slapped gentile palms to seal bargains, haggled, chewed kernels of grain.

From there the boys headed for construction sites where masons slaked lime and toted bricks in hods. Lodz was still growing street by street, and new stores, bazaars, and warehouses were always going up.

They proceeded to Balut with its narrow alleyways where from all sides, looms and sewing machines clacked and the songs of the workers filled the air. They bought sticky almonds in tiny stores thick with flies, as well as all kinds of cloying cookies and candies.

Simha Meir collected the groschens from the boys and entered the shop of the Turk with the red skullcap to buy a slice of raisin bread. The boys hesitated to taste it since it was probably not kosher, but Simha Meir had no such compunctions, and he chewed with relish. Each raisin he found sparked a light in his darting eyes.

They proceeded to the cropped fields where goats grazed. They stretched out on the grass and played cards. As always, Simha Meir won all the money.

The day was long, but for the boys it was never long enough. They crawled over the sand flats where dragoons drilled while noncoms pounded their legs with their scabbards. They assembled in the marketplaces where the town crier beat his drum and reported all manner of official tidings: who had been the victim of a burglary, who had lost a pig, who had been sentenced to prison, whose candlesticks or bedding were being sold in lieu of taxes.

Finally, they entered the red-light district—a narrow street where only recently brothels had sprung up. Prior to that, people had gathered here from all over to fulfill their natural functions under the open sky. Now small flimsy shacks with slanted attics and low windows stood here. If someone came to urinate or defecate out of old habit, the pimps and brothel owners would beat him up.

The brothels were staffed by cheap whores to accommodate soldiers and peasants who had left wives behind to work in the city. They also serviced the young Jewish journeymen who manned the city's handlooms.

The boys knew that this street was out of bounds to them, and this very fact drew them here. They ran through the narrow little street, stole covert glances at the bedraggled Jewish and gentile wenches sitting on the thresholds, cracking seeds. Not that they had any intentions of coming close to these girls, God forbid. Still they loved to hear the girls' entreaties: "Come on in, boys, you'll enjoy it. . . ."

And they raced home at dusk in time to say the afternoon prayers, when across the poorly paved streets, lamplighters, dressed all in black and carrying long poles, lit the streetlights scattered sparsely through the city. It was miraculous the way the lamplighters used their long poles to hook the ropes holding the lamps, pull them down, and ignite them with their torches. The boys looked on enraptured as the men cleaned the sooty chimneys, poured out kerosene from their cans, turned the wicks, and hauled the lamps back into place with the ropes.

"A good week!" the boys exclaimed in Yiddish when the lanterns were lit. "A good week!"

The lamplighter was vexed. He thought that the Yids were making fun of him and chased after them. He seized the slowest and hauled him to the top of a lamppost.

The boys fled, the skirts of their gabardines and the fringes of their ritual garments fluttering behind them.

"Bat!" they hooted at the pursuing lamplighter. "Angel of Death!"

And in the midst of the teenaged youths raced the flushed, tiny ten-year-old Simha Meir.

At home, he would find Jacob Bunem down on all fours, giving his sisters piggyback rides. Little Dinele was there, too. She no longer lived nearby, but she still came to visit her girl-friends and, more important, Jacob Bunem. Although he was already a big boy, he enjoyed playing with his sisters. He ignored the fact that it didn't behoove a boy his age to be with girls. He would get down on all fours when his mother wasn't looking and play the horse. He would tell all his sisters and Dinele to climb on his back, and he would gallop across the floor, supporting the whole crew. He would even rear like a real horse until the girls squealed in fear. Dinele would tighten her plump little arms around his neck to keep from falling and cling to him, laughing till tears came. Jacob Bunem gamboled with enthusiasm and whinnied like a colt.

"Jacob Bunem," Dinele asked, "are you afraid of a lion?"

"No," Jacob Bunem said resolutely.

When Simha Meir came in and saw his brother with the girls, he would try to shame him. "Jackass, I'll tell Father. . . . Dunce, you'll forget all your lessons!"

Jacob Bunem blushed. He was mortified to be called a dunce before Dinele, especially since it happened to be true. "You'll hang by your tongue in the other world, tattletale!" he warned Simha Meir.

But he was afraid to have their father find out, and he dickered with his brother, offering him anything he wanted if he would only keep silent. But Simha Meir wouldn't be bribed with mere objects, and he offered to play cards with Jacob Bunem. Naturally he quickly won all of his brother's cash, while his sisters, and Dinele most of all, glared at him and chanted as they once had in the courtyard:

> Simha Meir is a liar,
> Watch him jump into the fire. . . .

SEVEN

———◆———

ABRAHAM HERSH ASHKENAZI GOT HIS WAY.

Heinz Huntze ranted, raved, and stamped his feet, vowing that he would sooner go begging than take in that swine and snotnose Fritz Goetzke, but in the end, Abraham Hersh prevailed. He shuttled between Huntze and Goetzke, reasoning, appeasing, quoting parables from the holy books, until he arranged the partnership linking the two houses into one mighty firm bearing the name Huntze and Goetzke.

On account of this billing, the partnership almost ran aground at the last minute. Each partner was adamant that his name should come first, and Abraham Hersh had to employ all his tact and diplomacy to get Goetzke to yield the honor to Huntze.

His reward was his appointment as sales representative of the combined firm.

In a section of Wilki previously barred to Jews, on a street named Piotrkow, Huntze built a big stone house with iron-barred windows and massive metal doors for his representative. It contained deep cellars, vaults, and high lofts and was crammed from ceiling to floor with bales of goods produced by the Huntze and Goetzke plant. The sign outside featured all the gold, silver, and bronze medals the factory had won, along with the names of the partners and of its new representative. The sign painter even included the factory's emblem—two bearded Teutons nude except for fig leaves and spears—but Abraham Hersh made him remove it since it violated the second commandment. For him, his name and the medals sufficed.

For a long time Huntze's daughters, who wouldn't allow their father to speak Low German, had been wrinkling their noses at the Jewish scum scurrying around the factory courtyard and their father's offices. They made too much noise, these Yids; they talked Yiddish to their father, seized him familiarly by the lapels, or tugged at his buttons. You couldn't put a foot out of the palace—which adjoined the factory—without stepping into a pack of them in their long gabardines, jabbering their jargon.

For years now the daughters had been badgering their father to appoint a sales representative so as to spare himself such filthy company, but the old man had resisted. Beside being able to save the commissions he would have had to shell out, he relished the give-and-take of business, the haggling and excitement. Nothing pleased him more than outfoxing the sharp Jews.

He was beyond salvation, Old Man Huntze. You couldn't get him to appreciate the fine things of life. He preferred a stein of beer with a friend to champagne, a stinking clay pipe to imported cigars. He even used Yiddish for sparring with the merchants.

But when the business grew and the Jew Ashkenazi had to be compensated for arranging the partnership and saving the business from ruin, Huntze relented and appointed him the sales representative.

The great warehouse on Piotrkow Street now hummed with activity. Jews milled around the bales of goods stacked from floor to ceiling in every corner of the building. They converged upon the office where Abraham Hersh sat, skullcap on head, poring over heavy ledgers reminiscent of volumes of the Gemara. "Reb Abraham Hersh," they pleaded, "when will you give us a few minutes already? Time is money!"

The clerks, young men in swallow-tailed gabardines and pencils tucked behind ears, tried to serve the lesser merchants themselves. "The boss is busy," they would say. "We'll take care of you personally."

"What do I need with a tail when I can have the head?" the merchants countered.

Occasionally an out-of-town merchant remembered that he had neglected to say the mourner's prayer after a departed parent, and right then and there he would rub his hands in the dry dust and recite the prayer along with a hastily assembled quorum mumbling impatient "amens," eager to get back to business. The clerks grumbled, but they dared not voice their displeasure since upon such occasions Abraham Hersh himself set the books aside, quickly made the ablution, and joined in with thunderous "amens." Only Goldlust the bookkeeper growled in Germanized Yiddish, "A place of business isn't a Hasidic clubhouse, you pack of rustic beasts. . . ."

* * *

Abraham Hersh's home was always filled with strangers—Russian and Lithuanian Jewish salesmen, merchants, factors, and agents who converged by the hundreds upon Lodz to buy up goods at cheap prices which they then sold from China to Persia—wherever the Russian flag flew.

Dressed to modern garb, with beards trimmed or totally shaved, so indifferent to their faith that they didn't mind skipping a prayer or a blessing, or even taking a ride on the Sabbath, they despised the Polish Jews with their long gabardines, narrow caps, drawn-out Yiddish, and piety, just as the Polish Jews loathed *them* as schemers, connivers, and near gentiles. But when it came to business, all such distinctions were laid aside.

There were few hotels in Lodz, only some ratty inns and boardinghouses, so most of the strangers stayed with the merchants with whom they were dealing.

There was always a crowd for lunch at Abraham Hersh's table. Jews in derbies smacked their lips over the fat Polish roast geese and the sweet gefilte fish few could afford in Lithuania. Out of deference to their host, they made their ablutions, mumbled the benedictions, dipped bread in salt, and even interposed snatches of Judaic wisdom, mostly passages from the Scriptures with which they were quite conversant.

But mainly they talked business—about the legendary Russian merchant princes, about remote cities, exotic peoples and customs. At night, sofas were set up in all the rooms to accommodate the horde of visitors.

Abraham Hersh was most anxious to guard his sons from half-assimilated strangers, and he dismissed the boys from the table early. Jacob Bunem went off to his games, from which he still hadn't weaned himself despite his age, but Simha Meir lingered, his ears cocked like a hare's, drinking in every word.

"Simha!" his father exclaimed, employing the boy's first name only out of respect for the memory of the Przysucha Rabbi. "Go study! Don't waste your time on idleness!"

But Simha Meir was in no hurry to leave the table. He used various pretexts and excuses, at which he was so adept, to gain a little more time with the fascinating strangers. Without his father's knowledge, he guided the guests about the city, giving directions to streets, marketplaces, and stores, for which the strangers pinched his cheek and tipped him a half or even a whole ruble. They also encouraged him to acquire a secular education and to become a man of the world.

"The only thing that counts is *prosveshtchenie*—education," they told him, "you hear, lad?"

The boy didn't fully grasp the difficult Russian word, but he gathered its meaning and the message stuck in his head.

He also made it a point to visit his father's place of business, even though the father had strictly forbidden it. Under various pretexts, he kept dropping in and winking at the clerks to keep his secret.

Abraham Hersh warned his employees not to let his son in, but Simha Meir pleaded with them not to betray him, and they hid him among the bales of goods, where he sat happily reading the labels attached to the bolts. He tore off the seals, studied the various patterns and colors, and absorbed the smell, sight, and din of business, relishing them more than the raisins in the Turk's raisin bread.

When his father was away, he would steal into his office, glance into the thick ledgers, question Goldlust, the bookkeeper, about everything, badger the clerks to explain this or that. Nothing escaped his attention. He envied the grown-ups who didn't have to attend school and who were free to do as they pleased.

"The boy will get me with calf with all those questions," Goldlust, the bookkeeper, would complain as the youngster pored over the books.

"He's growing up a regular smart-aleck," the clerks remarked, pursing their lips. "Hoo-hah!"

Simha Meir's thoughts were years in the future. When he was grown, he would sit in an office just like Father's, but without a skullcap—bareheaded like the German merchants across the street. He would not admit the kind of riffraff his father did, either. They would have to doff their caps to him first and address him in German, not Yiddish.

EIGHT

THE LARGE DINING ROOM of the manufacturer of women's kerchiefs, Haim Alter, was bright and warm. It was late Saturday—actually long past the appearance of the three stars signifying the end of the Sabbath—but Haim Alter was only now conducting the ceremony of ushering out the holy day. He liked to linger in the Hasidic prayerhouse over the Sabbath meals. He had a yen for music, and he enjoyed singing chants in front of an audience. He was also eager to say the benediction, and he constantly bid for the honor with bottles of beer. Afterward, he said the evening prayers before the pulpit so that by the time he ushered out the Sabbath, it was already late in the day.

"A good week, a good week," he would say expansively, smiling sweetly at his wife, his daughter, and his sons gathered in the large, overstuffed dining room, which was brightly illuminated by the many candles in the silver holders and the large copper lamp suspended by heavy chains above the enormous oak dining table.

He filled a large carved silver goblet with wine, letting some spill over into the saucer as a symbol of the overflowing prosperity and abundance he had been enjoying. Humming a chant under his breath, he took out of the sideboard the tall carved silver spice box with its green turret and silver flags and bells. He folded back the sleeves of his silk gabardine over the hairy, plump, pampered hands, to protect the garment from spilled wine, and told his only daughter, Dinele, to hold up the twisted Sabbath candle.

"Higher, Dinele," he said to the thirteen-year-old girl with the chestnut braids, "this will bring you a tall bridegroom."

A blush suffused the girl's soft cheeks, and she made a face at her father, but she lifted the candle higher. Haim Alter raised the goblet high. He looked over the room to see if everyone, including Hadassah, the maid, was present. Satisfied, he launched into the ceremony in a loud chant, enunciating each word so that its sweetness permeated everywhere. The flickering candle illuminated his soft, fleshy hands as he praised the Almighty for having created fire. He shook the spice box at length to extract more flavor from the spices, and he inhaled with relish the sweet scents that exuded from the opened lid.

"Oh, ah!" he exulted, praising God for having created such redolent spices. He passed the spice box to his wife and children, so they, too might sniff, and waited until he had heard everyone make the blessing.

"Well now." He lightly rebuked his daughter for mumbling the benediction too quickly and merely going through the motions. "Blessed be He who has created fragrant plants," he intoned pointedly for her benefit.

Even the maid was handed the spice box to sniff after everyone had had his turn. But Hadassah invariably grew rattled and forgot how to poke her nose inside the silver lid, and this made them all laugh.

Haim Alter himself barely refrained from smiling as he concluded the ceremony. He folded back a corner of the tablecloth, spilled a quantity of wine over the table, doused the flickering candle, then dipped both hands into the wine and touched the wet fingers to every pocket of his gabardine, velvet vest, and broadcloth trousers as an invitation to a prosperous good week, portending a generous inflow of cash into the pockets, with God's help. He touched his olive eyes with the wine and crooned; "A good week, a joyous week, a pleasureful week, a prosperous week, a lucky week."

He took off the silk gabardine and cried loudly, "Samuel Leibush, my robe!"

Samuel Leibush, a young man with a trimmed blond beard and a paper collar, ran up quickly. He snatched up the silk gabardine Haim Alter had discarded and helped him into a flowered cloth robe.

"Your cigar, Reb Haim," he said with a smile, holding out the humidor of imported cigars.

He knew the terrible deprivation his employer had suffered during the Sabbath, and he was ready the moment the ceremony was over.

Haim Alter beamed with contentment over his man's devoted service. He bit off the tip of the cigar and drew in the flame the servant held to the other end. Puffing away, Haim Alter intoned: ". . . and He shall give unto the . . ."—the words of the concluding prayer. He savored the sweet words of the Sabbath-night prayer and actually smelled the aromas

of the dews and oils God bestowed upon those Jews who
hewed to the path of righteousness. And still reciting the
gratifying phrases, he opened the letters and telegrams that
had accumulated over the Sabbath.

When he reached the last lines of the prayer, he hurried
his pace, he couldn't wait for a glass of the fresh-brewed
aromatic tea for which he had been yearning all Sabbath.

"Privehshe," he called to his wife, "Priveh love, you'll tell
the maid to bring me tea with lemon, won't you, Privehshe?"

Priveh, a plump, striking, clear-skinned matron in a silk
dress with a train, pearls around her neck, diamonds on every
finger, and a fair curly wig which made her look like an opera
diva, came mincing up and, with the sweetest smile on blood-
red lips, held out a coquettish hand for her weekly allowance.

"Money, money," Haim Alter grumbled good-naturedly.
"For what do you need so much money, Privehshe?"

Within a second, her sweet smile vanished. "*You* run the
household," she snapped hurling the ring of keys to all the
closets and pantries at her husband.

Haim Alter squirmed with contrition. "Privehshe, Priveh
love," he pleaded. "You know I didn't mean anything by it.
It was just a little joke. . . ."

But Priveh wouldn't let him off the hook that easily. She
knew that her Haim was crazy about her, and she wanted
to teach him a lesson so that in the future he would know
how to act toward a daughter of Ansel, the Warsaw Rabbi.

Haim Alter nearly burst into tears. He couldn't stand anger
or resentment, the very opposite of Priveh, who delighted in
confrontations. At the least provocation she would tell Hadassah to make up the master's bed on the dining room sofa, and
she wouldn't let him near her.

When this happened, Haim Alter suffered grievously. He
yearned for her soft, warm flesh, her delectable neck. He was
too weak and too self-indulgent for prolonged spats, and he
would give in, begging her forgiveness with handsome presents,
something Priveh really appreciated—a new dress or a piece of
jewelry.

He was especially irked that a thoughtless remark had slipped
out now, at the beginning of the new week. It was true that
Priveh was most extravagant in running the household—he
couldn't figure out how she managed to spend so much money
—but he should have bitten his tongue before sounding off.
He made up to her. He stroked the golden curls of her wig
and offered her his purse—all the cash he had on him.

"Here, Privehshe, take whatever you want," he cajoled, "all

the money in the world isn't worth a moment of your displeasure. . . ."

Priveh relented and finally accepted the roll of bills that he had forced on her, uncounted.

"Everything all right now?" he asked, and in front of the servants he patted her pouting face.

"Drink your tea before it gets cold, Haimshe," Priveh said, appeased at last.

Haim Alter gulped the tea in huge swallows, content that all was peaceful in the house again. He went over the accounts for the week with his man, Samuel Leibush. For a long time they pored over the stacks of papers—searching, figuring, growing more and more entangled and unable to arrive at any conclusion.

Haim Alter kept his books in traditional Lodz-Jewish fashion —which is to say, in an erroneous Yiddish and broken Hebrew. One side of the page was marked "incoming," the other, "outgoing." But nothing tallied, and the servant was of no help at all.

Lazy, placid, absentminded, Haim Alter kept sloppy books. His pockets bulged with papers, figures, notations that should have been entered—but somehow he never got around to doing it.

The ledgers were a mess—blotted, erased, the margins full of numbers and annotations which he couldn't figure out. So many entries accumulated by the end of the week that Haim Alter took the easy way out. He threw the ledger aside and told his man to escort him to the factory, which lay deep within the courtyard.

"The less figuring, the more prosperity," he observed. "Isn't that so, Samuel Leibush?"

"Absolutely, Reb Haim," Samuel Leibush concurred as he turned up the wick in the lantern.

The clacking of looms echoed in the courtyard. Haim Alter loved his factory. These weren't numbers and figures to boggle the mind—this was something real and tangible. The more the looms rattled, the more work the weavers turned out, the more profit flowed in, the better this was for business—it was as simple as that.

On Saturday nights the weavers worked longer than usual to make up for the time lost during the holiday. By the dim light of tallow candles affixed to looms, they sat—fifty men in all—and turned out women's kerchiefs. The workers supplied their own candles, a precedent established by the earliest employers who had maintained two- or three-man shops. Even though Haim Alter's factory was a big one, the old custom prevailed.

Haim Alter disliked progress. He liked things just as they were under his father and grandfathers. That was the reason he hadn't converted to steam despite pressures to do so.

His factory was Jewish through and through. There were amulets on every doorpost. He had even set up a small lectern among the bales of wool and crates in his storeroom, with a tin candelabrum so that the workers could recite their afternoon and evening prayers without having to leave the premises. In winter, when they reported to work before the morning star came out, they conducted their morning services there as well.

He also saw to it that his workers observed all the laws of Jewishness. No young worker dared sit at his loom bareheaded, even in the worst heat, be it only a makeshift paper cone that covered his skull. Ritual garments were a must. Haim Alter took care that the younger men didn't trim their beards or wear short secular jackets instead of the traditional gabardine. He knew that the Jews had been redeemed from bondage in Egypt for three reasons—because they hadn't changed their customs, their language, or their attire. He knew from the holy books. that sin was as contagious as the plague and that one sick sheep could infect the whole flock.

"If I wanted gentiles, I would have hired real gentiles and converted to steam. Whoever works for me must remain a Jew," he was fond of saying.

"A blessing upon your head, Reb Haim," the older weavers bleated fawningly. They were lean, broken men with faded beards, weary faces, and eyes red from the years of working in semidarkness.

Haim Alter made a contribution to their weavers' synagogue, Love of Friends, in Balut, which was crammed among factories, lumberyards, and coalyards. He also maintained a tutor who instructed them on Sabbath afternoons—"Ethics of the Fathers" in summer, chapters from Psalms in winter. The teacher was a learned man with a thorough knowledge of the other world. He sat tightly squeezed among the exhausted weavers and lectured on the follies of human life and the triviality of flesh.

"From where dost thou issue, man?" he asked in a chanting tone, and answered, "From a stinking drop. To where goest thou? To a place of worms and worms. . . ."

Outside Balut stretched open fields where Jewish teamsters sprawled on the sweet grass, dozing, while their horses grazed. Beyond the pastures lay a shady and redolent pine forest, but

Haim Alter's weavers didn't go there. Haim Alter checked with the teacher as to which of them had played hooky, and whoever repeated the offense was fired, for it was forbidden a Jew to wander through field and forest on the holy day in a place frequented by gentiles and other riffraff. No, a Jew had to study on the Sabbath, just as he, Haim Alter, did.

All Sabbath afternoon he sat on the veranda of his summer villa, reading the holy books and discussing Jewishness with fellow Hasidim. How did the Holy Torah put it? That a Jew who walked outside and exclaimed, "How lovely is the tree!" or "How luscious is the field!" had forfeited his life. . . .

Besides, all these walks tended to make workers lazy, and on Saturday nights they had to work until midnight or later to make up for the time lost on the Sabbath.

Haim Alter was like a surrogate father to his men. When a worker's wife bore a son and the father came with cake and whiskey to Haim Alter's house to invite him to the circumcision, where he would be accorded the honor of holding the infant during the ceremony, Haim Alter never refused, busy as he might be. Even though he was, thank God, a man of substance, he didn't hold himself above his employees, for it was written that all Jews were brothers. Nor was the privilege of holding the newborn infant something to be sneezed at. His presence lent grandeur to the occasion; he ate the meager cake even though it offended his taste, and he left a gift of three rubles.

Likewise, when a weaver married off a daughter, Haim Alter sent a nice wedding present even if he was too busy to attend the ceremony. On Passover he gave each worker a bottle of the raisin wine that he bought cheaply from a fellow Hasid at the studyhouse. On Succoth he provided the ceremonial citrus fruit for the weavers' synagogue. True, it wasn't as handsome as the one he bought for himself, but it served the purpose. In the event one of his men died, God forbid, he dropped whatever he was doing and went to the cemetery since escorting a Jew to his eternal rest was a good mark on one's record of good deeds. He contributed toward the cost of the shrouds, and he also sent Samuel Leibush with some money for the bereaved family.

Yes, he did everything he could for his people, for which he was lauded in the Hasidic prayerhouse he frequented. For these reasons, he loved his factory, and he listened with pleasure now as it hummed with activity—every loom clacking away and making money.

Still in his robe and skullcap, he went inside to have a look at how the work was progressing. Samuel Leibush walked in front, lighting the way.

"Is everything in order?" Haim Alter asked as they paused on the threshold.

"Everything is in order, Reb Haim," Samuel Leibush assured him. "Two looms were out of commission, but they're all right now."

"Who fixed them?" Haim Alter asked.

"Tevye, the one they call the World Isn't Lawless, did," Samuel Leibush replied. "He fiddled and fiddled with them until he got them to run like they were greased."

"The lad has golden hands," Haim Alter said. "But he's a rebel and a knave. He tears the guts out of young and old alike."

"What can you expect when you spoil him so? . . . Five rubles a week! Whoever heard of paying such wages?" Samuel Leibush said with assumed outrage as he opened the door for his employer.

"A good week! A good week!" Haim Alter greeted one and all. The half-dim factory burst into sudden frenzy. The older workers, who had been discussing the problem of marrying off daughters, turned back to their looms and hurried their movements. They adjusted the sidepieces of their glasses and let their pale, veiny hands fly over the looms as they pumped their weary feet and swayed up and down on their seats.

"A good week, Reb Haim, a good week," they responded without looking up from their work.

The younger men, who had been chanting, "Be not afraid, my slave, Jacob," with intricate cantorial embellishments, were left with the unsung chorus still on their lips. They accelerated their pace so that the thread was fairly flying.

Haim Alter walked from loom to loom. He touched a kerchief here, made some observation there, checked the output. Spotting a stain from a sweaty hand, he wagged a threatening finger. "No botching, boys, and no eating at work. You see to it, Samuel Leibush, you hear?"

"I hear, Reb Haim," Samuel Leibush replied, glaring at the weavers. "How many times have I told you to keep those hands clean?"

Actually no one had ever heard him say this, but the looms kept on clacking. The rhythmic pounding was like music to Haim Alter's ears. It brought to his mind the sound of money being minted. He poked his nose into all the stockrooms, which were crammed with raw goods and finished kerchiefs, and his heart soared.

"Let people say what they want," he mused, "let them say handweaving is finished and steam is the wave of the future —I'll stick to my handlooms." And why shouldn't he? They'd provided him a handsome income, blessed be His name. If things remained just as they were, he would be content. His women's kerchiefs were the rage of Poland and Russia. The gentiles literally snapped them up. So many orders were coming in that it might be necessary to lengthen the workers' hours. His weavers turned out a better product than any machines could. Let the Germans and the Jewish heretics put up plants and chimneys; he'd stick to his handlooms.

For what did he need smoke and chimneys and whistles? His weavers managed to report to work on time without whistles. Nor did his devotion to Jewishness stand in the way. Nothing prevented a man from being a good Jew and wealthy at the same time—Torah and *srorah* were the answer—the Good Book and business together.

Smug with pride and a sense of accomplishment, he walked the length of the looms, his olive eyes glinting with pleasure as the kerchiefs took shape with every minute, every second. Trailing him like a shadow was the ubiquitous Samuel Leibush. Finally, they came to the loom of Tevye, nicknamed Tevye the World Isn't Lawless.

He was the only one who hadn't acknowledged the boss's presence. Slight, with sharp yellow eyes beneath bushy eyebrows and a fair, sprouting beard slightly trimmed at the sides, he stood at his loom and fed red thread into the borders of a black shawl. A paper collar surrounded his scrawny neck, inside which his Adam's apple bobbled. His lean hands flew as swiftly as a magician's as he sang not a cantorial piece, but some secular Yiddish song.

Sensing the boss near him, he lowered his tone so that the words could be heard, yet could not be clearly discerned.

It was an odd little ditty Tevye had introduced into the factory some weeks earlier. It quoted a rich employer who took offense when his workers wept at their jobs even as he was guzzling his beer and smoking his cigars. Part of it went like this:

> Stop pissing with the tears, you fool,
> You're staining the cotton and wool.
> Your belly is empty? So what?
> I'll fire you on the spot.

Haim Alter had heard from his lackey about the seditious song being sung in his factory. He couldn't quite make out the words Tevye was humming, but he suspected that the song somehow mocked him, Haim Alter.

"What's that you're singing there, Tevyele?" he asked with an affected smile.

"Just a song," Tevye replied, keeping his eyes on his work.

"A Sabbath hymn?" Haim Alter probed innocently. "So why don't you sing it louder? Let us all hear it—after all, it's the Sabbath night. . . ."

Tevye didn't respond. He stopped humming.

Haim Alter glanced at Tevye's ritual fringes, so shrunken and snarled from repeated washing as to be almost meaningless, and he left the factory in a huff.

"Oy, Tevyele," he groaned, not finishing the sentence, "my, my, my. . . ."

Everyone's eyes were immediately riveted on Tevye. He stuck in the boss's craw and ruined his post-Sabbath glow.

But Haim Alter's mood didn't last; there was someone he had been anxious to see waiting for him at home.

"Ah, there you are, you rascal. A good week!" He welcomed his guest and paternally tweaked his ear.

It was Simha Meir, Abraham Hersh's elder son. He was playing cards with Haim Alter's sons. They were fleshy, overgrown youths and big for their age, but they let the little sharpster push them around and win all their money.

Haim Alter was flattered that Simha Meir associated with his lummoxes, for Simha Meir was known as a lad with a sharp head for everything, including business. He could master the most difficult calculations, and each time Haim Alter was perplexed by some mathematical problem he turned to Simha Meir for help.

Mumbling to himself, wetting the tip of the pencil on his tongue, the boy would add, subtract, divide, and multiply until everything tallied. Himself a thundering booby, Haim Alter would chastise his sons for being such dummies.

"You see, you knuckleheads," he would say, indicating Simha Meir, "here's a genius growing up. One day he'll lead all Lodz by the nose. . . ."

Inside his head there had already blossomed the notion of corralling the little prodigy as a husband for his only daughter, Dinele.

True, he was only a boy, not yet thirteen, and the wedding would have to be put off a few years, but it was high time to propose the match since such a prize would not lie long unclaimed. And for this reason Haim Alter was pleased to find the youth at his house.

"Dinele, daughter of mine, serve our guest some tea with strudel," he said.

Reluctantly Dinele brought tea to the little Hasid with his satin Sabbath gabardine, satin hat pushed back on his head, and sly, darting eyes. His head jerked like a bird pecking kernels, and his fair earlocks cast comical shadows upon the wall.

She had never liked him from the days when he used to loosen her hair ribbon or pour sand on her head. Besides, for years now she had been attending a gentile girls' academy, where her head was constantly filled with tales of kings and heroes and where she, the daughter of a Hasid, was instructed in social graces and customs. She studied piano and dancing and was always the court lady in the school plays, dressed in crinoline and waving an enormous fan.

Brown-haired, blue-eyed, pretty, pampered, she was very popular with her gentile classmates. Barely thirteen, she already read German and French novels about princes, duels and love affairs, and she dreamed of a knight who would carry her off to his castle on top of a mountain.

She found it amusing to watch the little Hasid who couldn't sit still a moment and who cast his eyes everywhere at once, as if eternally searching, probing, sniffing.

Dinele put the glass of tea before the boy, then hurried away, eager to get back to her books.

Her father tried to detain her. "Don't you recognize him, Dinele?" he asked. "This is Reb Abraham Hersh's Simha Meir. He is a brilliant fellow—writes a beautiful letter."

He turned to the boy. "Show her how you write a letter in German, Simha Meir. Let her not think that only gentile schools can train a person. You can learn much more from the Gemara, beg the comparison, than all the *goyish* schools put together. . . ."

Employing his finest script, Simha Meir composed a business letter addressed to an imaginary Mr. Goldman in Leipzig, just as his father's bookkeeper, Goldlust, had taught him.

"*Hochwohlgeboren* Herr Solomon Goldman," he began anxious to show off to the girl, but she—barely able to contain herself—raced to her mother's bedroom and flung herself into her mother's arms with such maniacal laughter that Priveh's artificial blond curls began to bob.

Haim Alter admired the boy's handwriting. He clapped his fleshy hands and decided to send for Samuel Zanvil of Alexander to propose the match to Abraham Hersh Ashkenazi before it was too late.

The next day he acted on his decision. "Samuel Leibush," he ordered his man, who was still struggling with the account books, "tomorrow, God willing, you'll go to Reb Samuel Zanvil of Alexander and ask him to come see me. I need him for something important, you hear?"

"I'll do it first thing in the morning, Reb Haim," the servant replied.

"Add, 'God willing,' you boor!" Haim Alter cautioned him. "How can sinful man be sure that there will be a tomorrow?"

"God willing," Samuel Leibush said, appalled at his own ignorance.

NINE

———◆———

PRIOR TO THEIR BAR MITZVAH, which happened to
fall on Passover, Abraham Hersh went to present his twin
sons to his rabbi. The Warka Rabbi was no longer living,
and Abraham Hersh had transferred his allegiance to the
Rabbi of Alexander, a town close to Lodz.

As usual, his wife wept about being left alone on the holiday,
and as usual, Abraham Hersh ignored her. He was anxious
to have the rabbi meet the boys and instill within them a love
and respect for Jewishness. He remembered the Warka Rabbi's
prophecy that his sons would grow up men of wealth, and he
brooded about the omission of any reference to their piety.
For all his absorption with business, Abraham Hersh knew
that wealth and business were temporal, while God, the Torah,
and heaven were eternal.

Thus, he asked God—whom he deeply feared—that if indeed it was destined that his sons be wealthy but impious, He
take them before they reached manhood.

Now that they were about to be confirmed, he wanted to
discuss and resolve this issue with the Alexander Rabbi. He
also wanted to consult the rabbi about Simha Meir's education.
Even Baruch Wolf of Leczyca was too limited for the boy. He
would have to be placed into the hands of a more learned
master. Abraham Hersh was sorely tempted to send him to a
yeshiva, a talmudic academy, where he would be forced into
contact with poor youths, forced, like the very poorest, even
to take his meals at the homes of affluent householders. This
would take him down a peg or two and make a true Jew of
him. Abraham Hersh knew that it was better for a boy to go
out on his own, as his father had compelled him to do. Only
through hardship did a youth arrive at true faith and the fear
of God.

His wife had already gone on record that she would never
subject her little Meirl to the mercy of strangers, but this didn't

concern Abraham Hersh. When, however, his fellow Hasidim dissuaded him, contending that a boy should live at his father's house, he reconsidered. Now he wanted to hear what the rabbi had to say. And whatever the rabbi decided, Abraham Hersh would do.

Then there was the matter of the match. Haim Alter had sent Samuel Zanvil with a proposal of a match between his daughter and Simha Meir, but Abraham Hersh felt no compunction to respond. He wouldn't say yes, and he wouldn't say no. There was plenty of time to decide.

But Samuel Zanvil wouldn't be put off, and he plagued Abraham Hersh's existence. A learned man, once considerably wealthy and still brimming with arrogance toward one and all and not in the least awed by affluence or status, he kept calling on Abraham Hersh, demanding an answer. He knew everyone in Lodz; he knew what was cooking in everyone's pot; he was able to bring mountains together and wasn't afraid to fling the truth in anyone's face.

"I want you to agree to this match," he commanded rather than urged Abraham Hersh. "I'm no lackey of yours to be shunted aside. Sign the articles of engagement, and let me earn my fee because I have a daughter of my own to marry off and I can't wait. . . ."

Abraham Hersh couldn't evade him—not at home, not at the prayerhouse, not even at business. Samuel Zanvil would push his way into his office, bowling over the clerks who tried to stop him. "The gall of those flunkies!" he raged. "Who do they think you are, the governor-general?"

Actually it wasn't a bad match. Haim Alter was wealthy; the girl was his only daughter; the dowry would be substantial, the gifts lavish, the groom's board generous. Because Haim Alter was simply dying for the match, he would allow himself to be squeezed. True, his wife was said to wear a wig instead of a bonnet like a truly pious Jewess, and to put on airs, but the household was run in proper Jewish fashion and was always full of Hasidim. Still, it would be up to the rabbi. He, Abraham Hersh, wouldn't make a move without the rabbi's recommendation.

He ordered the German coachman to hitch up the carriage and to drive him to Alexander.

He packed his finest clothes and the new satin gabardines and velvet hats he had ordered for the boys' confirmation. Into three brand-new red kerchiefs he placed a quantity of matzos specially baked of black flour—hard crooked matzos to last each of them through Passover. He also brought baskets containing several bottles of good Passover wine for the rabbi.

He picked up so many poor Hasidim along the way that the driver seemed on the verge of apoplexy. "Ah, sweet Jesus," he groaned, "my poor horses will croak from all these Jews. . . . Off with you, you rabble!"

But the Hasidim kept piling on, tasting Abraham Hersh's Passover whiskey, and chanting hymns. "Who cares what a dumb gentile says?" they observed with contempt.

Throughout all Passover Abraham Hersh didn't let his sons out of his sight, particularly Simha Meir. He made him listen to the Hasidim quoting the rabbi's wisdom and relating past and present miracles performed by saints. He drew him into the circle of dancing men. He placed his thick, tanned hand on Simha Meir's narrow shoulder, seeking to permeate him with the Jewishness seething and foaming all around.

"You see how Jews serve their Creator?" he lectured his son. "Be a Jew, Simha!"

As they were leaving, the rabbi jovially pinched Jacob Bunem's cheek, but he spoke at length to Simha Meir, the prodigy. He tried to catch him in a tricky question, but the boy wouldn't allow himself to be tripped up, and the rabbi praised him highly to his father. "You have a fine boy there, Abraham Hersh," he said, stroking the youth's cheek. "He's got a head on his shoulders. Bring him along whenever you come. And I approve of the match. But don't send him to any yeshiva. Take him to Reb Nuske in Lodz. He isn't a follower of any court, but he is a great scholar and a saint of a Jew."

Abraham Hersh left a donation of thirty-six silver rubles and started out for home, satisfied that his problems were solved. He treated the men to cake and whiskey, and they toasted Simha Meir. "Congratulations, bridegroom. May the match be a successful one. To your health!"

They held out their hands to Jacob Bunem. "To the bridegroom's brother! May you be next, boy."

Jacob Bunem was deeply depressed. For the first time in his life he tasted despair. He had been miserable the entire holiday. The Hasidim barely glanced at him and concentrated on Simha Meir, conversing with him as if he were an adult. The rabbi himself paid no attention to him, Jacob Bunem. He merely pinched his cheek as if he were some child and lauded Simha Meir to their father. And this left Jacob Bunem feeling unworthy and embarrassed. This wasn't the courtyard where children appreciated his strength, fleetness of foot, and agility. Here the emphasis was placed on intelligence, and Simha Meir took full advantage of the situation and lorded it over his younger brother.

But what really made Jacob Bunem's heart lurch was the match between Simha Meir and Dinele. Already at home he had heard hints of it, but he had never believed that it would happen. Now he saw that it was a fact, and he wanted to die.

"Why the long face, boy?" the Hasidim taunted him. "With God's help, it'll be your turn next. Shake the bridegroom's hand, and wish him well."

Jacob Bunem held out his hand to Simha Meir and mumbled "good luck." A single meaningful glance passed between the brothers—they understood each other better than anyone.

It wasn't the gold watch or the new set of the Lemberg Talmud that Simha Meir would get that aroused Jacob Bunem's envy—it was Dinele, his brother's intended bride. To accentuate his anguish, he bit his lip until it bled.

He had always loved Dinele, ever since they had been children. He loved the feel of her plump arms around his neck as he carried her piggyback and she clung to him like some frozen little bird seeking warmth from a human hand.

Later, when they were older, she would visit their house, and although it was no longer proper, he still played with her. He would bribe Simha Meir with his most prized possessions not to tattle to their father. But it was all worth it to feel the soft, warm touch of her. Each time Sarah Leah said, "What a fine couple you'd make," his heart would lurch and a flush would spread over his cheeks.

Later they stopped seeing each other. Dinele made new friends, and she felt it beneath her to associate with the Ashkenazi girls. But Jacob Bunem never stopped longing for her, and he hung around her house for hours, hoping for a glimpse of her coming home from school in her brown skirt and blue cape and carrying her books, so that he might tip his silk hat to her. Jacob Bunem at thirteen was already a man. Unlike the other boys, he didn't subvert his masculine stirrings with leering allusions to sex or by mouthing the forbidden words, but longed with healthy yearning for Dinele, the girl with the brown ringlets that gleamed like copper and gold.

When Samuel Zanvil called on his father for the first time, Jacob Bunem was sent from the room. His heart pounded with barely suppressed expectation, and Sarah Leah winked at him knowingly. But as it soon turned out, he wasn't the one to rejoice.

No one in his family took any notice of his anguish. He couldn't verbalize his feelings to his parents, nor would it have done any good. His father considered him a near dolt; his mother was concerned only about her favorite, Simha Meir, who was puny, delicate, and forever down with some children's disease. He, on the other hand, was never sick. The only one who shared his grief was Sarah Leah, whose favorite he had always been.

"Don't fret, Jacob Bunem," she comforted him, bringing him a glass of milk, "lots of things can happen between now and the wedding."

But he only lost his temper and slammed the door in her face because she knew his feelings.

He hated his father for favoring his brother; his mother for bringing him into the world a few minutes later; the Hasidim for shining up to Simha Meir; and ultimately himself for being so stupid. "Dummox!" he castigated himself. "Peasanthead!"

But most of all, he hated his brother with a passion that was totally foreign to him.

Dinele wept her own tears when her father took her on his lap, as he had done when she was a little girl, stroked her cheeks, fingered her curls, and told her softly, "You know, daughter, you have congratulations coming for being betrothed to Simha Meir? Aren't you overjoyed, Dinele?"

She sprang from his lap and ran screaming to her mother, who turned pale in alarm. "What is it, child?"

"I don't want it!" Dinele shrieked.

The mother took her daughter in her arms and showered her with kisses. "Silly goose, we only want your happiness. People will envy you such a bridegroom."

For eight days running, Haim Alter's house was in a state of turmoil. Dinale firmly refused to be engaged. She was deeply ashamed to have her new friends discover that she was marrying a Hasidic youth in a long gabardine. She had already confiided to them that she would wed only a knight, a nobleman. She couldn't stand the Jews who came to her house. They amused and repelled her. She couldn't stand her own brothers—blowsy dullards who pulled her braids and looked down on her for being a girl. Her mind was far away in a world of castles, balls, and duels. She couldn't abide her Jewish name, and she called herself Diana.

When she launched her campaign against the match, her father looked at her with disbelief. "Silly girl," he chided her. "Do you know what you are getting—a prodigy?"

He had no hint of her inner feelings. He knew that a girl had no intellect, and could spend her childhood idling away her time, but as soon as she reached maturity, she had to marry a scholar, be given a handsome dowry, bear her husband sons, and provide her parents with grandchildren. This was the way God had intended it, and this was the way it would be.

"Wait till you see the presents you'll get," he consoled her.

The girl ran to her mother. Priveh was a worldly woman, well read and sophisticated, but she, too, scoffed at the maidenly tears.

"I cried the same way, too, Diana," she said, employing her daughter's gentile name. "I was a bright girl who could speak French. Still, I've had no regrets. May you only have such luck with your husband as I've had with your daddy."

"But I don't love him!" the girl said with feeling.

The mother laughed until all the curls of her blond wig quivered. "After the wedding, you'll come to love him."

Realizing that her fate was sealed, Dinele asked but one concession. "Mommy, I'll become a bride . . . but not his. I *hate* him!" She bowed her head and barely mumbled, "His brother . . . talk to Daddy. . . ."

And between tears she rained kisses on her mother.

The mother dried her daughter's tears with a tiny embroidered handkerchief and went to talk things over with her husband. "The girl prefers the other brother, Haimshe."

Haim Alter stuffed up both his ears with his fingers to avoid hearing such drivel. "Priveshe, what are you saying? Simha Meir is a prodigy. People envy us. And the other is a nothing, a blockhead. . . ."

When Priveh tried to say something else, Samuel Zanvil intervened. "It's not the custom to marry off the younger sibling before the elder," he said. "Just as Laban told Jacob when he chose Rachel over Leah."

"Younger by five minutes," Priveh added.

"Doesn't matter," Samuel Zanvil barked. "I wouldn't even propose such a thing to Abraham Hersh. He'd throw me out on my ear."

Priveh dropped the matter. Within days a horde of aunts, grandaunts, nephews, nieces, and cousins from both sides of the family descended upon the house. They didn't stop talking, praising the prodigy, pleading, blessing, and preaching to Dinele—urging, nagging, and adjuring her until she weakened and gave in.

Eyes red from crying, she sewed a velvet phylactery bag for her intended, embroidered upon it a gold Star of David, the groom's two names, and the Jewish date of the creation of the world. Her father bought her many costly presents, and her mother ordered a long pretty dress for her betrothal.

The engagement was celebrated with great pomp at Haim Alter's house. The town's magnates, scholars, and Hasidim from the Ashkenazi and Alter sides attended. Haim Alter even dispatched Samuel Leibush with cake and whiskey for his workers and let them go home right after the afternoon prayers.

Upon the occasion the prospective father-in-law deposited 5,000 silver rubles in the bridegroom's name in the bank and signed a pledge for an additional 2,000 to be paid prior to the wedding. These had been Abraham Hersh's terms, and Haim Alter had had no choice but to comply. An additional 3,000 rubles would come from Abraham Hersh. He didn't have to pay the full 3,000 since the groom's side was obligated to pay only a third of what the bride's side paid, but Abraham Hersh preferred round figures, and he pledged the 3,000 so that the full amount would total 10,000 rubles.

The bride signed the articles of engagement in every language she knew—Yiddish, Polish, Russian, German and French—so that she could receive a present for each signature. She was showered with diamond rings, earrings, brooches, and a heavy necklace. The wedding was deferred for several years.

Right after the betrothal had been sealed, the Hasidim ripped down the flowers Priveh had set out upon the tables, swept away the costly glassware and china, and commenced dancing on the tables. Priveh was enraged, but Haim Alter encouraged them. "Dance, Jews! On the tables and on the chairs. . . ."

Jacob Bunem sat at the foot of the table like a mourner amid the festivities. He paid no attention to the sweaty palms held out to him, the wishes for his speedy betrothal. He didn't taste the fancy foods the waiters in silk skullcaps served him; he didn't answer the loutish Alter brothers, who whispered snatches of law relating to marital conduct in his ear, their pimpled faces beaming with drunken vulgarity.

He fixed his eyes on the other side of the room, where through the opened door the bride-to-be could be seen surrounded by women. He yearned to look into her eyes, but she kept them lowered. Only once their glances met, and they both looked swiftly away.

TEN

THE DAY AFTER THE PARTY Abraham Hersh turned Simha Meir over to Nuske as his rabbi had instructed him. Haim Alter took his own sons out of Baruch Wolf's classroom and enrolled them with Nuske so that they might study alongside Simha Meir.

In a low, squat shack in Balut, among weavers, tailors, street magicians, coachmen, and beggars, lived the scholar Nuske, to whom rich men sent their sons to be instructed in the Jewish Law. He was actually a rabbi, not a teacher, but he was temperamentally unsuited for the rabbinate and for Lodz.

In the ferment of the growing city, rabbis did very well for themselves. There were constant lawsuits, disputes to be settled, moneys to be held in escrow, partnerships to be formed or dissolved.

Jews traditionally turned to rabbis rather than to Christian courts to settle their disagreements. A Lodz rabbi needed to know more about promissory notes than about the Torah. He had to be knowledgeable in all the complexities of mercantile affairs, in contracts, in the ins and outs of wool and cotton, and Nuske neither knew nor wanted to know such things. His only interest lay in the holy Torah.

Although of Polish origin, he was a Misnagid, or opponent of Hasidism. He lived only for God and His wisdom and wouldn't stray from His laws by even a hair, hewing to the absolute and not accepting any compromise or diversion. Within his long, bony skull there was no room for anything but the Torah, the thousands of commentaries and annotations he had committed to memory and in which he immersed himself. He knew that there was only right or wrong, no in between, for to be partly wrong was to be totally wrong. All the smoke screens and sophistries put forward by the litigants in lawsuits didn't even penetrate his consciousness.

"Reuben is guilty, therefore, Simon is innocent, and there's no deviating from that," he would declare firmly. Those against whom he found shouted, raged, and screamed for justice, but Nuske remained unmoved and turned back to his sacking-bound volumes.

The merchants quickly perceived that Nuske wasn't attuned to the ways of Lodz, and they turned to rabbis who knew more about bankruptcy than God's laws. The women who came to him with questions regarding religious law abandoned him as well.

The Torah clearly stated that if a dairy dish somehow became mixed with a meat dish, the meat dish remained pure only if the ratio of meat to milk didn't drop below sixty to one. But since Nuske couldn't rely on the word of the women who were anxious to save the dish, he invariably judged the dish *tref,* impure, not even fit to feed a dog.

The women were sad, but no more so than Nuske himself, who knew that he was costing poor Jews money, a sin punishable in Gehenna, and he couldn't put his mind at rest. After a while the women stopped coming to him and consulted rabbis who were known to shut an eye to such things.

The Lodz rabbis made money arranging spurious sales by Jewish bosses to gentile employers so that their factories could operate on the Sabbath, but Nuske wouldn't take part in a subterfuge designed to circumvent the teachings of the Torah. The Law was the Law, not something to be trifled with.

His wife, whose wealthy father had laid out a fortune to acquire such a paragon for a son-in-law, sneered at and derided her husband. A sprightly, capable, mannish woman, she listened to the lawsuits presented to her husband and grasped every nuance of the complicated disputes. In her mind, she even worked out compromises that would have satisfied both parties, but she was helpless to do anything about it. A woman's place, she knew, was in the kitchen. Business and Torah were the province of men.

But her husband knew nothing of the first and too much of the latter.

The dowry had long since been used up, and the household suffered a privation that was particularly hard for her, a rich man's daughter. The landlord of their house in Old City wouldn't wait for the rent, and Nuske had been forced to vacate the big house in the city and move to a tiny shack in Balut, among the workers and coachmen. His wife bewailed her lot among paupers, but Nuske found peace here. No one in the deprived neighborhood disturbed him at his task of

serving God and studying His Torah. The men were away
all day at work; the women were so poor that they seldom
interrupted him with questions concerning the purity of meat.
The only time they came to him was to question the presence
of a drop of blood in an egg or to have him fix the date of a
mourning period. If a master weaver consulted him about a
contract with an apprentice, he would pay a mere pittance, and
Nuske wouldn't even take notice of it.

"Put it on the table," he'd say, keeping his eyes averted and
calling to his wife to take the abomination away since he was
reluctant to handle such a filthy thing as money.

Cranky and haggard from years of poverty, she would
sweep the few coins from the table and fling them at her
husband's feet.

"Idler!" she scolded. "Fool! Do you expect me to feed the
children on *this?*"

He didn't respond. He knew that the study of Torah could
be conducted only in a state of poverty. A Torah scholar was
obliged to subsist on bread and salt, sleep on the ground, and
live in dire need. Life on earth was nothing more than a brief
prelude, a vestibule leading to the true life. What did it matter
how destitute a vestibule was? . . .

He bore no resentments against his wife, for he knew that
women were immersed in the material world and were blind to
the Truth. And he accepted all her abuse, scorn, and mockery
with forbearance, not responding with even a word, which
served only to fire her temper.

"Say something at least, dummy!" she shrieked hysterically.
"Don't you even know when you're being insulted?"

He kept his silence. He *wanted* her to debase him as punishment for the sins in which he wallowed and which would
surely earn him a place in Gehenna. And when his wife grew
tired of abusing him, he went to his room, bolted his door,
and immersed himself in the great sacking-bound volumes in
the margins of which he wrote commentaries in a tiny script.
Full of allusions and abbreviations, they would have required
a genius to grasp their meaning.

The household was destitute. The children whined for a new
dress, a pair of shoes. Tradesmen pounded on the door for
money owed them and threatened to cut off further credit.
Nuske heard and saw nothing. He sat secluded in his tiny
room with only God and His Torah for company. The only
time he left the house was to go to services and to the bath.
But since he didn't pursue the duties of a rabbi, he gave in to

his wife on one point and consented to tutor wealthy youths, offspring of men who were eager to transform their sons into scholars.

From the very first day Simha Meir felt an aversion to Nuske. At first, he tried outshouting him and employing sophistry, as he had with his other teachers, but Nuske wasn't as easily duped. Although of Polish descent, he didn't believe in the Polish method of study just as he disclaimed Hasidism and wonder rabbis. He never argued. He rarely spoke since speech was a sin. The mouth had been created only to serve God and for studying, not for idle chatter. And the moment Simha Meir commenced his verbal pyrotechnics, Nuske silenced him. "Enough! The Torah must be explored straightforwardly, not casuistically."

Simha Meir wouldn't back off. "On the other hand, one can say—" he began, reversing his contention, but Nuske interrupted him again.

"The Torah is truth, and truth can't be batted back and forth. There is only one truth."

Simha Meir quickly formed a deep resentment for his teacher. "A crackpot," he whispered to his prospective brothers-in-law, irked that he had been prevented from demonstrating his erudition.

He saw that he wouldn't be able to dupe the teacher with specious arguments, but that it would be possible to avoid studying altogether since Nuske was innocent of guile and never checked to see if the students were following the text. Also, he would abruptly stop in mid-lesson to preach morality, something done only in Lithuanian yeshivas.

Simha Meir drew a deck of cards from his pocket and dealt out hands to the other students. They were mostly sated, pampered sons of the rich, considerably older than Simha Meir. They promptly recognized a kindred spirit in him and took him along to hidden pockets of Lodz where one could enjoy illicit pleasure. Haim Alter's sons inevitably tagged along.

Lodz seethed in ferment as the city grew day by day, hour by hour. Strangers converged from all over: German engineers and master weavers; English chemists, designers, and pattern-makers; Russian merchant princes in blue coats and wide trousers over short patent-leather boots; Jewish traveling salesmen and commission agents—gay, lusty young men who descended upon Lodz to make money and to have fun.

The youth of Lodz began to shave their beards and don worldly attire. Restaurants, cabarets, and gambling casinos opened and drew huge crowds. Hungarian dancers came to further their careers and fatten their purses. Circuses and carnivals arrived from Warsaw and Petersburg, from Berlin and Budapest. Russian functionaries and officers accepted bribes and kickbacks which they squandered on wine, women, and cards. Lodz drank, sang, danced, attended theaters, caroused in brothels, gambled. Wealthy Hasidim were caught up in the mood of revelry. They lingered in kosher restaurants, where waiters in silk skullcaps brought fat goose thighs and plump waitresses served dried chick-peas and foamy beer. Wastrel Hasidic youths, living on the largess of their fathers-in-law, ceased studying the Torah and surreptitiously played cards in studyhouses.

Business in the city was excellent, and orders kept pouring in. The prodigal Russian merchants didn't haggle and paid whatever prices were asked. Plants, factories, and workshops ran overtime, draining the workers' energy.

The affluent youths in their gleaming alpaca gabardines, kid boots, and heavy gold watches learned the meaning of fun. In illicit houses of pleasure they gambled, dined on roast goose and rolls, drank, and bedded the compliant servant girls who waited on tables.

A favorite of the idle youth was one Shillem the Sharper, a baker by trade who went about with flour in his beard, a paper cone on his head, and ritual garment dangling over long underdrawers. He spent little time in his bakery, which he left to his wife, children, and assistants, while he devoted himself to his main passion—gambling.

Just above the cellar bakery of his one-story wooden house, a game was constantly in progress. Hasidic youths feverishly slammed cards against the table and wagered heavily as their host swept away pot after pot. But the more they lost, the more they came back, for Shillem was an amiable fellow, merry, a jokester, and always ready to extend credit. He taught the youths how to sneak into their father's tills and make a score. He also lent money at high interest which could be repaid when the youths collected their dowries.

His large room, its walls hung with samplers of biblical scenes, was always crowded. At the head of the table sat Shillem with the paper cone on his head and in his underdrawers, and he swiftly dealt the cards as he fingered the one-, three-, and five-ruble banknotes that turned white from his floury hands.

His daughters, fleshy wenches, brought refreshments to the table—roast goslings, tripe, crisp cracklings, rolls, soft strudel, and mugs of beer. Cigarette smoke, clinking coins, Hasidic chants, gambling jargon, double entendre jokes, exclamations, and arguments formed a backdrop to the game. A youth sat at the window to guard against the sudden appearance of one of the players' fathers.

The two gentile servant girls already knew how to arrange a secret assignation with the youths. They would lead them to a cubicle in the cellar and give themselves on the sacks of flour.

Nuske's pupils were frequent visitors here. They spent more time with the baker than with their teacher. Haim Alter's lecherous sons, with their pimpled cheeks sprouting the first stubble of beard, had become more expert at stealing from their father than at anything Nuske might have taught them. They always had lots of money since their father left it around uncounted, and all of it passed into the baker's floury fingers. They also visited the dark cellar cubicle with alarming frequency.

As bad as was their luck at cards, so good was Simha Meir's. He quickly caught on to all of Shillem's tricks and manipulations, and he matched him card for card. The elder cardsharp came to respect the cunning youngster, and he dealt him straight hands as he would a contemporary. Within a short time Simha Meir had accumulated a roll of several hundred rubles that he promptly lent out at interest, actually to his prospective brothers-in-law, who promptly lost it all back to him.

Nuske sat over his Gemaras and didn't even notice who was or wasn't present. Only on Thursdays, the last day of the week assigned to study, when a student was obliged to learn a portion of the lesson in case a father tested him on the Sabbath day, did the boys begin to apply themselves. As usual, Simha Meir sought to show off his erudition, and he raised his voice to confuse and outshout Nuske. But the teacher cut him short. "Recite the lesson, Nissan," he ordered his son, "and explain it all to them."

Nissan, a thirteen-year-old as lean, brown-skinned and dark-eyed as his father, opened to the proper page and in a loud, clear voice repeated the lesson for all the boys.

Out of vexation, Simha Meir kicked Nissan under the table. Nothing enraged him so much as having someone outdo him at anything.

ELEVEN

———————

EVEN AS HIS PUPILS DECEIVED NUSKE, his own son, Nissan, did the same.

He wasn't fond of his father; he held him in great contempt. He couldn't forgive him for the fact that his mother went about forever weeping and with a rag wound around her aching head or that his sisters never had a new dress or a pair of shoes. Nor could he forgive him for the life he had imposed upon him, Nissan—a life lacking a shred of joy. All his father knew was the Torah, moralizing, and gloom.

From the time Nissan could reason—he could do so while other boys his age were still playing tag—the burden of supporting the household had fallen upon his shoulders. He had grown up listening to his mother and sisters railing and grumbling against the father. His mother, raised in the lap of luxury, could never endure the housework, their coarse neighbors with their earthy ways, the whole bitter lot that impoverished women bear so patiently.

She laid blame on her own father for selecting a son-in-law destined to ruin her life. But mostly she vented her rage on her bungler of a husband who was fit for nothing, who avoided people, and who disdained money. She maligned him before her own children, mocked him, held him up to ridicule. Most of all, she belittled him before their son, Nissan.

"There he goes, the good-for-nothing. . . . Stark, raving mad!"

From earliest childhood he had heard the threats and laments of the tradesmen demanding payment and vowing to cut off the family's credit. Whenever it was time to celebrate the Sabbath, to pay rent, to buy a child a dress, tears and accusations ensued. But his father simply turned his back on it all. He sat in his room with the door bolted and studied or wrote commentaries on the margins of the Torah in his tiny, cramped script.

And the whole burden of supporting the family fell upon the

only male in the house, him, Nissan. He had to go with head bowed to his rich, spiteful uncles and beg for money. He had to scrounge firewood for the house. He had to call in a handyman when something went wrong, pound a nail into a wall, fix a falling board, push a wardrobe away from a wall, do all the work of which there was always a surfeit in an impoverished household.

No one ever visited the house beside the few ragged women with questions concerning religious law. No one ever laughed; no joy was ever displayed. The father spoke only of the Torah, of the vanity of this world, the transience of human life, the folly of pleasure. Each sigh he issued was like a knife in Nissan's heart.

"Fear God!" Nuske would enjoin him in the midst of a lesson. "You hear, Nissan?"

Even more dismal were the Sabbaths. Nuske found quantities of prayers to recite, countless books to study. He read the weekly portion of the Pentateuch for hours on end, recited portions of the Zohar, swayed over the ancient volumes. With Nissan at his side, he paced through the house of prayer, mumbling the words in a mournful, monotonous tone. The boy felt hungry and oppressed by the bleakness of the deserted house of worship, but the father went on long after the other Jews had eaten their noonday meals and taken their naps.

The mother and daughters couldn't wait, and they ate the Sabbath meal without hearing the benediction. By the time Nissan and his father sat down the food was cold, unappetizing. Just as unsatisfactory were the hymns that followed. The father grunted rather than sang. As soon as he had eaten and recited the blessings, he lay down for his nap with a holy book on his chest to dream of the Sabbath as the Law directed.

"Nissan," he said, "you take a book in hand and nap, too. A Jew must sleep on the Sabbath."

Yes, he hated his father, and along with his father, he hated his holy books that spoke only of pain and were steeped in morals and melancholy; his Torah, so complex and convoluted that it defied all understanding; his whole Jewishness that oppressed the human soul and loaded it down with guilt and remorse. But most of all, Nissan hated his father's God, that cruel and vengeful being who demanded total obeisance, eternal service, mental and physical self-torture and privation, and the surrender of all choice and will. No matter what you did for Him, it wasn't enough. He was never satisfied, and He punished, condemned, and raked man over the coals.

It was because of God who demanded so much that their

house was so dark and decrepit. It was because of God that his mother was sick and prematurely aged. It was because of God that he and his sisters went barefoot and hungry. It was because of God that there was only worry, gloom, and despair in the house. And he hated God even more than he hated his father. Out of this rage at the Almighty, he intentionally jumbled the prayers, tore paper on the Sabbath, glanced at the cross on the church, ate dairy without waiting the required six hours after meat, didn't observe the fasts, and read heretic books at Feivel the rag dealer's.

Feivel lived on the edge of town. Pits had been dug in his courtyard and girls sat there sorting and grading rags, using iron combs to rake through the huge piles of rags that were constantly being brought in on carts. These rags were washed and cleaned before Feivel sold them back to cheap factories, which transformed them into inferior yarn. But just as Feivel's hands were immersed in rags, his head was immersed in heresy and Enlightenment.

Short, quick-moving, with a greasy derby upon his curly, dusty head; with shining eyes peering out of a merry, puckered face; with tufts of hair and lint clinging to his curly beard; beleaguered by his workers, the teamsters, and merchants, he still managed to find time to travel for miles in search of a new heretic book.

In his large house, strewn with daughters, papers, promissory notes, and bedding, stood bookcases filled with books for which he had paid fortunes. Others lay stacked on all the tables, in closets, cabinets, and on shelves.

His pious wife and blowsy daughters burned and discarded the books, which they despised as much as they did Feivel himself. But as fast as they threw them out or destroyed them, he bought new ones. In the midst of a profitable transaction he would drop everything and race off to some book peddler who had a rare find for him. His eyes would gleam out of his dusty face as his gnarled, stained hands fingered the pages of the new acquisition.

In the same way, he always found time to convert a Hasidic youth, to yank him out of the studyhouse and plant within him the seeds of heresy and Enlightenment.

In the evenings, on Sabbaths and on holidays, Hasidic youths sat in Feivel's house, reading forbidden literature. Feivel would roam from studyhouse to studyhouse, from house of prayer to house of prayer, recruiting youths, proselytizing, displaying erudition in both the Torah and in worldly knowledge. He gave the youths money; he fed them; he let them sleep in his house; he literally offered them the shirt off his back in his quest to set them against God and transform them into unbelievers.

He was unable to keep his mind on his rags; he kept running inside to check on his disciples. "Are you reading? Are you absorbing?" he asked with satisfaction. "Good, fine. . . ."

Exulting in his mission, he called to his wife and daughters to bring the boys a glass of tea, a bite to eat. But since they weren't about to listen to him, he dashed into the kitchen himself and brought out slices of bread with chicken fat with the same joy of service with which pious Jewesses fed poor yeshiva students dining on their husbands' charity.

Often Feivel sat down with the boys and studied the more complex texts with them, interpreting the philosophical systems and doctrines. Eyes shining, shoulders swaying, voice chanting, he preached heresy with the fervor of a pious teacher exalting the Torah.

On Sabbaths, his house filled with youths wearing silk gabardines, velvet hats, and skullcaps. Since Feivel's wife and daughters were observers of the Law and wouldn't think of cooking on the Sabbath, they all partook of the warmed-over Sabbath meal with Sabbath tea.

Feivel sat at the head of the large table in his greasy suit and, eyes flashing out of the withered face, expounded on philosophy, mathematics, history, astronomy, geography, and exegesis. He interpreted obtuse portions of the Scriptures, explained the difficult points in the Gemara, and encouraged his audience to pursue worldly education, accept Enlightenment, and renounce the ways of their fathers. "Education, logic, and work. That's the only way, my children," he proclaimed again and again.

Drawing the curtains and bolting the door on his own wife, of whom he was afraid, he lit a cigar and passed out cigarettes to the boys. Not all of them were yet ready to smoke on the Sabbath, but when those who were lit up and blew rings of smoke at the Sabbath candelabrum, Feivel's curly beard bristled with satisfaction. Gazing around at the smokers, he was convinced that their souls had been saved.

Among the youths sat Nissan, son of Nuske the rabbi, who haunted Feivel the ragmaker's house, digesting book after illicit book.

Instinct had guided Feivel to the rabbi's son, who displayed symptoms of unrest, a curiosity for something outside the house, the need to broaden his horizons. Feivel hadn't been wrong, and the youngster had taken to his reeducation

with the zeal of a dog attacking a bone. He raced through the
forbidden books under Feivel's enthusiastic tutelage. Feivel
realized that his new protégé was a genius. Before a single
word was uttered, Nissan grasped the meaning of the next
ten. Feivel treasured him as he would a costly gem. He taught
the boy, encouraged him, spent hours talking to him and
praising his intellect. "Nissan, next to you I am like nothing—
a dunce."

Nissan's father remained, as always, completely oblivious to
all this. Preoccupied and removed from the world, he didn't
notice his son's gradual estrangement, didn't notice him disappearing for hours at a time, reading heretic literature under
his very nose.

"Nissan," he mumbled often, "fear the Almighty, you hear?"

"I hear," Nissan replied mockingly, turning the page of a
forbidden book. Duping and betraying his father provided him
enormous satisfaction.

He read for hours on end. He lay awake nights on his
narrow bench bed, and by the light of candle stumps that he
stole from the house of prayer, he digested the books. He read
everything without system or order, whatever was available at
Feivel's house. He studied German from Moses Mendelssohn's
Bible commentary printed in transliterated Hebrew, and he
struggled over Maimonides's *Guide to the Perplexed*. He read
the articles in the Hebrew monthly *Ha-Shahar*. He reveled in
the nationalistic stories and poems by Smolenskin, Mapu,
Gordon, along with the articles of Krochmal and stories in the
Kuzari, fantastic travel accounts, books on astronomy and
higher mathematics. In German—which was still alien to him—
he read the philosophers Mendelssohn and Maimon, Spinoza,
Kant, and Schopenhauer. His brain was as chaotic as Feivel's
bookcases, which Feivel's wife and daughters were constantly
disrupting.

For all that, he still managed to learn the weekly lesson
from his father, and he repeated it to the students whose
minds were fixed on Shillem the baker's entertainments.

There was instant friction between his father's pupils and
Nissan, the teacher's son. The pupils envied Nissan his intellect, the fact that he always knew his lesson, that he didn't
subtilize and could explain everything clearly and succinctly,
making them appear dense. Simha Meir, most of all, hated and
envied Nissan, who had shown him up before the others and
diminished his reputation.

From his side, Nissan couldn't forgive the pupils their
handsome gabardines, their silk hats and neckerchiefs, their

soft, smooth boots and gold watches. He was the only one in the class forced to go about in garments that were patched and outgrown and a hat with the cotton lining showing. Their elegance accentuated his poverty. Most of all, he was disturbed that they mocked his father, duped and tormented him. And that his father was oblivious to it all compounded his vexation.

At first, the boys tried to draw Nissan into their circle so that he wouldn't snitch on them. But Nissan had no desire for gambling or carousing. He even tried to sway them to his ways. Just as unswervingly as his father was devoted to the holy studies, so was Nissan totally addicted to his newfound faith. Its every word was gospel to him, not to be deviated from by even a hair. And with the same fervor that his father preached the holy Torah, Nissan tried to convert his classmates to heresy.

He did this surreptitiously and with the total support of a delighted Feivel. But the wealthy youths merely glanced at the forbidden books and promptly threw them aside. As far as they were concerned, they represented as much bother as the Torah. They much preferred to play cards at Shillem's.

Only Simha Meir took an apparent interest.

One day in the midst of a lesson, he asked the teacher, "Rabbi, is it true that the Torah was given by God on Mount Sinai?"

Nuske blanched in fear. "What kind of question is that?" he asked in alarm.

"I only asked it because Nissan says that Moses made it all up himself out of his own head," Simha Meir replied with complete innocence.

A hush fell over the classroom.

Nuske sat there as if stricken by lightning. After a long while, he regained his speech. "Is this true, Nissan?"

Nissan would neither admit nor deny it.

His father gripped the edge of the table to keep from toppling. "Jeroboam, son of Nebat," he thundered. "You may not be in the same room with Jews!"

Nissan got up and left the house for good.

He apprenticed himself to a master weaver. At first, the man wouldn't agree without the father's signature on the contract and a fee, but Nissan offered to teach his daughters Hebrew and how to sign their betrothal papers and his sons a little arithmetic and writing, and the weaver agreed to take him on for a period of three years.

Nissan wasn't allowed near the loom. Like all apprentices, he was given cotton to wind. The mistress made him sit on a three-legged stool and rock her baby, which squirmed in its cradle from the heat and dampness.

In the long, low-ceilinged room crammed with looms and bench beds, a number of journeymen sat in only their pants and skullcaps, weaving and chanting cantorial hymns. The boss, a man in a greasy skullcap and a tattered cotton jerkin that he wore winter and summer, cast his bloodshot eyes everywhere to make sure the work was proceeding properly and no pilferage was taking place. If one of the men stopped to mop a brow or roll a cigarette, he promptly intervened. "Keep those hands moving! Every minute you loaf is like stealing bread from my mouth!"

The mistress of the house sat by the stove in a mangy black wig through which poked red tufts of her natural hair. A gang of black- and red-haired wenches sat around her on low stools, peeling potatoes with sharp knives. The acrid smell of frying fat, oil, and onions blended with the dense steam issuing from a huge iron kettle.

"Mistress, what's for dinner today?" shouted a journeyman, emerging from his tangle of thread like a spider from its web.

"Keep your eyes on your work, black tomcat!" she replied from out of the steam. "The pot is none of your business. . . ."

The "black tomcat" suddenly began to quote from the Book of Esther: "That shrew, Zeresh, wife of Haman—" he chanted in a Purim-like trill. The other workers quickly grasped the allusion and burst into laughter.

The mistress scraped with the sharp knife and hurled the half-peeled potatoes into the pot, splashing the water all around.

"Like fun you'll get dumplings and beans out of me!" she shrieked at the howling youths. "Potatoes and oil you'll eat till it comes out of your ears. . . . Then you'll know what Zeresh can do. . . ."

In her rage, she cut her finger and promptly went wild. With the black wig askew on her saffron head, she ran to the bench beds lined against the wall and stripped them of the stained bare pillows. "Father in heaven, may I not live to lead my daughters under the canopy if I give you my pillows tonight! The bare floor is good enough for the likes of you hooligans!"

His foot rocking the baby his mistress had borne in her late years, one hand tangled in cotton, Nissan sat winding away. The journeymen made fun of him, called him by nick-names, sent him to the store for a piece of bread or herring. The mistress scolded him, the baby screamed at him, but he stuck to it. Day after day he sat observing the work, watching the looms, confining to memory every rod and shaft in order to understand their function. At the same time he thought about his books.

His mother came to see him and wrung her hands to find him in such surroundings. "Nissan," she wept. "Is this what I've lived to see? *You,* a common worker? . . . Come home with me!"

But he didn't go with her. He learned the trade, he tutored his boss's children, and whatever spare time he had, he raced to Feivel's house to bone up on the latest heretic books. At night, lying on his filthy pallet in the corner, his blanket a yard of finished goods, he studied by the light of a forbidden candle and prepared himself for some goal of which he was yet uncertain.

In all the synagogues and studyhouses in Balut, parents held up Nissan as an example to their children. "That is the fate of all those who would stray from God's path. . . . Neither this world nor the world to come will they enjoy. . . ."

"Nissan the depraved," his coworkers dubbed him, since it was the custom for every worker to have a nickname.

The wealthy youths sat in Nuske's classroom and played cards under the table. Their teacher was more depressed than ever. He envisioned the flaming Gehenna already awaiting him for the sins of his son, who had abandoned God. "Boys, be good Jews," he admonished his students just as he had Nissan. "Fear the Almighty, you hear?"

"We hear," Simha Meir grunted, skillfully palming a card. He was again the leader, the prodigy among his classmates.

TWELVE

—————◆—————

FOLLOWING A NUMBER OF PASSOVERS AND SUC-
COTHS, on which the groom-to-be was invited to his prospective bride's home and she to his, the eighteen-year-old couple
was joined in matrimony.

The half-French, half-German Mademoiselle Antoinette, who
made clothes for the Huntze girls themselves, sewed Dinele's
wedding gown. When his wife, Priveh, told him how much
money the woman demanded for the trousseau, Haim Alter
opened his olive eyes wide. "What's the matter with you,
Privehshe?" he asked in alarm, tugging a coal black beard
with fleshy hands. "I never heard of paying such a fortune to
some seamstress!"

Priveh promptly assumed the expression of an irate queen.
"Mademoiselle Antoinette is no *seamstress*," she corrected him.
"She is only the finest dressmaker in Lodz, and it's a privilege
to have her prepare your trousseau."

Haim Alter grew so distraught by the amount he'd have to
shell out for the supposed privilege that for once he lost his
fear of his wife. "She'd be grateful to take a third of the
amount, the *shiksa!*" he said. "She isn't the only dressmaker
in Lodz, you know. Such bargains I don't need. . . ."

Priveh's china-blue eyes began to gush tears. "Mama!" she
lamented to her long-departed parent. "I'll never live through
this!"

During the long years of the engagement she had persuaded
herself that no one but Mademoiselle Antoinette would do to
prepare her Dinele's trousseau. It wasn't so much the quality
of the work—she knew full well from her own experience that
the precious silks, satins, velvets, and laces prepared for a bride's
trousseau seldom saw the light of day and molded away in
closets once the wedding was over. What *did* concern her was
to show all Lodz that the haughty Mademoiselle Antoinette,
who refused to kowtow even to the wealthiest ladies and who

sewed for the Huntze girls themselves, would deign to prepare her Dinele's trousseau. Wouldn't *that* turn all Lodz green!

What she had gone through to arrange this! What devious devices, intrigues, and machinations to make the connection! It was a secret she had confided to only half the women in Lodz. And now her Haim proposed haggling over the price and he dismissed all her efforts with a wave of the hand!

"Mama!" she weepingly implored her mother in the other world. "I'll never bear the disgrace! I won't live to see my only daughter stand under the canopy!"

Haim Alter grew so unnerved by his wife's words that he almost started crying himself. "Bite your tongue!" he said in a quavering voice. "How can you say such things on such a festive occasion? May they be scattered over all the distant forests and over all the empty wastes. . . ."

This time she didn't pout and bristle as usual. She was so elated that he had given in so quickly that she fell on his breast and showered him with kisses in full sight of Samuel Leibush.

"Privehshe." Her husband blushed. "In front of the servants?"

Samuel Leibush grew so flustered that he forgot himself enough to say "It doesn't matter, it doesn't matter. . . ."

With the same lavish disregard for extravagance, the bride was outfitted with dozen upon dozen of silks, satins, lace, furs, hats, silverware, jewelry, and pieces of furniture, for which there wasn't even room in the house. Haim Alter rented the biggest wedding hall, hired the finest band, wedding jesters, and caterers. Hundreds of invitations were sent out. He wanted his daughter's wedding to be the talk of Lodz—of all Poland— and he invited the cream of Lodz's wealth, religious society, and aristocracy.

Not to be outdone, the groom's side presented to Haim Alter a staggering list of its own guests.

In the huge wedding hall, with its gilt mirrors, red plush, gold chairs and magnificent chandeliers gathered the mélange that was Lodz.

There were great-bearded magnates; wealthy Hasidim in gleaming silk gabardines and shiny boots; clean-shaven double-chinned manufacturers in black top hats and white gloves; distinguished rabbis in sweeping satin gabardines and fur caps; Lithuanian traveling salesmen in derbies and elegant frock coats; ultrapietists in broad-brimmed velvet hats, shirts undone at the necks and ritual garments dangling; blond German industrialists in starched shirts and high stiff collars; and even a bewildered Russian police commissioner with sweeping muttonchops and a chestful of medals over a colorful dress uniform.

The same exotic mix existed among the women. There were stout, bustling female relatives in tightly waved wigs, vivid silk gowns with trains and bustles, heavy gold chains, and diamond rings and earrings; ancient crones in satin bonnets and outmoded dresses still saved from their own trousseaus; décolleté young matrons in stylish white gowns; gawky German ladies with long blond braids and lots of rouge over pale cheeks. Yiddish, Polish, German, and Russian blended in a deafening cacophony. Female eyes took measure, diamonds and gold flashed, silks shimmered, fans fluttered, mutual compliments flew back and forth as ladies teased, jibed, needled, scored conversational points.

Carriages drawn by teams of white horses came cantering across the narrow, ill-paved streets of Lodz to disgorge a steady stream of guests. The bride sat enthroned amid garlands of flowers. The groom's sisters had woven a wreath of roses for her chestnut hair that would be shorn the next day. The bride's brothers in their new gabardines and satin hats seated themselves next to the top-hatted coachman as he picked up party after party of guests. Although they were themselves old enough to marry, they couldn't pass up the opportunity to ride in a fancy carriage, and on the coachman's box at that.

The policemen with their curved swords pushed, chased, and prodded the hundreds of indigent girls and women who assembled outside the wedding hall to gawk at the guests, listen to the music, and push to get a glimpse of the inside.

As at most Jewish weddings, quarrels erupted at the last minute. Haim Alter had failed to hand over the 2,000 rubles due on the dowry, as had been agreed. He was short on money after the fortune he had paid out for the wedding, and he couldn't lay his hands on the required amount.

"Reb Abraham Hersh," he implored, "I give you my word of honor that I'll settle up directly after the wedding, so help me!"

"With a dowry, there are no promises," Abraham Hersh said. "Unless the two thousand is on the table, I'm taking the groom straight home."

Haim Alter took the groom aside and urged him to work on his father. "Simhele," he cajoled, "you're a man with heart, after all. You're going to be my son. Do me the great favor so I can savor your goodness. The minute the wedding is over I'll bring you the money without fail."

Simha Meir solemnly promised to speak with his father, but he never even approached him. He had lived long enough in Lodz to know that vows, pledges, and promises weren't worth a groschen and that whatever wasn't paid out in cash before the ceremony would never again be seen by human eyes.

"I begged and begged Papa," he lied to his prospective father-in-law, looking him straight in the eye, "but he won't give an inch. What can I do? Honor thy father, you know. . . ."

Samuel Leibush ran his feet off collecting the 2,000 rubles, which he brought back in various denominations of crinkled banknotes.

When all seemed ready, new complications arose, this time not fiscal, but moral.

From the start Abraham Hersh Ashkenazi had been looking askance at all the Germans and clean-shaven Jews Haim Alter had invited to the affair. He, Abraham Hersh, had brought the Alexander Rabbi himself, and he felt disgraced by the presence of infidels.

The rabbi had been escorted by a palace guard of a hundred uninvited Hasidim. A ragged, uncouth crew, they lunged toward the tables and, before the distinguished and impeccable industrialists and bankers knew what was happening, began singing at the tops of their lungs.

Haim Alter was beside himself. "Reb Abraham Hersh!" he wailed. "You're killing me without a knife. . . . You're driving away all my guests—the cream of Lodz's society!"

"I don't need any beardless heathens," Abraham Hersh replied vengefully. "Let them go straight to hell!"

Soon after, he charged into the women's hall, where he had heard mixed dancing was taking place. He snatched off his fur-edged cap, remaining in only his skullcap, and commenced to break up the couples.

"Out, gentiles and reprobates!" he shouted. "This isn't a German wedding!"

The bride's female relatives fainted; the bride suffered a fit; women shrieked; girls laughed. Priveh raised bejeweled arms to protect her guests, but Abraham Hersh was not to be denied. Towering, furious, beard ruffled, eyes shooting fire, he whipped the dancers with his cap. "Respect for the Alexander Rabbi!" he roared. "Reverence for an assembly of Jews!"

The aroused Hasidim extinguished the lamps and doused the waxed floors with pitchers of water to render them unfit for mixed dancing. The crones in the bonnets clapped in approval. "That's the way! Serves them right!" Brimming over with righteous joy, the Hasidim slid over the floor, making a shambles of the posh hall.

When it came time to stand under the wedding canopy, Simha Meir raised himself on tiptoe to appear taller than his bride.

Even though he had ordered the cobbler to put extra-high heels on his boots, she still towered over him. His lack of height vexed him greatly. Knowing this, Jacob Bunem made a point of standing next to his brother so that the difference between them was accentuated. Out of spite, Simha Meir made sure to step on his bride's foot before she stepped on his, a sign that he would be master of the house.

Later that night, when the two dotards escorted him to the wedding chamber, mumbling the secrets of marital relations, Simha Meir had to stuff his mouth with a kerchief to muffle his laughter.

The next morning, when his two brothers-in-law and his friends from the classroom and from Shillem the baker's came to him in a state of excitement to hear all about the wedding night, as they had arranged to do before, Simha Meir wouldn't even speak to them. Like all Hasidic youth, he felt a deep disdain for bachelors.

"I don't mess around with snotnose boys," he said, waving them away and tilting his hat rakishly to the side like a Cossack.

THIRTEEN

———◆———

Amid all the joy and celebration, Dinele suffered. She looked on in a daze as men congratulated her father and women wished each other the same good fortune that had befallen Priveh.

Dinele couldn't grasp what possible coup snaring the youth with the darting eyes represented. His erudition meant nothing to her. Jewishness in general bored her. When Hadassah, the maid, helped her put on her stockings in the morning and urged her to say the morning prayers, Dinele became hysterical at the comical way the maid extended her neck as she drew out the sacred words. It reminded her of a hen drinking.

And just as silly and laughable was the Torah her father tried to teach her. He was forever nagging at her to observe the laws. "Dinele, you mustn't comb your hair on the Sabbath! Dinele, you mustn't eat milk chocolate until six hours after meat! Dinele, don't drink without a benediction!"

She loved her father. He was very good to her. Still, he was alien to her with his constant "you mustn'ts" and with his hearty renditions of the Sabbath hymns. And just as weird and exotic were the Hasidic banquets he conducted. She was appalled by the Hasidim, and she shared her elegant mother's disdain for them. They made havoc of the waxed parquet with their muddy boots, and they spat on the floors.

"The pack of animals is already gathered," Priveh would quip with the forbearance of wives long inured to their husbands' idiosyncrasies.

"Hadassah," she instructed the maid, "make an onion borscht for that gang. I'm leaving. I can't stand their gabble."

And she was off shopping for bargains.

Dinele gazed at the hirsute, disheveled, perfervid crew with loathing. They were rude, uncivilized, boorish. They danced like savages, howled like wolves, scampered through the room with unkempt beards and earlocks flying. She held her breath and recoiled when they passed by.

Even less appealing were the pious spongers who were her father's guests at mealtimes. They demanded cake, whiskey, delicacies. They spoke in loud voices; they told outlandish stories, blew their noses into their fingers even as they tore great chunks out of the Sabbath loaves. Despite their eternal ablutions, their hands and nails were filthy and nicotine-stained. They openly discussed prospective matches for her, Dinele, and she fled the table blushing with embarrassment.

No better were the rabbis who stayed at the house from time to time. Her father would surrender the place of honor to the visitors and fawn over them as if he were a schoolboy. The mother would be barred from the room lest her sight defile the saints' presence, and she, Dinele, would be brought in briefly to be blessed by them.

It wasn't that Dinele was an unbeliever, for she feared God who sat up in heaven and made a note in His fiery book each time she ate a piece of chocolate after meat or combed her hair on the Sabbath. She also feared his representatives on earth, the long-bearded saints at her father's table. But she feared them as sorcerers capable of punishing and performing deeds of black magic, and she despised and avoided them.

She much preferred her school, a place of decorum and gentility, where etiquette and social graces prevailed. There was as much emphasis there on manners as on mathematics. The French-speaking teachers were as polite and genteel as the subjects they taught, and despite her heritage, they all liked her.

"Diana, you have nothing of the Semite about you. You're as fair and blue-eyed as any Christian," they assured her.

Because she was quiet, gentle, and compliant, her classmates were drawn to her, too, particularly the strong, mannish girls. "Diana, why don't you convert?" they urged her. "With your looks, you'd snare a count at the very least."

But she wouldn't consider such a drastic move. She feared the wrathful Jewish God too much. Still, when her classmates invited her to accompany them to church, she went. Standing in the darkness of the cavernous chamber, she gazed wide-eyed at the stained glass and carved statues. She listened to the sonorous chords of the organ, marveled at the forest of candles and banners, the priestly vestments and rites, the genuflecting and the Latin, and tears came to her eyes before all this splendor and glory.

It was so different from her father's Hasidic prayerhouse with its grime, noise, chaos, and disorder. Women were allowed in there only once a year, on Simhat Torah. She was afraid of

the scroll of Law that the men carried, just as she was afraid of
the blast of the ram's horn on Rosh Hashanah and the candles
on the Day of Atonement. But accompanying the fear was a
sense of the ridiculous, of something alien and repugnant that
made her flee from it all as if it were infectious.

Everything in her household was alien and strange to her—
her father, his guests, her loutish brothers who regarded her
as something inferior, good only to bully and tease.

She felt ashamed before her schoolmates if they encountered
her in the company of her parents in the street. She also made
sure to avoid her brothers lest they recognize her and approach
her. She envied her classmates, who could feel proud of their
families. She was too embarrassed to invite any of her friends
home.

Like all pubescent girls, she lived in a state of constant turmoil. Each day she grew infatuated with someone else—now
a French teacher, now her piano teacher, but mostly with her
girlfriends, as did they with her. They constantly kissed,
hugged, shared secrets, laughed, and cried together.

When she turned thirteen and became engaged to the Hasidic
youth with the particularly funny name, she was disconsolate.
He was hardly the hero of her novels. But she wasn't strong
enough to resist her parents.

During the years of the engagement she put the whole thing
out of her mind. She kept going to school and continued her
detached, dreamlike existence. She never exchanged a word
with her fiancé. They saw each other only when they exchanged
visits on the holidays. When he came to her house, she served
him his meals, as her mother forced her to do, but they never
spoke.

Even more she hated to visit his family. They were a cold,
solemn bunch. Her prospective mother-in-law prattled on about
religion and stuffed her beyond satiety. The father was an
awesome figure. One glance from him, and Dinele's blood
would freeze. The first chance she had, she fled from there as if
from Gehenna.

She retreated deeper and deeper into her fantasies and thought
no more about the wedding than she did of her inevitable
death. Just like her father, she enjoyed a fool's paradise and
avoided facing the future.

Thus, when it finally came, it was a particular shock, and she
felt deeply depressed on what should have been the happiest
day of her life.

She flushed with embarrassment over the wifely duties and
obligations hammered into her. She was repelled by the ritual

bath and the various attendants who blessed, poked, and prodded her.

She was mortified by her father-in-law's outlandish response to the mixed dancing. Most of all, she was terrified of her first encounter with her husband. She didn't utter a word to him when they sat down to eat the so-called gold consommé traditionally served to a newlywed couple.

Simha Meir turned to her. "How did the fast affect you?" he asked in his singsong just for something to say.

She didn't respond. She had nothing to say to the skinny youth with the great fur hat falling down over his ears.

When the women escorted her into the wedding chamber, whispering all kinds of advice into her ears, and then left her alone to await her groom, she became alarmed. She cowered on the edge of the bed as if to guard against an assault upon her body.

"No," she pleaded with the stranger approaching her, "no!"

But he ignored her. He didn't even make an effort to appease her, to establish some sort of intimacy. Like all Hasidim, he considered women inferior creatures put on earth to be wives and mothers, and he was deaf to her pleas. "What's the matter with you?" he asked harshly. "Why are you carrying on this way?"

Seeing that her words made no impact, Dinele tried to keep him at bay physically, but this served only to exacerbate his impatience. He hated to be thwarted, to be deprived of what was his. Most of all, he didn't want to lose face. How would it look the next day if people found out that he had failed to take her? He would become the object of their derision.

He therefore dismissed all her objections and took her by force, as befitted a good Jewish husband. He was crass, brutal, and she despised him. In the morning, when her mother came in to her and found her crying, Priveh burst into laughter. "Silly girl," she said, stroking her daughter's cheeks. "Don't be such a ninny. You'll grow to love him, just as I came to love your father."

But it didn't happen as her mother predicted. This wasn't the love of which she had dreamed from the day her friends at school had confided its secrets to her. This was a coarse, revolting experience that evoked only pain and shame, and she wallowed in her misery even as the others celebrated her joy.

She was so shattered that she didn't even resist when her mother-in-law came to her, accompanied by the woman who would snip off her long, shiny brown hair, as was the custom. But it was her mother now who took a stand.

Her mother-in-law, a pious woman who kept her skull shaved, was determined to impose the same condition upon her daughter-in-law. She knew that her in-laws wouldn't tolerate shaving the girl clean, but she did demand that the hair be cropped short enough so that not even a curl showed beneath the wig. But Priveh would have none of it.

"Leave that to me," she insisted, "I'll take care of it myself already."

She had only her daughter's braids shorn, leaving the rest of the hair untouched.

The mother-in-law was horrified. "Such a thing is unheard of among Jews! You've left all her hair! I won't stand for it. I want you to know that I'm the Ozorkow Rabbi's daughter. . . ."

"And I am the daughter of Reb Ansel of Warsaw!" Priveh responded with such vehemence that the other woman promptly retreated.

With skilled fingers Priveh put up Dinele's hair and set a small blond, wavy wig similar to her own on top of it. By the time she was done you couldn't tell which was the real hair and which was the wig.

She summoned her daughter to the large mirror. "Dinele, come see for yourself. I'll be blessed if they won't take it for a set straight from the hairdresser's."

The mother-in-law sighed. "Better your own hair than such a mockery. That way, at least, you don't fool anybody. . . . That the Ozorkow Rabbi's daughter should live to experience such sacrilege . . . !"

Her mother-in-law's high satin bonnet bobbed in unison with her mother's curly wig, but Dinele herself stayed out of the conflict. When her mother handed her the two shorn braids as a memento of her maidenhood, she accepted them with total indifference.

With equal uninterest she listened to the long list of laws her mother-in-law recited passionately to her, but once again Priveh bristled at what she considered an incursion into her province.

"See here, I don't need any lessons in Jewishness," she snapped, narrowing her lips, "even though I don't sport a satin bonnet. . . ."

And with a regal gesture she led her daughter away.

Just as Simha Meir's friends had done, Dinele's girlfriends came to her with flushed faces to learn the secret of love. But Dinele wouldn't say a word. She merely hugged them and sobbed. "Never, never marry without love!"

She couldn't stand to look at her husband or at her own father and brothers. More than ever she felt close to her girl-friends and was convinced that only toward them could she feel true love.

Simha Meir tried a friendly approach, but she didn't even look up from her book when he spoke to her. He felt rejected, and he snatched the book from her hand. He quickly scanned the few lines in German which revolved around some Alfred and Hildegarde.

"What is this?" he asked.

"A novel."

"Fairy tales . . . fabrications," he mumbled under his breath, and threw the book back at her. He tried to say something else, but she looked away. He turned on his heel, his pride dented.

"Are you so absorbed in that 'Torah' that you can't even answer?" he asked, rubbing his palms together as if anxious to remove all traces of the abomination.

After he left the room, she burst into tears. She realized that there could never be any intimacy between them, and this thought clamped her heart like a vise.

She wanted someone in whom to confide, but there was no one. All the hundreds of people who had danced and rejoiced over her happiness had no thought whatever about her feelings. Her mother was busy with the hordes of guests and relatives who had descended upon her from all over Poland. She dashed about with keys jangling, making arrangements, showing off, preening herself, making sure that the affair would be the talk of Lodz for years to come, that news of it would spread to Warsaw and other cities until the name of Alter became a household word throughout Poland.

As for her father, he was too involved with his own matters, Dinele knew, to listen to her. Right now he had worries enough of his own.

FOURTEEN

———◆———

THE HARROWING WEEK OF FESTIVITIES, visits, parties, banquets, and celebrations left the Alter family exhausted and misanthropic. All the congratulations, kisses, blessings, and handshakes evoked within them an enormous aversion toward people, felt most of all by the head of the household, Haim Alter himself.

True, all Lodz echoed his triumph, and not only Lodz but the neighboring towns as well, but the thousands of rubles he had been forced to lay out left a huge gap in Haim Alter's coffers. In addition, the season was slow, and the banks had grown leery about lending money. Because of this, Haim Alter felt vexed these days and unconsoled by his momentary success.

And as if out of spite, the thought of his indebtedness assaulted him just as he paused for the silent rendition of the eighteen benedictions at morning prayers.

True, he had no exact knowledge of the extent of his losses since neither he nor Samuel Leibush could decipher the ledgers, but he knew that things weren't going as usual. Cash was constantly short; notes fell due and went unpaid. In addition, the payrolls could not be met on Thursdays, and the workers were prevented from observing their Sabbaths.

Not that they dared complain. But they sighed aloud, and this upset him. Worst of all, he couldn't pray in peace. At a time when a Jew must divest himself of all extraneous thought, business took precedence in his mind over piety. He no longer even enjoyed his meals or his naps on the soft, plush ottoman.

Haim Alter racked his brain for a way out of his dilemma. The factory was working full time as usual. Whether their wages were paid on Thursdays or a few days later, the workers did what they were supposed to. They worked late on Saturday and Thursday nights, as they always had. They continued to buy their own candles. Samuel Leibush was as faithful as any dog. What other savings could be effected?

No matter how hard he thought, Haim Alter couldn't come up with the answer. Why had the profits diminished? What was wrong?

Even more than he hated being forced to think, Haim Alter abhorred worry. Ever since his marriage (he had used his dowry to open the factory), he had known no serious problems to speak of. He had always lived well, as befitted a man of his station. Things were sometimes a bit better or a bit worse, but he had never taken such fluctuations to heart. He knew that this was normal in business. He didn't even concern himself with an occasional bankruptcy by a debtor. He merely absorbed the loss and raised his prices to make up the difference. It became a part of the overhead, along with the payroll, the raw goods, and the rest. Then again, you could always come to some kind of arrangement with the bankrupts—sometimes for half the amount due, sometimes for a third—however God ordained it. You couldn't have business without bankruptcy or bankruptcy without business. It was all part of the game.

Things had gone along this way for years. He didn't keep accounts for the simple reason that the more you figured, the less profit you ended up with. He knew that he was comfortable, one might even say rich. There weren't too many men of his standing in Lodz, and people knew him. When he entered banks, the managers bowed deeply. Even the bank presidents, those clean-shaven snobs, invited him into their offices and offered him cigars.

Someone else in his position might have grown corrupt and surrendered his beliefs, but Haim Alter had remained a Jew, a Hasid. The Hasidim knew this and respected him accordingly. The rabbi himself paid him his due.

Nor was he parsimonious. No one could accuse him of that. He was forever making contributions toward the prayerhouse or financing the wedding of some indigent bride. He donated generously to his rabbi's court. He wasn't like other rich men who pinched their pennies, for he knew that there was not only a material world but also the world to come, one much more grandiose than all the money ever minted. And a Jew had to prepare for the other world. He had to enter it with a record of good deeds. Otherwise, God forbid, one had to be ready to face Gehenna with all its fires and tortures.

He therefore spent with a generous hand and never regretted a groschen laid out for charity, for he knew that a Jew must be a Jew. God, the Almighty, required everything in this world—rich men and paupers, philanthropists and spongers. In His infinite wisdom, He had selected him, Haim Alter, to be among the rich. The Creator had arranged it that money should pour into Haim Alter's pockets so that he might spread charity among the poor, see to it that his workers had a house of worship, a reader to lead them through the prayers, and citrons for Succoth. It was also his, Haim Alter's, God-given obligation to pay for his inferiors' weddings, funerals, and circumcisions.

There were also his own household expenses of which he never knew the amount. Each time Priveh held out her bejeweled hand, he filled it with money. And she knew even less than he precisely how much she spent. The money simply dribbled between her fingers. She forgot where she mislaid it; she often lost it, then sent her maids into tears, accusing them of robbing her. If the banknote or piece of jewelry turned up, she only lost it again moments later.

She loved shopping for bargains, and she bought whatever caught her eye, whether she needed it or not. Her house was always filled with tradesmen demanding payment for articles she didn't even remember buying.

She also loved to visit spas and to consult foreign specialists whose expertise served as a topic of conversation for the whole following winter. She went from resort to resort and from physician to physician. All her dressers and bureaus were filled with phials, ampules, jars, and boxes of variously tinted medicines, tonics, and pills that she never took. She also brought back bargains from abroad—suitcases full of silks, jewelry, lace, crystal, antiques. She always tried to smuggle these items past the customs officials, and she was always caught, and from the subsequent squabbles she grew sick again, compelling her to visit new spas and new specialists and to repeat the whole cycle again and again.

The house was in a perpetual state of disorder as Priveh was eternally replacing the furniture and tapestries. Since the other Lodz ladies were forever redecorating, Priveh refused to be left behind.

Haim Alter knew that all this took lots of money, but he couldn't refuse his Priveh anything. He loved her too much for that. Despite her grown children, she was a handsome woman and one with excellent taste. When he walked with her in the street or at the spas, men turned to look at her, and this filled him with pride. Therefore, when she held out her plump, dimpled hand for money, he gave her whatever she wanted.

Besides, he was no mean spender himself. In addition to contributing to his rabbi and the house of worship, he himself took the baths every summer and enjoyed other luxuries.

But Haim Alter knew that all this was as it should be and that even the money squandered on clothes and redecorating wasn't a sin. Because, first of all, why skimp? What was man, after all, if not temporal? Here one day, gone the next. Why then live like a pig?

Secondly, it was good for business. Lodz admired nothing more than wealth. Lodz knew what was cooking in everyone's pot. It sufficed for a Lodz businessman to skip one season at the spa or have his wife attend a party minus jewelry for gossip to begin that he was on the verge of bankruptcy, ready for the poorhouse.

Haim Alter didn't *want* an accounting. He knew that the factory was rolling along nicely, that the workers weren't sitting around idle, that the looms were clacking away, that people in the street looked at him with awe, and that he lived like a *mensh,* a person good to God and to man.

Nor would he skimp on his children. Hadn't he sought out the best match in Lodz for his daughter? Hadn't he provided the biggest dowry, the most princely wedding? In all this time he had never even considered the cost of the affair. Priveh had thrust her hand out, and he had filled it with money again and again.

Now, after all the fuss and bother, Samuel Leibush came to him with a long face. From all sides, artisans and tradesmen Priveh had engaged at fees she herself couldn't recall were descending upon him. Bills flooded in from all over. Tailors, cobblers, seamstresses, rugmakers, grocers, butchers, fishmongers attacked like a swarm of locust.

Samuel Leibush couldn't assuage them. In the factory the workers sighed and grimaced, anxious for money for the Sabbath. From abroad came huge bills for the raw materials. No cash was coming in, and the banks had cut off Haim Alter's credit. The ruble was hard to come by in Lodz, and Samuel Leibush bowed his head before his employer as if it were all his fault.

"Reb Haim," he said, averting his eyes like some thief, "I'm afraid we're in a tight squeeze."

At first, Haim Alter waved a fat, hairy hand in disdain. He was too tired from the wedding to listen to any sob stories. "You don't know what you're talking about," he said.

But Samuel Leibush wouldn't be put off. For days he had pored over the ledgers, adding, subtracting, multiplying, moving the beads on the Russian abacus, each time arriving at a new total and beginning anew. His head began to ache, his eyes grew bloodshot, but he couldn't get the figures to tally.

Finally, he tossed it all aside and advised Haim Alter to call in a bookkeeper.

Haim Alter wouldn't even hear of it. "I hate bookkeepers!" he exclaimed. "You know what I always say: the more you count, the less you have. . . ."

He couldn't stand those Litvaks, those enemies of Israel, who had become the bookkeepers of Lodz. But Samuel Leibush persisted and persisted until Haim Alter gave in.

"All right, all right," he finally said. "I need it like a hole in the head, but bring in one of the dunces. . . ."

For eight days the scrawny Litvak with the pince-nez affixed to a thick black ribbon pored over Haim Alter's ledgers, groping among the additions, notations, and erasures.

"Incoming, outgoing . . ." he kept muttering, as he calculated. "The devil take it. . . ."

Haim Alter couldn't stand looking at this pauper with the stubbly jaw and rubber collar over the knobby neck. He could accept manufacturers and bankers abandoning their faith, but that such a ragamuffin should do so was beyond his tolerance. The Litvak was good for neither this world nor the next. He, Haim Alter, wouldn't go near him, with his tattered jacket with its skimpy sleeves and the stink of Lithuanian garlic. But the Litvak wouldn't leave him alone.

"What's this?" he asked in a grating voice, pointing to a row of convoluted numbers.

Haim Alter said whatever came into his head, but the Litvak wouldn't let him off the hook.

"Expense isn't income, after all, the devil take it!"

After eight days the Litvak finally emerged from all the allusions, abbreviations "incomings," and "outgoings" and produced a clear and accurate balance sheet with credits and debits, with rows of neat figures as level as troops lined up for inspection before a general.

He stood up, stretched his skinny arms, straightened the dangling pince-nez, and, in his pronounced Lithuanian accent, announced with deliberation, "You are broke, Gospodin Alter."

Haim Alter leaped from his seat with even more fervor than he did at his rabbi's table on Rosh Hashanah. "You don't know your ass from your elbow, Litvak swine!" he shouted in a rage, and slammed shut the covers of his new account book that the bookkeeper had so painstakingly prepared.

The Litvak didn't take offense. He opened the ledger and with a bony finger pointed to the evenly aligned columns. "You are bankrupt, Gospodin Alter. Ab-so-lute-ly. . . ."

His final word, issued in a drawn-out Russian, served to

convince Haim Alter. The latter thrust his hands into his trouser pockets, pulled them inside out along with all the pockets of his red and blue dotted vest, and turning on his servant with fury, he demanded, "Well, what do you say to the state of *your* business, Samuel Leibush? What do you say?"

Samuel Leibush's face broke out in splotches as if indeed it were all his fault. And Haim Alter paced through his rooms unable to get the Litvak's words out of his head: "You are broke, Gospodin Alter. . . . You are bankrupt. . . ."

At first, Haim Alter tried to consult with his wife. But she didn't have the patience even to let him finish. "You know that I don't understand these things, Haimshe," she said. "You'll manage by yourself already."

Realizing that he wasn't making any headway, he got down to brass tacks and asked her to lend him her collection of diamonds for a brief time so that he might arrange with Samuel Leibush to pawn them discreetly until things straightened out a bit. This would afford him at least a brief breathing space from the smaller creditors, all those pesky craftsmen and shopkeepers who were so persistently snapping at his heels.

The blood drained from Priveh's face, leaving her wide-eyed and with sickly red patches on her cheeks. "Mama!" she wailed, resorting as usual to her long-departed parent, blue eyes gushing tears. "I can stop eating. I can stop buttering my bread or drink tea without sugar. Is that what you'd like?"

Haim Alter saw that he would get nowhere with his wife— it was all beyond her. Her only concern was whether she would be able to go to the spas that summer. Haim Alter reassured her and walked away.

Early the next morning he sought out his rabbi for advice. But the rabbi was no more help than Priveh. To all of Haim Alter's complaints he merely responded that the Almighty would help.

Neither were Haim Alter's sons of any assistance. All they knew was how to drag money out of their father. Haim Alter then turned to his last resort—his son-in-law's father, Abraham Hersh Ashkenazi.

Following the ceremony of ushering out the Sabbath, he went to his in-law's house. Abraham Hersh placed his red kerchief between the pages of the Gemara as a sign that he was merely postponing his studies temporarily and calmly, mutely, and without interruption listened for an hour to his in-law's impassioned words.

Although the Ashkenazi house was cold and forbidding with its massive furniture, brown tapestried walls, huge iron safe, and the murky light of the kerosene lamp, Haim Alter sweated freely. He didn't drink the glass of tea that was served him, but kept on talking with fervor and conviction. When he finally grew silent, Abraham Hersh fixed his dark eyes upon him and uttered a single word: "No."

Sweat drenched Haim Alter. "You would let me go under?" he blurted. "To whom then can I turn if not to you?"

"He who lives without reckoning dies without confession," Abraham Hersh responded with a parable.

When Haim Alter resumed hotly and even seized his in-law familiarly by the beard, Abraham Hersh removed the red kerchief from the Gemara and resumed studying the laws regarding the number of lashes a sinner had coming. "How many lashes are forthcoming?" he chanted, oblivious to the other's presence.

Haim Alter left his in-law's house so distraught that he even failed that night to recite the closing hymn, "And He shall give unto thee," that he chanted each Sabbath night with such relish, and he spit out with rage the usual cigar Samuel Leibush brought him. "Lousy cigars!" he snarled. "Bitter as gall. . . ."

He was just as displeased with the glass of sweet aromatic tea Hadassah brought him on a silver platter. "Couldn't you make a fresh pot?" he raged. "Do I have to drink warmed-over tea?"

Hadassah flushed deeply. "May my luck be as good, dear Father in heaven, as this tea. If the master would only taste—"

But Haim Alter wouldn't taste. Instead, he glared at his loutish sons as they played cards with unconcern. "Lousy wastrels!" he screamed, tearing the cards from their hands as if this were the first time he had caught them at it. "You and your cards will send me begging door to door!"

At night he tossed on his three soft down pillows that had suddenly grown hard as stone. All Lodz passed before his eyes in the sleepless night, but he couldn't choose the one person to whom he could turn in his moment of need.

Only as dawn was breaking did it come to him suddenly— the very person he needed, one who had the money and yet had no immediate need for it. And he cursed himself for not having thought of it sooner.

Mind relieved, spirit unburdened, Haim Alter sank into deep, dreamless sleep.

FIFTEEN

SIMHA MEIR LISTENED to his loquacious father-in-law's troubles with an attitude different from his father's. Haim Alter's urgent words were appended with aphorisms, maxims, and parables, but they all ended on one note: "I tell you, Simha Meirshe, I'll pay you a much higher interest than the bank. And you can rest easy. I wouldn't hurt my own child, after all, God forbid!"

"Of course not, Father-in-law." Simha Meir nodded sympathetically.

Haim Alter exulted inwardly over his son-in-law's swift acquiescence. "Your money will grow, Simha Meir, darling. You'll get interest over interest, and you can still board with me for as long as you please. Do you understand, Simha Meirshe, darling?"

"I understand, Father-in-law." Simha Meir nodded amiably.

But when it came time to go to the bank and withdraw the 10,000 rubles, he hung back. "I must consult with Daddy first," he explained sanctimoniously.

"Why burden your father?" Haim Alter asked, trying to mask his anxiety. "You're not some simpleton, after all. You know yourself what you must do."

"Honor thy father!" Simha Meir quoted piously. "Without Father's advice, I wouldn't dare make such a move."

Haim Alter walked him through the house for hours, stroking and flattering him, praising his sharp brain and common sense, but Simha Meir remained obdurate. "Believe me, Father-in-law, I would trust you with my life. But without Daddy's consent, my hands are tied. Honor thy father, you know. I'll see him this very day about this matter."

Naturally he never consulted his father. He never even considered such a step. He had been under his father's dominance long enough. Now he was free of him. The dowry was deposited in his own name, and he knew better than his father exactly what to do with it. But it was a good ploy to use against his father-in-law, and he let him stew a few days more until he was nearly jumping out of his skin. Only then did he come to him with his father's alleged advice.

His face serene, his words crisp and direct, his manner airy but resolute, he broached the matter during lunch. After buttering a roll, he bit into it zestfully, and with a mouth full of food, he enumerated his father's demands: "Daddy says I should get collateral—guaranteed collateral."

Haim Alter jumped to his feet, face burning. "You'll get IOUs, Simha Meir. I wouldn't have it any other way!"

Simha Meir sliced himself a piece of cheese, laid it on the roll, and waved away his father-in-law's suggestion. "Daddy insisted I not take IOUs. Daddy wants me to take a mortgage on Father-in-law's house."

"A mortgage?" Haim Alter bristled. "What favor are you doing me with a mortgage? I can go to anybody with a mortgage."

"Then why doesn't Father-in-law do so?" Simha Meir asked, looking ingenuously into Haim Alter's eyes.

For a full day Haim Alter worked on his son-in-law. He tried to impress him as to his solvency; he pointed out how unseemly it was for a son-in-law to distrust his own father-in-law's promissory notes, particularly a man of his reputation, to whom people had always been eager to entrust their money.

Simha Meir remained adamant. "What can I do?" he said. "My hands are tied."

Even when Haim Alter finally agreed to the mortgage, Simha Meir was in no rush to conclude the transaction and explained that he must again talk things over with his daddy.

Haim Alter exploded. "Again with the daddy? It's becoming a story without an end already. . . ."

Simha Meir washed his hands and didn't answer. From his gambling days at Shillem the baker's, he knew that when an opponent was at his most frantic, that was the time to play a waiting game. No, he hadn't been able to catch his daddy at home; yes, he *had* found him, but he had been too busy to talk. . . .

Haim Alter fumed until Simha Meir finally came to him with an answer. "Daddy says that I shouldn't settle for anything but a first mortgage. Otherwise, it's no deal. . . ."

Haim Alter raged and ranted. He couldn't let Simha Meir have a first mortgage for the simple reason that someone else already held it. Naturally Simha Meir had known this all along. He had made inquiries into his father-in-law's affairs, and in a city where everyone knew everybody else's business, people were only too delighted to transmit the bad news. The fact that he knew about the first mortgage was the very reason he had demanded it. He was after bigger game.

Ever since childhood he had had his eye on Haim Alter's factory. Not that he had any use for handlooms, for his sympathies lay with the New Lodz, with modern Lodz, with steam. He had always been intrigued by the huge mills with their sky-high chimneys. Nothing smelled so sweet to him as the smoke pouring from these chimneys. The shrieking sirens were like music to his ears.

The ancient handlooms, with their bearded, skullcapped operators, repelled him. They reminded him of the despised study-house. He was always drawn to the newest, the latest, the biggest and best. He envisioned himself as one of the magnates of Lodz, attended by mobs of flunkies awaiting his every command.

But he also knew that Rome hadn't been built in a day. All of Lodz's industrialists had started with handlooms and worked their way up to steam.

He was also keenly aware that his own progress need not be so gradual. Lodz was no longer what it once had been. Everything moved more quickly now. And he would skip the first step. He was, after all, the son of Abraham Hersh Ashkenazi, the son-in-law of Haim Alter, and the possessor of 10,000 rubles (plus interest). With such a start, you could do something, assuming you grasped the essence of business. With such a sum, you could begin with fifty, not five handlooms.

He had already deduced the full measure of his father-in-law's character. He was soft, weak, lazy—devoted to luxuries and comfort and wholly under his wife's thumb. Even as a boy Simha Meir had known that Haim Alter wouldn't fit in the New Lodz. He also knew that eventually, he, Simha Meir, would somehow become part of the factory. He had observed it in all its disorder, and he knew that one day it would fall upon someone of business sense, innovation, and daring to turn it into the profitable venture it could be. It was for these reasons that he had refused to accept notes in lieu of cash as part of his dowry. And the wisdom of his judgment was becoming evident now.

Clearly his chance had come. He was sick of hanging around the house, swaying over the Torah like some schoolboy. He knew that the season had been a disastrous one for the weaving industry and that cash was short. He, therefore, expected little opposition to the terms he now broached to his father-in-law.

At first, Haim Alter blustered, accused his son-in-law of having a heart of stone and of being totally corrupt.

Simha Meir kept silent. He suddenly grew inordinately devoted to his studies. Haim Alter avoided him, but as his creditors began to grow more and more insistent and Samuel Leibush could no longer keep them at bay, Haim Alter came around and agreed to all of Simha Meir's conditions.

For the sum of 10,000 rubles, Simha Meir became a one-third partner in the factory. At his insistence, a contract was drawn up between the pair which was filled with provisions, clauses, and various "whereases." It took so long to complete that Haim Alter was slavering by the time the money flowed into his fat, eager hands—money that had been his in the first place, money for which he had gone into hock to purchase a brilliant scholar and prodigy for his only daughter.

"You're a hard man, Simha Meir." He sighed as they left the musty notary's office and shook hands on their new partnership.

Having gotten what he wanted, Haim Alter now sought to keep his son-in-law out of the factory and to send him back to his studies. But Simha Meir had other plans. "If we're partners, then we're partners in fact, not in name only," he said with assumed righteousness. "I wouldn't let Father-in-law carry the entire burden. I'll hold up my end of the bargain."

When Abraham Hersh learned of his son's actions, he promptly sent Jacob Bunem to fetch him. Jacob Bunem was anxious to get the errand over with. In the Alters' dining room, he chanced upon Dinele sitting as usual with her legs tucked under her on the ottoman and reading one of her novels.

"Good evening," he said in a reserved tone.

She seemed taken aback and began to tremble. He grew confused as well, and his fingers flew to the peak of his cap, as they used to in the past when he encountered her in the street. She, in turn, blushed.

"How is Jacob?" she asked in the formal third person.

"How is Dinele?" he responded.

They both dropped their eyes and kept silent.

Simha Meir didn't greet his brother too warmly. He knew that his visit boded trouble.

His father laid the kerchief between the pages of the Gemara, as was his custom, and let his son stand for a very long time.

As always when in a rage, he spoke softly. "Simha, did you ask me if you could withdraw the money?"

"No, Father."

"Then why did you do it without my knowledge?"

"Father-in-law was pressed for money," Simha Meir replied piously, "and I took pity on him."

"You wanted to perform a good deed, was that it?" Abraham Hersh asked with narrowed eyes.

"Yes, Father," Simha Meir replied naïvely.

"Well then, and obeying your father is *not* a good deed?" Simha Meir didn't answer.

Abraham Hersh pushed the skullcap back on his head and regarded the youth. It would have helped if his son had at least lowered his eyes as he lied to him, but he didn't even blink and kept the same sanctimonious expression on his face until his father lost his tightly controlled composure.

"Listen here, saint of mine, I order you to go back to your studies!"

"I will study whenever I find the time," Simha Meir said. "That's a promise, Father."

"No, you will study the full five years of your board!"

"I can't lay the whole burden on Father-in-law. Is it not written: 'Though shalt not see thy brother's ass or his ox fallen down by the way, and hide thyself from them; thou shalt surely help him to lift them up again'?"

The blood rushed to Abraham Hersh's head. "Despoiler of Israel, don't you dare set one foot inside the factory until your five years are up! I want your word on it now!" And he extended his hairy, sinewy hand.

Simha Meir let his father's hand dangle in the air.

It grew so quiet in the room that the only sound heard was Jacob Bunem's heavy breathing. Abraham Hersh endured his humiliation for a full thirty seconds; then he raised his hand high and let it fall with all its might against Simha Meir's cheek.

"Out of my house, reprobate!" he exclaimed.

Silently Simha Meir picked up his silk hat which had been dislodged by his father's slap, rubbed his reddened cheek, and left the house. Outside of the physical pain, he felt fine. He even smiled, walking home.

What was a father's slap to the junior partner of the firm of Alter and Ashkenazi, to an independent businessman about to take on Lodz not with five, but with fifty looms right from the start and aiming at the very highest smokestacks? . . .

With wide, eager nostrils Simha Meir drew in the sooty air of Lodz and walked confidently across the ill-paved sidewalks.

SIXTEEN

———————————

WITH ALL THE FERVOR of his energetic youth, with the same zeal with which he had manipulated the cards at Shillem the baker's, Simha Meir threw himself into the task of taking over the factory that adjoined his father-in-law's house. He was everywhere at once—ears cocked like a hare's for every sound; deceptively mild, darting gray eyes observing everything; long, thin nose sniffing everywhere.

First, he tackled the books, the messy ledgers that had sent the Litvak bookkeeper into such a tizzy. To Simha Meir they presented no mystery. He added, subtracted, multiplied, and divided in highly unorthodox but eminently practical fashion until everything balanced to the groschen.

After he had concluded, he forbade everyone, including his father-in-law and Samuel Leibush, to touch the books again.

Next, he addressed himself to the pile of letters, misplaced orders, overdue bills, and receipts that lay scattered everywhere and usually ended up forgotten in his father-in-law's pockets.

He knew no other languages except a scattering of German he had picked up from Goldlust the bookkeeper and from primers. His Russian was even more fragmentary, only the few words he had picked up from the Litvak traveling salesmen at his father's house. But he had the native ability to use one word to explain ten and with it, supreme self-confidence. He pitched right in and wrote replies to customers' letters, letters that were misspelled and ungrammatical, yet concise and to the point.

When he was through with the paperwork, he focused his attentions on Samuel Leibush. First, he took over the safe that Haim Alter had entrusted to his servant for all the years. Samuel Leibush didn't give in easily. He was used to taking full charge of the factory and supplying his employer with cash on demand, and he was loath to yield to a new authority—a callow youth who plucked at his sprouting beard as if seeking to hurry its growth, a snotnosed boy with his mother's milk still fresh upon his lips.

He flatly refused to listen to Simha Meir or to surrender the keys to the safe. "I'll pay the boss myself," he insisted. "Don't let it become your concern, Simha Meir."

His tone indicated that the only boss he would accept was Haim Alter, regardless of any private arrangements the old man might have made with his son-in-law. Haim Alter silently backed his man's revolt all the way and relished his resistance against his new and unwelcome partner.

Simha Meir launched his campaign. He made sure to get to the factory before Samuel Leibush, arriving with the workers before dawn and staying long into the night. He ignored all calls to lunch and dinner, and Hadassah had to come running to fetch him to the table.

He distributed the work to the workers. He saw to it that the work wasn't botched. He counted the threads through a magnifying glass. He kept an eye on the shirkers and made sure the men didn't weave the yarn too loosely.

The workers acknowledged his expertise as a born manufacturer who knew his business and wouldn't allow himself to be deceived, and they learned to depend upon him. They obeyed his orders and ignored those of the ineffectual Samuel Leibush, who would make a brief appearance and fall into senseless rages for reasons he himself didn't fathom.

"Be off with you," Simha Meir dismissed him. "I've got things under control here."

Samuel Leibush turned away in a pout and, after a while, stopped coming to the factory altogether.

In no time Simha Meir relieved him of his other duties. He began to meet personally with the merchants and buyers, he took over the correspondence, and he oversaw the shipment of the goods.

The merchants and buyers, who for years had been compelled to give kickbacks to Samuel Leibush, welcomed the chance to speak directly to a principal of the firm who conducted business on the up and up. Besides, he was sharp, agile, and understood a problem before it was even verbalized.

Simha Meir quickly let it be known that henceforth Samuel Leibush was to be skipped over and that no money was to be paid into his hands. Only he, Simha Meir, was empowered to accept payments.

Samuel Leibush went on as before, but at every turn he was informed that young Ashkenazi had already taken care of the matter. Seeing the way things were going, Samuel Leibush decided to get in good with the new boss, who obviously had his wits about him, but Simha Meir kept him at a distance. He sent him out on simple errands until Samuel Leibush put his foot down.

"I'm no errand boy," he griped. "I've been running the factory all these years by myself, Simha Meir!"

Simha Meir stuck his hands in his pants pockets, rose on tiptoe to appear more impressive, and snapped, "If you don't like it, go get a better job. And while we're at it—where do you come off calling me by my first name? I don't recall us having slopped hogs together. . . ."

Samuel Leibush promptly climbed off his high horse. "No need to take offense, Reb Simha," he said, bowing his head. "I'm leaving straight off!"

Simha Meir enumerated what his tasks would be henceforth, and Samuel Leibush stood trembling in his new boss's presence. Haim Alter felt mortified for his retainer, but there was nothing he could or would do about it. He was simply too timid to confront his strong-willed son-in-law, and his solution was to show up less and less frequently at the factory. Whenever he did show up, Simha Meir came running up with affected concern. "Father-in-law can go lie down. I'll take care of everything already."

And the older man gratefully accepted the suggestion. He napped, read Hasidic storybooks about squires who assumed the guise of werewolves in order to harm Jews and about the saints who used sacred blessings to frustrate these wizards and transform them into dogs and tomcats.

Reclining on his soft ottoman, he kept chastising his good-for-nothing sons for their laziness and lack of will, traits that were exactly his own.

"You should follow Simha Meir's example," he bleated at them as they smirked in secret knowledge of their brother-in-law's intentions. "He never rests, like the River Sambation. . . ."

Simha Meir no longer showed up in the studyhouse except on rare occasions. He spent more and more time in the cafés among the merchants, traveling salesmen, brokers, moneylenders, and others who loitered on the fringes of the Lodz business establishment. They sat over glasses of beer and plates of hard-boiled eggs, talking business, making deals, figuring, scheming, trading information, quoting the price of wool and cotton, discussing everyone's joys, sorrows, gains, and losses.

By the hundreds they scribbled figures on beer-stained table-tops, enveloped in the noise, smoke, and dust of the city the fortunes and fate of which were their lifeblood.

Here it was known who was accumulating a fortune and who was losing his shirt; who was really solvent and who only presented a front and couldn't be trusted with a bundle of goods. Here cotton fields thousands of miles away were bought and sold. Here the prices of goods were fixed and manipulated. Here yarn was unraveled and graded.

In this vortex of Hasidic catchphrases, Lithuanian street wisdom, and salesmen's jokes, the fruit of the toil of thousands was transformed into cold figures scrawled swiftly over dirty tabletops.

And amid it all skulked Simha Meir, ears and eyes alert for every useful tidbit of information, every morsel of gossip. He wasn't well known yet, this puny youth, who kept tugging the hairs on his chin as if to hurry their growth, and the others paid him scant attention, but he didn't let this disturb him. He knew from experience that one must force oneself to wait for the opportune moment to throw the trump card.

So he kept his lips sealed for the present and didn't mix in, merely hovered around the edges, absorbing everything like a sponge.

Gradually he began to toss in a word or two, inquire about some deal, feel a swatch of goods, unravel a thread. He acquired the appropriate jargon and mannerisms. He learned when to speak and when to keep silent, when to play dumb and when to avoid an answer. He even learned to seize a man's lapel and finger the material of his garment, in the way of the Lodz merchant. People began to take notice of him and to ask about him.

"Abraham Hersh Ashkenazi's son," they informed one another, "Haim Alter's son-in-law." And they turned their heads to catch a better glimpse of such a privileged young man.

Before they knew it, he had already insinuated himself into their circle and was joking, quipping, and joshing with the best, cleverly countering the sallies of the old-timers, who tried to initiate the fresh young upstart.

"He's got no flies on him, the little twerp," they said admiringly. "He doesn't need anyone to take up for him. . . ."

And word spread in the dingy restaurants that the young fellow wasn't only well connected but quite a shrewd little operator on his own.

"He's the real goods, all right," Jews said with a wink, and welcomed him with open arms. He fitted right in, and in no time, men twice his age were taking him aside to discuss some juicy deal to be pulled off on the sly.

"A shrewdie, sharp as a tack," they said. "But you've got to watch him like a hawk. . . . The guts of a burglar and crooked as a corkscrew. . . ."

He didn't rest on his laurels. Behind the high forehead framed by the short-clipped hair and the uptilted hatbrim, his brain didn't cease churning, scheming, speculating. One day he came to the conclusion that the kerchiefs his firm turned out were too long and too wide and used up too much wool. Sure, they sold well and made a profit, but who said they had to be the size they were? Would it be a tragedy if they were a touch shorter and narrower? No dumb Russian peasant or market-woman would catch on. What was an inch? Nothing to a customer, but to the manufacturer—a great deal. . . . With the pencil he always kept tucked behind his ear, he calculated swiftly.

Each worker finished 3 kerchiefs per day, which came to 150 or so kerchiefs in all, more than 1,000 per week, and about 50,000 per year, counting days lost for holidays and such. By trimming just one inch from each kerchief, he could effect a most respectable saving over the year.

The very next morning he ordered the weavers to drop an inch from the kerchiefs.

"Hey, the boss wants we should circumcise off an inch," Tevye the World Isn't Lawless remarked with a wink.

Simha Meir promptly cut him short. "I don't want to hear such talk. The kerchiefs are too long and too wide. Do what you're told, and don't talk so much. No one has to know what goes on inside the factory."

The weavers did as they were told and stretched the ker-chiefs out sufficiently to make up for the missing inch of material. No one caught on to the deception—not the cus-tomers or even the retail merchants—and it all went off as smooth as butter.

Simha Meir began to scheme ways to achieve additional savings. He had a kerchief made of a blend of virgin wool and recycled yarn. Only an absolute expert could detect the differ-ence between this and the pure wool product, and only after he had unraveled the kerchief between his fingers.

Simha Meir instituted other innovations. He designed a kerchief that was wool at the borders but cotton in the center. To mask this discrepancy, he had the border handsomely dec-orated with colorful flowers by Tevye, who was adept at this type of work. The Russian women seized upon the item, and Simha Meir began to manufacture them in quantity. He even took on additional help to weave the flowered borders. The mongrel kerchiefs became the rage of Lodz, and soon other manufacturers pirated the design, but not before Simha Meir had reaped a handsome profit.

At the same time he began to turn out an all-cotton kerchief, one that was very thin and flimsy, but so cheap as to be affordable by even the poorest woman. The workers were able to finish these kerchiefs at a rate of seven or eight per day. On the principle that the cheapest candy deserves the fanciest wrapper, Simha Meir arranged for the kerchiefs to emerge very colorful and patterned in loud designs.

The cotton kerchiefs made an enormous hit, but Haim Alter began to grumble about his firm's reputation's being damaged by turning out such a shoddy product. He spoke of "integrity" "responsibility," but Simha Meir quickly challenged such ridiculous pretensions. "If Father-in-law would be good enough to show me where it is written that weaving wool will bring greater rewards in paradise than weaving cotton, I'll be grateful," he said in singsong. "Besides, why bother your head about these things? I'll take care of it already."

And he elbowed Haim Alter away from buyers with whom he had business to discuss.

Haim Alter vowed to himself to reassert his authority. From time to time he burst into the factory, shouted, and threw his weight around, but no one took him seriously. Simha Meir was the only acknowledged boss here.

Not that Haim Alter had any complaints against his son-in-law. Just as Samuel Leibush before him, Simha Meir shoved all kinds of papers in front of him, and he signed without even reading them. Nor did he ever refuse to give him whatever cash he demanded. The only difference was that unlike Samuel Leibush, Simha Meir marked down every ruble, every groschen. He didn't share Haim Alter's view that the less figuring, the greater gains.

Samuel Leibush tried very subtly to instigate trouble. "Reb Haim," he grumbled, "I don't trust that runt. Best keep an eye on him."

But Haim Alter wouldn't do anything to disturb his own equanimity. He much preferred to follow his regimen of banquets, naps, and other material comforts. Most of all, he was reluctant to let his darling Priveh go all alone to the spas, where the men literally devoured her with their eyes. He placed his trust in God, with whose help everything would turn out all right.

"Father-in-law can go away with an easy mind," Simha Meir assured Haim Alter. "Why stay here in all this smoke and noise? I'll take care of everything already."

At the end of the year, when Simha Meir made the annual audit, it turned out that the factory had done quite well indeed. The new cotton kerchiefs, the savings on wool, the accurate bookkeeping, the time spent in the noisy cafés, getting the orders off on time and supervising the help closely had all paid off handsomely. Besides, Simha Meir had pulled off some nice little deals on the side that he didn't enter in the firm's books. He had bought several lots of cotton on credit and had disposed of them, sight unseen, at a nice profit. Since these were personal deals and the risk had been entirely his own, he felt that the profits belonged to him alone. Besides, his father-in-law had drawn far more than his share of profits for the year.

With relish, Simha Meir scribbled figures everywhere—on tablecloths, on swatches of goods, on walls and doors. He had every reason to be pleased. The year's efforts had been most lucrative. Still, he was discontented. He couldn't stop brooding about Jacob Bunem, who, just as in the courtyard years ago, had again scored a tremendous personal victory over his elder brother, and Simha Meir's guts churned with envy. He couldn't sleep nights on account of Jacob Bunem's incredible stroke of luck.

SEVENTEEN

SHORTLY AFTER SIMHA MEIR'S WEDDING, the matchmaker Samuel Zanvil came proposing a spectacular match, one that left Abraham Hersh Ashkenazi temporarily and untypically dumbfounded.

"With *whom* do you propose to match my son?" he asked in disbelief. "With a granddaughter of Reb Kalman Eisen?"

"Yes, yes. Kalman Eisen's granddaughter," Samuel Zanvil said, drawing out every word and gazing triumphantly at the father. "Just as I've told you." He even neglected to add the honorary title "Reb" to the great man's name.

To heighten the effect, he grew emboldened and boasted of his gall in arranging the match, which wasn't exactly the truth. "I went there," he bragged, "and said, 'Look here, Kalman, I want to join your family with that of Abraham Hersh Ashkenazi of Lodz—'"

Abraham Hersh could listen to no more of the matchmaker's self-approbation, and he interrupted. "Said this, said that, the main thing is—was it at your instigation that this happened or were you told to arrange the match?"

"Told, told to—" Samuel Zanvil repeated crabbily, furious that his word had been doubted. "The bride's side asked for it. . . ."

"Hard to understand," Abraham Hersh observed, reaching for a hefty pinch of snuff with which to clear his head.

Even though Kalman Eisen lived in Warsaw, there wasn't a Jew in Poland who hadn't heard of him. He was known to be worth millions. Besides, he was a man of such monumental ego that people trembled in his presence. He was also a follower of the Ger Rabbi—and therefore an opponent of the Alexander Rabbi—and Abraham Hersh couldn't understand the reason for the proposal. Kalman Eisen's household had put out the feeler. And for whom—Jacob Bunem? He might have understood had it been Simha Meir, the prodigy, but Jacob Bunem? . . .

The only one who knew the secret was Jacob Bunem himself.

At his brother's wedding, actually right by the wedding canopy out in the courtyard, a thin, sallow girl, whose white gown made her appear even leaner and more sallow, struck up a conversation with him. "Maybe you'd move a bit, sir," she drawled. "I'd like to see the ceremony, too, but you seem to be blocking the whole yard."

He moved aside, but she persisted. "Maybe you wouldn't mind raising me up a trifle?" she asked, laughing to her girl-friends. "And don't shake that candle so, you'll drip wax all over my dress."

He blushed, only making her laugh harder.

"Are you afraid I'm going to bite you?" she asked. "I don't bite."

He replied earnestly, "I'm not afraid of anything."

The girl giggled at his bashfulness. "You don't seem as pious and fanatical as you're trying to make out," she observed, moving closer and pressing against him in the crush. Without quite knowing how it happened, they suddenly found themselves holding hands.

"Why did you let your brother marry first?" she asked. "You're bigger."

"He's older," Jacob Bunem replied.

"Oh? And do you want a bride, too?"

Jacob Bunem was too embarrassed to answer.

The girl squeezed his hand. "Would you like me for a bride?" she asked, laughing slyly.

Jacob Bunem flushed all over.

"You're quite the cavalier," she observed. "But you'd appeal to me more if you shed that Hasidic attire and put on European clothes. Do you think I'm pretty?"

He didn't answer. He was too shy. Besides, there were people all around, and he was afraid that someone would notice how close he was standing to a girl. But she wouldn't let go of him, and she paid no attention to the others.

"You must tell me if I appeal to you," she insisted.

"Yes," he said, even though it wasn't so.

"My name is Pearl, Pearl Eisen of Warsaw," she said with pride. "One might even consider us kinfolk since I'm related to the bride on my mother's side. I came here specially for the wedding from Warsaw."

As the crowd began breaking up, the girl squeezed his hand for the last time and drifted away.

Jacob Bunem didn't see her again, but he recalled the incident. She was the first girl to hold his hand, to speak to him in such fashion. He hadn't thought any more about her, but she thought about him a great deal. The towering, dark-eyed youth, from whose glance fire seemed to emanate, had aroused every desire within her virginal, sickly being. And she began urging her family to send a matchmaker to the youth's father.

When she first proposed this to her own father, he blanched. "Perele, don't even utter such words!" he pleaded in alarm, and stopped up her mouth with his hand. "All we need is for your grandfather to hear!"

The grandfather, Reb Kalman, a man in his late seventies, ruled the household with an iron hand. Boys and graybeards alike withered before his steely glance.

He was a millionaire many times over. It was said that he himself didn't know just how much he was worth, and this was true. He owned buildings by the hundreds, one whole block of houses in Warsaw being called Kalman Eisen Street. He also owned many tracts of timber and conducted huge business transactions with the authorities. He provided ties, poles, and other lumber for all the railroad tracks and telegraph lines built by the government. But he conducted all his business in old-fashioned style—the same as when he had first married and owned a small lumberyard on Warsaw's Iron Street. He didn't believe in boards of directors or in accountants. Just as he had built his business with his own two hands, so did he run it by himself, scorning the new methods and the gentiles with all their ledgers and account books.

He hated innovation. He had his own way of doing things, from which he didn't deviate by even a hair.

So long as he lived, he wouldn't let his sons near the business even though they were already middle-aged men themselves. He kept them all domiciled within his great court, apportioned a large apartment to each, and covered all their and their families' expenses. But he wouldn't let them do anything on their own. They generally had no say in the house, nor did they dare arrange matches for their children, leaving all that to him, their father, who also provided room and board for the young couples. Each time there was a marriage in the family, Kalman Eisen had a new story or addition built onto the house, which now extended for two blocks.

Nor did his sons and sons-in-law preside over their own tables on Sabbaths and holidays, but they had to sit at the patriarch's table along with their children and grandchildren. This table ran the entire length of the enormous dining room and was filled by a throng of relatives, besides the usual quota of impoverished Sabbath guests, saintly Jews, and tutors of the household's children. Male and female servants served the large crowd.

Each person sat with a prayer book in hand, positioned according to his age and status. At the head of the table on an elevated throne sat the tall, distinguished, white-bearded Kalman Eisen himself, and ruled his roost. No one dared touch a finger to knife or fork until the old man picked up his; no one dared utter a word until he spoke first. He addressed his sons, gray-bearded men, as if they were boys.

He was held in the same awe by all the Jews in Warsaw, including the richest and most scholarly. He rode in a carriage drawn by a team of white horses. When he traveled to spas in the summers, an army of servants, including a personal ritual slaughterer, attended him. And although he was pious and a good Hasid, he wore a stiff collar and a hat of his own design, a kind of silk kepi with a glistening lacquered visor of the type worn by gentiles. Because of his near-royal status, he was beyond censure, and he did exactly as he pleased. It was rumored in Warsaw that he used silver cuspidors and that when he went out for a stroll, he was accompanied by a servant carrying such a silver spittoon.

He was feared most of all by his youngest son, Solly. No scholar, not particularly bright, the least physically prepossessing of all his brothers, he was terrified to catch his father's eye. He never spoke up or ventured an opinion. "I'm no expert, after all," he would say deprecating himself, and turn away to avoid contact.

He was a widower, having lost his sickly wife and all his children except for Perele, who was as sickly, obstinate, and imperious as her late mother. Her father was afraid of her, too, and began twitching when she expressed her infatuation with the Lodz youth and her intention to send a matchmaker to his father.

"Bite your tongue, I didn't hear a word you've said!" he said to quell his own fear. "God forbid your grandfather should hear!"

Matches were strictly Kalman's province. The family matchmaker, Asriel Cohen—a man of acid tongue who could wreck a match if it suited his purpose, a vicious slanderer and gossip —arranged all the matches for the Eisen family.

He knew all Poland. He was acquainted with everyone's income, status, family ties. He could rattle off everyone's genealogy going back to the first generation. He considered

Kalman Eisen's house his own, kept his eye on everyone, and as soon as it came time to marry off a grandchild, he arranged a consultation with Kalman.

He was never wrong in his evaluations, and Kalman relied upon him. And if, occasionally, following a wedding, Kalman took a dislike to some son-in-law, he promptly told the wife to discard her husband, and a divorce was quickly arranged. The women may have cried, but they obeyed. A self-arranged match was, therefore, out of the question. Such a thing was unthinkable, and Solly Eisen trembled at the mere thought of proposing it to his father.

But Perele was made of sterner stuff. Determined to get her way, she went straight to her grandmother, Tirza.

Tirza, paralyzed, sick, and old, was the only one able to sway Kalman. They had made their fortune together. She had worked side by side with him, advised him. She was a shrewd woman, and even though she had been confined to bed for years, she kept herself apprised of everything that went on in the house, all the business and personal affairs, all the joys and sorrows.

Lying in her wide four-poster bed, enveloped in tulle and lace, she reigned no less than her husband over the family. Each child and grandchild had to stop by to say good morning and kiss her hand. On every holiday, each family member had to come and pay his or her respects. All the male and female servants had to consult her about marketing, prices. She held the keys to all the china closets and the silver. A quorum of men drawn from among the courtyard spongers assembled by her bed on every Sabbath and holiday so that she could recite her "Blessed be He's" and add her "amens."

It was to Grandmother Tirza that Perele spoke as one woman to another.

"Fallen in love, have you, you *shiksa?*" she asked, shaking all the laces and tulle about her aged head.

Perele began to shower her with firm, ardent kisses. "Granny, dearest Granny, my treasure. . . ."

The old woman summoned her strength to extend her paralyzed hand as she admonished her granddaughter. "Wouldn't rely on your grandfather, eh?" She sighed. "Well, so be it. I'll speak to him. But why are you so green? A bride should have cheeks like red apples, just like I had for my wedding. . . ."

Perele was her favorite grandchild. She was the only one left of a whole brood and the daughter of Solly, the butt of everyone's humor, but his mother's favorite son for that very reason.

When she summoned her husband to her side, asked him to sit down on the bed, and began discussing Perele, the old man grew enraged. "What's this—love in my house? Like with musicians! I won't hear of it!"

His wife made him sit down again. "Kalman," she warned, "you're playing with fire. She is the only one left of a household of children, a poor orphan, more's the pity. . . ."

Kalman raged, but the old woman let a tear fall. "Kalman, let me live long enough to see the poor child married off. I've got a feeling I won't be around for long. . . ."

The old man grew so despondent that he began to blow his nose vigorously. "It's probably fated this way in my old age," he said as he stroked his wife's wrinkled face with a calloused hand.

He promptly sent for Asriel Cohen. "Tell me, Asriel," he began. "You know a certain Abraham Hersh Ashkenazi of Lodz?"

"What do you mean, do I know?" Asriel Cohen snorted. He commenced to enumerate the other's lineage going back ten generations. He also threw in the genealogy of all of Abraham Hersh's relatives, including their offspring, their mates and in-laws.

"Lodz, Lodz," the old man muttered angrily. He held a low opinion of that upstart community, which he still remembered as a tiny village.

"And who is his rabbi, this Abraham Hersh's?" he wanted to know.

"The Alexander. When the Warka was still living, he went there."

"Alexander . . . Warka. . . ." The old man grimaced.

As a true follower of the Ger Rabbi he was contemptuous of all other rabbis, but he had no option.

When Asriel Cohen found out what was wanted of him, he became enraged. He had already selected a mate for the girl, and the match was as good as arranged. It was a much better match, one befitting the honor of the Eisen family. Nor could he stand the fact that some snit of a girl dared circumvent his authority, for when it came to matchmaking, only he, Asriel, had the say. And he promptly began to malign, manipulate, and obstruct, to demonstrate his power. But Kalman himself ordered him to desist.

"Asriel," he said to him in a quavering voice, "this time, we must give in. You'll earn your fee in any case."

But since it wasn't fitting that the first overture should issue from Kalman Eisen's house, Asriel was dispatched to Lodz.

There he met with his worst enemy, Samuel Zanvil, and he dropped a hint about the match which wouldn't be acceptable to Reb Kalman under any circumstances but which it couldn't hurt to discuss. With God's help, there'd be no reason to have a rabbi settle the matter of fees should anything come of it. But in the meantime, mum was the word.

Samuel Zanvil promptly grew suspicious as to the reason his foremost enemy and defamer had suddenly grown as sweet as honey to him—and he divined that the other side was eager for the match. Smelling a juicy fee, he immediately ran to Abraham Hersh and finally revealed that the other side had made the overture.

Abraham Hersh summoned Jacob Bunem and measured him from head to toe. He knew the matter wasn't as simple as it appeared; he guessed that his son wasn't Kalman Eisen's choice, but the girl's, and that somehow Jacob Bunem wasn't as innocent as he tried to appear.

"Tell me," he said sternly, "what kind of monkey business has there been between you and Kalman Eisen's granddaughter?"

Jacob Bunem blushed. "I saw her only once at Simha Meir's wedding."

Abraham Hersh sighed. "You can go," he dismissed him.

It was the second time he had been disappointed by a son. The Warka Rabbi's prediction was apparently coming true. But he couldn't honestly say that he opposed the match. After all, Reb Kalman Eisen's grandchild! And although he needn't have considered for even a second, he didn't say yes immediately but indicated calmly that he was amenable to further discussion.

The articles of engagement were drawn up without fanfare since Kalman Eisen was reluctant to publicize his disgrace, even though the match was already being talked about with astonishment all over Warsaw. Still, when the wedding was made, it turned out as elaborate as any Eisen family affair. The ceremony was held in Warsaw following the Shevuot holiday. The Rabbi of Ger himself performed the rites. The dowry presented to the bridegroom was huge, in the many thousands. The bride also had a large inheritance from her late mother, bank accounts, and apartment houses. The couple received an additional fortune in wedding presents.

Simha Meir, along with Dinele, his in-laws, and his parents' whole family, traveled to Warsaw for the affair. Simha Meir bought an expensive present for his brother. Intuition told him that since Jacob Bunem had become part of an influential family, it would be beneficial to stay on good terms with him, but this accommodation did nothing to quell Simha Meir's envy.

That which he, Simha Meir, achieved with will, energy, and intrigue fell into his brother's lap with no effort at all simply because some silly girl had grown infatuated with his looks.

Simha Meir felt deeply wronged. What did his 10,000 rubles mean now against Jacob Bunem's fortune? Zero, chaff, dust scattered by the wind. And the envy gnawed away at his guts until he couldn't eat or sleep. He skipped meals and calculated frantically on every available surface. He compared his brother's worth with his own, and the disparity pierced like a bone in his craw.

More than ever he spent sleepless nights, scheming how to squeeze even more profits out of the factory. He knew that there was no future in handlooms. They were only a stepping-stone. His destiny lay in steam. He knew that all his little ploys with the kerchiefs were but a drop in the bucket. Lodz was a city of sharpsters, ready to knock off any new idea or innovation. As soon as he made a move, others quickly followed and flooded the market, forcing down the prices. He would be constantly pressed to come up with new ideas if he wanted a jump on the others. But in the meantime, he had to find ways to effect new savings.

He decided to stop using brokers and jobbers and deal directly with the retail merchants. This would eliminate commissions. He visited several small towns near Lodz and found subcontractors who would make up his kerchiefs at lower cost per unit than the factory.

His next innovation was to drop his workers' wages a half ruble per week. This would save more than 1,000 rubles a year, not counting the amount he could earn by lending it out at interest.

In his fanciest handwriting he drew up a notice announcing the wage drop and had Samuel Leibush post it on the factory wall.

The workers wailed and pleaded. Their wives came to grovel at Simha Meir's feet, but he wasn't moved. "Whoever wants can quit any time he pleases," he said, tucking his hands into the pockets of his trousers and rising up on tiptoe. "I'd just as soon convert to steam anyway."

EIGHTEEN

———◆———

INSIDE THE WEAVER'S SYNAGOGUE, Love of Friends, squeezed in among the squat shacks, lumberyards, and coalyards of Balut, it was hot and tense. The weavers had long since finished their Sabbath prayers and had spat from every angle in derision at the heathens who worshiped dumb idols that couldn't respond to man's prayers. The married workers had already tucked their cheap prayer shawls away inside their prayer shawl bags; the bachelors had stuck their prayer books in the pockets of their Sabbath swallowtail gabardines.

Still, no one rushed home to the Sabbath meal, but they milled around the reader's lectern, where Tevye the World Isn't Lawless rapped his hand against the worn velvet cloth covering the pulpit. "Silence, men!" he cried. "Let a person speak!"

This time it wasn't matters of religious nature that concerned Tevye, but a secular matter—Simha Meir's evil decree to sever a half ruble from the workers' salaries.

"Let us have silence already!" the assembled men in their green faded gabardines cried. "Let's hear what the man has to say!"

But it was no simple matter to quell the noise and excitement that buzzed like a beehive when the keeper comes to remove the wax and honey.

The pale, gaunt men seethed with outrage and indignation. Life had been hard enough as it was. Their tiny salaries didn't even begin to cover their weekly expenses, and there was the additional burden of supplying their own candles for the factory. The later they worked, the more candles they needed.

In addition, there were weeks, even months when there was no work and therefore no pay. On what were their families supposed to live then? So it was a steady diet of grits with potatoes and barely fried not in fat but in oil, which left one with a hollow stomach and heartburn.

Meat? Only the cheapest tripe, legs, or lungs and livers even on the Sabbaths. Fresh fish? Maybe in summers when the fish was plentiful and sold cheaply since it couldn't be kept for long. But usually a piece of herring would have to do, with a bit of onion or some so-called Balut scratch borscht —beet soup as thin as water. Nor was raisin wine always available except for a drop reserved for the blessing over the Sabbath loaves. Neither were there there enough candles to light for each member of the household, of whom there were always more than enough.

The free community schools for the workers' children were packed and detestable. The sons of the more affluent citizens, who attended private schools, mocked their less privileged contemporaries. The teachers, who were underpaid and were invariably owed money by the community, took out their frustration on their pupils and beat and cursed them mercilessly. On Fridays they sent them begging from door to door to raise their fees.

But even though the weavers' children came home bruised and battered and despite the frightful conditions, there weren't enough of these schools to accommodate all the Balut youngsters, and those left out had to be turned over to private tutors, whose fees had to be subtracted from the families' already strained budgets.

Just as scarce was hospital space in the Aid to the Ill Society building for sick members of the community, of whom there were always more than enough. The area's rickety, bloated, bowlegged, malnourished children dropped like flies from lack of proper food and fresh air; the women suffered from excessive childbearing; the men ruined their lungs with the eternal dust and stinking fumes from old rags used for waste or recycled yarn.

The men of the Aid to the Ill Society had no inkling of medical knowledge except that during times of epidemic they rubbed the bellies of the sick with alcohol.

To buy medicines you had to go to the Christian pharmacy where you couldn't haggle, and what was even worse, you had to doff your cap before the picture of the Holy Virgin illuminated by the red lamp. Nor would Sender the leech come down by even a groschen though he had but two remedies— cupping glasses and an enema—for every complaint for which he charged a whole gulden.

The price of potatoes and vegetables kept rising, for as the city grew, so did the inflation.

Fathers took sons out of school before they had even been confirmed and put them out as apprentices in order to eliminate another mouth at the table. Mothers sent their daughters into domestic service, where they were made to lug buckets of water from wells and carry strangers' children in their own scrawny, childish arms. It was impossible to feed everyone, but new mouths kept constantly appearing as God blessed the wombs of Balut's women.

The housewives worked miracles trying to feed their families. Dresses and shirts were darned and patched until they fell apart. Landlords kept pressing for the rent. Few of the weavers owned their own houses; most rented a room or two, and the first few guldens of the salary were always set aside for the rent. The coins were collected in a prayer book and bound in a kerchief, so that the landlord would be sure to get his rent on the first. Not even in times of greatest need, was this prayer book tapped. And now there would be a half ruble less weekly!

The women howled, cursed, slammed down the chipped black iron pots, and refused to cook. "Cook yourself on what you bring me!" they shrieked at their breadwinners.

The elderly weavers—broken, defeated men, inured to every indignity—kept their silence, but the younger men seethed with indignation. Most enraged of all was Tevye the World Isn't Lawless. Lately he grumbled more than ever and sang his little ditty of unknown origin. But while before the men had been afraid of the song, from every second or third loom now could be heard the sound of its lyrics. At first, it was only a hum, but soon the bolder among them began to sing louder and more clearly, drowning out the convoluted cantorial chants of their more docile coworkers.

Samuel Leibush wagged a threatening finger. "Sing! Sing!" he muttered. "Just let Simha Meir catch you, and you'll be singing from the other side of your mouth."

But they didn't stop.

No matter what time it was, Tevye no longer went home to his wife and family but dashed from house to house, agitating, inciting, conspiring, sowing the seeds of dissatisfaction, feeding the flames of unrest.

His embittered wife—a big, prematurely aged woman with children clinging to her apron from every side and perpetually nursing the latest arrival at her drooping, blackened breast— spewed a stream of curses on her husband up and down the streets of Balut.

"Tevye!" she bellowed. "Tevye, may you yourself grow as dried and withered as your dinner waiting for you! . . .

May your soul blow away like the breath I waste trying to keep your bit of slop warm for you!"

She dragged her whole brood as she went, pregnant belly jutting, in search of her husband, and they all helped her call his name. But Tevye ignored them as he ran from house to house with all thought of food, drink, and sleep suspended, and he talked, agitated, and incited until he had roused the householders to fever pitch.

"Solidarity!" he cried. "Only with solidarity will we overcome the exploiters!"

It wasn't easy to win over the workers. Weary, shattered cowed by the bosses' authority and their own uselessness in light of the coming era of steam; saddled with large families; indifferent toward everything but a little peace and quiet and a filling meal, they remained largely unmoved.

"How can you fight fate?" they countered. "It's God's will, after all."

Each was concerned only with his own piece of bread. Each dreamed of the time when he himself would become an employer with a few looms of his own. Bachelors hoped for a dowry that would allow them to become bosses. Others consoled themselves with the fact that they weren't seasonal workers, on whom they, the full-time workers, vented their own rage and frustration. The seasonal workers, in turn, bullied and tormented the apprentices. The prevailing attitude was: "I've suffered; now it's your turn. . . ."

The only one who supported and understood Tevye was Nissan the depraved, the rabbi's son. Himself a seasonal worker who toiled all day and studied all night, he was intelligent enough to gain a broad overview of the Balut worker's existence. Although his initial intention was to become independent enough to pursue an education, he had been so totally drawn into the routine of work that he was now just another weaver of Balut.

His father had eventually forgiven him. He came to him without recriminations and groaned at the sight of his son. "Oy, Nissan, oy!" He sighed so piteously that Nissan's guts turned to jelly.

He couldn't stand his father's sighs. He would have preferred blows, abuse, reprimands. For all his contempt toward his father, he still loved him, and his sighs tore him to pieces.

Of all the employers in Balut the worst were the subcontractors, petty bosses who operated home workshops where they contracted to do piecework for the factory owners. These petty tyrants bullied and exploited their journeymen viciously. They themselves were at the mercy of the manufacturers and their foremen, most of whom demanded kickbacks. If none were forthcoming, they either boycotted the offenders or were super-critical of the finished product and flatly rejected it.

Another ploy was to issue to the subcontractor a bundle of inferior wool that split and tore when it was woven. Often the subcontractor had to wait by the foreman's door like some beggar to pick up the raw material, and when he delivered the finished goods, he was paid with a promissory note that had to be cashed at a moneychanger's, who naturally subtracted his commission.

The subcontractors took all this frustration out on their workers. The bosses' wives fed the workers army issue bread, which they bought from soldiers in the marketplace and which was so stale and inferior that it could be consumed only a little at a time. Each morning they set out a meager portion on each worker's bench. But the workers didn't practice restraint, and by evening they were ravenous.

"Mistress, bread!" they whined shamefacedly. "Just a crust— I'm starving."

They got no bread, but curses. "Drop dead!" the women responded with feeling.

The more agile among the workers managed to filch some bread from the pantry, but those less bold starved. A piece of meat was never seen; the chicory substituting for coffee was served with a mere lick of sugar. The work went on all through the night by the dim light of oil lamps and smoking wicks. The smoke from the stoves irritated the eyes; the boss's children cried; the women cursed and bickered. When the red eyelids could no longer be held open, the men stretched out on the dirty floor with a piece of goods as a pillow and dozed off, freezing in the winter, steaming in the summer, eaten alive by fleas, flies, and bedbugs.

Often the goods were wet and sandy because just as the foremen cheated them, so did the subcontractors cheat the foremen. They were issued the wool and cotton by weight and were supposed to return goods in equal weight. So in order to pilfer a little wool, they doused the goods down with water or weighted them down with sand. The wet goods penetrated the bodies of the sleeping workers; the sand rubbed their skins raw; the dye from the cheap materials ran so that they awoke looking like chimney sweeps.

Besides, the men had to work in collusion with their bosses in swindling the factory owners. They stretched the thread so that it wove more loosely, yet covered the required quota of fabric, and in order that the manufacturer not catch on, only the ends were woven densely and smoothly.

Everyone had to cooperate in this subterfuge on the threat of not receiving wages on Thursday. And when the finished goods were ready for delivery, the workers had to tote them on their shoulders across all Lodz since no subcontractor would think of wasting money on a droshky.

Like true slaves, the subcontractors starved and degraded their own slaves—the seasonal workers. It happened that having worked a whole season, a worker didn't receive his wages. The matter was submitted to arbitration by rabbis, but regardless of the findings, the money was never paid.

"Here, drain my last drop of blood!" the subcontractor cried, baring his chest beneath the cotton vest. "I don't have it. . . . I'm a pauper myself!"

It was, therefore, very hard for Tevye to convince all the embittered, toil-worn men to stick together against the bosses.

"Tevye!" people warned him. "Don't get involved. You'll be the first to be fired."

But Tevye didn't take the advice. Weary from the day's toil, rubbed raw by his wife's abuse, his mind deadened by his children's eternal crying, he didn't cease his agitation. "Only solidarity!" he cried in a grating voice.

At his side walked Nissan the depraved. Just like Tevye, he found time after a day's labor and an evening of study to preach rebellion.

He was popular with the weavers, who felt proud that a rabbi's son had become one of them. They greeted him warmly when he dropped by their synagogue on a Sabbath. The women respected him, too, but they couldn't understand why a youth who might have married a wealthy girl would choose the life of a worker. Still, they looked up to him, as if his presence among them elevated the status of their own husbands.

Besides, he was very handy to have around. He read to illiterate mothers the postcards sent by daughters put out to service; he wrote letters for wives to husbands conscripted into the Russian Army; he taught brides to sign articles of engagement and translated Russian documents issued by the courts or the police.

Inured to the burdens and degradations of poverty from childhood, endowed with the ability to reason and speak logically, his head filled with religious and secular knowledge, trained in interpreting and verbalizing concepts, he made a deep impression on the weavers and, even more so, on their wives.

"Some tongue on that one," people said admiringly. "He could talk the birds out of the trees. . . ."

Mothers of marriageable daughters drooled at the sight of him. Even Tevye's virago wife restrained herself when Nissan was present.

Simha Meir's decree had promptly caught Nissan's attention. He remembered Simha Meir well from their days at his father's table. Even then he had hated him for his arrogance, slyness, and ruthlessness. Now he was a manufacturer proposing to starve the families of Jewish workers. And although he didn't work for him, Nissan took the matter as a personal affront and challenge. Every injustice affecting Balut was also his injustice, and he placed himself squarely on Tevye's side and called a meeting of not only those directly involved, the workers in Haim Alter's factory, but of all the workers of Balut.

They came by the droves to the little synagogue: the full-time workers and the seasonal, the apprentices, and even the exploited subcontractors. The tiny synagogue seethed with jostling, gesticulating men all eager to have their say.

Tevye stood at the pulpit in his faded Sabbath gabardine and paper collar. His yellow eyes flashed through his wire-rimmed glasses so that they seemed to be shooting fire.

"Solidarity, men!" he cried. "Only with solidarity will we overcome!"

Nissan unrolled a sheet of paper on which he had written in an elaborate script, and read to the audience.

" 'Articles of the association of the weavers of Balut,' " he began in a fiery voice, enunciating each word separately. " 'A. We the weavers who worship in the synagogue Love of Friends, in conjunction with the other weavers of Balut, do not consent to any reduction of our already miserable wages. This is equivalent to highway robbery, and we adopt a self-imposed ban against further work. No man among us shall encroach upon another man's province and take his job during this period since such transgression is as if man were to rise up in a field and slay his brother.

" 'B. On Thursday nights, work shall not be performed around the clock but until midnight only. The same shall apply to Saturday nights: work shall be conducted only from the time the Sabbath is ushered out until midnight.

" 'C. No more than fourteen hours of work shall be performed on any weekday, from six A.M. until eight P.M. The time taken off for afternoon and evening prayers shall not be deducted from this total. In winter, when it is too dark for morning prayers to be said prior to going to work, time off shall be granted at work for such prayers, and this time too shall be considered part of the overall workday.

" 'D. On Fridays, work shall be stopped two hours before candle-lighting time, and on the eve of holidays, two hours before sunset, to allow the men time to clean up and prepare for the holy days.

" 'E. The salary for any workweek shall not be deferred to the following week but shall be paid promptly on Thursday nights so that the workers can make proper preparations for the Sabbath. The salary must also be paid promptly before holidays, for he who neglects to pay his employee on time is likened to a robber.

" 'F. Candles for work shall be provided by the employer at his own expense.

" 'G. The employers may not insult their employees since it is forbidden to degrade a fellow human being or raise a hand to him, for he who raises a hand to his fellow man may be likened to an evildoer. Nor may the full-time and seasonal workers abuse each other or, God forbid, strike each other or the apprentices, since everyone must remember his own years of degradation. Whoever is guilty of this act shall be removed from the society.

" 'H. On fast days, the workday shall not continue past the afternoon prayers.

" 'I. Likewise, on the intervening days of Passover and Succoth, the workday shall not continue past the afternoon prayers.

" 'J. The full-time workers, seasonal workers, and apprentices who board at their employers' must receive food that is fattened; likewise, their coffee must contain milk and sugar, for he who does not feed his workers and demands of them work may be likened to the Egyptians who did not supply straw, yet demanded bricks.

" 'These ten terms have been issued on the Sabbath when the weekly portions referring to the purity of mothers and to lepers are read in the synagogue Love of Friends in Balut.' "

A roar went up.

"It'll never work!"

"It will work if we stick together!"

Tevye slammed the pulpit and waited for the noise to die down, at which time he launched a sermon spiced with quotes from holy volumes, with aphorisms and homilies. He very neatly compared Balut's workers with the Jews in Egypt who had built Pithom and Ramses. He compared the employers to the Egyptians and their flunkies to the Jewish taskmasters whom the Egyptians used to torment and beat their own brothers. With verbal dexterity he concluded that just as the Egyptians entombed the children of Israel inside the walls of Pithom and Ramses, so did the bosses of Lodz force the workers to stifle their own children inside the bundles of goods by failing to provide their offspring the milk and medicines they needed to survive.

"Words of wisdom!" voices cried. "It's as true as the fact that it's the Sabbath today. . . ."

Having won the crowd over, Tevye demanded that those present submit the ten demands to their individual bosses at the end of Sabbath and refuse to report for work until the terms were met.

Again, an uproar ensued.

"We'll be left without bread!"

"They'll never give in!"

"We have to approach them with goodness, not make them mad!"

"No one will do it! The first to be fired will be the instigators!"

"We've got wives and children to think of!"

Tevye smote the pulpit so forcefully that the crooked chandelier trembled overhead.

"That's how the slaves in Egypt spoke, too!" he cried. " 'We remember the fish that we ate in Egypt,' they said. You are worse than they because you don't even get fish . . . not even bread do you get! But Moses ignored the fact that the slaves grumbled and he delivered them out of Pharaoh's clutches. . . ."

The men grew ashamed and fell silent. Tevye gazed triumphantly down at them and raised his hand.

"I will go to our pharaohs and speak in the names of you all. But no one must go to the bosses behind our backs. No one must report for work. Let us not lose heart. Let us stick together. Let us maintain solidarity, and we shall overcome!"

"No one will sell you out!" voices cried.

"I demand an oath!" Tevye cried. "An oath right here in the synagogue that no one will go to work until mutually agreed, or steal another man's job."

An elderly weaver with a beard like a wad of dirty cotton, bloodshot eyes, and a back stooped from years of travail leaped up to the pulpit and began pounding the lectern with trembling hands. "Men! Jews may not take oaths on the Sabbath regardless of the reason. . . . It's a mortal sin!"

Nissan the rabbi's son sprang forward. "When life is endangered, you can even desecrate the Sabbath!" he pronounced. "Lack of bread for women and children constitutes a danger to life, and for such a thing, you can swear an oath even on the Day of Atonement!"

Tevye quickly approached the ark, took out the congregation's scroll of Law wrapped in its mean velvet mantle, and laid it fervently on the pulpit.

"Swear on the holy scroll in this place of worship that not one of you will without the knowledge of the others report for work. This is equivalent to an oath. Give me your word!"

"We swear!" they exclaimed together.

NINETEEN

———————————

SIMHA MEIR MET THE CHALLENGE flung down by the workers in his father-in-law's factory with characteristic vigor and obstinacy.

As usual, at this time of year, Haim Alter was away visiting spas. Right after Shevuot he packed his high silk top hat and donned it the moment his train crossed the Austrian border so as not to embarrass his wife before the lordly Germans.

Simha Meir was delighted by his father-in-law's absence. The less time Haim Alter spent in the factory, the better. And particularly so now, during the strike. But he wasn't pleased that Dinele had accompanied her parents abroad.

His brilliant business coups, his inspired dodges and innovations that left the other merchants and brokers aghast, made no impression upon his pretty young wife. He even took time at dinner to explain to her how shrewd he had been. Chewing noisily, dribbling food, displaying all the crude table manners of the Hasid, he desperately sought her approval, but she barely understood what he was saying. The Lodz business ruses were as alien to her as he himself. All she saw was a slovenly, uncouth little man who squirmed in his chair, gulped his coffee, dunked his roll in the butter, poured on too much salt, and generally behaved like a boor. Throughout the meal he scribbled on scraps of paper, talked nonstop, then hurried back to the factory with his fly unbuttoned.

"Do you get it—do you get it, Dinele?" he persisted. "Your husband is a shrewd man, isn't he?"

"Wipe the crumbs from your face," was her only comment. "And don't scribble on the tablecloth. You've ruined every tablecloth in the house."

Simha Meir felt whipped, humiliated. Despite his inborn contempt for women, he wanted his wife to look up to him. His crazy, darting eyes relished her lush beauty. He wanted her badly, more so each day. But she remained distant, superior, aloof.

Not that he could find any fault with her, for she performed all her wifely duties. She saw to it that his meals were served on time, that he had clean shirts and underwear, that he brushed himself off before leaving the house. She kept after him to stop dropping cigarette ashes on his lapel. She even accompanied him to his family's house on the holidays, but beyond that, she withheld all warmth, all tenderness. She wouldn't even grant him a smile.

For all his apparent yeshiva-student abstraction and lack of perception, he knew precisely how she felt toward him, and this puzzled him, for he knew that all Lodz held him in esteem.

When he came upon her as she sat reading one of her novels, she jumped. "God, but you startled me!"

"What are you reading?" he asked, knowing full well what it was.

"A book," she replied without even looking up.

The more she kept him at a distance, the more drawn he was to her. He looked hungrily at her soft white arms so dazzling against the black silk sleeves, her lovely neck, the delicious symmetry of her limbs, the womanliness that seemed to bloom from day to day. He trembled with excitement every time he came near her.

True, he never relinquished that which was his, but all he had was her body, never her love.

Spurned, he directed all his energy to business, taking but a few minutes for lunch and dinner at home and rushing right back to the factory, where he counted for something. But even the nights when he took her at will were frustrating. Although he had never been with another woman, he sensed that he was missing something.

One day Dinele came running to her mother and confessed with tears that changes were occurring in her body. Her mother laughed, hugged her, and wiped the tears from her daughter's eyes.

"Silly," she whispered, "is this any reason to cry? Run tell Simha Meir the good news."

"I won't, Mama!" Dinele cried, and clung to her mother, unable to stop the torrent of tears.

Simha Meir felt a surge of manly pride when his mother-in-law—blushing like a maiden—informed him that his wife was expecting. "Maybe now she'll put away those silly books," he said.

He was convinced that motherhood would rid Dinele of her

silly notions and transform her into a loving, obedient wife. He would be master of the house in every sense of the word.

But Dinele remained as withdrawn as ever and centered her attention on the coming child. For hours she reclined on the divan as if eager for some manifestation of its presence. "Mama, I feel it," she cried. "Listen!"

"Silly, you're only imagining it." Her mother laughed. "It's much too early yet. . . ."

"I feel it!" Dinele insisted with a blissful smile.

She didn't develop the usual flecks and blotches of pregnant women. On the contrary, she seemed to grow even more radiant. Her blue eyes were warmer, more lustrous. A smile seemed to hover perpetually over her lips.

Her mother kept muttering incantations to drive away the evil eye. Simha Meir couldn't keep his eyes off Dinele in her new glow. "How are you, how are you?" he blurted, seeking some pretext to lead her to the bedroom.

But she wouldn't even allow him near her in the nights. "I'm tired," she mumbled, and turned to the wall.

And when Shevuot came and her parents made ready to go away, she packed her things and joined them without even asking her husband. "Good-bye," she said, neglecting to say his name and keeping her eyes averted.

He felt deeply offended and alone. He stared at her empty bed, which mocked him with its neat, unruffled covers. He was plagued by all kinds of evil notions and fantasies. A married woman alone in a strange country among so many fops and gigolos. . . .

During the week the work kept him busy, but the long summer Sabbaths were interminable. You couldn't chivy the help or flimflam the brokers and sharpsters on the holy day. The holy books bored him. There was nothing to do but sit, stare, and think.

It was on one of such Sabbaths, as he sat impatiently awaiting the appearance of the first three stars signifying the end of the holy day, that Tevye the World Isn't Lawless and Nissan the depraved came to him with their list of demands inscribed on a sheet of ruled paper torn from a notebook.

For a moment Simha Meir looked at them blankly. Balut workers weren't welcome in the homes of their employers. To their credit, the two men didn't enter with swagger or bravado. "A good week," they said quietly.

Drawing deeply on his first after-Sabbath cigarette, Simha Meir didn't respond to the greeting. "I'll see you in the factory," he grunted.

"We can't go to the factory. Be good enough to read this first," Tevye said extending the list of demands.

Simha Meir snatched the paper from his hands, glanced at it swiftly, and looked up again. "You wouldn't be Nuske the rabbi's boy?" he asked, studying Nissan from head to toe.

He turned to Tevye. "What's his connection to this?"

"I'm a weaver," Nissan said.

"So," Simha Meir grunted, plucking at his beard. "You've become a worker? And what does your father say to this?"

Nissan didn't answer. Simha Meir thrust his hands into the pockets of his silk Sabbath gabardine and said angrily, "Why are you here? You don't work for me."

"I come in the name of the weavers," Nissan said. "They've delegated me to speak to you in their behalf."

"But I don't want to speak to *you*," Simha Meir replied curtly. "I don't accept you as anybody's spokesman."

Nissan grew momentarily rattled. To begin with, he didn't know whether to address Simha Meir in the familiar "thou" or the formal "you." Nor had he counted on such a rebuff. He also felt overawed by the elegant house, which reminded him of the times he had gone to his rich uncles as a boy to beg a loan. Besides, Simha Meir had let the sheet of demands fall to the floor, and Nissan could only stand there and do nothing.

Tevye picked up the list, smoothed it out, and said to Simha Meir, "We weavers stand together. Read!"

Simha Meir glanced at the paper. "So," he asked in singsong, "it's more money and less work you want?"

"That's it. More money and less work," Tevye agreed.

"Well, and what if I don't go along? What will you do then?"

"We won't work," Tevye said.

"And who'll feed you?"

"We're starving anyway. So why work besides?"

"These are your swinish tricks, Tevyele," Simha Meir said, wagging a finger. "Yours and this boy's. You turn the people's heads and steal the bread from their mouths."

He couldn't imagine people not wanting to work. Ever since he could remember, men had stood by their looms and worked. This was as basic as getting up in the morning and expecting to see daylight. The whole thing boggled the mind.

"Wait until Thursday when there's no money for the Sabbath. You'll come crawling to me to take you back."

For a whole week the factory stood idle, yet no one came to grovel at Simha Meir's feet. Just as before the women of Balut had reviled their husbands for their inadequate earnings, so they were the first now to bemoan the good old days when the men had brought money home. "Murderers!" they shrieked at their mates, "Have pity on the little ones at least. . . ."

But the men held firm.

Simha Meir went around in a daze. He couldn't sleep without the rattle of the looms. Life lost all flavor without the daily routine of work. Thursday passed, and the men still didn't report for work, and as if out of spite, orders for goods started pouring in from all over.

Simha Meir sent Samuel Leibush out into the streets to recruit replacements, but all he could come up with were several elderly German women, who moved at a snail's pace, and a drunk or two, who were totally inadequate.

On the Sabbath, Simha Meir sent for the teacher his father-in-law maintained for his workers' synagogue and ordered him to convince the weavers to return. He was to tell them that if they went back to their jobs immediately, no reprisals would be taken against them.

But the weavers wouldn't listen to the teacher's preachings. Instead of the "Ethics of the Fathers," Tevye treated them to a sermon urging solidarity until victory was theirs.

"I pawned my pillows for a piece of bread," a weaver moaned.

"I bartered my copper candelabrum for potatoes," complained a second.

"I hocked my prayer shawl and phylacteries to prepare for the Sabbath," said a third.

"With solidarity, we shall overcome," Tevye exhorted. "Let a few more days go by, and they'll send for us. Mark my words. They're going broke with their factories standing idle."

He knew his Lodz. Even better, he knew Simha Meir.

For days Simha Meir sat calculating, totaling his daily losses at a time when orders were pouring in. It was maddening. True, he had never believed in handlooms. At the first opportunity he would switch to steam. But in the meantime, he had to save every groschen he could lay his hands on. A factory standing idle was intolerable, particularly now that people were clamoring for goods, and Simha Meir didn't cease wetting the tip of his pencil and scribbling figures on every scrap of paper, every tablecloth before him.

From the other side, if he gave in now, it would cost him dearly. Outside of the 1,200 rubles (not counting the interest) he would be losing annually, the nervy beggars demanded a shorter workweek, free candles, and all kinds of other preposterous concessions. Besides, eating only intensified the appetite. Once they got a finger, they would demand the hand. True, he was suffering financial losses, but once they came crawling back, these losses would be more than made up. He would get his revenge. Then, after a few more years of hustling, he would switch over to steam and throw them all out on their behinds.

"I can bide my time," he told the other merchants in the taverns, sipping beer and chewing on peppered chick-peas. "Let them get a sniff of hard times. . . ."

And hard times they sniffed in Balut. Each day Samuel Leibush reported the latest news to Simha Meir.

In the small Balut groceries with the swarms of flies buzzing about the bins of candy, the grocers wouldn't issue so much as a slice of bread on credit.

"The account books are already swollen from credit," they cried, pointing to the stained, greasy pages. "No more bread on account. The bakers don't extend *us* credit."

The weavers dug up articles to be pawned—a torn pillow-case, an old-fashioned wedding gown, a winter shawl, even a woman's prayer book. But soon they ran out of pawnable items. The days stretched seemingly without end and the children kept tugging at their aprons: "Mama, bread!"

The men milled through the narrow streets in their Sabbath gabardines that they no longer bothered to remove. Excitement ran high. Groups assembled on every corner to wrangle, debate, gesticulate.

"Tevye is right," the younger weavers said. "If we don't give in, we will overcome."

"That's easy for you to say," the middle-aged workers complained. "You don't have kids crying for bread. If you were in our shoes, you might think different. Simha Meir will replace us with scabs, and we'll be left high and dry."

The old men were even more concerned. "We must go to him and say we had nothing to do with it . . . that it was all Tevye and Nissan's doing. If not, we'll end up begging from door to door in our old age. . . ."

"But we took an oath," others pointed out.

"Any rabbi will absolve us from it. We're dealing with a life-and-death matter, after all."

Without their husbands' knowledge, women began coming to Simha Meir, begging the loan of a few guldens to tide them over the crisis.

"My old man will work it out," they said. "The children are starving for a crust of bread. To whom then shall we turn if not to you? You are like a father to us, after all!"

Simha Meir gave them neither sympathy nor cash. Money was like a bird, he knew. Once it left the hand, it seldom came back. But he was more than generous with advice.

"Those outcasts, Tevye and the rabbi's whelp, will be your husbands' death," he said with feeling. "They'll rob them not only of this world but of the world to come."

"May their mouths be twisted around to their backsides for the cunning words with which they duped our men," the women cursed.

"Next thing they'll do is persuade them to convert," Simha Meir predicted, trying to keep from laughing. "They'll convince them to desert their wives and children, wait and see."

"Woe is us!" the women lamented, wringing their hands just as if their husbands had already left them. "Those reprobates should be run out of town. One leprous sheep infects the whole flock. . . ."

The aroused housewives began to trail Tevye and Nissan through the narrow streets and belabored them with curses. The most vociferous of all was Tevye's own wife, Keila. Accompanied by her brood of children, an infant nursing at her flapping breast, she dragged herself through the hot, dusty streets, pelting her husband with sulfur and fire.

"Communal billy goat!" she screamed. "May the blood drain from your throat! Alien broom that sweeps out all the corners, then is chucked out into the street, may they fling you as high as the rooftops! Why must you worry about the world when your own wife and children are starving before your eyes, you filthy animal?"

Her children launched a chorus of heartrending shrieks.

She was no more sparing of Nissan. "It's all your doing, too! I'll douse you with boiling water if you ever dare cross my threshold again, devil's imp!"

But Tevye ignored her and kept talking, persuading, cajoling, urging solidarity.

The second Thursday rolled around, and still no one reported for work.

By the third week Simha Meir began to knit his brow and pluck at his beard nervously. His losses were enormous. Customers threatened to switch over to other manufacturers. He began to wonder whether he had gambled and lost. In such cases, the best course was to cut your losses and wait for a better opportunity. But at the last moment he got a sudden flash of inspiration, one so clear and obvious that he almost laughed aloud.

"Samuel Leibush," he called to his man. "Run and fetch

me Lippe Halfon. Tell him I need him right now. Very important."

Lippe Halfon was a Litvak with a trimmed pointed beard, a Russian accent, and great ingenuity. He had arrived from Lithuania with a teapot in one hand and an umbrella in the other and had promptly launched his personal conquest of Lodz.

He began by peddling shoelaces, paper collars, needles, and pins in the street. He subsisted on dry bread and herring and hot water that he brewed in his teapot. Gradually he came to perform errands for storekeepers—matters dealing with the post office, with the railroads. He had the knack of getting along with Russian officials, and he rented a flat where he could pursue his affairs. In no time he hung out a shingle listing his accomplishments, which entailed writing petitions to courts and to other official Russian bodies. Few people in Lodz knew Russian, and Lippe Halfon prospered.

He soon became a confidant of the police and of all the functionaries. Whoever had dealings with the authorities came to Halfon with the bribes, which he then channeled to the proper official. He gave satisfactory service and spared his clients needless time and bother. He dressed like a man of the world and was never seen without a thick portfolio stuffed with all kinds of official-looking documents. He greeted all the officials in the street, even the police commissioner himself.

Although the lawyers looked at him askance and made fun of his ungrammatical speech, they couldn't do a thing to stop him. He had a larger practice than any of them. What they couldn't accomplish with their beautifully composed petitions, he managed with his, errors and all.

"I've got the police right here," he boasted, pointing to his pocket. "What good are all those shysters? For nothing with nothing. . . ."

His area of expertise encompassed a broad range of interests. He discounted bad IOUs, collected delinquent debts, advanced cash on pawn tickets, called the railroads to task for failing to provide services, represented clients in court without the official right to do so, lent money at high interest, and, if necessary, even trumped up charges against a client's enemies.

"The world is founded on just three things," he liked to say, "money, money, and money."

It was this man Simha Meir sent for and eagerly awaited now.

The Litvak patiently heard out the nature of Simha Meir's problem and didn't interrupt with a single word except to correct Simha Meir when he called him Reb Lippe instead of Gospodin Halfon.

When Simha Meir finished, Lippe Halfon reached inside his portfolio for a sheet of paper, and in Russian, he carefully noted down the names of the troublemakers. "They're as good as out of your hair already, Gospodin Ashkenazi. Now, as to the matter of the fee—"

Simha Meir drew a wallet from his pocket and counted out several crisp banknotes. The Litvak scooped them up without argument.

"This is clearly a violation of Article One Hundred Eighty-One of the Imperial Criminal Code," he announced. "You no longer need bother your head about those two."

"Naturally no one must know about this," Simha Meir said, escorting the Litvak out.

"Naturally," Lippe Halfon agreed. "Mum's the word."

Late that same night policemen dragged Tevye and Nissan out of their beds. Although it was late, the news of the arrest spread through Balut. People congregated in the streets, and the policemen scattered them with their curved swords.

Tevye's wife, wearing only her shift and surrounded by the brood of crying children, accompanied her husband as if he were being taken to the cemetery. "Jews take pity!" she cried, wringing her hands. "Who will take care of my little worms now?"

The prisoners were thrown into a cell among drunks, thieves, and men without proper papers. "Why did they shove you in stir?" the thieves asked Tevye and Nissan.

"We don't know. We haven't done anything," the two men replied.

"Jerks." The thieves laughed. They flung rags at the two new prisoners' heads and made them take out the slops.

After two days Tevye and Nissan were led to the office of the police chief himself.

"'Tention!" that worthy cried. "Don't you dare twitch even a whisker!"

They didn't understand and tried to mumble something about being innocent, but the policemen expedited their chief's order with whacks to the ribs. "Like this!" they taught the terrified men, pounding their chins and bellies with fists.

The chief fingercombed his bristling side-whiskers and came up so close to the men that he nearly trod on their toes. "So, that's how things are?" he asked with the air of a cat toying with a mouse. "Rebels, is it? Rising up against the authority, eh?"

They tried to explain, but this only exacerbated the chief's rage. "Silence, sons of bitches!" he roared. "You'll rot in chains! I'll strip the hide from your backs for trying to overthrow a peaceful government!"

At a gesture from him, an elderly hunchbacked policeman sat down at a table and began to fill a sheet of paper with complex Russian characters as the chief dictated, pacing through the room.

When he was through, the correspondent read the charges to the prisoners, enunciating the difficult Russian words in a nasal snort. The prisoners understood none of it except the word *rebels,* which was repeated every third sentence or so.

"Sign!" the police chief thundered. "If you can't write, make an X."

The prisoners exchanged glances, but the policemen slammed their legs with their scabbards.

"Sign as His Excellency told you!" they grunted. "Move it!"

One after the other, they signed.

"'Toviah Melech Mendeliev Meirev Buchbinder; Nissan Nusiniev Shliomovich Eibeshutz,'" the police chief read with difficulty. "Take them back to their cell."

The very same day the police chief wrote to the governor in Piotrkow describing the two dangerous rebels who had been inciting the peaceful workers of the industrial city of Lodz to riot and clearly posed a danger to the populace. He begged His Excellency to petition Petersburg to have the two rebels exiled for a period of time outside the ten provinces constituting the Polish kingdom and to do this without benefit of trial but as an executive order. Until such directive arrived from Petersburg, he would keep the two men under temporary detention.

"By the time an answer comes from Petersburg, they will have served a year, if not more. They'll think twice before they'll start up with the police again," Lippe Halfon assured Simha Meir.

The Balut weavers ran from synagogue to synagogue, calling on rabbis to speak out against the injustice, but no one would get involved. "For something like theft, we might possibly pay a ransom to free them," the community leaders told them. "But sedition is a dangerous business. All you can do is get yourself in trouble."

Within a few days Simha Meir's factory was back in full swing. The starved workers worked with such zeal that they quickly made up for the losses incurred during the strike. Not one of them so much as sighed when he received the reduced wages. They were grateful to be getting anything. To effect further savings, Simha Meir fired the teacher Haim Alter had engaged for the weavers' synagogue.

All Lodz spoke of Simha Meir's victory. "Shrewd as they come . . . smart as salt in a wound. The guts of a pickpocket!" people said.

In Lodz this was the highest possible compliment.

TWENTY

NEVER IN HIS LIFE had Haim Alter suffered so much grief and joy in a single year as he did that year.

It began with joy. His only daughter provided him with his first grandchild, and a boy at that. As usual, Haim Alter went overboard and spent a fortune on the party celebrating the circumcision.

"Haimshe, money, more money," Priveh crooned, extending bejeweled fingers.

"Simha Meir, darling, money, more money!" Haim Alter crooned, extending fat, hairy hands to his son-in-law, the business manager.

Simha Meir doled out the rubles, more even than his father-in-law asked for, and he had him sign for every last groschen. Because Simha Meir's first child was a boy, his former friends from the studyhouse forgave him for having estranged himself from them and from the Torah.

"You're lucky it was a boy," they said half in jest. "Had it been a girl, we would have laid you across the table and whipped your behind!"

Even his father, who had ordered him out of the house, had agreed to a reconciliation on account of the grandson and had come, wearing his fur-edged cap.

Predictably a controversy erupted between the grandfathers concerning the naming of the child. Each wanted the infant named after his own rabbi. Haim Alter raved and whined, but Abraham Hersh wouldn't give an inch.

"Because yours was the mother, you can name the girls," he argued. "When it comes to boys, I'll have the say!"

Haim Alter proposed a compromise—one name for each faction—but Abraham Hersh was adamant. He wouldn't stand for the name of any rabbi but his own. And it ended up with the boy receiving a single name after the Rabbi of Warka—Isaac. Abraham Hersh personally circumcised the boy and danced so violently with his cronies that Priveh stopped up her ears.

"Reb Abraham, the mother is still weak. . . . She can't stand this," she objected.

"Livelier, Jews, faster!" Abraham Hersh encouraged the Hasidim, ignoring her.

Lying pale and frightened in her bed, Dinele pressed the crying infant closer and drenched him with her tears. "Murderers!" she wailed. "The poor little precious, pity upon him. . . ."

"Hush, a Jewish daughter dare not say such things!" her mother-in-law chided. "They danced this way when your husband was circumcised, and it didn't hurt him any. . . ."

Pious women clucked. "May you live to enjoy your grandchildren, with God's help. . . ."

Haim Alter felt belittled in front of his friends, but the lavishness of the occasion made up for it to some degree.

"When the second boy comes with God's blessing, Abraham Hersh can stand on his head before he gets his way. I'll show that pigheaded ass!" Haim Alter blustered.

But soon after the joy a great mishap befell the household. Hadassah, with her experienced eye, noticed that the new maid who had been hired a few months before seemed to be hiding something under her apron. What's more, she often got a yen for some delicacy and would reach right into the pot to keep from getting nauseated.

Hadassah tried to question the girl, but she resisted, whereupon the older woman felt her belly and started screaming. "Fie! Me, a mother of nine children—five living and four dead—me you'd try to fool, you slut? Say this minute who gave it to you, whore that you are!"

"The young masters!" the girl whined. "They kept harassing me. . . ."

The pimply louts, naturally, denied everything, but their parents knew that the girl was telling the truth, even though they wouldn't admit it.

"You can't take the word of some slut!" Haim Alter protested. "No one would believe such a thing about my boys. . . ."

"Leave the house this minute, you baggage!" Priveh ordered the girl.

But since they were deathly afraid that she would make a scandal, they gave her 100 rubles and sent her back with Samuel Leibush to her uncle, a tenant farmer in her native village.

Haim Alter sent for Samuel Zanvil and ordered him to find wives for his sons. "I want to wash my hands of those bums," he said. "And the fact that they haven't been rejected from conscription need not be an impediment. For another hundred rubles or so, this can be easily arranged."

"You won't regret this, Haim," Samuel Zanvil said with his usual overfamiliarity. "Since you're satisfied with Simha Meir, I seem to have done all right by you."

Samuel Zanvil took to the task with his customary energy, and he managed to find wives for the sons. In a matter of months they were engaged and married.

Again the house filled with guests, in-laws, Hasidim. Again Priveh stretched her hands out to her husband for money, and again Haim Alter turned to Simha Meir. Simha Meir doled out whatever was asked and had his father-in-law sign for every groschen.

Lodz was impressed with the magnificence of the double wedding. Haim Alter demanded only the best from his two sets of in-laws and more than matched their extravagance with his own. He spewed gifts and provided dowries, even though it wasn't his obligation. What was money, after all, but to be spent?

The weddings made up for the grief he had suffered on account of the maid. Now, with God's help, all would be well, and he would enjoy nothing but satisfaction.

With the coming of winter, the conscriptions began. Because so many of the Jewish youths were incorrectly entered in the municipal register, Haim Alter's sons were listed as older than they actually were and were called to present themselves before the army commission.

In Lodz, as in the other towns and cities, Jews went about with worried faces and bowed backs, gazing fearfully at sons who had reached twenty-one and who now had to serve a full five-year term of conscription in some far-flung outpost. Many of the prospective draftees already had wives and children. The Hasidic youths maimed themselves, fasted, drank salt water, and ate lots of herring in order to ruin their health and fail the physical examination. The rich bribed the doctors and other officials to reject their sons for some imagined defect. The only ones to be conscripted were the working-class youths.

Resigned to their fate, they ordered wooden boxes from carpenters and had them painted green. Inside, they would store their possessions when they went to serve the tsar.

Long before they were scheduled to report, the young workers quit their jobs and hung out in houses of prayer, where they allegedly prayed to God to keep them out of gentile hands. Actually they pelted each other with towels and prayer shawls and roasted potatoes in the huge prayerhouse ovens.

They knew full well that prayers wouldn't help, just as they hadn't helped their friends before them. Nor would complaints to the military doctors about deformed hearts and weak eyes do any good. They knew that their fate was sealed, and unlike the scholars, who inflicted wounds on themselves, or the rich youths, who bought their way out, they knew that they would have to serve out the full five years of degradation and abuse.

They drank whiskey, wrestled, marched with sticks substituting for rifles. Some took out the ram's horn and blew blast after blast into the night. Some actually prayed. Others went to affluent and Hasidic households to rouse those who had dodged conscription and drag them along to the houses of worship.

The terrified Hasidic youths hid themselves, but the workers pulled them out from under their beds and forced them to accompany them. The wealthy youths bought off the incensed workers with whiskey, with money and delicacies.

Aroused, embittered, filled with the abandon of those who have nothing more to lose, the young workers paraded through the streets, crowing like roosters, rousing respectable householders, frightening young matrons, banging on shutters and singling with bravado:

> Better you should have been born without a head
> Than wear brass buttons, my lad.
> Woe is us, we are as good as gone,
> Better we had been never born. . . .

Haim Alter had nothing to fear about his sons. Wealthy youths weren't drafted, God forbid. Still, he worried. They were so big, so disgustingly healthy it would be a mockery to attribute weak lungs to them. For this reason, the members of the commission demanded a particularly fat bribe to reject the bruisers. In addition, the youths' new fathers-in-law refused to contribute to the expense, leaving the entire burden to Haim Alter. He had promised them sons-in-law freed of their military obligations, and they held him to his word.

Again he turned to Simha Meir for cash, and again he signed notes that he never even read.

The doctors rejected the Alter boys and, in their place, conscripted two puny, undersized weavers. This called for a celebration, and Haim Alter threw another party.

Infuriated by the fact that the rich youths had freed themselves through subterfuge and then added salt to the wounds by throwing banquets, the workers took up a collection and

engaged Lippe Halfon to denounce the slackers to the governor.
The result was that the Alter boys had to present themselves
before a second military commission, this time in the provincial
capital city of Piotrkow.

The workers didn't get their way since the new set of
doctors again rejected the rich youths, but the effort cost Haim
Alter additional sums of money.

Right after Succoth came Simha Meir's turn to stand for
conscription. Of all the rich youths in Lodz, there were more
complaints of chicanery lodged against Simha Meir than against
all the others combined, and Lippe Halfon was kept busy com-
posing petitions and denunciations against him. Simha Meir
knew full well where these complaints originated. All three
commissions that he faced found enough wrong with him to
turn him down, but before he emerged with the red ticket
signaling his rejection, much money passed under the table.

Simha Meir insisted that Haim Alter bear part of the
financial burden, as was the custom in wealthy Lodz households that boarded sons-in-law, Haim Alter had no option
but to agree, and in lieu of cash he signed additional IOUs.

The coming of Passover again brought joy to Haim Alter.
As if by agreement, both daughters-in-law bore grandsons. This
time the choice of names was strictly his, and he even managed
to include the name of a grandfather in addition to that of
his rabbi.

Full of gratitude to God, Haim Alter felt that all his troubles
were now behind him, and he settled down to the good life
that a man who had done right by his children and grandchildren had earned.

"Praised by the Almighty," he said as he pressed a generous
donation on his rabbi. "May the evil eye spare us, God forbid.
I have, thank God, lived to enjoy satisfaction from my sons,
my daughter, and my son-in-law."

But the ax fell soon enough.

One Saturday night as Haim Alter chanted the hymns
ushering out the Sabbath, relishing the sweet taste of the wine,
grain, and oil that God had bestowed upon His chosen people,
Simha Meir came to him with a thick stack of papers in hand.
"I would like Father-in-law to meet these notes," he said. "I
can't wait any longer."

Haim Alter didn't quite grasp what Simha Meir had in
mind. "Notes? What notes is that?" he asked in a singsong.

Simha Meir calmly spread out the IOUs, which he kept
tied in ribbons, and began to read from them.

"On the tenth of the first, Father-in-law took eight hundred forty-three rubles; on the eighteenth of the second, Father-in-law took—"

Haim Alter was reluctant to listen to monetary matters, particularly at the conclusion of the Sabbath, but Simha Meir persisted. He read, and the stack of papers mounted.

"Well, let's hear the total already," Haim Alter said with impatience. "Is there no end to it?"

"It's coming," Simha Meir assured him.

When he finished reading, he tied each bundle separately and came up with a total that was so mind-boggling that Haim Alter recoiled.

"Lies!"

"I have Father-in-law's signature on every one," Simha Meir responded calmly.

Haim Alter extended a fat, hairy hand for the IOUs, but Simha Meir stuck them away in his breast pocket.

"Does Father-in-law deny his signature?"

Haim Alter paled. This was a new Simha Meir—a calm, composed, ominous stranger.

"So you've trapped me, eh?"

"I advanced Father-in-law money," Simha Meir said evenly. "Now I want it back."

"What if I don't pay you? What will you do to me then?"

"Father-in-law knows what's done with IOUs."

"You want to ruin me? You know very well that I can't pay you at this moment. You want to bankrupt your own father-in-law?"

"Business and family don't mix," Simha Meir said.

Haim Alter had no recourse but to rail. "Robber! . . . Highwayman!"

Priveh came running, Dinele behind her with the infant at her breast. Even Hadassah rushed in, holding a dripping pot.

Haim Alter pulled aside his velvet vest. "Go ahead! Take a knife and stab!"

The three women clasped his arms and led him to the sofa. "What's happened?" they asked. "God in heaven!"

Simha Meir left the room. He didn't go to the factory but headed for the studyhouse, where friends he hadn't seen for a long time were enjoying their customary post-Sabbath banquet. He sat with them until dawn, chanting, telling stories, exchanging witticisms. He was in no hurry to go home.

Together with the new week came the accusations, litigations, and denunciations between the two men. Haim Alter spent days running here and there, seeking redress against the son-in-law he had spent thousands to snare for his only daughter. The first one to whom he came crying was Simha Meir's father.

As was his custom, Abraham Hersh placed his bandanna between the pages of his Gemara to indicate that he was merely interrupting his studies momentarily and listened to his visitor's complaints without a word.

When he had finished, Abraham Hersh said coldly, "Who told you to take him in as a partner? I wanted him to study. Without my knowledge or consent you took him away from his books and drew him into a partnership. Now lie in the bed that you made yourself. I don't want to know the boy any longer."

Haim Alter began to pound the table and demand justice, but Abraham Hersh removed the bandanna from the Gemara and turned back to his studies.

Seeing that he was getting nowhere, Haim Alter dashed to the Alexander studyhouse to seek justice from Abraham Hersh's Hasidic cronies. But none of them would get involved. Next, he went to the Alexander Rabbi himself, but it was the rabbi's practice to keep out of money matters and concern himself only with affairs of the spirit.

"Jewish law provides for such contingencies," he said. "Convene a board of rabbis."

Haim Alter took the advice and sent a beadle to summon his son-in-law before a rabbinical court. Simha Meir appeared and resorted to his usual tricks. Just as he had done to his teachers in boyhood, he now outshouted and flustered the rabbis until they could no longer make sense of anything. Wise to the ways of Lodz lawsuits, he unloosed a flood of sophistry, offered precedents by the dozens, quoted a host of laws from the Breastplate of Judgment—a part of the Jewish codex, the Shulhan Arukh—and created such a morass that the rabbis couldn't decide on anything.

For months Simha Meir dragged his father-in-law from court to court, bullied and harassed him until he caved in and agreed to all his demands. Ultimately Haim Alter ended up with just the wooden looms, which were practically worthless anyway, while Simha Meir got everything else. The factory was now his, and Haim Alter was additionally obligated to pay off his debts to him for years to come. Haim Alter was left with a tiny percentage of the business and a small salary to live on.

Simha Meir didn't respond when Haim Alter cursed him or even when Priveh allowed herself to descend to the level of a marketwoman and doused him with a glass of tea. He only wiped his face and told himself that curses, childish acts of violence, even a slap were the impotent weapons of weaklings. A slap passed; money stayed.

There was only one person before whom he felt uneasy, his wife, Dinele. He knew that her parents were maligning him to her, and he was eager to move out, leave the house, even though he was entitled to the full five years of board as specified in the articles of engagement. He felt uncomfortable here. Even Hadassah glared at him and served his meals with such resentment that the plates and glasses rattled. But Dinele's parents wouldn't let her move out.

"That'll be the day, when I let you go to that murderer," Priveh said, pressing her daughter to her breast as if she were still a little girl. "Never mind, we can still afford to feed a son-in-law, even one like him. I'll keep my child with me for the full five years, thank you!"

Simha Meir wanted Dinele to take an interest in the dispute. After all, he wasn't doing it for himself alone but for her as well, for their future. And she, his wife, should have taken his side. She was no longer a child clinging to her mother's apron strings. A wife was supposed to stick up for her husband, no matter what. Her place was at his side. That's what the Torah said—that was the reason a man left his parents and got married so that he and his wife could become like one. She should have learned from his, Simha Meir's example. Even though his father had tried to tell him what to do, Simha Meir hadn't listened. Once married, a person had to be for himself only. Business and family didn't mix.

But Dinele didn't utter even a word. She kept silent as always and occupied herself with her child and her books.

Simha Meir wanted to explain to her, to tell her about the dog-eat-dog philosophy that prevailed in the outside world, but she merely gazed at him with derision and wouldn't listen. She wouldn't even give him the child when he asked to hold it. "He needs his sleep. I don't want you to keep him up," she said.

Simha Meir knew that her parents were inciting her against him, and he wanted to tell her his side of the story. Was it his fault that her father lived beyond his means? All he, Simha Meir, had asked for was what was legitimately due him. It was all legal and above board, correct down to the last groschen. But she wasn't interested. "Let me read," she interrupted the moment he started stating his position.

He had hoped that she would plead with him on behalf of her parents, even though he wasn't sure he could resist her and refuse to give up all he had gained with so much effort. At the same time he wanted her to approach him. More than ever these days he desired her.

He found all kinds of childish pretexts to go to her—he needed a handkerchief; a button was loose—anything to lure her out of the dining room and into their bedroom. Like a dog sniffing around a bitch in heat, he nervously milled around his own wife.

He waited for her to come to him on behalf of her parents. At first, he speculated that he wouldn't yield to her entreaties. Soon, however, he feared that he would give in. He was sure that this was one way to win her over completely. All he had to do was show his magnanimity, and she would be his.

Dinele knew that if she deigned to make the effort, her husband would do whatever she asked. But she couldn't bring herself even to think about it. She couldn't humiliate herself before such a boor. When her parents spoke to her about it, she burst into tears.

Her mother couldn't understand her attitude. Accustomed to using her charms to get what she wanted from her husband, she was puzzled by Dinele's refusal to save her own parents.

"You're a silly little girl," she complained. "Go and talk to him. After all that we've done for you—"

"I can't do it. . . ." Dinele sobbed. "I loathe him!"

Her father interceded. "Imagine that you had to ransom your parents from some murderer."

"Take my jewelry, take my pearls. . . . I'll work as a maid, but don't make me go to him," Dinele sobbed.

But when her parents contended that it had been for *her* sake that they had gone into hock in the first place, she lost her customary apathy and began to scream. "It wasn't for my sake but for yours! You did it to satisfy your own vanity and pride . . . to show everyone what a genius you snared, to show off to the world! I didn't want him, but you forced him on me!"

She knelt like a child before her parents. "I'll do anything you ask but this. I can't. . . ."

They understood. "Let's not talk any more about it. . . ."

Their daughter's pride restored their own and gave them back some self-respect.

Simha Meir waited, but she remained as aloof as ever, as if nothing had happened between him and her parents. She brought him clean clothes, saw to it that his meals were on time, and performed all her wifely duties as the Law dictated.

Simha Meir felt his resolution waver. Perhaps he would go to her and tell her that he was ready to make peace with her parents. Let her not think that he was the villain they made him out to be. Even though business and family didn't mix, he was ready to surrender the IOUs and restore peace in the house. He knew that this would be an expensive gesture, but he was ready to make it.

"Dinele," he approached her, ready to tell her the good news, but she looked up at him with such a surly, disdainful expression that he caught himself on the edge of the abyss. "Nothing," he mumbled. "I thought I didn't have a handkerchief." And he raced from the room with a sigh of relief at having nearly given up everything for some silly romantic notion.

In the cafés and exchanges, the younger men spoke of him with awe. "He's a man to watch," they said. "He's going places."

The older merchants were appalled. "To do such a thing to your own father-in-law? Where's the justice therein?"

"Idiots!" their younger counterparts sneered. "Justice isn't a commodity in Lodz. It isn't wool or cotton."

"Nor is it listed on the exchange," the brokers confirmed as they doused their cigarette butts in the last of their beer.

TWENTY-ONE

HEINZ HUNTZE'S PALACE, fenced in by heavy iron pickets and guarded by two huge watchdogs, rang with dissension between the old man and his sons and daughters.

For all his seventy-odd years, Huntze was still a robust, vigorous man. He spent his days in his mill, wending his way among the machinery, peering into storerooms, sticking his nose into the ledgers he didn't understand, testing dyes, probing and supervising every aspect of the operation.

Although somewhat deafened by age, he was alert to every rustle, every comment. The assistant directors had to consult him about every batch of wool or cotton they brought back from England. The engineers had to submit to him every plan and innovation. The chemists didn't dare choose a color without his approval. The designers couldn't introduce a new flower or stripe into a pattern without his consent. The firm's attorney couldn't institute a lawsuit without first going over its every detail with him.

He had to be told about everything from a million-ruble transaction to the pettiest incident in the mill, a worker's cut finger or an accidental death.

Partially deaf, obstinate, full of the peasant's slyness and suspicion, he managed to run the mill almost single-handedly and brooked no interference. He came to work with the workers, and he stayed long after they went home.

Because of his impaired hearing, he questioned every word he didn't happen to catch. "What's up, Albrecht?" he kept asking the plant director, an immense, sweating German under whose bulk chairs groaned in protest. "What's that you're babbling, you tub of lard?"

Barely able to stand on his gross, distended legs, encased in enormous checked trousers, the director had to shout into his employer's ear the gist of his most recent conversation with some subordinate.

"Don't shout!" Huntze admonished him. "I can hear fine!"

Everyone in the sprawling mill, from the director down to the lowliest stockboy, lived in terror of the old man who shuffled about with a meerschaum pipe filled with the cheapest tobacco stuck between his lips. He would plant himself in someone's chair, command him to light his pipe, and spit on the floor. He took inordinate pleasure in humiliating his employees, especially the educated among them.

But as the years went by, he felt that his days were numbered and his power was slipping away from him. This caused him to exert his authority all the more forcefully and to grow progressively more pigheaded. No one dared disagree with him in the plant, but it was different at home.

For years already, Huntze's children had been voicing their growing displeasure with their father. True, he would leave them a huge inheritance, but with it came the disgrace of common blood, plebeian lineage, an undistinguished surname.

His daughters, especially, yearned to rise in the world. Freckled, buck-toothed, pale, vapid, watery-eyed, chinless, they couldn't be distinguished from the women who worked in their father's plant. To compensate for these deficiencies, they wanted at least the benefit of an elegant surname.

In Lodz the name Huntze evoked instant respect, but the Huntze children cared little what Lodz thought. They had nothing but scorn for the stinking, smoky pesthole where their father was still remembered from the days when he had arrived from Saxony in his little horse-drawn cart. The younger Huntzes spent most of their time abroad, where they purchased for themselves ancestral estates complete with retinues of lackeys. In the grand hotels and clubs where they congregated, the name Huntze sounded woefully out of place. The moment they came home to scrounge additional capital, they started in on their father. They didn't like the way he conversed in Saxon Low German; they despised his meerschaums, his crew cut, his execrable table manners, his entire way of behavior that accentuated his, and their, common stock.

Old Huntze wanted to marry his daughters to sons of wealthy Lodz manufacturers. He was prepared to pay out sizable dowries but he wanted a return on his investment. As a shrewd businessman he felt that money should flow to money.

He was eager to bring into his family young men who knew manufacture and who could be trusted to run the plant after he was gone so that he could die with an easy mind, knowing that the business wouldn't fall into strange hands. He also hoped to merge his firm with others through marriage and thus forge an empire that would rule Lodz and defend it against all interlopers.

But his daughters wouldn't hear of it. They'd sooner remain old maids. Being female, they could at least marry up and acquire names that sounded more genteel.

The old man swore he'd go to hell before he laid out good money for titled sons-in-law who would contribute nothing to the family fortune. The daughters grew hysterical and threatened to go on the stage and completely disgrace the family, at which point Huntze's elderly wife burst into tears and pacified her husband just as she had in the old days when he got drunk and threatened to make a scene.

"I beg you, Heinzchen," she pleaded, groveling at his feet like a peasant wife, "do as the girls ask. . . ."

Ultimately the old man gave in, and both daughters married aristocrats. The elder, Elsa, snared her baron abroad. He was a surly, pompous snob with a title as long as himself—Baron Konrad Wolfgang von Heidel-Heidellau. Even longer than his name was the list of debts accumulated against him and his estate in East Prussia hard by the Russian border.

On the very first day he arrived in Lodz, accompanied by his valet, his hound, and his hunting rifles, he turned up his long, lean patrician nose at the city he described as a "Polish-Jewish pigsty," at the mill that stank of smoke and dye, and at his in-laws and their repulsive jargon.

"I won't remain in this garbage dump even a single day!" he announced with feeling.

Old Huntze paid him out every groschen of the enormous dowry, upon which his tall, erect son-in-law made a curt bow, brushed this mother-in-law's hand, and, along with his hound, valet, and wife, fled to his estate.

He never added a greeting to his wife's letters home, but when he had accumulated new debts, he addressed a letter on stationery bearing his crest to his father-in-law, demanding cash, and signed it with his long and aristocratic title.

When Old Man Huntze finally put his foot down and refused to squander any more money on the wastrel, the baron badgered his wife until in desperation she packed a valise (naturally, with a crest, too), took along a liveried servant as befitted her station, and went home to wheedle the required sum out of her father.

The younger daughter found a less forbidding spouse. He was a young Baltic officer with a hussar mustache and a very elegant name, too—Baron Otto von Taube. He served in the Imperial Guard in Petersburg, where, after the wedding he gathered a group of his high-living friends around him to carouse and gamble, constantly demanding money to pay off debts, under the threat that he, as an officer and gentleman, would otherwise have to resign his commission and put a bullet in his brain.

Thus, it evolved that the two daughters spent more time in Lodz now that they were married than they had when single. They flaunted their newly acquired titles shamelessly and cadged money from their father to maintain their husbands' insatiable profligacy.

As if this weren't enough, all three of Huntze's sons ganged up against their father and demanded nothing less but that he acquire his own barony.

Just as a former Piotrkow governor had for a considerable bribe arranged for an Order of St. Anne for Huntze, the present governor dropped a hint that for a consideration, Petersburg might be persuaded to settle the title of Baron upon the old man. He had earned such an honor for his outstanding contributions to the commercial development of the land and for helping establish the weaving industry in Poland. However, this would require numerous trips to the capital, along with additional expenditures associated with establishing the proper contacts and connections.

The Huntze brothers were enthralled. Just like their sisters, they despised everything about Lodz. Their father had sent them to Germany to study business administration, modern weaving techniques, and chemistry, but their flaxen, florid heads couldn't absorb numbers, machinery, or chemical elements. Instead, they were drawn to horses, hounds, cards, and women. Their father's money got them into the best places, but the advantage of their father's money was outweighed by the drawback of his plebeian name, which shamed them in the rarefied company they were keeping. And since they couldn't marry titles, they were damned to bear their disgrace until death. They, therefore, launched a concerted campaign against their father and would not give him a moment's peace until he agreed to purchase a barony.

On the one side, their father's age presented an obstacle. Their needs were enormous, what with their private stables, gambling losses, their mistresses, and the sums they had to force upon impoverished aristocrats in order to retain their friendship.

But the old man refused to meet their debts and instructed his cashier not to issue so much as a groschen to his sons without his personal signature. This didn't always help since the sons constantly threatened suicide unless their debts of honor were paid, but it did represent a nuisance to them since it always took a considerable amount of shouting and table pounding before their demands were met. The brothers, therefore, looked wistfully ahead to the time when their father croaked and they became the masters of their own destiny.

"The old shithead intends to live forever," they said with indignation, watching him flourish from day to day.

On the other side, their father's advancing age alarmed them. If they were ever to inherit his title, they needed him alive long enough to become a baron, for it would be most difficult to acquire this title on their own. Besides, even if they did manage it, the title would go to only one brother, not to all three.

The best and easiest solution would be to inherit the ready-made title from the old man along with his millions. The plans had already been laid. All that remained was the transfer of a sum of money to the governor. But the old man obstinately refused to turn over so much as a groschen.

"I shit on this!" he growled in his earthy fashion. "I wouldn't give a plug pfennig for it!"

Besides the sheer waste of money, he felt offended by his children's contempt for the name Huntze, which was held in high esteem not only in Lodz but even in such far-off places as Russia, Germany, and England. He had invested enough sweat, toil, and effort to make the name widely known and respected, but for all his wealth he had remained the same common worker he had always been, one who instinctively despised aristocrats and the educated. He went out of his way to be rude to his managerial help and to keep them hopping, and they—the trained engineers, chemists and managers—cringed before him like whipped curs. He was equally rude to the Polish counts and princes who came to him for favors. He wouldn't speak a word of Polish to them, only Low German out of sheer spite.

To him, the name Huntze was handsome and distinguished enough all by itself. And it enraged him that his sons sought to adorn it with a title. The sons knew full well that if they missed this opportunity, they would be stuck with their burden forever. You never could tell about old fogeys like their father. One moment they were full of life, and the next—they were no more. And they intensified their campaign for what they believed was rightfully theirs.

Old man Huntze fought back like a tiger. "After I die, you

can do whatever you like, but so long as I live, I'll be the boss. Me, Heinz Huntzel!"

His temper drove him to odd behavior. He came to dinner in his shirt sleeves. He chewed his bones with loud relish just as in the old days. He spit on the costly rugs, used the most vulgar expressions, even went to the tavern in the evenings for a beer.

The elderly weavers grew so petrified when he joined them at their tables that they couldn't even respond to his *prosit!* and he had no choice but to leave his beer and go back to the palace, where there was no peace for him either.

His elderly wife wandered in a daze through magnificent halls hung with elaborate draperies and antlered deer heads. That which her children hesitated to tell their father they heaped upon her head without restraint. She, a simple peasant woman awed by her affluence, unable to cope with the staff of servants, lost in the presence of strangers whose words she didn't understand, terrified of the airs put on by her own sons and daughters, longed for the days when she had sat at her spinning wheel, when she had cooked huge pots of food for her husband and his assistants, when she had gossiped with neighbors about homemaking, children, and other familiar subjects.

She never got accustomed to the fancy carriages, the lackeys, the salons, and the gentlemen who kissed her hand. This made her think only of the times she herself had kissed the hand of the doctor to whom she took the children when they were ill.

She liked it best when she was alone with her husband. He then filled his pipe, threw off his jacket, and chatted with her in a Saxon Low German while she darned a stocking. But this happened seldom now. He was always busy. And the children shunned her, unless it was to nag her into getting something they wanted out of their father, whom they called "the old shithead."

She would blush, take offense, and feel like telling them what a shocking thing this was, a sin before God, but she didn't dare. She was afraid of them, as a peasant woman fears the imperious squire.

"Oh, sweet Jesus," she would lament, wringing her hands. "I'll talk to your father about it. Only don't call him names. . . ."

Now the sons gave her no rest, and out of desperation, she pleaded with her husband on her knees to give them whatever they wanted. The fact that this would entail her becoming a baroness was as inconceivable to her as if she had been told that she would become the Holy Virgin.

"Heinzl," she pleaded, "do it for your old wife's sake."

Huntze was touched, but he wouldn't yield. "Everything they want ready-made!" he raged. "Everything I've worked for all my life. Let them go after things on their own, the lazy bums. . . . I've done enough for them."

When conditions at home grew intolerable, Huntze tried to seek the advice of others, but they dared not tell him a thing. They held their tongues and agreed with everything Huntze said. He spat in disgust and went to consult his sales representative.

As was his custom, Abraham Hersh listened without interruption. When Huntze finished, he asked, "What will this cost, Herr Huntze?"

"A fortune. . . . tons. . . ."

"And what will you get out of it?"

"Nothing."

"Then what's the point of it?" Ashkenazi asked in bewilderment.

Huntze came home more determined than ever. "Not another word about it! The subject is closed!" he said, and slammed the table.

The war went on.

TWENTY-TWO

━━━◆━━━

QUITE THE OPPOSITE OPINION to that of his father was held by Abraham Hersh's son, the manufacturer of women's kerchiefs, regarding the barony. Although Simha Meir rarely entered his father's house these days, he was cognizant of everything that went on there and at his father's place of business on Piotrkow Street. He got his information partly from his father's clerks, from Goldlust the bookkeeper, and from his sisters, whom he often invited to his own home for the specific purpose of pumping them about their father's affairs.

Simha Meir's sisters were like strangers to him. He had never needed them before, so he had avoided them, but now they could prove useful, for even though he had his own business, he always kept an eye open for better things. He knew if his father had had a good or poor season; he knew which of his out-of-town buyers were reliable and which risky; he knew which of the Huntze goods moved and which didn't; he even knew the exact total of his father's estate. As in everything else he did, he had an ulterior motive in all this. Ever since childhood he had fantasized about taking his father's place as sales representative of the Huntze mill, and all of his father's efforts to keep him out of the office had merely firmed this resolve.

True, he was doing well enough on his own. Besides his kerchiefs, he occasionally turned a handsome profit trading in cotton and wool. With his quick perception and keen mind he had grasped all the intricacies of trade and knew the right time to buy and the right time to sell. At the same time he was sober enough not to be reckless, not to put all his eggs in one basket, and always to leave himself a way out.

He was the complete man of Lodz, familiar with its every ruse and wile, attuned to its ebbs, flows, and rhythms. No, he couldn't complain. His investment of 10,000 rubles had already doubled many times over. He never for a moment regretted having disobeyed his father by abandoning the scholar's desk for the life of commerce. He already boasted a name among the merchants and small manufacturers of Lodz, but this was scarcely enough for Simha Meir.

He had never believed in manual production. He knew that the city's future lay in steam. The handlooms were only a bridge to further accomplishments, a scaffolding upon which to build and expand. Once the structure itself was finished, the scaffolding could be discarded.

True, he could have switched over to steam now and ended up with a small factory that he could gradually expand, but he had never been one for slow advancement. He wanted to take a giant step forward, one that would take the city by storm. But so far he lacked the resources for such a move. He knew from the holy volumes that the tiniest moth was stronger than the largest garment once it penetrated the closet—that a tiny spark could burn down the biggest house if only it found a chink through which to enter.

He set his sights high, this young man of Lodz. His darting eyes never gazed lower than the tallest chimneys, and looming above all were the stacks of the Huntze mill. For now, its gates were barred to him, but there was a chink through which he could inveigle his way inside. And that chink was his father's position as the firm's sales representative.

With greedy eyes Simha Meir gazed at the Huntze warehouse, jammed from ceiling to wall with costly fabrics. He deduced that his father ran it too conservatively and that newer, more daring methods were called for. But his father was solidly entrenched. Old Huntze was completely satisfied with his representative, who was as cautious and prudent as he himself.

Simha Meir grasped what the full potential of the position would be in the hands of a younger, more vigorous and imaginative man. Were he, Simha Meir, allowed free rein, he would show the world what could be accomplished there. He would move goods as no one believed possible. But his father didn't want him around now, any more than he had when Simha Meir had been a boy.

And there was nothing he could do about it. He knew how bullheaded his father could be, and he knew that he would get nowhere with him. Still, he kept his eyes and ears open.

At every opportunity he questioned everyone close to his father's affairs. His sisters, who still lived at their father's home with their husbands and who had little to do with their time, were eager to tell Simha Meir about every visitor to the house, every conversation held there. They mentioned Huntze's recent visit to their father as if this were just another bit of insignificant gossip. Simha Meir perked up immediately.

"Huntze?" he repeated. "Huntze personally came to ask Father's advice?"

He shut his mind to the rest of their chatter, seized upon the one significant fact, and turned it over in his head. He couldn't have cared less how much the barony would cost the firm. He also knew how devoted Huntze was to his father, even though others offered fortunes to replace him as his sales representative. But Huntze was old, and his days were numbered. It would be foolish to stake one's future on the whims of an old man who was liable to go at any time, leaving heirs with modern, progressive ideas. Simha Meir knew that it made more sense to hitch one's wagon to those to whom the future belonged. His father failed to grasp this. He tied his destiny to that of an old dodderer whose own end was near. He didn't even bother to shine up to the heirs but did everything possible to antagonize them. Just now, for instance, he had advised Huntze against the barony that the sons wanted so desperately.

Simha Meir chortled to himself. No, his father wouldn't fit into the New Lodz. So long as Old Man Huntze lived, he would hang on, but Huntze couldn't live forever. And his heirs would have nothing to do with such an old-fashioned representative and would replace him with a more modern, more worldly individual. There would be thousands of applicants for the job. But it would be a great folly to allow a stranger to fall into the ready-made gravy pot which rightfully belonged to the Ashkenazi family. Had his father understood this, he would have personally invited him, Simha Meir, into the business and groomed him for the position since he, the father, was already a man along in years himself. He had no need to work so hard. He no longer had the strength or the aptitude for this. But his father was obstinate, and he did everything possible to keep his son out of the business. Therefore, it fell upon him, Simha Meir, to seek some way to keep the job that was rightfully his from going to a stranger. True, this wasn't possible now, but one had to plan ahead. It would be politic to cultivate the heirs, the Huntze brothers, and thus lay a foundation for later.

Simha Meir racked his brain for some way to approach the brothers, to become their confidential agent just as his father was to their father. But this wasn't easy. They were seldom home. They had nothing to do with the business. And what could possibly draw them to a young Hasid whom they had seen around the plant but who, to them, looked like the hundreds of other Jews that congregated there?

Maybe he, Simha Meir, could do something to help them get the barony they wanted so desperately, although only God knew why they did. For several nights he lay awake, his brain churning. He actually talked to himself, and didn't even notice, in his self-absorption, when Dinele awoke and watched him. His gray, darting eyes saw nothing but the warehouses jammed with goods, customers by the droves, coffers full of money, and, more than anything, the red-brick walls of factories abuzz with work and chimneys looming—a forest of chimneys belching smoke into the skies. . . .

The next morning he sat down at the table, and choosing with care German words he still recalled from the correspondence primers, he composed a letter to the Huntze brothers in which he proposed to lend them cash without limit for as extended a period of time as they elected and at a rate of interest they themselves determined.

Employing the fanciest German script appended with all kinds of spirals and curlicues, he wrote the letter again and again, then signed the final version with his name and with that of his father, the sales representative of the Huntze firm.

The letter hadn't come easy to Simha Meir. For all its handsome and generous offer, he had to make it patently clear to the thickheaded gentiles that they would be doing *him* a favor by accepting since he could think of no safer place to invest his money than with the esteemed gentlemen. He might have found someone to help him with the grammar and phrasing, but he was loath to let anyone else in on such a confidential matter. In cards and in business it was better not to have anyone looking over your shoulder.

For the next twenty-four hours he waited in a state of fevered anticipation for a reply from the palace. His impatience and anxiety made him squirm. He felt hemmed in inside the factory, in the small cafés, at home. He kept glancing at the gold watch that had been his wedding present, and every ring of the doorbell brought him to his feet.

Finally, when Melchior came in his forest green hunting costume to deliver a brief note to him, he grew so rattled that he tipped the huge German a whole ruble without even knowing the contents of the letter.

It contained a few brief words. It lacked any salutation and preamble, and curtly, as if it were a telegram, it bade the recipient present himself the following day at the palace at four.

There was no signature, only a scrawled initial.

Simha Meir read and reread the note. Having digested it to his satisfaction, he picked up a mirror and looked at his beard with distaste. At first he tried to get it to lie flat against the collar so that it appeared less blatant and less Jewish. Failing this, he picked up a scissors and committed his first outright desecration against Jewish custom. The first snip alarmed him, and his hand trembled as if he were cutting into his flesh. But when no lightning came to strike him down, he went on. In order to get it just so, he had to keep on snipping. Next, he lopped off the earlocks until no trace remained of them.

He polished his boots carefully and pulled out his trouser legs, which had been tucked inside, allowing them to hang outside so that it looked as if he were wearing European ox-fords, not boots. He tugged at his trousers to press the long-established wrinkles out of them and to form a crease.

Next, he went unobserved to a side street, stole into a haber-dashery, and bought a stiff collar and a black tie that resembled a swallow in flight. It took plenty of effort before he managed to affix the collar and tie, which seemed reluctant to adapt to his Hasidic neck. He drew on his shortest swallowtail gabar-dine, which he seldom wore since it was too small for him. Under it he had donned a red velvet vest. He let the heavy gold watch chain dangle across his belly, dropped a silver cigar case into his pocket, and picked up a slim black walking stick with a silver knob.

He hailed a closed droshky to avoid being spotted and ordered himself driven to the Huntze palace. "Keep the canopy up!" he told the driver when the man tried to lower it.

Lodz seethed in the late-afternoon rush. People jostled each other on the sidewalks. Teamsters spewed deadly oaths and swung whips, trying to push through the dense traffic. Keening women shuffled in a funeral cortege. But Simha Meir saw and heard nothing.

"If you get me there in a hurry, there's a nice tip in it for you," he said, prodding the driver's blue-clad shoulder with his cane. "Make it snappy!"

TWENTY-THREE

———◆———

THE YOUNG HUNTZES weren't yet presentable when Simha Meir called at the palace door precisely on the dot of four.

"Wait here!" the lackey ordered, rather than asked, looking down his nose at the stripling, who long before had snatched off his hat and now stood gazing about with darting eyes.

They had been out all night carousing, the young Huntzes, and they were sleepy now, queasy and hung-over. Their heads felt light, but nowhere as light as their wallets after the hours of heavy gambling.

Things couldn't have gone worse for them. It started with the fiasco at the Renaissance.

For the past few weeks the cabaret Renaissance had been featuring a Hungarian dancer who had taken Lodz by storm. Night after night the place filled with merchants, manufacturers, officers, government officials, plant superintendents, traveling salesmen, even ordinary clerks, whooping and whistling each time she stepped out on the floor.

From her very first night she was assailed with presents, bouquets, and invitations from Lodz playboys, vying to outdo one another. She accepted the gifts and flowers, but not the propositions. She was even more adamant about barring the young rakes and old roués from her tiny dressing room. An elderly lady with eyes and diamonds flashing kept stern watch at the door and politely but firmly kept everyone out.

In a hodgepodge of Hungarian, German, and Russian she demanded that her daughter's privacy be respected. "No, no, it's out of the question, gentlemen!" she insisted, hands held out to block the onslaught. "My daughter is resting, and no one can go in."

If some of the more rash among them still refused to back off, she summoned a swarthy, sickly young man who was always dressed as if on his way to a wedding. Bowing low and speaking in the same polyglot jargon as she, he said in a low but sinister tone, "Messieurs, my wife begs your indulgence, but she is exhausted and soon she must do another show. Please. . . ."

Something about his presence made the men retreat, but the momentary frustration served only to ignite their lust and competitive spirit. Lodz wasn't used to such behavior. Lodz knew that with money you could buy anything.

Once the small fish had failed with their puny offerings, the sharks of Lodz moved in. These were sons of the wealthiest industrialists, to whom diamonds and pearls were like trash.

The dancer kept their gems, but the attached calling cards ended up in the wastebasket. Following her final performance of the night, she dressed very modestly and headed straight for her hotel on Piotrkow Street, the old lady on one arm, the sickly young man on the other.

"Nothing doing. . . . Not a chance in the world," the cabaret owner told the ardent suitors when they tried to slip him a bribe to gain some advantage with the dancer. "She doesn't take a step without her mother and husband. There isn't a thing I wouldn't do for my guests, but this is out of the question."

"I can't help you, gentlemen, much as I'd like to," the hotel manager in the green frock coat reiterated, spreading his hands in tragic dismay. "They've given strict orders not to be disturbed. The moment they come in, they retire. I must say, for actors, they live very, very simply."

Lodz was a town without secrets. Everyone knew down to the last kopeck the price of every gift offered the dancer and the exact measure of her rebuff. In their rage and frustration, the competitors turned on each other. Men neglected their homes and businesses to spend night after night at the Renaissance, indulging their fantasies and planning new stratagems to break down the dancer's resistance.

"A saint," the Germans raved. "A nun. . . ."

"A *rebbetzin*," the Jews half jested.

Inevitably legends sprang up about the young woman. The gentiles claimed she was a Hungarian countess who had eloped with the sickly young man after her father, the count, had renounced him. The old lady was really the young man's mother, who called her daughter-in-law "daughter" to allay suspicions.

The Jews came up with another tale. The girl was a Galician rabbi's daughter who had fled home on account of her Hungarian lover.

Others had a more cynical explanation. This was merely a gang of con artists setting up the suckers to fleece them out of their last ruble.

Its equanimity shattered, its assurance threatened, Lodz smoldered. Its women felt insulted and betrayed. They couldn't go to the cabaret—respectable women didn't even show their faces in cafés—so they strolled the sidewalks of Piotrkow Street for hours, hoping for a glimpse of the source of the men's infatuation.

Ultimately news of the dancer reached the young Huntzes at the palace. It was brought there by the Swiss chemist in their father's plant, who revealed that the girl had taken him into her confidence since he spoke French and she wanted to practice the language.

When they heard of the sensation created by the lady and of her intransigence, the Huntzes' florid faces turned even more scarlet. "What crap! No wonder she won't give in. Sending boys to do a man's job. . . ."

They hadn't the slightest intention of pitting themselves against the young bloods of Lodz—it was beneath them to rub shoulders with tradesmen, drummers, and junior clerks. They took over the cabaret for the night and gave strict orders that no one be admitted except a select group of invited guests, including some high-ranking Russian officers, several picked industrialists' sons and members of the local Polish gentry, and the French-speaking chemist.

Each Huntze, unbeknownst to his brothers, arranged for a handsome gift of expensive jewelry and an intimate supper in a private dining room.

It started out as a gay, festive evening. The owner personally stationed himself at the front door and kept everyone out. Handsomely attired waiters served the fanciest dishes and finest wines. The dancer was at her most seductive. She writhed like a sinuous snake, cast alluring glances, teased and flirted with every curve of her shapely body.

She even made an exception this time and joined the brothers for a glass of wine at their table. But everything suddenly turned very ugly for the young Huntzes.

Like true Germans who abjure diplomacy for direct action, they began to discuss in coarsest terms how they would succeed where all Lodz had failed.

"A hundred rubles for the first kiss," a Huntze offered.

"Two hundred!" bid a second.

"Three hundred!" shouted a third.

The dancer smiled. Her frail, dapper husband sat beside her, brooding silently.

"Look here, little one," a Huntze said, flashing a diamond ring. "All you got to do to earn this is be a nice little girl. . . ."

"I got you beat!" his brother said, shouldering him aside to display an emerald nestling against a black velvet background.

"That's all junk next to mine!" the third Huntze said, and without even awaiting a response, he slipped a string of pearls around the dancer's neck, letting his hairy paw dangle across her bosom as he did so.

The sickly young man stood up. "Monsieur, mind your manners."

"And a hundred rubles thrown in!" the inflamed German added.

"Monsieur, I demand an apology this instant!" the young man said with unblinking eyes.

"If that's not enough, make it two hundred—five hundred!" And he pawed the woman with a drunken leer.

The young man seemed to stretch to twice his height as he slapped the smirking German so hard the glasses on the table toppled.

The Huntze brothers sat stunned. No one had ever dared raise a hand to them. And now this—a cabaret floozy's pimp?

A moment or so later they leaped to their feet to stamp the fellow into the ground, but he was already gone, along with the two women.

First, the affronted Huntze smashed every glass on the table. Next, he shattered the biggest mirror in the place with a bottle. Finally, he doused the proprietor's dazzling shirtfront with the nearest glass of wine. He then flung a roll of bills at his feet and snarled, "You'll never catch me in this cathouse again!"

To break the mood, the officers invited the brothers to walk them to their camp on the outskirts of town. Once there, they drank heavily for a time, then broke out the cards.

"Unlucky at love, lucky at cards," the officers joked.

The Huntzes recklessly bet thousands after thousands, but they couldn't seem to win a pot.

Incensed, besotted, they didn't get home until dawn. Still wearing their tails and starched linen, they dropped where they stood and fell asleep right there on the floor. They first awakened late in the afternoon—stiff, crabby, covered with vomit. They beat, cursed, and abused the servants who tried to undress them. They recalled the slap and brooded over the fact that by now all Lodz was enjoying their humiliation.

Besides, they had lost many thousands of rubles in markers that would have to be redeemed in cash since the officers were to be transferred, and not to pay a gambling debt promptly was for gentlemen unthinkable. Getting the funds together, however, was another matter altogether. Their father wasn't one to let go of money so easily. Besides, they had been feuding with him for months already as a result of his obstinate refusal to lay out even a pfennig for the barony they so eagerly yearned for.

It was at this time that Simha Meir showed up at the palace —flushed, awed by all the opulence around him, anxious, yet full of confidence in his own future and that of Lodz.

When the spectacularly liveried servant first informed them about the little Jew waiting on the front stairs, the Huntzes couldn't even recall making an appointment for this hour. "Jew? What Jew? Throw the swine the hell out!" they roared.

But the man, whom Simha Meir had had the foresight to bribe, gently reminded his masters that this was the same Jew they, the young gentlemen, had personally invited. Only then did the Huntzes recall the letter, and they ordered that the Jew be brought to them.

Simha Meir followed the lackey gingerly through room after room, gazing nervously at the huge wolfhound which trotted behind him, all the while sniffing with obvious mistrust at a gabardine which, although cut down, still wasn't short enough for him.

"Good day, esteemed gentlemen," Simha Meir said, bowing low to the three naked individuals who received him in the bathroom, where they were trying to sober up by having the servants pour cold water over their heads.

No one responded to his greeting.

Simha Meir gazed with apprehension and embarrassment at the gross, bloated bodies of the three gentiles, who apparently lacked all shame, and he shifted the brim of his hat between his fingers. He didn't know what one did about hats in such company. Finally, the brothers stood up and let the servants wrap them in large bath towels, glaring all the time at the youth in the gabardine.

"You there," the eldest said. "You're the son of Old Ashkenazi, Father's court Jew?"

"Yes," Simha Meir said. "My father is business representative for the factory."

"And you want to become our court Jew, is that it?"

"I want to lend you gentlemen money," Simha Meir said.

"How much have you got?"

"All you gentlemen need."

The brothers exchanged glances. The eldest Huntze flipped back his flaxen, ropy gentile hair and shook himself like a dog caught in the rain.

"We don't know when we can pay you back."

"I can wait."

"Our father mustn't know."

"You can count on my discretion."

"We can't figure to pay you back till our father is gone. And that's not liable to happen for a long, long time."

"I have patience."

"We need lots of money. Many thousands now and more later."

"I am always ready to accommodate the gentlemen," Simha Meir said boldly, even though he had no inkling where he could lay his hands on that kind of money. "All I ask is two weeks' notice."

"Agreed," the half-naked German said, performing his calisthenics. "Get some cash to us at once. By two weeks from tomorrow. Good-bye."

Simha Meir walked out in a daze, irked by his rude reception, yet buoyed and exhilarated. The first breach had been made in the wall. True, he could only crawl through it on all fours, but that's how it always was at the start. Even the Sages said so. But wise was he who could see beyond—into the future. And that something would come of this Simha Meir never doubted. Never had he felt such power in his hands, such faith in himself as he did now, striding along the wide, dusty suburban road running alongside the red fence that surrounded Heinz Huntze's plant. Never had the soaring chimneys blackening the skies loomed so close. . . .

Some workers passing by snapped at his coattails and growled like dogs. "Here, sheeny, sheeny, sheeny!" they taunted. *"Oy veyl"*

Simha Meir never even heard them. He was up high somewhere among the tall chimney tops. . . .

With the same haste and zeal with which he had inveigled his way into his father-in-law's factory right after the wedding, he now left it. He didn't even wait for more favorable circumstances but sold out at a lower price in order to lay his hands on the ready money he needed. He borrowed more at inflated interest, went into hock, bartered objects and goods for cash. He forced himself to cultivate the callow youths at the studyhouse whom he had so assiduously avoided, sons-in-law living on their fathers-in-law's bounty—and he cajoled them into investing their dowries with him, making them partners in the sweet deal he was putting together and promising them a share of the profits. He also resumed relations with his brothers-in-law, his sisters' husbands, whom he had neglected till now. Using all the guile at his command, he whetted their greed and convinced them and his sisters to entrust their dowries to him.

"I can't tell you at this time what the deal is," he said conspiratorially. "It has to remain a secret for now. But I promise you juicy returns. With God's help, we'll all be swimming in gravy. I wouldn't do anything to hurt my own flesh and blood, after all."

But when even this didn't prove enough, he took up his briefcase and umbrella, as he always did when he had a hard nut to crack, and decided to pay a short visit to Jacob Bunem in Warsaw.

For two days Simha Meir put on his best face in Jacob Bunem's elegant quarters in Reb Kalman Eisen's mansion. He displayed so much wit, logic, and erudition that everyone from his sister-in-law to Reb Kalman's sons, those snobs and faultfinders, fell under his spell. "A genius, no less!" they raved. "A head for business and Torah both. . . ."

Even Jacob Bunem's father-in-law, who walked in fear of everyone and kept to himself, took cognizance of the brilliance of his son-in-law's brother. "God knows I'm no expert," he said, denigrating himself as usual, "but I'm simply mad about that Simha Meir!"

He knew how to make an impact when he chose to, Simha Meir did. Just as he could remain isolated from people when he didn't need them, he also knew how to turn on the charm and be as cordial, sweet, and caring as necessary when he was after something. He was never at a loss for an apt quote, parable, or aphorism. More than anyone, he was able to manipulate Jacob Bunem, who promptly forgot any resentments and recriminations he may have borne his twin brother. Gay, lusty, relishing life, and anxious for others to do the same, he couldn't remain angry or bear a grudge for long. He listened to his brother briefly and lent him the money he asked for.

Actually Simha Meir could have raised all the capital he needed by discounting the Huntzes' IOUs at high interest. But this was precisely what he didn't want. It wouldn't have served his purpose to have their notes floating around town. A crux of his scheme was to keep people away from them and to remain their confidential aide and personal banker.

He didn't sleep; instead of eating, he scribbled rows of figures on the tablecloth and raced through his prayers, unwinding the phylacteries from his arm before he had even properly wound them.

He presented himself on the dot with the first installment and earned the grudging praise of the Huntzes. "Very nice work," they acknowledged, negligently signing note after promissory note.

Once they had taken care of their immediate problem, they turned to a more pressing task—the barony they were so eager to acquire. They realized now that they could arrange the matter by themselves without going to their father. They would use their own friends to approach the Piotrkow governor. They knew that the sums they would have to lay out would be enormous, but what would that matter once the old man dropped dead?

This was exactly what Simha Meir had been counting on, and he was there again with the money at the appointed time.

The Piotrkow governor left his province in the hands of deputies, and traveling at the Huntze brothers' expense, he took the first train to Petersburg.

TWENTY-FOUR

———◆———

THE BARONY WEIGHED like an oppressive yoke on the shoulders of Heinz Huntze. It had cost a fortune, far more than anticipated. Also, in keeping with their new station, his children demanded huge sums, as befitted the sons and daughters of a baron. Their gambling losses alone were staggering.

Finally, the director of the mill, Fat Albrecht, beneath whose bulk the sturdiest chairs groaned, gathered his courage and confronted his employer with some unsettling news. "Excuse me, Herr Baron," he began apologetically, "but I felt it my duty to inform you that our treasury has been severely depleted and Herr Goetzke insists on drawing out his corresponding share immediately."

"That filthy swine!" Huntze raged. "That scum!"

Goetzke was now as resentful of Huntze as he had been before their partnership. The barony his partner had acquired kept him awake at night. Throughout their partnership he had been silently brooding, for even though they were contractually equal, everyone referred to the plant as the Huntze factory, and Goetzke's name was never mentioned.

As if this weren't enough, the title of Baron served to accentuate the inequality between them. True, he, Goetzke, didn't acknowledge the title. To him, it was as if it didn't exist. He never attended Huntze's balls, nor did he once make use of the title in speaking to his partner directly or in referring to him to others. He recoiled when others insisted on calling Huntze Herr Baron.

No matter what he, Goetzke, did to equalize the relationship, it always turned out that he emerged second. His only victory had been to force his former employer into a partnership, but since then it had all been downhill. As far as the world was concerned, Huntze was the King of Lodz, and Goetzke was some nonentity.

Not that he had taken this lying down. He built a palace

every bit as grand as Huntze's and rode in an equally ornate carriage. But people still thought of him as an upstart, if they thought of him at all.

And now Huntze had taken a giant step toward leaving him even further behind. He seethed with rage and could neither eat nor sleep from envy and frustration. He had eagerly sought an opportunity to puncture Huntze's balloon, and now it had come.

The business was in trouble. Goetzke could have easily waited for things to return to normal before drawing his share of the money due him, but he wouldn't agree to this despite all of Albrecht's pleas in Huntze's behalf. "Let him become a baron on his own money, not on mine!"

If Huntze had come to him personally, he might have relented. The very act of having him beg a favor would have been worth everything. But the old man wouldn't stoop to such humiliation, and he, Huntze, and Albrecht were forced to bring the situation to a head.

Of course, Huntze could have obtained unlimited credit to tide him over—his signature was like money in the bank. But it was his principle never to sign anything. It was a standing Lodz joke that the reason for this was that he couldn't write, but Huntze couldn't have cared less what people said. He knew that kings didn't sign IOUs, and he was the King of Lodz, indeed, of all Poland.

At home his life was a continuous hell. His sons and daughters were forever teaching him manners and social graces. They kept entertaining aristocrats, who then invited him, Huntze, to their estates for hunts and parties.

He hated this. He knew nothing of horses, hounds, shooting, gambling, and dancing. His greatest pleasure was to sit in his office and banter with merchants and foremen, to insult his chemists and engineers. Title or no, he didn't want to change his routine. He wanted to rise at dawn, put on his loose jacket and baggy pants, and be at work on time with the first worker. But his daughters wouldn't allow this. "You are now a baron, Father," they reminded him. "You may no longer mix with rabble."

They wouldn't let him exchange a word with anyone, wouldn't let him go anywhere on foot but made him ride everywhere in the carriage, even though he loved to walk.

Worst of all were the honors heaped upon him. He was forever being appointed honorary director of this or that institution and dunned for donations to various churches and hospitals.

He hated to dole out charity. He had made his fortune with his own two hands, and he felt that all others who hadn't done so were stupid, lazy, and inept. He particularly despised the poor, who, he firmly believed, were lazy drunks who only wanted to sponge off others, and it drove him wild when he was approached for a donation. "I pay enough taxes to the government!" he roared. "Let the government take care of that scum. . . ."

Now that he was a baron, his children forced him to give generously to all kinds of leeches. They insisted that it was his duty—*noblesse oblige*.

All these expenditures placed a severe financial strain on the factory, and he and Albrecht spent several sleepless nights agitating about the problem. Finally, after lengthy deliberation, Albrecht came to the conclusion that the remedy would have to come from the factory itself. When a body fell sick, the best solution was to allow it to heal itself, and this was true not only of human beings but of institutions.

"Well put, Albrecht," Huntze concurred. "For once in your fat life, you speak words of wisdom."

Having received his employer's approval, Albrecht considered the various approaches open to him.

Reducing the quality of the finished goods was out of the question. Baron Huntze had worked too long and too hard to have his reputation so casually ruined. His product was known and respected everywhere. The gold and silver medals earned by the factory were ample proof of this. No, the solution lay elsewhere.

True, Baron Huntze could have cut down on expenses at home. Tens of thousands of rubles could be saved annually without the slightest inconvenience. But Albrecht was reluctant to propose this to the baron. Actually, this was out of the old man's hands—it was the work of his daughters, sons, and sons-in-law.

The only remaining source of savings lay in the help.

Here savings could be effected. True, wages didn't constitute the major source of the operating expenses, but there were so many workers, thousands of them, and only one treasury to carry them all. If each worker drew a little less, the savings would be enormous. In the course of a year all these losses could be made up. Those workers who objected were free to quit. There was no lack of available help in Lodz. Each day hordes of peasant men and women poured into the city in search of work. They would be content to work for pennies, particularly the young girls, who were every bit as capable as any man. The automatic looms required only hands to work the levers, and female hands were no worse than male. Besides, the young country girls were subservient, didn't drink, and were conscientious about the work.

The next day Albrecht directed his foremen to fire as many men as possible and hire girls in their place—the younger the better. Next, he instituted an overall 15 percent cut in wages.

"Good work, Albrechtschen," Huntze said. "Since I've had a new carriage made with the coat of arms and all, I'm giving you my old one along with the team and driver."

"Thank you, Herr Baron!" Albrecht said, clumsily bowing his huge bulk.

The very next day the new changes were instituted. More and more men were discharged and replaced by peasant girls in flowered head kerchiefs who were paid a third of the men's wages.

Long lines of men, mostly Polish peasants, who anxiously fingered their blue caps waiting for their final wages, queued up before the paymaster's window. "Where to now, Jesus?" they muttered, having already doffed their caps long before reaching the paymaster's grille.

The German workers, who hadn't been let go and who lived in dormitories built on the factory grounds, cursed into the goods they were weaving, twisting their oaths along with the yarn and gazing around to see if the foremen had overheard.

At Albrecht's suggestion, the foremen's pay wasn't cut. This assured their loyalty, and they supervised the workers with redoubled suspicion. The humble Polish girls were too frightened to resist when the foremen led them to a bale of goods in the corner, and the foremen sniffed around like bloodhounds to catch the remaining men in a dismissible offense.

Nor did the change in personnel bother Melchior, the attendant, and his friend, Jostel, the watchman. The former frisked the workers as they left the factory to make sure they hadn't filched anything, and the latter was responsible for the plant's security. Together, they had a moneylending sideline going. There were men who liked a beer or two after work; others lost their week's pay gambling; still others had to visit the leech about some venereal affliction without telling their wives.

None of this could be deducted from the salaries the men turned over intact to their wives, and they turned to Melchior, who charged only ten kopecks' interest per week. He, Melchior, also collected tips from businessmen who came to visit Huntze and earned additional income procuring for Director

Albrecht, who kept bachelor quarters close to the factory. Only the very youngest and freshest girls would do for Albrecht, and Melchior was very popular with the female sex because of his position, his splendid forest green uniform, and his gigantic proportions. As if this weren't enough, he played a clarinet and had a steady supply of wine at home that he collected from the Huntze palace following the parties and balls, and the female workers flocked to him, providing him a splendid crop of girls to choose from for himself and for the director. The girls inevitably came back from Albrecht's quarters with bruises about their necks and arms and a cheap dress or a ruble in payment. The director paid Melchior handsomely for his good taste and the endless variety of girls he provided him, and everyone, except possibly the girls, was content.

The workers to whom he, Melchior, lent money would have been astonished to learn that the rate of interest he charged them came to nearly 500 percent; but they didn't bother their heads about such things.

Melchior's friend Jostel had his own little rackets. He took money from the commission salesmen whom he admitted into the factory; from buyers of waste who pulled up with huge wagons at the factory gates; from peasants who came to cart away the manure from the stables; from drivers who delivered the raw materials; even from peasants who made the mill their first stop upon their arrival in Lodz.

He also lent money at interest, but to the wives of workers when there was no bread in the house, when a husband had drunk away the week's pay, or when the midwife had to be paid for an abortion resulting from an illicit affair.

Just like Melchior, he enjoyed females visiting the quarters he maintained in a corner of the factory. But he was already too old for women, and he could only enjoy little girls who were willing to kiss an old grandpa for a piece of candy and even play games with him. Not all the mothers were willing to send their daughters to Jostel in lieu of repaying their loans, but there were always enough who did so without the knowledge of their husbands. They recalled their own childhoods when they, too, had allowed themselves to be fondled by such an old "uncle," be it the village teacher, a storekeeper, or whoever. They knew that they hadn't been seriously harmed by this since they had married, borne children, and become good wives.

And they sent their little daughters to Uncle Jostel, cautioning them to do as they were told and to tell no one afterward.

Now that notices were posted in the factory announcing the 15 percent cut in wages, business for the two entrepreneurs was excellent. In the dormitories where the workers lived, times were harsh. The wives no longer added fat to the soup, and they kept serving the same millet with potatoes, which left their husbands unsated and irritable so that out of frustration, they beat their families and got drunk in the taverns. The wives sought to earn some side money, and they sold themselves to the young bachelor weavers who boarded in their kitchens. Children were torn from their dolls and put to work in the factories to bring home a few guldens.

The factory pastor made frequent visits to the workers' quarters. He escorted their children to their final rest with prayers to the Eternal. The police came to search for chickens and piglets appropriated from neighbors. Even dogs started disappearing. It was rumored that the weavers trapped them for their Sunday dinners.

More than usual now the weavers came for loans to the two factotums. Because of the rapid rise of business the usurers raised their rate of interest by several groschen. Melchior didn't stop blowing his clarinet for the stunning young women who visited his rooms and served them wines left over from the baron's parties. Old Jostel had all the little girls he wanted for his peculiar games.

The mill worked around the clock to make up its losses. Just as Albrecht had predicted, it was curing itself without resorting to outside means.

"By the end of the year things will be back to normal," he assured his employer. "Possibly even sooner."

"You're a clever rascal, Albrechtschen," Huntze grunted, treating him to a cigar. "Just don't break my couch with that fat behind of yours. . . ."

"Oh, I won't, Herr Baron," the director assured him, his bulk quivering over his employer's joke.

TWENTY-FIVE

———◆———

EVEN SOONER THAN the young barons had anticipated the "old shithead," as they called their father, departed the world, leaving them his huge inheritance along with the title.

So long as he was able to wander through the factory, peering everywhere and sticking his nose and half-deaf ears into every corner, feeling the goods, dipping his fingers in the dye, trying to make sense of the complicated ledgers, giving advice on designs, correcting plans, haggling with merchants, puffing away on his pipe, arriving with the first workers and leaving after the last—so long as he was able to do all that, his health held.

Doctors warned him not to walk on the cold stone factory floors lest he become rheumatic. They predicted that the dust and lint would damage his lungs, that the fumes from the dyes would be bad for his heart, that the roar of the machinery would shatter his nerves. They advised him to leave town, particularly in the summers. But he would have none of this. His response to all the medical advice was *Quatsch,* bunk.

The older he grew, the more he was drawn to his beloved factory and the better and more energetic he felt. But now that he was a baron, his children no longer allowed him near the factory. They wouldn't let him smoke his pipe—only Havana cigars. They kept urging him to go to doctors and spas.

This evoked all the weaknesses of old age, and his bones began to ache, his legs swelled, his skin dried up, his spine hurt. He suffered constant headaches. He would doze off in the midst of a conversation or lose his train of thought. He raged at people for interrupting him even though they hadn't uttered a word.

He became unbearable at home. He drove the servants to distraction, insulted his wife, hurled plates and glasses on the floor, and didn't stop spitting on the Persian rugs and tiger skins covering the parquet.

At first, he fought against his indispositions. Racked with pain, his legs wobbly, he dragged his body through the huge factory, giving advice, muttering, losing his temper, tormenting the help, and supervising everything as before.

Albrecht would try to reassure him. "Herr Baron, we will take care of everything already. Herr Baron should stay in bed."

"Shut your snout," the old man snarled, "and take your hands off me—I can walk perfectly well by myself!"

Often the doctors and his children would put him to bed by force. But he refused to take medication, spit it into the doctors' eyes, and spilled it on the floor. The designers, chemists, engineers, and managers had to come to his bedside. He rambled, blabbered, interfered with the running of the factory. Then, quite abruptly, his mind would clear, and he'd come up with solutions so brilliant and incisive that people were astounded.

From time to time he rallied sufficiently to tear off his covers, drive away the nurses, and—dressed in his bathrobe and slippers—pad to the factory. This would throw everyone at the plant into a stew since he shouted and caused scenes, claiming that the plant was being run into the ground and that he had no one to depend on. "Stop the machines!" he roared. "Who started the machines without my permission?"

The people knew that his mind was affected, yet no one dared stand up to him. For all his advanced age, physical debilitation, and senility, he was still the king. And when his children forced him back to bed and locked his doors, he would toss, tear his clothes, and shred the pillows like some wounded caged beast.

"I want my factory people here!" he roared, foaming at the mouth. "Why aren't my people here so that I can give them the orders for the day?"

The sons kept everyone away. They knew that his days were numbered, and they wanted him isolated. They knew the extent of his authority, and they feared lest he direct some final shattering catastrophe. Most of all, they were afraid that he would change his will. The old man understood, and he tossed in rage.

"Murderers!" he screamed when they came to his bedside. "You want to poison me!"

In the nights he was frantic from the pain. He threw whatever came to hand at those looking after him and strained only to go to his factory.

His elderly wife pleaded with him. "Heinzschen, what do you want?"

"To burn down the factory!" he told her. "I want to leave

nothing behind me . . . let everything go up in smoke!"

Abruptly he would fall into an apathy, not utter a word or get out of bed even to perform his natural functions. He whimpered like a child and allowed himself to be used at will.

On his last night the doctors wanted to shut down the factory to spare him the noise of the machinery, but despite his deafness, he detected the unaccustomed stillness, and he raised himself up from his pillow. "Why isn't the factory running?" he asked in distress. "It's no holiday today."

The doctors informed him of his condition.

"I'm ready to die," he said, "but I want to hear the factory running. Otherwise, I can't die in peace."

They did as he asked. The whistles commenced to blow wildly; the machinery hummed and buzzed.

The dying man cocked his ears, a lopsided smile formed on his face, then froze forever.

The sons knelt around his bed, then rose quickly, smoothing the creases in their trousers. "Well, finally," they said with a sigh, as if a heavy burden had fallen from their shoulders.

They sent for Albrecht to arrange a handsome funeral. All the factory sirens and whistles screamed the passing of the King of Lodz into the grimy, smoke-filled skies.

Right after the funeral, which bored the young barons to distraction, they summoned Albrecht and ordered him to discard everything that didn't fit in with the modern methods of factory operation. Everything was changed, from the ponderous furniture in the old man's office to the factory help.

"Youth, bring in youth!" the barons insisted. "Enough of tradition . . . we're not running some old folks' home here."

Along with all the other changes was the one replacing Abraham Hersh Ashkenazi with his own son. This was the latter's reward for lending money to the heirs with which to purchase the barony.

Abraham Hersh didn't react as Haim Alter had when Simha Meir had deposed him in his old age. Very calmly he heard out Albrecht, who came to inform him of the developments.

"I'm very sorry to have to be the bearer of such news, Herr Ashkenazi," the ponderous director apologized. "But the young barons want to be rid of all the old employees. They believe your son will serve them better."

"Koheleth, who was King Solomon, said that there is a time to plant and a time to pluck up that which is planted; a time to build up and a time to break down. Nothing occurs without the will of God, Herr Director, not even the tiniest scratch of a fingernail," Abraham Hersh said in Yiddish.

"Yes, and my turn will come next, Herr Ashkenazi," the director said wearily. "There's nothing we can do."

The two old men shook hands mutely.

Abraham Hersh quietly put his records in order, locked the office safe, and turned the keys over to the director. The only thing he took from the office was the volume of the Gemara that he kept there. He thought about removing the doorpost amulets, but he decided against it. He kissed them for the final time and said good-bye to his associates.

They wept, but he shed not a tear.

The very next day Simha Meir brought in a crew to remodel the office from top to bottom. He even installed gas illumination, something seen only in the wealthiest Lodz palaces.

On the new signs, which already carried the Huntze crest, the name of the new sales representative, Max Ashkenazi, was printed in gilt in three languages—German, Russian, and Polish. The same new name was also imprinted on all the factory stationery.

When Jacob Bunem heard what his brother had done, he took the first train to Lodz and went straight to Simha Meir's office.

"Herr Ashkenazi is busy," a skinny clerk said, trying to block Jacob Bunem's way. He pushed him aside and stormed his way inside the office.

"Greetings, Jacob Bunem," Simha Meir said, extending a hand.

"Where is Father?" Jacob Bunem asked.

"Am I my father's keeper?" Simha Meir joked.

Jacob Bunem moved closer to his brother, who retreated as far as he could go.

"Is it for this you wheedled money out of me—so that you could throw Father out into the cold in his old age?" Jacob Bunem asked, spitting the words into Simha Meir's face.

Simha Meir turned white and began to stammer. "Your money is yours any time you want it. . . . I swear it. . . ."

Jacob Bunem raised his hand and slapped Simha Meir's cheeks, one after the other. "This is for Father," he said as he dealt slap after deliberate slap.

Simha Meir made no move to fight back. He merely picked up his hat that had fallen off during the scuffle and wiped his inflamed cheeks.

"You'll pay for this!" he warned, waving a finger at his brother's retreating back. "Just you wait! And this is what you'll see of your money!" And his fingers formed the fig.

Out of rage, he shouted at the clerks, who had gathered to see what all the fuss was about, "Get back to work! You're not being paid to gawk."

They fled back to their cubbyholes.

Just as if nothing had happened, he turned back to the books, determined to wipe away every trace of his father's influence.

Along with his old name, Max Ashkenazi discarded his Hasidic garb and donned the attire of the man of the world. He shaved off what was left of his beard, leaving the barest tip at the point of his chin. He exchanged cigarettes for thick cigars and Yiddish for a broken Lodz German. He retained the Yiddish only for counting money so as not to make a mistake, God forbid.

Learning of his son's deeds, Abraham Hersh took off his boots and tore the lapel of his gabardine. He ordered Sarah Leah to fetch him a low stool, and he sat down to observe a period of mourning for a son who had left the faith, which was tantamount to dying.

He sat on the low stool and studied the Book of Job.

II

CHIMNEYS IN THE SKY

TWENTY-SIX

THE TSAR'S COURT IN PETERSBURG was torn by unrest and intrigue.

Following the assassination of Alexander II, the tsar who had freed Russia's serfs and been inclined toward liberal reform, two opposing factions of the court locked horns in an effort to exert influence over the new tsar, Alexander III.

The liberals advised the new tsar to follow in his father's ways and to institute even more liberal policies which would win him the support of the people and stifle the revolutionary spirit, while the reactionaries under Pobedonostsev urged him to be stern and root out all the enemies of the monarchy and the church. The minister of the interior, Ignatiev, belonged to the liberal faction, but he lived on a grand scale and spent far beyond what his estates earned him. He assembled the Jewish millionaires of Petersburg and proposed that they raise a half million rubles in his behalf, for which he would serve as an advocate for the Jews at court. If his demands weren't met, he would go over to the side of Pobedonostsev.

The Jewish millionaires could have raised the sum, large as it was, but they were reluctant since once the precedent was established, the courtiers would keep bleeding them under the threat of depriving the Jews of the few rights they now had. This view was shared by the rabbis.

Out of rage, Ignatiev did just as he had threatened, and he persuaded the tsar to bar the Jews from Moscow.

Moscow Jews by the thousands were expelled from the city, along with their wives and children. Some of them went to America, a greater number took refuge in Warsaw but most went to Lodz, the center of Polish industry and commerce.

Bringing along cratefuls of furniture, bedding, Sabbath candelabra, iron safes, huge samovars, and Russian abacuses, they settled on Piotrkow, Wschodnia, Poludniowa, and surrounding streets.

They promptly opened shops, offices, agencies, and commission houses and brought much Russian trade into the city. Lodz soon grew overcrowded with the strangers, whom the local residents called Litvaks even though they weren't from Lithuania.

Accustomed to a broad, free-spending Russian life-style, they took over the city's best establishments, creating a shortage of residential and commercial quarters. Their wives didn't haggle in the markets, serving to turn the grocers, butchers, and fishmongers against their old customers, who, in turn, grew even more resentful of the newcomers.

They were even more disturbed by their non-Jewish ways. Russian-Jewish boys and girls paraded boldly through Jewish neighborhoods in school uniforms. They conversed in the alien language of the police and the bureaucrats. And the Polish Jews' animosity was not untinged with envy.

"They'll grow up gentiles," the Lodz parents said. "Primed for conversion . . . "

But even the older Litvaks who spoke Yiddish and attended synagogues weren't accepted by the natives. Their Yiddish was queer, unintelligible, particularly when they spoke fast. Their praying and studying lacked the true Jewish flavor. The Lodz synagogues and studyhouses grew very crowded on account of the influx, and services were conducted from before dawn until late evening. The moment the last quorums concluded the morning prayers, other Jews were already beginning afternoon services.

Traditional Lodz Jews were outraged. The elder Litvaks wore short gabardines, derbies, and fedoras. The younger were clean-shaven. They didn't sway at prayer. They were more like gypsies than Jews. It was rumored that they could cast spells. When a Litvak moved into a house, all those who could afford to moved out. The Lodz men wouldn't include a Litvak in a quorum. The Lodz women wouldn't lend a pot to a Litvak neighbor lest she render it impure. Lodz youngsters taunted Litvak children:

> Litvak swine, choo choo choo
> Go to hell, do, do, do. . . .

But when it came to business, all distinctions were forgotten. The newcomers had excellent connections in Russia. In spring and fall, swarms of wide-trousered, broad-bearded Russian merchants descended upon Lodz, and they preferred to deal with their fellow countrymen. They sat drinking gallons of hot tea, snacking on jam, playing cards, and closing deals. Litvak salesmen sold Lodz goods from the Persian to the Chinese borders and boosted the local economy.

But even though the Lodz Jews did business with the Litvaks, they avoided social contact with them. The feeling was mutual. Litvaks mocked the natives' old-fashioned dress and accents and referred to them as Itche-Mayers, hicks who still reckoned money in groschen instead of in rubles and kopecks.

The local resentment grew even more intense when a new wave of settlers arrived from the towns and cities of Lithuania to compete for a livelihood. In contrast with their profligate Muscovite cousins, the Lithuanians were dour, dry, and notoriously tightfisted. All they brought with them to Poland were their teapots and razors with which to shave once a week.

They did everything possible to make a living—sold needles, shoelaces, soap, cheap shoes. They bought up every remnant and scrap at the factories and hawked them in the streets in grating Lithuanian accents.

The poorer Lodz women rented them living space in corners of their kitchens. Squeezing every kopeck, the Lithuanians existed on bread and herring only.

They couldn't understand Polish Jews, who thought nothing of eating meat daily. They stared in disbelief when local housewives roasted a goose for the Sabbath and baked trays of cookies. They wondered how the Polish Jews could go to a restaurant to drink beer or whiskey, munch on chick-peas, order chopped liver. They gaped when grown women went into a confectionery for a bar of chocolate.

"Polish gluttons," they sneered, "savages. . . ."

"Lithuanian onionheads," the Polish Jews responded. "Borscht with herring. . . ."

What's more, the newcomers looked down on factory work and waited for better things. Local employers hired them for their stores and offices because of their knowledge of Russian and bookkeeping, and they gradually pushed out the native employees. But what irked the Polish women most was that the newcomers had no compunction about fooling around with their daughters, but when it came to marriage, they sent for their sweethearts to join them—plain, hard-faced girls, nothing like the soft, pampered Lodz maidens.

The strangers swiftly overran the city. As soon as they moved in, the local residents fled, offended by the Litvaks' habits of going bareheaded, singing Russian songs on the Sabbath, and generally behaving in rude, rowdy fashion. They took over house after house, street after street, and soon dominated the city. They built their own synagogues and brought in a rabbi who seemed more like a priest than a rabbi.

A struggle for supremacy evolved. The old settlers' cause was weakened by the fact that their wealthiest and most influential members gravitated to the Lithuanian rabbi, who fulfilled their yearnings for an enlightened, contemporary spiritual leader. Foremost in this campaign was Maximilian—formerly Mendel —Flederbaum, the town's leading magnate and community leader.

He had long sought a rabbi whom he could invite to his soirees without feeling repulsed and embarrassed. The current chief rabbi was a wild-bearded fanatic, while the new candidate spoke Polish and Russian and was the recipient of an imperial medal. Rumor even had it that he had received a gold sword from the tsar, even though no one had actually seen it. The Lithuanian rabbi had his official meeting with the police chief and became the chief rabbi of Lodz.

After this, teachers and bookkeepers, female dentists and midwives, preachers and sewing machine salesmen, insurance agents and commission men from every part of the far-flung Russian Empire poured into Lodz. Along with this wave, two strangers appeared one freezing winter day in Balut.

It was early evening, when Jews, hunched over from the cold, with their beards tucked inside their lapels, were making their way to combined afternoon-evening services. The two strangers, wearing European dress, fur caps, bashlyks, and kits behung with teapots, brought to mind demobilized soldiers, but when the people took a closer look, they saw that there was nothing military about them. One was already middle-aged; the other, still young, but with a brooding face unlike any soldier's.

The older man stopped under a lamppost and by its dim light squinted at a scrap of paper.

"Who are you looking for?" men asked the stranger.

"Could you tell me the way to Keila Buchbinder's place?" the elder man asked in a half-Lithuanian, half-Lodz accent.

The men looked puzzled.

"Keila, the wife of Tevye the weaver," the stranger amended.

"Why didn't you say so in the first place? Tevye the World Isn't Lawless's Keila? Come, we'll show you. She lives right on the corner in a cellar by the baker's."

The strangers had hefted their kits and started to follow when suddenly one of the men turned around, looked sharply into the older stranger's face, and clapped his hands. "Tevye, may I have such a good year if it isn't Tevye himself! Greetings!"

Before Tevye could get there, several boys beat him to Keila's cellar and shouted breathlessly, "Keila, your husband has come! Keila!"

It was even harder for Keila to recognize her husband. She gazed in shock at the stranger, glanced at his companion, blushed deeply, crammed the tip of her apron into her mouth, then commenced nervously to wipe off a bench.

Tevye removed his bashlyk, but Keila still couldn't believe her eyes. He was nothing like the man who had been torn from her side that night.

"How have you been, Keila?" he asked.

Even his voice rang strange to her. It had turned somehow sharp like a Lithuanian's. Even after he had taken a kerchief from his kit and made her a present of it, she still couldn't stop staring at him, her hands folded over her massive bosom. Nor could she bring herself to believe that the other man was the rabbi's son, Nissan the depraved.

He was so different now—older, taller, with a stubble upon his cheeks and the beginnings of what resembled Jewish earlocks. Actually he looked a lot like his father. He had the same bony, ascetic face, the same big black eyes that seemed to be gazing off into the beyond as if seeing celestial scenes hidden from all others. Rarely did a smile cross his sharp-featured, dark-skinned face. He wore a Russian blouse draped over black trousers. It was embroidered in gentile fashion around the collar and cinched with a colorful belt. His curly hair—so black that it seemed blue—covered his head in glossy waves. His thick brows were sharply etched and grown together over the bridge of his nose to lend him a stern, forbidding appearance.

As if this weren't enough, he kept removing book after book from his kit and satchel—densely printed Russian tomes that he wiped with the devotion pious Jews offorded a holy volume. When he spoke, it was more in Russian than Yiddish.

"Can't make head or tail of a single word," Keila complained.

The rest of Balut was just as puzzled. People came running from all over. Men greeted them; women measured them up and down; children stood with mouths open and fingers thrust up noses.

Returning soldiers were greeted in the same fashion, but their strangeness wore off after a few days, when they donned their old Jewish clothing, let their beards grow, and lost their foreign accents. But the two men made no effort to turn back to their old ways.

On the Sabbath, when the congregation sought to honor Tevye by granting him the privilege of reading from the Torah, he didn't even show up for the services. The men assumed that he was praying at home, and they came to invite him to the benediction that had been prepared for him and Nissan, only to be told by Keila that neither of them any longer observed the Sabbath. "All they do is whisper, read books, and go around bareheaded like gentiles. . . ."

"They've turned into real Litvaks." Pious Jews sighed. "Forgotten God. . . ."

For a while the people of Balut assumed that the men had brought money back from Russia. It happened more than once that exiles came back from Siberia with a bundle, and because of this, they were forgiven their non-Jewish ways. But when Tevye went immediately back to work in a factory and Nissan started giving Russian lessons to poor families, Balut concluded that they were only indigent heretics who had forfeited not only this world but the world to come, and the two were promptly forgotten.

Soon queer-looking youths and girls began congregating in Tevye's cellar. They had come with the wave of Russian and Lithuanian newcomers. The young men had great shocks of hair, wore glasses, Russian tunics, and soft broad-brimmed hats. The girls wore their hair short, acted tough, and smoked cigarettes. What they did in Tevye's cellar, no one knew, but it was understood that they weren't there for the purpose of praying. Soon after, young Balut weavers began to come as well, particularly on the Sabbaths and holidays. The neighbors tried to question Keila, but she could tell them nothing.

"All they do is gab and read books," she said. "I can't make out even a word of what they're babbling. . . ."

Each Sabbath the congregation Love of Friends lost more and more young worshipers to Tevye's cellar. Tevye, the former reader at the synagogue, and Nissan, the rabbi's son, told them startling things which initially struck them as outlandish, but the more they thought about them, the more convincing they sounded.

Tevye spoke to them about the life of workers in the Lithuanian cities, of their struggle against their bosses, of their solidarity, and of the funds they contributed to the fight against their exploiters.

The young weavers in their Sabbath gabardines sat with mouths agape, trying to absorb all the new concepts to which they had never been exposed. "We'll raise funds, too!" they said. "We vow to pay our dues on time!"

Nissan spoke of more exalted matters—of the French Revolution, of the socialist movement abroad, of the valor of the Russian fighters for equality, of the struggles between capital and labor as well as tidbits of natural science and the history of peoples and races. Speaking simply and in easily understandable terms, employing the practiced orator's warmth and sincerity, he explained to the weary, downtrodden men what went on in the great world outside Balut. The weavers sat with bedazzled eyes turned upward and mouths agape.

"True!" they said. "Pearls of wisdom. . . ."

They felt their insignificance melt away in the dark cellar and their spirits soar. For the first time in their lives they weren't reminded of their worthlessness and vanity, which the preachers and rabbis constantly hammered into them. Instead, they were told of their strength, their importance, their esteem. Their life seemed to assume new purpose, and this feeling grew even stronger when Tevye and Nissan confided in them and drew them into their conspiracy. The very word, so strange and secret, sent shivers through them and burned itself into their blood and marrow, and they accepted the pamphlets and brochures distributed by Tevye's disciples. Later, reclining on bundles of goods following the day's mind-numbing labors, they turned down the wicks of smoky kerosene lamps so that the boss wouldn't see and eagerly absorbed the context of the poorly printed booklets.

Tevye formed study groups and circles, enlisted new converts, and collected ten-groschen pieces from the weavers for the fund. Even the old weavers, shattered, toil-worn men, contributed their coins every Friday. Tevye's cellar room grew so crowded on the Sabbaths there wasn't even standing room for all those who sought to attend. Young weavers stopped taking strolls through the fields on Saturdays and instead came to listen and learn the new Torah.

Like the wake caused by a rock thrown into a pond, the circles spread from the cellar through all Lodz. Workers met to discuss the new views in teahouses, in the Konstantin Forest, but mostly in the large, messy rooms of Feivel the rag dealer, which were stacked from ceiling to floor with books and more books.

Feivel had no respect for the workers. What could those clods know of Enlightenment and heresy? His argument wasn't with bosses, but with God. After all, he himself employed girls to grade his rags, and he was an employer like all other employers. Nissan's theories, which he had brought back from abroad, meant nothing to him—he wanted to know only one thing: "Are you or are you not spreading heresy?"

"Of a certainty, Reb Feivel. Very much so."

"In that case, my house is your house," Feivel said, his face creased into a network of happy wrinkles. His large, neglected house was thronged with people on the holy days.

Nissan even managed to enlist a number of wayward yeshiva students to the cause. Having been one himself, he knew the best way to approach them. He knew of their thirst for knowledge, and he taught them Russian and mathematics, natural science and history. At the same time he introduced other ideas —deep, forbidden, but logical views that fulfilled the emotional and intellectual needs of the scholars.

He had gained extensive knowledge during his years of confinement. He had acquired it from university students who shared his exile and from his own studies. With his father's zeal he probed and investigated. Just like his father, he wrote on the margins in a tiny script, making commentaries, annotations, additions.

He had been strongly drawn to the Marxist dogma, which was still new in Russia but which had been enthusiastically taken up by Jewish revolutionaries in Lithuania's towns and cities. To Nissan, its logic and depth, its directness and ingenious construction seemed to answer all his eternal questions. He never let his copy of *Das Kapital* out of his sight and carried it everywhere, as his father had carried his prayer shawl and phylacteries. And just like his father, who held that the Torah wasn't to be studied only for one's own edification but disseminated to all, he felt it his mission to spread the new Torah and to deride and belittle all those who refused to acknowledge its truth. Even in exile, he had used cold logic to discredit the narodniks with their silly romantic notions and had heaped scorn upon all those who dared refute the prophet Marx.

Now he proselytized among the yeshiva students at Feivel the rag dealer's, and they—with their minds honed by years of study and receptive to philosophical notions and abstract concepts—became true believers.

Feivel beamed through all the tufts and bristles of his curly beard. He was as proud of Nissan as if he were his own son. "Light up, boys!" he encouraged them as he distributed cigarettes. "It's good to smoke on the Sabbath. . . ."

Inside the factories, new songs were heard, songs directed against the tsar which made the foremen blanch with fear. "Loafers!" they cried. "Walls have ears! Because of you, we'll all go to Siberia in chains!"

They grew even more enraged when the songs made ugly allusions to them and to the bosses. "May your mouths be twisted around to your backsides for biting the hand that feeds you!" they cursed the young men.

The derogatory songs spread quickly, leaping from factory to factory like sparks. The bosses threatened to denounce the young workers to their fathers and to the rabbi, but the youths couldn't care less. "We are our own masters now!" they replied. Such defiant words had never before been expressed in Lodz.

Gradually the young weavers began to disobey their bosses' orders. They refused to haul goods on their backs; they wouldn't work long hours. "Enough!" they declared. "Time to knock off for the night."

Seasonal workers no longer cowered before their employers. They refused to take out the garbage or take the Sabbath meals to be warmed at the baker's. In synagogues, fathers anxiously sighed about the sinful generation that rebelled against its parents.

"They defy God and the Messiah!" some said.

"They malign the tsar himself!" others whispered, looking around.

"It's all the fault of the Litvaks," pious Jews observed bitterly. "One rotten apple spoils the barrel."

Police began to appear more frequently in Balut and to peer suspiciously into the open doors of the factories. "Just you wait, Jewboys," they warned, waving threatening fists but leaving with nothing more than that with which they had entered.

TWENTY-SEVEN

———————

THE WARKA RABBI'S PROPHECY, which had so alarmed Abraham Hersh Ashkenazi, came true. Following his elder brother's defection, Jacob Bunem too abandoned the ways of Jewishness.

So long as his father lived, he took care to be discreet. In Warsaw he adopted European garb and caroused in cabarets, but when he came to Lodz, he put on the traditional dress and even accompanied his father to the Alexander Rabbi's court. As soon as the father died unexpectedly of a heart attack, directly after the period of mourning, Jacob Bunem accomplished the total transformation and took the Polish name of Yakub.

Simha Meir (now Max), despite all the modifications, had remained the quintessential Hasid. He still talked to himself, plucked at his wisp of beard, spoke in singsong (albeit in German), answered questions with questions, resorted to half words and insinuations. He still seized people by their lapels or buttons when addressing them, groped for their beards regardless if they wore them. His lapels were always sprinkled with ashes, as was his vest; his tie lay inevitably askew; the European fedora or top hat he now affected sat well back on his skull, as had his Hasidic hat. The checked English suits he now favored in order to lend his figure dignity and elegance quickly assumed the shape of a Hasidic gabardine upon his stooped shoulders.

Jacob (now Yakub) Bunem on the other hand, seemed to be made for modern attire. He wore the half-bohemian outfits with verve and dash. Even his black Vandyke lent him a rakish, debonair, un-Jewish air. In his top hat, with his broad black cape thrown over his shoulders, white gloves, and cane, he resembled some wealthy patron of the arts to the manor born.

Just as he had been the favorite of the children in his father's courtyard, his popularity with adults was legendary, and Max spent sleepless nights writhing over his younger brother's successes.

To begin with, he couldn't forgive him their father's inheritance. Following the period of mourning his father had observed over him, the old man had cut Max out of the will without leaving him so much as a shoelace. The entire inheritance now went to Yakub and the sisters. It came to quite a sum, more than Max had conceived, and Yakub's share alone totaled in the tens of thousands.

Max went about in a stew. He had made quite a show of grief at his father's funeral; he had torn the lapel of a perfectly new suit and even observed the seven-day period of mourning. But the heirs wouldn't even answer when he tried to discuss his claims with them. Besides, he still owed them money from the sums he had borrowed in behalf of the Huntze brothers. No court would find in his behalf, but he did consult rabbis in an effort to break the will. None of his old obfuscating tricks had any effect, however, and in the end, Max collected nothing.

He was also disturbed that Yakub had made the transition from Jewishness with so little difficulty, while his had evoked such animosity and ill will. The injustice of it all rankled within his bosom. Everything that came so hard to him evolved to Yakub without a hitch. Surely his brother had been born under a lucky star. He was handsome, rich, popular. He was welcome in the wealthiest homes, to which, he, Max, couldn't even aspire.

Yakub now spent more time in Lodz than in Warsaw. He maintained a handsome pied-à-terre in the city's most extravagant hotel, drove a fancy coach over Lodz's poorly paved streets, greeting passersby with regal geniality. He quickly became a member of the city's fast set, socialized with artists, writers, and actresses. He was known in the best restaurants, theaters, cabarets, and nightclubs. Headwaiters and doormen greeted him by name; ladies gazed at him with burning eyes.

His wife, Pearl, was his direct opposite. While he loved life, she hid from it. She was forever ailing, sour, depressed. She took no joy in the material pleasures her wealth might have afforded her, and she resented others who did. She adored her husband, but she couldn't keep up with him. She couldn't bear his enduring joy, his abounding good humor. Even as she couldn't swallow a bite, he ate with a wolfish appetite. When she tossed and turned despite the sleeping potions, he snored through the nights, and this drove her to fury.

"Yakub." She prodded him awake and asked irrationally, "How can you sleep like that when I can't even close an eye?"

She couldn't stand the people who flocked around him or his unfailing geniality toward one and all. She was jealous of everyone, of women to whom he indolently tipped his hat, of actresses he applauded lustily in the theaters. "And who is that flirt?" she would ask, eyes narrowed, guts churning.

She wouldn't accompany him when he went out, yet she threw tantrums when he went without her. He therefore stayed away from Warsaw and ran to Lodz, in the raucous, flashy atmosphere of which he could indulge his senses.

Women, from nightclub singers to bored young matrons, were drawn to him. As they strolled Piotrkow Street, he tipped his hat to them from his flying carriage. He reserved his most extravagant greeting for his sister-in-law, Dinele, whenever he chanced upon her strolling with her mother, both of them elegant in their high feathered hats.

Just as he had waited for her as a boy, hoping to catch her coming or going to school, he now drove his carriage up and down Piotrkow Street, hoping for a glimpse of her. He still recalled her warm arms clasped around his neck as she rode him piggyback, still remembered her adoring laughter.

He couldn't forgive his brother for robbing him of the one he had always thought of as his bride. He wasn't happy with his own wife, who could neither live herself nor allow anyone else to live. He looked for Dinele so that he might somehow express his intense feelings for her with the tip of his hat. She, in turn, arranged to be there so that she might see him. He was every bit as handsome and dashing now as the heroes in her novels.

She now lived in her own apartment, which Max had leased following his break with her parents. Max had changed, too. He dressed like a worldly man, spoke to her in German, called her Diana instead of Dinele. But she still couldn't stand him as he sat at the table dribbling food, calculating, figuring, mumbling to himself, unable to stay put a moment.

"Where are you off to now?" she asked when he rose from the table. "You haven't had your dessert yet."

She also tried to dissuade him from scribbling all over every tablecloth and napkin he could lay his hands on. "You might take a lesson from your children," she chided him. "See their table manners?"

"Children?" Max Ashkenazi asked blankly.

He often forgot that he had children, a daughter in addition to a son. He rarely saw them, seldom spoke to them. If they asked him to dandle them on his knee or throw them in the air, he shooed them off to their mother. "Frightfully busy," he mumbled.

He only wanted to know how they were doing in school, especially the boy, Isaac, whom he called Ignatz. "Well, show me your notebook, boy," he said. "I'd like to see your marks."

The boy brought the notebooks reluctantly. Max snatched them from his hands, glanced at them swiftly, and grimaced at the atrocious grades, particularly the one for mathematics, which was Ignatz's poorest subject.

"I don't understand how little he takes after me," he said, glaring at his wife.

Gertrud, a carbon copy of her mother, was very happy to show her notebooks to her father. She was a capable child who painted very pretty flowers and butterflies. Such things, however, had barely any meaning to her father, who expected little from girls anyway.

"Very nice," he said perfunctorily.

The children felt as alienated from him as he did from them. They laughed at the way he mumbled to himself, plucked his beard, scribbled on the tablecloth, noisily picked food out from between his teeth.

Dinele took offense. Even though she herself found him disgusting and comical, she resented it when others did so, too, since this was a reflection on her, Haim Alter's daughter. She also made sure that he was presentable when he left the house.

"Simha Meir!" she scolded him. "Look at you, you're a mess!"

Even though he despised the discarded Hasidic name—especially from the lips of his wife—he welcomed her concern. "Put me to rights, Diana. I can't seem to knot my tie."

She knotted his tie and brushed the ashes off his lapel, but when he tried to slip an arm around her waist, she recoiled and looked at him so coldly that his blood froze.

He dropped his hand, crushed by her contempt. She stubbornly refused to call him by his new name or to speak German. She insisted on speaking Yiddish even when there was company present, much to his distaste. He had literally forced everyone in the envy-filled city to respect him, except his own wife. She wasn't impressed by his business acumen or by his rapid advance up the ladder. She never listened when he boasted of his latest accomplishment.

"Don't throw your cigar butts on the floor," she would interrupt him, "and don't drop your ashes on the tablecloth. . . . Use the ashtray like a human being."

Nor would she take any steps to become a Lodz society woman, as he strongly urged her to do. She wouldn't even discard the traditional wig, although she had always despised it, and he couldn't understand her attitude. "What is it, have you become so pious all of a sudden? It doesn't suit you to wear it."

"It suits me!" she replied spitefully.

Nor would she accompany him to the homes of his nouveau riche friends but kept herself busy with her children, with the running of the house, and, most of all, with her books.

She had never stopped living vicariously among her heroes and heroines. She exulted in their joys and commiserated with their sorrows. She spent more time in her parents' home than in her own and took daily walks with her mother. There was little to differentiate between them, both elegant and trim. They might have been sisters, rather than mother and daughter.

Priveh had barely aged over the years. Men still turned to look at her, even though she was already a grandmother. As always, she couldn't pass a store without buying something. She even dragged her daughter along to the confectionery for chocolate.

Max was irked by his wife's devotion to her parents. He felt that they were robbing him of what was legally his. Each time she went to her parents, he said again, "Again to your mother's? I wonder what there is there to draw you so urgently?"

He wasn't entirely convinced that she wasn't slipping money to her parents, but he was afraid to say anything to make her angry. He was anxious to wean her away from her mother and to befriend her with his new acquaintances. She was the wife of one of Lodz's most important men, and it wouldn't hurt him to be seen with a beauty other men envied.

But she wouldn't agree, and he threw himself into his work with renewed zeal, coming home late and leaving long before daylight.

His fortune grew, but he found neither rest nor satisfaction. He was resentful of his in-laws, his sisters, and, most of all, Yakub, who again had become the talk of Lodz. Max couldn't go anywhere without hearing of his brother's excesses.

"He'll end up begging door to door," Max predicted darkly. "It's only a matter of time."

But Yakub's phenomenal luck held out. Somehow he made contact with Maximilian Flederbaum himself, and between the card games, drinking bouts, and balls, he was appointed sales representative of the Flederbaum manufacturing firm.

Max turned pale as death when people gleefully brought him

the news of his brother's latest triumph. "A lie!" he shrieked, forgetting his German and reverting to homey Yiddish in his agitation.

Directly across from Max's office, Yakub opened his own offices and warehouse. Sparing no expense, he had signs erected displaying the Flederbaum medals, citations, and trademark— an anchor and key intertwined. A uniformed flunky guarded the portals and leaped to attention when the new sales representative pulled up in his splendid carriage, which he drove himself in the latest Lodz fashion with his coachman beside him.

Max ordered all his windows draped in green curtains to block out the sight, but wherever he looked, huge advertisements carried the name of Yakub Ashkenazi.

"He's turned the town on its ear!" people exulted to Max, recounting Yakub's successes by day and conquests by night. But even more startling triumphs were in the offing.

TWENTY-EIGHT

———

THE PALACE OF MAXIMILIAN FLEDERBAUM was alive with lights, brilliant company, and music. There was good reason to celebrate—the newly appointed governor, von Müller, had chosen to attend his first function in Lodz at the Flederbaum mansion instead of with the Barons Huntze.

For years the families had been waging a bitter feud for social and industrial supremacy. Just as elderly Germans recalled Heinz Huntze's humble beginnings, elderly Jews remembered when Mendel Flederbaum first came to town—a powerful, lusty youth wearing metal-reinforced heels on his heavy boots and carrying a stick with which to beat off gentile dogs and shepherds who combined to harass any passing Jew. He had walked all the way from the village of Wulka to seek his fortune in Lodz.

His father, the village innkeeper, had lost his livelihood when he had been outbid for the privilege of operating the tavern, granted by the local squire. Left without means of feeding his wife and dozen children, the father took his eldest son, Mendel, a cheese and a bottle of honey and went to Kazimierz to ask advice of the rabbi. The rabbi took the cheese and honey, invoked God's blessing on the two, wished them luck in whatever they undertook, and gave each a three-kopeck coin to carry on them at all times except for the Sabbaths and holidays.

The father took to the road, buying up wool and flax from the peasants. He wanted Mendel to help him, but Mendel had bigger ambitions. Robust, broad-shouldered, able to lift the heaviest cask and eject the most obstreperous bully from the tavern, filled with a lust for life, he felt destined for bigger things than toting a peddler's sack through villages.

From visiting Jews who stopped at the inn, he had heard tales of Lodz and its phenomenal growth, and his interest had been piqued. Into a bundle he packed a prayer shawl and phylacteries, several patched shirts, a loaf of bread, a hard cheese, some scallions, a pinch of salt, and a jackknife that a gentile had left in lieu of payment and that he, Mendel, had let stand point down in the ground for several days to render it pure.

Carrying this bundle, his gabardine cinched at the waist, thick pole in hand and several coins knotted in a corner of a red bandanna, he set out on his way. He roasted potatoes in fields, slept in barns or under the open sky, and directed his steps toward the alien, magnetic city where he would carve a life for himself. He was twenty years old, and he carried the rabbi's good-luck piece in a little pouch around his neck.

That was how the Jews of Lodz remembered him.

Heinz Huntze never forgave him his success and addressed him by his Jewish name. "How goes it, Mendel?" he would ask when they passed each other in their carriages. "I've got some nice remnants to sell you, dirt cheap. . . ."

"And I can sell you my horses," Flederbaum countered. "I'm buying a new team, and I can let you have the old ones at a bargain."

They had been needling each other this way for years, playing tricks on one another, each doing his best to make the other look bad. But while Huntze surpassed Flederbaum in the volume of business he did, Flederbaum more than outdid him in the opulence of his life-style.

He, Flederbaum, could never aspire to a title because of his religion, but he did wear an Order of St. Anne next to the good-luck piece the Kazimierz Rabbi had given him so long ago. He also proudly bore the title Meritorious Citizen, which had been conferred upon him by the imperial court and which he could pass along to his heirs. Likewise, the gold and silver medals earned by his factory decorated all his stationery.

To make Huntze even more jealous, he frequently redecorated his palace, always had fancier teams of horses, bigger and better pedigreed dogs, costlier wines, and more distinguished guests at his balls and parties. Ever since childhood, when his father had taken him to the squire's manor, Flederbaum had been drawn to wealth and luxury. He recalled how his father had bowed and kissed the skirt of the squire's garment; now that he had the means, he indulged himself in every way to surpass them, the gentiles. He even grew a luxuriant mustache, the ends of which he curled up in true Polish fashion. And just like the gentry, he spent a fortune on horses, kept his own racing stables and an army of trainers and jockeys. It cost him plenty, but his horses were the finest in Poland, and they earned him great acclaim in the newspapers.

Despite his natural aversion to dogs, he ran the finest pack of hunting dogs in the area, buying up choice breeds from local squires. He also purchased estates of impoverished noblemen and invited the governor and high-ranking civilian and military officials on hunts.

Personally revolted by the sight of blood, he forced himself to become a good marksman and massacred hordes of hares, wild ducks, and foxes on his private hunting preserves. Afterward his gamekeepers in their forest green uniforms and with feathers in their hats sounded their horns, and servants roasted the slaughtered beasts over campfires so that the gentlemen could enjoy an outdoor feast.

In the winters, balls were frequently held at the Flederbaum palace. The host twirled his mustache and danced the mazurkas and polonaises with the aplomb of a genuine blueblood. Unlike Huntze, he slipped into his role without any traces of his humble beginnings. But for all his assimilation, Flederbaum lived in dread of the Jewish God and strove to redeem himself in His eyes for the many sins he had committed.

Despite all his wealth and awesome power, he felt that he owed all his success to the lucky three-kopeck coin given him by the Kazimierz Rabbi. He tormented himself with the fact that he wasn't repaying this debt properly by shaving off his beard, desecrating the Sabbath, eating forbidden foods, committing adultery and countless other transgressions against God.

A superb businessman, he knew that books had to be balanced. God had bestowed so much good fortune upon him, and what had he done in return? He couldn't live the life of the pious Jew—he loved luxury and material pleasure too much for that. To make up for it, he devoted himself to charity. But since he wished no contact with the fanatic fringe, he appointed a man versed in Jewish matters to distribute his largess in the right places.

Besides Jewish causes, he had other obligations. When the workers at his plant needed a new church, he himself laid the cornerstone, for which the archdiocese put up a tablet on the building honoring him and his wife. But since he knew that the Jewish God frowned on this, he compensated by paying for the construction of a new synagogue.

He still recalled his teacher's lessons concerning the scale on which a man's sins and good deeds were weighed against each other. Lately the sins had begun to tip heavily. Two of his daughters had married converts and had promptly converted themselves. Considering everything, he could hardly observe a period of mourning for them but could only twirl his mustache and give his paternal blessing. Yet he trembled with fear. He knew that God took revenge on parents for the sins of their children. He knew that the fires of Gehenna stood ready to consume sinners while devils hung them by their tongues and tossed them from one end of hell to the other.

In the nights he shook with dread in his French four-poster bed and a cold sweat doused him. He screamed in his sleep until his wife, Elzbieta—née Elke—forgot her Polish and roused him in the more intimate Yiddish: "Mendel, Mendel, wake up! You frightened me so. . . ."

As if this weren't enough, his sons had turned out strange. Since childhood, their tutors and nannies had taken them to churches, taught them to genuflect, filled their heads with Jesus and Mary and tales of horror concerning Jewish ritual murders and such. At first, Flederbaum had thought nothing of this. He wanted the boys to grow up polite, inoffensive, presentable to the Polish world. But when he later asked them to accompany him to the synagogue on the Day of Atonement and to learn the mourner's prayer, they were horrified. They told him that the Jews had crucified Jesus, and they refused to eat matzos since it contained Christian blood.

Flederbaum was in mortal dread. He knew that a son's mourner's prayer could save a dead parent from the flames of Gehenna. Now even that avenue of escape was denied him. And he worried, for even though his hair and mustache were still coal black, it wasn't youth but the French barber's dye that kept them that way. He, Flederbaum, was already at an age when one had to contemplate the final, terrible journey, and he redoubled his charitable efforts in the hopes of rebalancing the scale.

He concentrated his philanthropy among the poor Jewish workers of Balut. He didn't hire them for his plant since they couldn't work on the Sabbath. Nor would he pay them the higher salaries they required to observe the Sabbath and buy kosher meat. Nor were they as physically durable as the gentiles, who didn't complain, weren't envious or disrespectful to their superiors, as Jews were wont to be.

But to make up for it, he strove to provide for their spiritual needs—gave money for Hanukah candles, for free infirmaries, for burial societies. He sent wagonloads of flour for the Passover matzos, and during periods of unemployment, he set up free soup kitchens.

Following his two daughters' conversion, he felt the urge to perform some enormous and compensating good deed with which to weigh the scale in his favor. He built a hospital for poor Jews, a Jewish hospital, where the food was kosher, where no crosses or icons were displayed, where an amulet hung on every doorpost, and where the male patients could wear their ritual fringes without fear of rebuke. There was even a little synagogue attached to the hospital where a quorum could pray for the sick.

No expenses were spared in building and equipping the hospital. The opening ceremonies were attended by the most distinguished citizens of Lodz. Dignitaries came from as far away as Warsaw. The driveway swarmed with carriages. The new chief rabbi of Lodz officiated with his imperial medal prominent upon his satin gabardine. All the youngsters from the primary and talmudic schools played hooky to catch a glimpse of the rabbi's legendary gold sword, which—although it was never seen—was a constant source of gossip.

The weavers of Balut left their looms and milled around their new hospital, where mounted police employed their trained horses to keep them at bay. A firemen's band sponsored by Flederbaum and attired in brass helmets played stirring martial airs.

But all this paled in comparison with the fact that the new governor himself attended the ceremonies.

For weeks, the Huntzes and Flederbaum had contested for the honor of being the first to entertain the new governor. Being barons, it might have appeared that the Huntzes had the advantage, but Flederbaum came up with the brilliant notion of naming the new hospital after the tsar and tsarina, and this patriotic gesture wasn't lost on the governor.

The Lodz Jews celebrated Flederbaum's victory over the Huntzes as if it were their own. In marketplaces, studyhouses, and bathhouses, people gloated over the victory over the gentile.

But on the forthcoming Sabbath much of this joy was vitiated.

Following the day's labors on Thursday, the longest workday of the week, Tevye and Nissan sat down and composed a biting proclamation against Maximilian Flederbaum, Governor von Müller, and the tsar himself. It contained the usual invective against the rich and powerful, couched in the customary bombastic language.

Keila shrieked at the men for wasting kerosene and threatened to douse them with a bucket of water, but they kept on writing, erasing, and correcting until at dawn they had the text ready. The whole following day Nissan made copies, assisted by several of his disciples. That evening, while Jews were visiting bathhouses, they sneaked into the synagogues and studyhouses and posted the proclamations. This way, even if the beadles caught them in the act, they would be prohibited by the laws of the Sabbath from tearing them down.

When the Jews at the houses of prayer read the proclamations, a great fear fell over them. The proclamations dared malign not only Flederbaum and the governor but the tsar himself. The Jews wanted to tear the terrible papers down, but they were prevented by the restrictions of the Sabbath. The problem was brought to the rabbi, and he promptly judged that the danger was serious enough to warrant breaking the law.

In the Flederbaum palace, all was gaiety and pomp. Yakub Ashkenazi danced with all the Flederbaum daughters, who insisted that he was much too dashing and attractive to be Jewish.

Governor von Müller enjoyed himself hugely, especially the thousands of rubles Flederbaum permitted him to win from him at cards. Warmed by the winnings, the wine, and the company of lovely ladies, the governor let it slip to his host that a new railroad line was soon to be built through the region. Flederbaum excused himself and sought out his new sales representative, whom he drew off to one side.

"I want you to buy up all the land in and around the city through which the line will be running," he instructed him. "This has to be done in the strictest confidence since no one but you and I know about it."

"I'll get on it the first thing in the morning," Yakub said.

"I know that I can count on you," Maximilian Flederbaum said in homey Yiddish, and put his arm around his young associate's waist. "And we won't have to go to the rabbi to arbitrate the amount of your commission. . . . And now you can go back to your ladies."

The orchestra struck up a polonaise.

TWENTY-NINE

———◆———

MAX ASHKENAZI TOOK THE SETBACK with the governor much harder than the Huntzes themselves. "Gentile louts!" he growled, thinking of his employers, who neglected business for women, hunting, duels, and other such passions of the blood.

True, the governor had paid a subsequent visit to the barons and had admired their collection of stuffed animals and weapons, but his visit had brought no financial gain, while Flederbaum had exploited his priority with an enormous windfall from the new railroad. Although this was supposed to be a secret, everyone knew of Flederbaum's preknowledge of the railroad's course—in Lodz there were no secrets.

Flederbaum had bought up all the adjoining parcels of land for a song, then sold them back to the government for tenfold the price. All Lodz spoke of Flederbaum's brilliant coup. The people who had sold him the land for next to nothing cursed their luck, and in the cafés and restaurants the merchants and brokers estimated the profits Flederbaum had made on the deal.

"His hospital was paid for in spades," was the general consensus.

"A millionaire has both this world and the world to come," others sighed with envy.

Max calculated his brother's share of the profits, and he plucked at his beard from frustration. "Those drunken bums," he muttered against his bosses, the barons, "those dunderheads. . . ."

Even though he was only their sales representative, he took a proprietary interest in everything that had to do with the factory. He was determined to become involved in its day-to-day operation.

He began, as usual, by making himself useful and available. In the very first year after taking over from his father, he in-

creased the sales volume several times over. He sent his salesmen to all parts of Russia; he wrote letters; he met with merchants and buyers; he ran around promoting the Huntze line,
urging, whetting appetites. He even went to Russia himself in
order to get a feel for the market.

With scant knowledge of Russian, by nature a man of sober
habits, he managed to worm his way into the graces of the
hard-drinking, gregarious, expansive Russian merchants. He
learned how to allow a companion to get sodden drunk while
he himself remained cold sober. He arranged things so that his
companions indulged their every folly while he avoided every
temptation offered him.

And although he was rewarded handsomely for his efforts
and even given a substantial bonus, he wouldn't be satisfied
until he supervised every step of the factory's operation.

From the very first day he set foot inside the plant, his darting eyes told him that its director, the ponderous Albrecht, was
lazy and totally inept. Albrecht's policy was to leave the factory
entirely on its own so that like a fine watch, it ran by itself.

Max made his initial inroads into the factory. He gave suggestions directly to the barons on how to achieve savings. when
to operate and when to shut down, what goods to prepare for
the coming season. His advice was inevitably correct, and the
Huntzes began to rely more and more on his judgment and not
make a move without first consulting him, their court Jew, as
they thought of him.

"Where actually did you learn all this, Ashkenazi?" they
asked in wonder.

"In the Academy Talmud under Professors Abbayeh and
Raba," Max replied, struggling to keep a straight face.

The situation began to irk the director. He perceived how
the little Jew was undermining his authority, but he didn't dare
bring about an open confrontation. He was too subservient to
his employers to do anything without their consent and too
lazy to bother. He took comfort in the young girls Melchior
provided him in steady profusion.

Max exerted more and more influence in the factory. No
longer even bothering to consult the barons, he did whatever
he considered necessary to enhance production and increase
profits. At the same time he kept providing his employers unlimited capital.

In time, Albrecht himself acknowledged him his superior
and did everything to curry his favor. Anyone who wanted
something from the barons now called on Max first so that he
might put in a good word for him with the Huntzes.

But the incident with Flederbaum and the governor served to negate all of Max's successes. Again Lodz spoke of Flederbaum and of his sales representative, who had been so instrumental in expediting the coup. Priveh made it a point to praise Yakub when she came calling. "You should have seen him, Dinele!" she gushed. "Like a prince riding down Piotrkow Street. Who could have dreamed it?"

Dinele listened and sighed, and Max's blood ran cold, even though he wouldn't let the women see his rage and jealousy. He lived for the day when the mill would be his. If his wastrel employers didn't give a hoot about the future of the firm, it behooved him to assume that burden.

First, he persuaded the barons to buy out Goetzke and to form a corporation. The barons seized upon this suggestion. They had long been anxious to be rid of that lowborn boor, who refused to acknowledge their title and continued to call them by their Christian names. But since they didn't want to take the time to carry out this action, they left it entirely to Max. For his efforts, he was awarded a large share of the stock in lieu of cash, at his own request.

Soon afterward he came up with a new and startling innovation.

Walking one day in the street, he suddenly spotted a woman wearing a red dress the color of which so dazzled his eyes that he was compelled to stop. The fabric was of such a vivid, bright hue that no dye known in Lodz could have achieved it.

Max stopped to look. The woman glanced back at him and moved on. He followed. Finally, she paused beside a factory fence. He stopped, too, but he said nothing to her, merely stared. She waited. She was plain, no longer young, but stoutly built.

"Why are you following me?" she asked.

"I like your dress," he replied quietly, embarrassed lest someone overhear.

"I'm a respectable woman," she said, and waited.

"Where did you buy that dress?" he asked.

The woman laughed. She knew that he was after something other than her dress but lacked the courage to say so. She noted that he was expensively dressed, and the situation struck her as comical.

"I'm no streetwalker," she said. "I'm a married woman."

"Maybe you would sell me your dress," he asked. "I'll pay you well for it."

The woman considered a moment. She knew that Jews murdered Christians for their blood, but she didn't think he appeared violent. She had also heard of queer men who made fetishes of women's garments.

"Why do you want my dress?" she asked. "Is the gentleman making fun of me?"

Max took out a gold ten-ruble piece and pressed it on her. Just as he had assumed, she couldn't resist and went with him.

She assumed that he would take her to some quiet place, but instead, he led her to his office. He sent out for a new expensive dress, and once she had changed into it, he took her cheap red one, which she had bought in Germany, where she had gone to work as a farm laborer, and handed her a gold imperial. She fled from the queer man, looking over her shoulder to make sure he didn't follow her and snatch back the money.

Max promptly sat down and unraveled the fabric. He knew little of women except that they loved bright, brilliant colors. He was constantly after his designers and chemists to come up with such a color, but they weren't sufficiently knowledgeable to give him what he wanted. Their reds always emerged dull, dark, and muddy.

He decided to go to Germany himself and learn their secrets of dyeing. Without informing even his closest associates, he acquired a foreign passport through Lippe Halfon and crossed the border. He went to Frankfurt am Main, which boasted a large colony of pious Jews. There, in the synagogues, kosher restaurants, and studyhouses, where even physicians weren't ashamed to be seen wearing skullcaps and where professors spent evenings studying the Gemara, he wormed his way into the confidence of the local inhabitants. Displaying his enormous erudition, he made a good impression on the local scholars. He didn't whine like the other Polish Jews who came to cadge money; on the contrary, he was always the first to pick up the check, and he bid a handsome sum for the privilege of reading from the Torah at the synagogue.

He was soon put in touch with a chemist, a specialist in colors and dyes despite his poor vision, which compelled him to wear dark glasses at all times. He persuaded the man to accompany him to Lodz, where he set him up in his own secret laboratory and where he kept him isolated from the world.

The chemist experimented until he came up with a color exactly matching that of the red dress. Once this was achieved, the factory went on round-the-clock shifts to produce the fabric for the upcoming season.

The red material caused an instant sensation, and orders started pouring in from all over Russia. The factory couldn't keep up with the demand, and soon the price of the fabric had to be raised. The women paid whatever prices were asked for the red fabric, which lent its wearer a younger, more alluring appearance.

Max took his share of the profits not in cash, but in Huntze stock.

Lodz forgot about Flederbaum and his sales representative and spoke of Max Ashkenazi's latest stroke of genius. "He's moving up," people murmured as he sat huddled and preoccupied in the huge carriage that he had received from his employers in reward for his services.

He would have felt more natural walking, but it was now beneath him to do so. He tried to interest his wife in taking advantage of the carriage. "Diana," he offered, "if you have some errand to do, I'll be glad to take you along. There's lots of room."

"No, I'd rather walk with Mama," she replied.

Out of rage, Max ignored the tipped hats of the passersby and made believe he hadn't even seen them.

THIRTY

LODZ CAME TO A COMPLETE STANDSTILL. Like a glutton who has eaten so much he can't take another bite until he has emptied his stomach, the city was bloated with goods.

Not only the large industrialists but the petty manufacturers as well had bullied and prodded their workers to increase production. And in all this ferment, no cash exchanged hands. Everything ran on credit, on IOUs.

A merchant's son married a merchant's daughter on IOUs. The young groom endorsed his father-in-law's notes and obtained yarn and cotton on credit. He let the yarn out to a subcontractor and paid him with IOUs. The subcontractor endorsed the notes and paid off his workers with them. The workers added their own clumsy signatures and used the notes to pay for all their necessities.

From cities and towns all over Poland came merchants and secondhand clothes dealers, to buy up wagonloads of goods for which they paid with IOUs. The sellers exchanged the notes for goods, services, labor. Notes were used to pay shop clerks, housemaids, tailors, teachers.

Jobbers and commission agents raced throughout Russia, buying up huge masses of goods, for which they paid with IOUs. Everything in Lodz was available for a signature. With notes, Jews bought honors in the synagogues and made donations to their rabbis. With notes, playboy-clerks caroused in restaurants and bought wedding presents for their brides-to-be. Even the whores in the brothels and the doctors who later treated their venereal diseases were paid off with IOUs.

Whoever was clever and cunning enough could establish a business, buy expensive furniture and jewelry, and put on a big front without possessing so much as a groschen. Each day ambitious weavers left their looms and became petty wheeler-dealers. All that was required was a bit of larceny in the soul, the ability to sign one's name, and the fifty kopecks needed to purchase a blank IOU, the only commodity in Lodz that couldn't be obtained on credit.

Independent of cash, fired by the prospect of quick riches, made reckless by the fierce competition, Lodz seethed and bustled without system or order and with total disregard for the rules of supply and demand. People schemed, finagled, wheedled, and conspired, caught up in the mad, headlong rush of the city. It was a sham existence built on dreams, artifice, and paper. The only base of reality and substance was the workers.

Suddenly it all ground to a halt. A large bone stuck in Lodz's throat, and the city disgorged everything it had swallowed through years of unrestrained gluttony.

To compound the problem, a drought settled over the land. The Russian Orthodox priests donned gold- and silver-embroidered vestments and carried their icons into the fields to ask Jesus and His holy mother to have mercy upon man and beast. But the sun didn't cease beating down day after monotonous day.

Cattle dropped from thirst and hunger. And when harvesttime finally came around, the rains came in torrents and turned the fields into soggy rot so that the little grain that remained couldn't be reaped. The unburied animal carcasses helped spread cholera, typhoid fever, and scarlet fever. In the villages of the Ukraine, peasants drove out the Jews, who—it was rumored—had poisoned the wells. Peasants used sticks and pitchforks on students who had come to the villages to root out the epidemics with lime, pitch, and carbolic acid.

The peasants stopped coming to towns to sell their produce, and the merchants were stuck with the goods they had imported from Lodz for the harvest season. No one had the cash with which to pay off due notes, and demands for payment began pouring down on Lodz by the tens of thousands. The manufacturers who depended upon banks for cash were left stranded as bank after bank failed.

The first to go under were the little fish, the small manufacturers, the subcontractors, the petty yarn and cotton dealers, the dry goods merchants, shopkeepers, commission agents, brokers, and the thousands of others who had gathered like flies around the jar of honey that was Lodz. All the credit-based enterprises went up like straw in the mighty conflagration. People scurried about like poisoned mice, trying to sell notes for a hundredth of their face value, but there were no buyers. The great paper chain that had held the city together crumbled, sending victim afer victim to his destruction.

The millionaire industrialists managed to withstand the shock. Sustained by their cash reserves, they merely waited for the crisis to subside. It no longer paid to operate when finished goods were worthless while raw materials soared in price from day to day. Tens of thousands of unemployed workers wandered idly through the streets.

In Balut the handlooms were silent. The tailors, hosiers, cobblers, and gaitermakers draped their machines like so many shrouded corpses awaiting burial.

"It's good only for toilet paper," grocers snapped when a worker timidly offered a note in payment for potatoes or a loaf of bread.

The more affluent pawned the gold and diamonds they had bought during better times and sold the goods in their warehouses for whatever they could get. Others managed in other ways. Although the weather was already on the cool side, fires started breaking out mysteriously in factories, warehouses, and spinneries. All night fiery tongues licked at the heavens, sturdy firehorses pounded over the poorly paved Lodz streets, firemen's trumpets roused people from their sleep, and as soon as the newsboys began to cry the day's headlines, people leaped out of bed to read who had balanced their books during the night.

Usurers and pawnbrokers made quick fortunes as people sold their remaining possessions to smuggle themselves across the border into Germany and, then, on to America.

Only the workers and artisans had nothing to sell, barter, or turn into food or a means of escape. Gentile weavers went back to their native villages. Unmarried peasant maidens went back to their parents to help out in the fields. Jewish youths from the provinces, who had come to Lodz to make their fortunes, went back to their hometowns. The young married men parted temporarily from their wives and children, whom they sent back to their in-laws until the bad times passed.

The local residents who had nowhere to go wandered around in a daze. Landlords evicted those who couldn't pay their rent, and the homeless were forced to sleep in empty cellars and hang around bakeries, trying to warm their chilled bones by the glowing ovens. People went out into the woods and dug pits to protect themselves from the cold.

Unemployed female workers sold their bodies for a crust of bread or a bed for the night. Poor Jewish mothers offered their

children to employers for something to eat. Workers begged
bosses for the chance to earn no wages but a plate of groats or a
cup of chicory.

In the poorer sections, typhus, diphtheria, and scarlet fever
raged. The police doused the gutters with lime and carbolic
acid to keep the epidemics from spreading, but to no avail.

Flederbaum Hospital worked day and night, but it couldn't
keep pace with the cemetery. The Jewish industrialists responded to the challenge. Flederbaum invited the wealthiest
people to his palace and organized a committee in behalf of
Balut's poor. Soup kitchens were set up for those still able to
eat; doctors and barber-surgeons were sent to attend the ailing;
shrouds were provided for corpses.

Flederbaum came each day to Balut in his carriage. He flung
mounds of change to urchins and visited the homes of the
most severely deprived to whom he personally dispensed one-,
five-, even ten-ruble notes. He even rolled up the sleeve of his
frock coat and helped members of the Aid to the Ill Society rub
down with alcohol the belly of a sick worker. He also helped
the members of the Burial Society prepare the corpse of a dead
weaver for burial. News of these acts of mercy swiftly spread
through Lodz, and in the synagogues and the bathhouses of
Balut, Jews felt as exalted as if their personal angel of mercy
had come to aid them in their hour of need.

They forgave Flederbaum his gentile ways and even his
daughters' conversions. They felt that he had earned his golden
throne in paradise, and he agreed with them. The only house
where his sainthood wasn't acknowledged was the dark cellar
room of Tevye the World Isn't Lawless. Like all the weavers,
Tevye was out of work. His wife stood in the street all day with
a basket of homemade pickles and came home at night with a
tiny handful of groschen and a large mouthful of imprecations
and curses. The smaller children hawked boxes of candy, while
the older ones roamed about on their own, seeking food and a
place to rest their heads. Inside the cellar it was damp, smoky,
and barren, but Tevye was oblivious to it all. There weren't
enough hours in the day for what he had to do.

Ragged, freezing, the Russian bashlyk wound around his
throat and a fur hat on his head, Tevye raced around all day,
exhorting the workers, blazing with the righteousness of his
cause, distributing proclamations he and Nissan had composed,
which revealed the causes of the crisis, calling for a struggle
against the manufacturers and merchants, the rabbis and clerics,
the police and the military, the governor and the tsar himself.

Elderly weavers laughed at him; women made indelicate

gestures to indicate that he was touched in the head.

"Tevye is displeased with the tsar—well, what do you think about that?" people jested.

His own wife cursed him and vilified him as if he were lower than slime. "Community billy goat!" she shrieked. "Jailbird! Burned-out torch!"

He didn't even hear her. Pale, emaciated, sharp Adam's apple bobbing within the bashlyk, eyes burning, he was everywhere at once, his nose thrust into every gathering, his ear alert for every remark. His words poured out sharp and angry and full of conviction. He concentrated most of his effort in the very soup kitchens Flederbaum had set up in Balut for starving workers.

As people sat around the bare tables, eating the black bread and groats from earthenware bowls, he harangued them mercilessly. When the elderly weavers blessed Flederbaum for the meager lunches they were enjoying, Tevye went nearly berserk.

Like seeds dropped into black, rich soil, his words fell upon the armies of Balut's poor and suffering Jews. Not only the workers but laid-off shop clerks, bookkeepers, cutters, and designers—who had always held themselves above the others—now listened to him with mixed emotions.

They realized that the paper notes for which they had sweated and bled had been nothing but a sham and a delusion. They had been cast out into the street alongside the common laborers, and the words of the agitators found a warm reception within their affronted souls.

More and more proclamations blossomed upon the peeling walls of Lodz. In synagogues, markets, train stations, offices, even on the walls of police stations revolutionary posters sprouted in the nights. People gathered before them until the policemen and janitors tore them down.

In the midst of eating, people leaped up to heap invective on the industrialists, the police, and the tsar. The wealthy ladies distributing the free meals were outraged and called the police to restore order.

On the outskirts of town, in Konstantin Forest, swarms of people gathered to argue and sing revolutionary songs. Hunger and need assumed a meaning, a justification. Out of the bitterness of deprivation, the people nurtured the sweet flavor of hope, which lent them the strength to endure the bad times.

"More literature, more, more!" Tevye demanded of Nissan. "The masses are finally waking up. . . ."

Nissan couldn't keep up with the demand. He translated, reworked, transformed the material into simple Lodz Yiddish so that the context would touch the heart and move the spirit. Everything had to be rewritten by hand. His disciples, the yeshiva students, couldn't work fast enough to keep up.

In the evenings Nissan dropped whatever he was doing and went to the German beer halls, where the weavers sat in their velvet trousers, drinking huge steins of beer and puffing on cheap cigars. Following Bismarck's persecution of the enlightened adherents of the Lassalle socialist movement, many German workers had fled the country. Some had gone to Amerca; others had settled in Poland. They were good workers, exacting and honest, and they promptly found employment in the Lodz mills. Some had even become bosses.

Corpulent, amiable, devoted to their beer and cigars, they spent their evenings in the taverns alongside their long-settled compatriots. But unlike the older generation, they didn't attend church, didn't join glee clubs, but kept together, read contraband books that they received from Germany, and sang revolutionary songs at their private get-togethers. Just as they had in Germany, they maintained their small Lassalle societies and stayed true to their socialist ideals.

It was to these weavers that Nissan now turned. In the broken German that he had taught himself from Moses Dessauer's commentaries and from philosophy books, he called on the weavers to join in the struggle, and although his manner of speaking was alien, his conclusions agreed with their own. "True, true," they acknowledged, draining the last of their beer.

Along with his former classmate Simha Meir (now Max) Ashkenazi, Nissan favored steam over handweaving. He knew that the manual loom had no future and had to give way to the machine, forcing the handworkers out of work and out of the proletarian class. He himself worked among the Balut Jews and incited them against their bosses, but he didn't deceive himself that this was a class struggle, a fight between the proletariat and the bourgeoisie. More accurately, it was a domestic quarrel between pauper and pauper.

He knew that most handweavers weren't workers in the true sense of the word. Each of them yearned to become a boss or a subcontractor. He saw what a bittter life the subcontractors themselves led, how they, too, were oppressed and exploited. The true proletariat was the workers in the steam factories, where no Jews were employed. Seeing them by the thousands, hurrying to work, carrying their lunch pails, he envisioned them as the cadres of the inevitable revolution predicted by the implacable laws of Marxism—the shock troops in the coming struggle for freedom. Let the factories proliferate for now; let the manufacturers thrive, build, grow rich. The future belonged to those who raced in the predawns to beat the siren's wails. In the tread of their wooden clogs he heard the echo of the liberation. It was for them that the industrialists built up and concentrated their capital so that when it grew huge, bloated, and overripe, it would burst like a balloon and pass over to the workers.

Balut, on the other hand, demonstrated poverty. Here there was no concentration, but decentralization, a deterioration which was unwholesome, unpromising.

No, he didn't believe in Balut. He was drawn to the chimneys, the smoke, the pounding of the machines, the call of the sirens. It was from there that the redemption would come. All that was needed was to educate the masses, to make them aware, and he met daily with the German refugees from Bismarck in their broad velvet trousers, haranguing them through the difficult days of the crisis to join in the struggle which was theirs by the nature of Marxist dogma.

The person entrusted with the task of transporting the illicit material between Nissan and the German weavers was Tevye's daughter Bashke, the only member of the household who didn't encourage her mother's diatribes against her father and hung on his every word. A spinner for a subcontractor, for whom she worked long hours without earning enough even to buy herself a decent dress or a pair of shoes, she understood her father's passionate call for justice and equality, although she was only fifteen.

"Mama," she defended him each time her mother vilified him anew, "you should be proud to have such a husband."

"Such pride will break me in little pieces," the mother mocked. "Remember, Bashke, don't let yourself be led astray by your loon of a father, or you'll end up in shackles next to him. . . ."

Bashke mended her father's clothes, patched his shirts, and cooked his meals while her mother was out hawking her pickles. When he finally came home nights weary and worn, she made up his bed.

Her father held her close. "*You* understand me, Bashke, you alone do. You don't consider me a madman, do you, daughter of mine?"

"Daddy," she replied tenderly, pressing her dark head to his breast, "I will always be with you."

In the murky cellar room, amid the gloom, hunger, and deprivation, Bashke was Tevye's only consolation. After the days of ferment against the unjust world, the swarthy girl with the green, mysterious eyes was his beacon, his only happiness.

"Bashke, come to Daddy's bed," he urged her. "You're still a little girl, after all; don't be ashamed to lie next to your daddy."

"Yes, Daddy," Bashke cooed, settling herself in happily beside him and kissing him quietly so that her mother shouldn't wake up and scream about the "honeymoon," as she indelicately described it.

Inside the room, it was moist, cold. Rats scurried and squealed out of a rage evoked by hunger. Often they leaped right over the sleepers. But the father and daughter didn't see or hear them. They were too caught up in mutual tenderness and affection.

No less than her love for her father was her love for Nissan, the frequent visitor at her house. For hours on end she lay awake on her bench bed and watched the tall young man sitting at the table and writing the subversive literature with her father. Never in her deprived life had she imagined that she would be brought in contact with such an intelligent, educated man. An ignorant girl barely able to sign her name, she didn't ever permit herself to think of herself in the same breath with Nissan. She only felt happy and warm that when lying on her bench bed next to a sister, she was privileged to watch him for hours on end as he scribbled away, handsome and romantic as any poet.

Now she came often to his room on her errands to pick up the subversive pamphlets and she was so thrilled that she prayed to God that the crisis should never end. With pounding heart she sat on the edge of the chair, unable to indulge herself the whole seat, and gazed at Nissan's bony, expressive hands as they flew swiftly over the paper. And as he placed the papers in her basket, she trembled with rapture when their hands accidentally touched.

"Be careful, Bashke," he cautioned her. "In the event you are caught, don't say where you got the material."

She yearned to tell him that she would let them strip the flesh from her bones before she'd do anything to cause him a moment's harm, but she couldn't bring herself to speak, and with head bowed, she left the house, clutching the basket to her breast.

THIRTY-ONE

IN THE ROOM OF former veterinary student Marcin Kuczinski, who had been expelled from the institute for his membership in the Polish Social Revolutionary party, Proletariat, the illicit printing press worked with swift efficiency.

"How goes it, Felix?" Kuczinski asked, flipping back the strands of flaxen hair that had a habit of falling down into his eyes.

"The first copies are smudging," replied Felix, a tall young Jew with a pince-nez clamped over his sharp beak of a nose. "But the subsequent ones will be fine. Hand me the paper, Marcin."

Off to the side by the kitchen sat two girls. The fair-haired one with the small cross around her throat was the teacher Wanda Chmiel, who lived with Kuczinski. Next to her on a small stool sat the biologist Maria Licht, dark-eyed, dark-haired, and swarthy as a gypsy. Together they dried the damp, poorly printed proclamations at the stove, then stacked them in even piles.

"Say what you will, Felix," Marcin said, shaking the hair from his gray eyes, "but I don't care for these proclamations. They won't grab the workers by the throat."

"That's what the *Tsay-ee-ḳah* has put together," Felix replied, coating the rubber roller with ink.

"The *Tsay-ee-ḳah*, the *Tsay-ee-ḳah*," Marcin mocked. "I don't like the *Tsay-ee-ḳah*'s style. Soft and intellectual. Not for workers."

Felix put down the roller a moment and looked at his friend evenly. "How can you say this of the *Tsay-ee-ḳah*?" he asked in a shocked voice.

"You remind me altogether of a Talmudist." Marcin laughed. "You speak of the *Tsay-ee-ḳah* in the same pious tone Jews speak of their lawmakers. If it were up to me, I'd write proclamations that would make the workers drool with pleasure. Something so gory that—"

"With you it's always blood, Marcin," Felix said, and grimaced, "carnage and murder. That's not the way. You must appeal to man's reason, not his instinct."

"That's because I'm a veterinarian and I know that a dead horse must be skinned without ceremony, while you're a lawyer who deals only in words and papers."

"I believe in the power of the word," Felix said, applying the wet roller to paper.

"Above all, you're a Jew who's afraid of blood," Marcin added, laughing. "With such appeals you might reach the anemic tailors and weavers of Balut, but not our crowd. To them, you have to talk their language . . . something really gory. The whole *Tsay-ee-kah* is made up of Jews and intellectuals. They don't know our workers. They preach morality to them like in a synagogue. . . ."

Felix put down the roller and wiped his hands on a sheet of paper. "Marcin," he said uneasily, "it's not the first time you've brought up the same thing already. I don't care for this kind of talk. It stinks of anti-Semitism, which has no place in our ranks."

"Oho!" Marcin sneered. "And in you the Jew is always ready to pop out. When it really comes down to it, you're like any sensitive Semite. . . . Well, you'd better print up some more of that crap, moralist of mine. It's getting late, and we still have lots to do. You give me the roller, and you do the setting!"

Felix stationed himself by the small tray of type, where he searched with unskilled fingers for each letter separately.

He wasn't an experienced typesetter. He was an ex-law student who, unlike his friend, Marcin, had given up his studies of his own free will, since like all the revolutionary-minded students at Russian universities, he considered it a sin to devote his time to studies and to prepare for a personal career at a time when the working classes were enslaved.

Even though his father was a rich man and the owner of several glassworks and brick factories, Felix Feldblum had set himself on the side of the poor. He stirred up the workers of his own father's factories to demand higher wages and shorter hours. He even led them in a strike against his father. After his father died and left his entire fortune to him, his only son, Felix, liquidated everything and turned all the proceeds over to the Proletariat party to be used in the task of liberating the Polish peasant and worker from the shackles of the tsar and his exploiters.

Although Felix Feldblum was the son of a Jew and he knew

that Jews were even more terribly oppressed than the Polish peasants and workers, he chose to devote his life to the Christian poor.

Even as he was growing up, he had been alienated from Jews, from their language and way of life. Everything in the village where his father's glassworks and brick factories were located was gentile—the maids in his house, his governesses, his teachers, all his father's visitors and friends. Even the parish priest was a frequent guest at the house. His father considered himself a full-fledged Pole, and the only Jews who entered his home were the merchants and brokers from the surrounding cities and towns or village peddlers, who came to buy raw goods from the peasants. And Felix felt no kinship toward these queer, black-garbed strangers, who stood with hats humbly in hand and who spoke such a fractured Polish.

When he grew older, his father sent him to his brother's place in Moscow to be educated first at the *Gymnasium,* then at the university. Just as everything at home had been Polish, everything at his uncle's house was Russian.

At the *Gymnasium* and later at the university, he was always among Christians. He knew that he was a Jew—the others often reminded him of this defect—but his Jewishness was like a plague or proud flesh that insinuates itself into the body and must be tolerated as some loathsome burden and nuisance.

The only thing that linked him with Jews was the inscription in his passport designating him as of the Jewish faith, but he had never believed in any religion, much less the one to which he was assigned. As soon as he was drawn into revolutionary circles, he lost whatever Jewish feelings might still have lingered within his consciousness.

He knew that Jews were oppressed, too, but he also knew from his teachers and friends that the Jews were mostly merchants, storekeepers, brokers, and black marketeers—a class that was unproductive, that didn't work the land and only lived off the peasants and workers it exploited.

Nor could the Jews be counted on to make the revolution. They were a weak, inconspicuous minority. The liberation of the land would be brought about by the millions of peasants who were the heart and the soul of the land, and freedom would then come to all, Jews included. The revolution wouldn't differentiate between peoples or nations. The revolution would free Poland as well.

Felix Feldblum became a narodnik—a populist. As soon as the Polish students established their own radical circles in the Russian universities and formed their own party, the Proletariat,

Feldblum joined them. He left the university months before earning his degree. He didn't want to be a member of the privileged class at a time when workers were starving. He went back to Poland, and with all his innately Jewish fervor he threw himself into his messianic task.

Following in the footsteps of the Russian narodniks, Feldblum went out among the Polish peasants to spread the word. When the party shifted its emphasis to the cities, he set up his headquarters in Lodz and launched his campaign to radicalize the Christian factory workers.

Although Lodz was full of Jewish workers of every kind, to Felix Feldblum's eyes the only Jews present were the shopkeepers, brokers, jobbers, and assorted tradesmen—a frenzied, oddly garbed gang of connivers, whose only interest lay in money, money, and more money. Opposed to them were the thousands of gentile factory workers, former sons of the soil whom deprivation had transported from their villages to the big city. In contrast with the haggling, wildly gesticulating Jews, they struck Feldblum as stalwart, direct, honest proletarians, and as usual, he firmly took their side against the exploitative Jewish bourgeoisie.

Not always was this devotion reciprocated. Although he spoke Polish as well as any Christian, without the trace of an accent, his name and appearance militated against him. Even as he had harangued against his own father, the local priest had gazed at him askance. "That's all very nice and fine of you, young man, but you should leave such matters to us. You simply don't understand the spirit of the Christian people. . . ."

Even within the party, Feldblum often heard pointed allusions to his heritage despite the fact that all comrades were considered equal. And although he yearned to address the workers, the party assigned him such internal tasks as writing articles, translating literature, and working the press.

When he poked fun at priests, the standard party line, the others appeared uncomfortable. "These are sacred things, after all," they mumbled

Feldblum knew that these vestiges would be rooted out in time; still, he felt a deep sense of hurt. Nor did he concur with Marcin Kuczinski that the way to win over the people was with blood and gore. For all his non-Jewish upbringing, he strongly believed in ethics and in the historical imperative of the revolution. And since he was assigned internal tasks toward that end, he performed them with fervently inbred zeal.

The time was particularly auspicious to foment unrest. Following the long period of unemployment, the workers were angry and embittered. There was another, most significant factor. Some years earlier the first of May had been designated a universal workers' holiday by the Second Socialist International in Paris, a day commemorating the struggle for freedom and equality.

For Feldblum, this was the first holiday of his life. Neither at his father's nor at his uncle's house was a Jewish holiday ever celebrated, and he wanted the coming festival to be particularly meaningful. All the workers in the city would stay out; all the factories would shut down. The workers would parade in closed ranks, demonstrating their power to their masters and exploiters. They would also voice Poland's protest against the tsarist slave masters. And Feldblum set the type for the proclamation with particular fervor.

"They will respond to our call," he assured Kuczinski. "All Lodz will come to a halt. Mark my words. . . ."

Late at night, when the streets were deserted and the March winds tore at the naked branches of the few isolated Lodz trees, Felix Feldblum went home. Ever the experienced conspirator, he first sniffed the area to see if anyone was following. Then, as an extra precaution, he and his companion, Maria Licht, each went off separately on a roundabout course to the residence that they shared.

"You weren't followed?" he asked the swarthy girl, who arrived after him.

"No," she said.

"Neither was I," he said, relieved.

Although they posed as a married couple—he as a commission agent and she as his wife—they slept in separate beds and never touched each other.

"I wish I were a few weeks older so I could see how the workers will react to our May Day call," he said in the dark. "What do you think, Maria, will they take a stand?"

"They'll take a stand," she replied with assurance.

From outside, the first factory whistles sounded. In the poor sections, kerosene lamps illuminated the windows as men and women rose to go to work.

THIRTY-TWO

———————◆———————

As MAY APPROACHED, Lodz grew uneasy.

The workers did go out, but it wasn't on May 1, as the revolutionaries planned, or even on May 3, which was the Polish national holiday secretly observed by the patriots. They struck on May 5, which was an ordinary working day.

After nearly a year of unemployment the factories had gone back on full schedule. But since the manufacturers wanted to make up the losses they had suffered during the crisis, they cut the workers' salaries by 10 percent. The workers, already in debt up to their ears and inflamed by the agitations of the revolutionaries and the patriotic societies, both of which, for their own reasons, called for an uprising and an insurrection, wouldn't accept the pay cut and struck.

As usual, there were scabs. When the striking workers couldn't verbally persuade those still working to walk off the job, they resorted to violence. Armed with sticks and poles, they stormed the factories. The stokers barely managed to restrain them from smashing the boilers, which would have caused the factories to blow up with everyone in them.

Weavers, spinners, stokers, and teamsters marched, accompanied by the usual street loafers and riffraff. Singing revolutionary and patriotic songs, they went from factory to factory, forcing workers away from their machines. The factory managers ordered their watchmen to bolt the gates, but the mobs smashed down all barriers.

"Death to the bloodsuckers and leeches!" voices cried.

The smaller manufacturers became intimidated and promptly capitulated, but the bigger ones wouldn't yield.

In the Huntze mill the workers sent a delegation, but the barons refused to meet with it.

Caps in hand, bowing and scraping their muddied feet on the threshold, the members of the delegation timidly approached Director Albrecht. "What do you want?" he asked them curtly.

"We humbly petition the illustrious director not to cut our pay," their spokesman said.

"I'll take it up with Their Excellencies the barons," the illustrious director said. "In the meantime, get back to work!"

"First, we would like some assurance of your intentions, Illustrious Sir."

"We give no assurances," the director muttered angrily. "That's a favor only Their Excellencies the barons can bestow, should they so desire. But first you must go back to work. Later we'll see further."

"Begging the Illustrious Sir's pardon," one of the older workers said, "can at least those with wives and children be spared the pay cut? We can't feed our families on the lowered wages. . . ."

"Who in blue blazes told you to marry and father brats if you can't feed them?" Director Albrecht blurted. "The factory isn't obliged to pay for your—"

The blood rushed to the workers' heads.

"Damn swine!" one of the delegation muttered.

"Swabian pig!"

"Trample the fat slob for our daughters he corrupted!"

"Kick in his beer belly for insulting decent women and children!"

Albrecht perceived that his situation had grown precarious, and he started to rise from his chair, but before he could move his ponderous legs, the workers were upon him. Melchior tried to intercede, but he caught a fist in the face for his troubles.

The workers dragged the terrified director out by his arms and legs like a steer to slaughter. The crowd in the courtyard sent up a chorus of jeers that sent a chill through Albrecht's heart.

"Hang him!" men cried. "Skin him alive!"

"Drop his pants, and flog him!" women urged.

The workers draped a sack over the director's head, thrust a broom into his hand, and after sitting him in a wheelbarrow used to cart bricks and dung, they wheeled him through the factory courtyard.

"Your mother!" the men jeered.

"For you!" the women shrieked, showing him their behinds.

Next, the mob headed for Flederbaum's mill. Their lust was aroused—they wanted blood.

"String up the damn Jew!" voices cried. "Smash his palace!"

They rushed the gate, but it was already guarded by a row of armed soldiers under the command of an officer and by a dozen policemen headed by a huge, bearded Russian commissary, whom Flederbaum had alerted well in advance. Flederbaum himself sat inside his luxurious office with a loaded revolver by his side. Next to him sat the police chief himself with several of his aides. As the policemen led the workers in one by one from the factory yard, the chief interrogated them on the spot. He only posed the questions; he didn't wait to hear the answers.

"Why aren't you at work?"

When the worker would try to justify himself, the chief cried, "Silence!" And he slammed the table.

If the worker still tried to speak, the policemen silenced him with their fists. The chief didn't even bother to question some of the workers. "I don't like the looks of that one," he would say. "Hold him on suspicion. . . ."

When the mob of detained workers filled the corridor, they were surrounded by policemen and marched off to the station. But the crowd gathered outside the factory closed ranks and wouldn't let the arrested workers be taken away. The officer guarding the gate drew his sword and ordered the mob to disperse. "Break it up, sons of bitches, or I'll give the order to fire!" he threatened.

The crowd didn't budge. The men pushed even closer toward the gates, and the women waved kerchiefs and cooed at the soldiers, "Lads, you wouldn't shoot down a fellow Christian. . . ."

The officer knew that soldiers were susceptible to female entreaties, and he was afraid to delay any longer. "Take aim!" he cried in a resounding voice.

Rifles were raised to shoulders.

The officer hesitated another moment to give the mob a chance to back up. When no one stirred, he barked curtly, "Fire!"

Several dozen shots shattered the strained silence. Smoke, shouts, cries, and the sound of running feet filled the air. With bayonets fixed, the soldiers prodded the human mass, clearing the square. Policemen seized people at random and put them under arrest.

When order had been restored, the police chief treated the officer to a real Havana cigar, which he had obtained from Flederbaum, and pressed his hand in congratulations.

"Tomorrow the factories will be back to normal," he said with a wink.

Despite his prediction, the factories weren't back to normal the next day. By the tens of thousands, the workers turned out into the streets in their Sunday best and began attacking policemen, gathering outside the jails and demanding the release of their comrades. Others demanded to see the police chief himself.

The night before, a worker had seized the chief's dog, a wolfhound of the purest breed, and had stabbed it in revenge for the beating his father had gotten at the station. The police seized the perpetrator and brought him before the chief. "A hundred lashes!" the chief ordered. "And don't spare the whip!"

By the seventieth stroke the victim no longer cried or kicked his legs, but the whipper didn't stop until he had recorded a full 100 strokes. When he ordered the worker to rise, the man was already dead. The chief berated the whipper. "Idiot, you should have given him a breather every twenty-five strokes or so!"

He had the dead man hustled out of town and buried in some deserted spot, but somehow, the news leaked out, and the strikers demanded their fellow worker's body. "He's got to be given a decent Christian funeral, not be tossed on some heap like a dog!" they growled.

The police chief called out the firemen to hose down the inflamed mob with cold water, but this served only to ignite the workers' ire. They grabbed cobblestones and began to smash the panes of the headquarters building.

In other streets, mobs attacked police stations and government liquor stores. The chief panicked and wired the governor in Piotrkow. "What orders?"

The governor wired the governor-general in Warsaw. "What orders?"

The governor-general wired Petersburg. "What orders?"

Petersburg wired Warsaw. "Crush without mercy."

Warsaw wired Piotrkow. "Crush without mercy."

Piotrkow wired Lodz. "Crush without mercy."

The police chief wired the governor. "Short of troops. Send Cossacks."

The governor wired Warsaw. "Short of troops. Send Cossacks."

Warsaw promptly dispatched a regiment of Cossacks, but in the interim, the rioters ruled Lodz.

First, they smashed open the liquor stores and drank up the wares. The party leaders pleaded with them in vain to conduct themselves with dignity. People stretched out in the gutters, lapping up spilled whiskey. When they were decently sodden, they lit torches and raced through the streets, looking for new sources of amusement.

They seized a Polish tailor, a hunchback with a great drooping mustache, and proclaimed him King of Poland.

"Long live the Polish king!" the mob cried, carrying the terrified wretch on their shoulders. "Hurrah!"

The women ran up to kiss the king's twisted feet.

The mood of the mob suddenly shifted.

"Let's get the Jews!"

"On to Balut—to Balut!"

The rioters poured into Jewish stores, dragged Jewish merchants out of droshkies, and beat them severely. The storekeepers fled their shops, leaving their goods to the mob's mercy. Jewish women swooned. The doors and gates of Jewish houses were nailed shut.

A number of Jews made a stand. Butchers, teamsters, blacksmiths, and porters used axes, clubs, and crowbars to fend off the attackers. On Feiffer Lane, which was inhabited by magicians, organ grinders, and assorted criminals, the residents poured boiling water down on the intruders. One young butcher swung his ax so zestfully that he clove a gentile's skull in two.

The gentiles drew back, but they took along their mutilated comrade and displayed his corpse in the streets. "See what the Christ killers have done to a good Christian!" they cried.

At dawn the Cossacks reached Lodz, accompanied by Governor von Müller. The police chief rode out to meet him.

"What's the situation in the city?" the governor asked.

"A pogrom against the Jews, Excellency," the chief reported, saluting.

"Excellent!" the governor said with a smile. "That should keep them busy for a while. . . ."

He leaned toward the colonel of the regiment who was sharing his carriage. "We'll camp here a day or two until the Polish dogs have had their fill; then we'll give them a taste of powder."

After three days of riot and carnage the Cossacks slowly rode into town. Sated with blood, besotted with drink, the rioters offered no resistance.

The Cossacks rounded up hundreds of men and women and packed them off to jails. The "Polish King" was brought before the governor. Trembling, his hair and mustache awry, he cowered before the magnificently uniformed governor.

"So you're the King of Poland?" the governor asked with a smile.

"I'm innocent, Your Worship," the terrified hunchback whined. "I'm a tailor by trade, a patcher. I was walking in the street when some people grabbed me and said I was the King of Poland. I swear before Jesus and His sacred wounds—"

"What's to be done with him, Excellency?" the police chief asked.

"Whip his Royal Majesty's ass; then send him home to his wife, the Queen."

Afterward the governor called on the Barons Huntze and Meritorious Citizen Maximilian Flederbaum. The latter came out to meet the governor with a bandaged head. For all his Christian attire and upturned mustaches, he had been beaten by the gentiles as if he were some common Jew.

"I'm dreadfully sorry," the governor exclaimed. "If you would point out the hooligans who did this to you, I'll see to it they're punished at once!"

Flederbaum knew that the governor knew that he, Flederbaum, knew what the story was, but he merely bowed his bloodied head and thanked the governor for his sympathy.

The Jewish stores slowly reopened. Glaziers replaced panes. Burial Society members rode about in their hearses, picking up corpses. Doctors bandaged the wounded. Rabbis fasted, and in the houses of worship, trembling Jews recited fast day prayers during the afternoon services.

The gentile workers, subdued and apathetic, stood with heads deeply bowed and pleaded with the factory directors to take them back. The directors took them back, but they cut salaries at their own discretion. Black smoke again belched in twisted whirls from factory chimneys, polluting the Lodz air as before.

In Jewish courtyards, blind beggars from Feiffer Lane sang "Pillage," the song that an enterprising street musician had composed to commemorate the orgy:

> Hear, oh, good people, of the fear,
> That befell the Jews of Balut.
> On the first day of Iyar,
> Gentiles came to rob and to loot.
>
> Like mad dogs off leashes, they ran wild,
> Biting and tearing night and day.
> Woe to any man, woman, or child
> Who happened to get in their way.
>
> Sweet God, whose mercy is so deep,
> Stretch out your divine hand.
> Gather up your stray, lost sheep,
> And lead us to the Holy Land.

THIRTY-THREE

———

SHAMEFACED, HORRIFIED, unable to look their fellow Jews in the eye, the strike agitators stumbled through the streets of Balut. Everything lay in ruins. Dazed, bloodied people staggered about, seeking their loved ones and their possessions. "It was our brothers, our fellow workers, who did this to us, not the police or the exploiter bosses . . ." the weavers taunted their leaders.

"A curse on you!" the women added spitefully. "You had nothing better to do than run around nights with secrets and plots? Didn't you know it always ends up with Jewish heads bleeding?"

The most depressed of all was Nissan, the rabbi's son, known as Nissan the depraved. In the first days after the workers, *his* workers, had so foully desecrated the honored day of freedom, Nissan couldn't get out of the bed on which he had thrown himself fully dressed. He wouldn't eat, wash, shave. He wanted to die, to shut out the shame and horror of what he had seen. Along with Tevye and the other leaders, he had been out in the streets, trying to bring the inflamed workers to their senses, but they had pushed him aside, and one had even punched him in the face.

His landlord, a Litvak, who had come to Lodz after the expulsion of Jews from Moscow, wanted to fetch a doctor for him, but he refused. The landlord brought him hot tea, but Nissan wouldn't touch a thing.

"To you, this is something new," the landlord said, "but to us it's ancient history. We had it in Russia; we have it here; we'll have it wherever we go. It shall be ever so, so long as we live among the gentiles. . . ."

Nissan sat up in a rage. "Not so! So long as we live among bosses and oppressors!"

In his distress, he broke the rules of conspiracy and openly expressed his revolutionary views to a stranger.

The landlord gazed at him sympathetically and shook his head. "You are young. I once thought the same way. But they will always beat us. When new machines were installed in Lodz, they beat us. When Russian students assassinated the tsar, they beat us. Now it's the workers who beat us. Later it will be the revolutionaries. It will never change. Not as long as we are Jews and they are Christians. . . ."

"Don't say that!" Nissan screamed, pressing his hands against his ears. "Shut up!"

"You'd do better to clear your room of the illicit material," the landlord advised. "They're conducting searches all over the city."

Nissan blanched. The landlord looked at him with knowing eyes. "Don't look so alarmed. I know how to keep silent. But take my advice—don't get mixed up in it as I once did. I, too, wanted to help the gentiles, but the first pogrom opened my eyes."

Nissan wanted to answer, but the man had left the room, and he was left alone with his pain and despair. From the courtyard echoed the dirges of beggars lamenting the pogrom. The landlord's words weighed on Nissan's breast like a heavy stone.

No, he wouldn't, he couldn't believe it! He knew that the road to redemption was a hard one, lined with thorns, obstacles, and sharp rocks over which the freedom seekers would stumble more than once until they reached the summit. He knew from history that all revolutions were drenched in innocent blood, pain, and tears. He knew that the pogrom had been the result of agitation by agents, provocateurs, criminal elements, who had duped the ignorant workers and misdirected their ire against the Jews in order to draw them off from their true enemies. He knew this in his head, but not in his heart.

The events of the frightful days passed before his eyes—the beatings, the maimings, the violations of women and children. It had been his proletariat that had perpetrated these crimes, and his landlord's comments refused to leave his conscience.

"To die . . . simply to die," ran through his mind. "There's nothing more to live for. . . ."

He didn't even bother to clear his room of the contraband material. He no longer cared what happened to him.

Maybe man was essentially evil. Maybe it wasn't the fault of economic circumstances, as he had been taught, but the deficiencies of human character. Maybe the Torah was right in its contention that man's heart was rotten from birth. Maybe his former idol Schopenhauer had been right, not the idealistic

Hegel or the pragmatic Marx. . . .

He drifted off and suffered terrible nightmares replete with blood and carnage. Behind it all resounded his landlord's words: "It shall be forever so. . . ."

Ungroomed, fully dressed, he lay on his cot for a day and a night as if in a stupor. He was roused by the morning sun shining as brightly as it could through the polluted Lodz air and dingy windowpanes. He no longer felt the despair that had consumed him, the apathy and loss of purpose. Instead, there surged within him a will to live, to restore himself, to forge something positive out of the tragedy and disappointment. Like his pious father, whose faith in the Messiah nullified all contemporary suffering, Nissan reaffirmed his faith in the validity of his ideals and pushed aside all negative thought.

He cleared his room of the compromising material, washed, dressed, and went to seek out his comrades in order to confer on future steps. But they were nowhere in evidence. They were hiding, unwilling to show themselves. The few he encountered wouldn't talk to him.

"Get away!" they said. "If you go near the workers now, they'll skin you alive. . . ."

He went to see Tevye, but he, too, was unavailable. "Papa is in the hospital," Bashke told him through her tears. "A gentile hit him with a rock. . . . And don't let Mother see you. She said she'd slap you silly if you dared show your face. . . ."

Nissan went back to his room and composed a proclamation addressed to the Jewish workers of Balut. It was filled with bitter denunciations of the capitalists, who had so cynically turned brother against brother. It directed the responsibility for the outburst against the police agents and provocateurs. It urged the Jewish workers not to surrender to despair, but to renew their faith in the solidarity of the proletariat. It concluded with a long series of "*down with*"s and "*long live*"s.

He spent a full day and night making copies of the proclamation, then waited until midnight to post them on the crooked walls and fences of Lodz. He had already posted a number of them and was taking a roundabout way home when two policemen slipped out of the shadows and seized him. They swiftly handcuffed him and drove him in a droshky to the station. Two rows of Cossacks with knouts in hand stood facing each other in the station courtyard. Nissan hesitated, but the policemen nudged him forward. "Move it, Moshe!"

This alerted the Cossacks that the prisoner was a Jew and that they didn't have to hold back. Nissan ran the gauntlet, trying to avoid the whistling thongs descending upon his head, arms, back, and shoulders. Policemen picked him up from the ground, where he lay bleeding, and led him before the night shift commander.

"Caught him posting proclamations in Balut."

They displayed one of the posters they had peeled from the wall.

"Search him!" the officer ordered.

They did so.

"You there, what's your full name and address?" the officer asked.

"Don't call me 'you'!" Nissan responded sharply.

The officer regarded him through narrowed eyes. "So, an intellectual." He laughed. "Your name and address?"

Nissan didn't answer. He wiped his bleeding face with a kerchief.

"Well, all right. We have our own ways of finding out such things," the officer said. "Throw him in the tank."

The large cell was filled with prisoners. There were thieves and men without proper papers, street brawlers and drunken cabbies, beggars and lunatics, and a mob of workers detained for rioting. New prisoners kept being brought in. The stench, noise, filth, and smoke were unbearable. The men yelled, cursed, laughed, cried. A tiny kerosene lamp barely illuminated the large room. A bunch of youths pounded on the cell door, calling for the jailer. They wanted to visit the latrine, but he had already been fooled too often by such requests.

All the bunks were taken, and Nissan sought out a corner of the cell and stretched out on the bare, dirty floor. Men came over, demanding money for whiskey, but he ignored them.

"Get the hell away from me!" he said curtly in the tough tone of the experienced jailbird.

"That's no fish," the men grunted. "He's done hard time already." And they went off, looking for "fish."

Nissan lay on the cold floor, aching in body and spirit. The green light of morning shone in through the barred windows.

After several days he was taken before the interrogator. In a brightly illuminated office a clean-shaven colonel of gendarmes wearing gold-rimmed glasses sat before a desk covered in green cloth.

"Have a seat," he said politely. "Is this your first time here? A Lodz citizen or a stranger?"

"A native of Lodz," Nissan replied.

"I don't know your name," the colonel said with a smile. "You wouldn't give it to the arresting officers."

"They beat me," Nissan said angrily. "Look at my face."

"I'm very sorry," the colonel said with an amiable smile. "But times are such that it's hard for us to maintain proper discipline. Surely you know how hard it is to control Cossacks. . . . This wouldn't have happened with gendarmes."

He pushed a box of cigarettes toward Nissan. "Would you care for a smoke?"

"Thank you," Nissan said, taking the proffered cigarette.

The colonel began to clean some penpoints. "You speak a very fluent Russian for a native of Lodz," he remarked. "Were you educated in Russia or in Poland?"

"I was for some years under police supervision in Russia," Nissan replied. "My name is Nissan Eibeshutz."

"Very nice to know you, Mr. Eibeshutz," the colonel said, enunciating the Jewish name. "That's the best way. We would have found it out anyway. You merely saved us needless effort."

In the same polite tone the colonel tried to ascertain from the prisoner to which party he belonged—the Proletariat, the Zwionzek, or perhaps some new offshoot? . . . "There's no unity in your ranks," he observed with a smile. "You keep splitting up into factions and making extra work for us. They say the Proletariat is on the verge of another split. What's your opinion?"

When Nissan offered no reply, the colonel turned his attention to the proclamation. He compared it with the Russian translation supplied him by the secretary of the Jewish communal society and went on to discuss the recent riot in the city.

"Very deplorable"—he sighed—"truly regrettable."

"It was your doing," Nissan said.

"No, yours," the colonel corrected him. "Jews have no business mixing into politics. You should stick to business, which is your specialty. This would be better both for you and for us. Think about what I'm saying."

"I have my own views on such matters," Nissan said.

"I hope that in prison, where you'll have lots of time to think, you'll muse some more on this and come to agree with me," the colonel said paternally. "You're tired now and sleepy, and I don't want to burden you any more than I have to. We'll talk again. In the meantime, is there anything I can get for you? Tell me, and if it's at all possible, I'll be happy to do it."

"One thing, Colonel. I don't want to go back to that cell. Please send me to prison instead."

"I've already arranged for that," the colonel replied, and rang for the guards.

The policemen seated Nissan in a droshky and drove him to

the prison on Dluga Street.

"They keep sending and sending," the warden raged, "and I don't have any place to put them. What a mess!"

Two sleepy guards stripped Nissan naked, made him stoop, and probed his orifices. They took away everything he had, including a pencil, cigarettes, matches, and loose change. They also took away his tie and suspenders.

"Take it!" they ordered, handing him a tiny kerosene lamp and leading him down a long corridor. "You'll be staying here for now. Later, we'll see further."

They tossed him like a corpse onto a bunk covered with a coarse gray blanket. After the crowded jail cell, the prison cell with its bunk, table, and bench was to Nissan like a palace.

Soon a message in prison code sounded from the adjoining cell. Nissan placed his ear to the wall.

"Good evening. Who are you?" the message tapped out.

Nissan gave his name.

"What's doing in the city?" the other asked, giving his own name.

Soon he added the news that the prisoners wouldn't be detained here too long. The trials would be held shortly, and the sentences would be stiff ones, up to eight or ten years.

Nissan asked about the prison routine, food, exercise time, sleeping time, but especially about reading matter.

The answer came that books were available in quantity, political literature along with a sizable library left by former prisoners.

Nissan was delighted. He anticipated a long term, and he looked forward to many years of uninterrupted study.

One day he was told that his bride had come to visit. He came out, puzzled, to find little Bashke with a package in hand. The guard took the package. "What's in there?" he asked.

"Food."

"We'll give it back after we've gone through it," the guard said. "In the meantime, you two can talk."

Nissan took the girl's hand, and she blushed fiercely. "Don't be angry," she apologized. "But they only let family visit, so I said that we were married."

"I thank you, Bashke," Nissan said, and stroked her head. He inquired about her father, about friends.

"Papa is already home," she said. "He's back working, and so am I. He sends his regards."

She mused a moment, then added, "He'll go on as before. Both of us will, even though Mother screams."

"You're a good girl, Bashke," Nissan said, "but be careful. And you mustn't bring me packages. I have everything I need here."

Then girl gazed at him with grateful eyes, then burst out crying.

"What is it, Bashke?" he asked, stroking her hair.

"They're so mean . . . so horrid . . ." she mumbled, averting her eyes.

"Who, Bashke?"

"During the search," she said, her face deeply flushed. "I was so ashamed. . . ."

Nissan nodded. He knew about prison searches of female visitors. "You shouldn't come here. You're only a child."

The guard cut the visit short. "Time to go," he said, clanging his keys.

Nissan kissed the girl's head and said good-bye.

THIRTY-FOUR

———

THE LODZ RAILROAD DEPOT was noisy and crowded. Around the third-class wagons, Jews and peasant men, women, and children milled and jostled one another. Although there was plenty of time until the train left, people scurried, shouted, pushed. Women fretted about their possessions. They didn't understand the conductor's Russian, and they wailed and lamented, pressing their bundles to their bosoms. They were on the first step of a journey to join their husbands in America. The only things they were taking with them were their bedding and their children, and they were terrified of losing one or the other. They shrieked each time the children left their sight anew. Besides, there were pickpockets about, ready to snatch whatever wasn't tied or nailed down.

"Help, my money!" female voices kept shattering the murky air.

Many Lodz citizens were emigrating to America these days. Following the crisis, many people had been left without a groschen. Others had been beaten and stripped clean during the pogrom, and they hoped to begin a new life in the New World.

For the hundredth time, fathers said good-bye to sons and admonished them, "Remember to remain a Jew! Observe the Sabbath, wear your phylacteries, and don't shave your beard, you hear?"

"We hear," the sons promised, counting their bundles yet another time.

Peasant women carrying baskets of chickens tried to sneak into the train and wrangled with the conductors. Hasidim with bundles bound in red kerchiefs on their way to their rabbis' courts traveled with their young sons, who were attired in long gabardines and looked like so many tiny old men. They chanted Hasidic songs even as they boarded. Litvak merchants, reeling under valises, teapots, and umbrellas, fought for berths so that they could sleep all the way home. They bickered with the

Polish Jews, shouted through the windows at the porters, and consumed oceans of hot tea they had brought along.

An uproar resounded through the wagons. People tossed bundles, argued, fought. Pious Jews donned prayer shawls and phylacteries and formed quorums. Women bared breasts and suckled screaming infants. Female Litvaks played cards. Hasidim offered toasts. Gentiles sliced pork sausages with jackknives, ate, spit, and laughed at the praying Jews. Children cried; hens clucked; a piglet in a sack squealed; a dog barked.

Through it all moved the so-called Whipper, a red-bearded bully of a Jew in a yellow gabardine who unofficially but brazenly collected fares. "Hand it over, Jews, whoever hasn't paid," he cried. "Hand over the cash!"

Not everyone bought regular tickets for the train. Some people sneaked aboard and hid under seats. But the Russian conductors didn't mind. They employed bouncers to extract payment from the stowaways, then split the take with them.

The red-bearded Whipper poked, prodded, crawled under benches to flush out hiding passengers, and shouted, "Make it snappy! Hand it over, or off you go!"

The Russian conductor walked beside him and lent an official hand. "Will he come alone?" he asked in a Hebrew quote from the Torah as his accomplice had taught him.

"He will leave alone!" the passengers countered, and paid for the privilege of traveling without a ticket.

The Whipper reserved his greatest scorn not for those hiding under the seats, but for those who had bought legitimate tickets.

"Look at the favor they've done the Russky!" he raged. "Couldn't let a Jew earn a few kopecks and travel cheaper? You're worse than any gentile!"

"Will the Angel of Death be coming?" Hasidim asked, referring to the conductor.

"No, the Angel of Death won't be coming," the Russian conductor assured them in Yiddish.

Men reluctantly drew money from purses; women groped in bosoms and stockings and haggled with the Whipper.

"This is no fish market," he grumbled, "no haggling here. . . ."

Before first-class and second-class wagons, well-dressed, self-assured passengers were gathered. Several army officers were traveling with their orderlies, who carried their luggage. Well-to-do merchants strolled expansively along the platform. They kept consulting gold watches and blowing blue rings of smoke from thick cigars. A brace of out-of-place Polish squires, holding hunting dogs on leashes and carrying rifles, talked and laughed too loudly. But the majority of the passengers here were matrons traveling to resorts. Porters struggled under mounds of trunks, valises, hatboxes, traveling cases, and portmanteaux filled with enough dresses and accessories for two weeks at a fashionable resort.

Dressed in their long gowns and huge plumed hats, the ladies minced along, conversing in German, even though they were still miles from the German border. They accepted bouquets and boxes of chocolate from husbands and swains amid tearful protestations of undying love.

Wearing a light checked English suit designed to make him appear taller and more distinguished, a Havana cigar in his mouth, Max Ashkenazi, sales representative for the Huntze Corporation, strolled to and fro, calculating rapidly with a pencil on any surface available—the margin of his German newspaper, the tiny notebooks he carried in every pocket, even on the cigar case. He moistened the tip of his pencil and quickly scribbled figures, oceans of figures.

"Good day, Herr Ashkenazi," men greeted him, tipping derbies and top hats. "Where are you bound for this time?"

"A pleasure trip," he lied to keep his destination a secret.

"Much pleasure," the men wished him, knowing full well that he was deceiving them.

Ashkenazi grunted in reply and resumed his calculations.

He wasn't going on any pleasure trip, even though it was already broiling hot in the stinking, smoky city. He was bound for Russia to sell goods and to establish connections with important merchants for his agency.

Good times had returned to Lodz following the crisis—even better than before. The city had purged itself. It was good for Lodz to cleanse itself regularly, Ashkenazi mused. This allowed the bad blood to escape and purified the system. The petty manufacturers and mechants had drained the city enough already. They competed too fiercely, dropping prices to rock bottom, selling below cost, granting every pauper and sponger credit, until it became nearly impossible to do business in Lodz.

Now the crisis had swept away the whole gang like so much dirt, and all that was left were the big manufacturers and merchants—those of solid, substantial background.

They, too, had suffered setbacks, but not sufficiently damaging to destroy them. Now they would make up for the losses in spades. The prices of goods had stabilized. The workers had been taught a good lesson. They would accept whatever wages were offered them. They would kiss the bosses' feet just for the chance to work.

Now that everything had been straightened out, Max Ashkenazi was on his way to Russia to cement relations with old customers, to establish new connections and open up new markets. He was raring to go, bursting with faith in himself and in the future of Lodz. The Huntze firm had suffered comparatively little damage. Governor von Müller had retained the Cossacks in the city and had promised that henceforth law and order would prevail.

Along with the other papers in his portfolio reposed a certificate attesting to the fact that Simha Meir Ashkenazi was a merchant of the first guild and entitled to travel the length and breadth of the Russian Empire despite his Mosaic faith. The fact that the passport still carried his old Jewish name displeased Ashkenazi somewhat, but his business cards identified him as Max.

He glanced at the gold watch he had received as a wedding gift from his father-in-law. It indicated that it was already time to leave, but still, the third and final bell hadn't sounded.

"Why aren't we moving?" he asked the conductor through the open window of his first-class carriage.

"Prisoners are being led aboard," the conductor replied. "It takes time to get them settled in the cars. We'll be plenty late. . . ."

Max nodded and with total indifference gazed along the platform.

A detail of black-clad military police stood lined up on either side with swords drawn as rows of convicts passed between them one at a time. "No staring, and keep your distance!" the soldiers warned those who had come to see the prisoners off.

Following the strikes and riots, a huge number of prisoners had accumulated in Lodz. Now they were being deported from the city to make room for others in the local prisons. By the hundreds they were being led to the trains to be sent back to their hometowns or into exile. There were professional criminals in gray convict uniforms and round caps, bearded peasants who had been picked up without proper papers, shackled lifers in wrist and leg irons, political prisoners in civilian clothes and carrying valises, ragged beggars, women with infants in arms, elderly Jews, and gentiles. A gang of vividly clad gypsies demanded something in their Romany dialect, but the soldiers silenced them with truncheons.

"Keep in line, filthy sons of bitches!" they growled.

Row after row the convicts mounted the steps into the barred wagons as relatives and friends waved and called their names. The prisoners were bound for various destinations.

Some were going to the Citadel Prison in Warsaw; some, to Russian prisons; some, to face trial; some, into exile in Siberia.

Those in civilian clothes included hundreds of workers arrested during the riots and students and intellectuals detained for revolutionary activities. Among these was Nissan Eibeshutz, who had but recently returned to Lodz from years of exile. Just like Max Ashkenazi, he was going to Russia, but he would be routed and rerouted many times before he reached his final destination in the frozen subarctic.

For a brief moment the two men locked gazes, but presently Max Ashkenazi sank back against the soft velvet of his seat and lit a cigar, and the convict, Nissan Eibeshutz, was pushed into a barred wagon jammed with men, women, children, and their possessions. The car resounded with cries and curses and exuded the foul stench of unwashed humanity.

The train started. Off to the side stood Bashke, who waved at the departing train, veiled in smoke and steam.

THIRTY-FIVE

BRIGHT, SUNNY DAYS filled the world. In fields groaning with grain, young peasant girls with heads bound in red kerchiefs sang as they tied the sheaves.

Inside the convict car it was stifling and foul. The whole tragedy and worthlessness of human existence were compressed within the wagon's metal walls,

On the floor squatted a young woman in tattered clothes, weeping bitterly. She had come from a distant village to seek work in Lodz, but on the way there she had been robbed of her few guldens and her train ticket. The conductor had turned her over to the police in Lodz. But along with her money she had lost her papers, which had been stamped for her by the village notary, and all she retained were her tin cross and the name of the village she came from.

Now she was being sent back to that village, a journey that should have taken a day and night, but that had already gone on for weeks. Shy, timid, unworldly, cowed, she had been bullied and bedeviled by the prostitutes, the female thieves, and the guards. Before leaving Lodz, she had been lured inside the guardhouse under the pretext of washing the floor. Frightened, she had obeyed, but the guards had doused the lights and had gang-raped her. In the morning she had been taken back to her cell, bruised and bleeding. Now she sprawled on the wet, soiled floor with red eyes and a swollen face.

"Jesus!" she wept. "Holy Mary. . . ."

Several prostitutes, who had been nabbed for not carrying their special books, sneered, "You won't die from it. Now that you've got the experience, you can become one of us—"

The guards laughed and nodded. "Right. . . ."

A young Jewish wife sat on a basket, wringing her hands. Her father had compelled her to marry an elderly man whom she couldn't abide, and she had fled to Lodz to work as a maid in an affluent home. But her husband had learned her location

and informed the police, who were sending her back to her
legal spouse as the law dictated, and she didn't cease bewailing
her fate.

"What shall I do?" she asked a group of Jewish female
thieves, sitting huddled in a circle and playing with a deck of
greasy cards.

"Poison him!" a woman in convict dress advised. "That's
what I done to mine, and that's why I'm here."

On a bundle of rags lay an old crone, groaning. In a city of
thousands of beggars it had been her misfortune to be arrested,
and she was being sent back to her place of origin, as the law
provided. But she was so senile that she had forgotten the
name of her hometown.

"I come from God's earth," she replied to all questions. "It's
got a church with such pretty pictures. . . ."

She had been riding the prisoner trains for years already.
No one was willing to accept her; no one would issue her a
passport. And she rotted away on her bundle of rags, unable
to get up even for her natural functions, surrounded by the
dried crusts of bread she could no longer consume.

"Get her out of here!" the other convicts cried. "You can die
from her stink!"

"It won't croak, the pile of shit!" the guards cursed, spitting
on the bundle of rags. "We'll have to drag her all over Russia
—and for what?"

The company included murderers who boasted of their
ferocity; horse thieves; a blue-eyed peasant with the face of a
saint who had hacked a neighbor to death in a dispute over
land boundaries; a huge mustached peasant who had picked
up a branch of wood in a squire's forest from which to make
a new wagon pole and who had been condemned for this
crime with a sentence of nine months' imprisonment; a Tatar
with high cheekbones who had worked as a porter in Lodz
and who had failed to deliver a bundle of cotton; several
gentile youths who had gotten into a brawl at a wedding;
thieves and prostitutes lacking proper credentials; arsonists
and smugglers; cold-blooded killers and total madmen; gypsies
and revolutionaries—a microcosm of sprawling, polyglot Russia
squeezed within the confines of barred wagons and wallowing
in stench, sweat, excrement, tears, and injustice.

In the midst of it all sat Nissan, trying to catch a breath of
air in the stifling, sweating crush. His prisonmates had been
correct about the swiftness of the trials and the severity of the
sentences. There had been a glut of arrests, and the authorities
had had to make quick work of the defendants.

For robbing and beating Jews, the sentence was six months, for organizing the strikes, three years. The revolutionaries all received from five to eight years' imprisonment, to be followed by an additional five to ten years of exile in Siberia under police supervision.

Like all political prisoners, Nissan had made a long impassioned speech in the courtroom in which he reiterated the usual charges and accusations. The judges let him continue uninterrupted, but they didn't hear a word he said. They dozed, yawned, and waited for him to finish. They had heard it all many times before. The sentence was preordained, and nothing the defendant said would make the slightest difference.

In the courtroom Nissan looked around for some people from Balut to hear his words, but none were present. Only policemen, agents, and several fashionable ladies were in attendance. The general public had been barred.

Now he was on his way to a prison outside Moscow since the authorities preferred to assign convicts to prisons far from their homes. The governor-general had also dictated that the convicts travel an indirect route that would involve months of stops and detours at various jails and detention halls abounding with filth, desperate criminals, and genuine lunatics. Nissan knew that months of travel on such trains were far worse than years of prison. He was also without money. His few rubles had been taken from him, and even though the jailers promised that they would be forwarded to him, he knew he would never see them again.

He now faced a long and difficult journey, but this did not distress him. Just like his father before him, he was willing to endure the worst hardships for his faith. He knew that physical anguish was the price one had to pay for the achievement of an ideal, and he was willing to pay this price. Besides, he was already accustomed to hardship. His first imprisonment had hardened him, and he was prepared for every indignity and danger prison life might proffer.

He made sure that all his rights were observed, and his demeanor was such that the professional criminals respected him and didn't try to bully him. He knew that wherever he might go, he would encounter fellow political prisoners, who would band together to assist each other. Nor were all wardens or guards the same. Some were decent people who treated convicts—especially political prisoners—strictly by the book.

Nor was he as naïve as he had once been. He had learned an excellent Russian, and his urge to learn, to study Marxism in particular, was as strong as ever. Ironically, there was no place in tsarist Russia that offered such splendid opportunity to study Marxism as its prisons.

For Nissan, as for all political prisoners, prison served as a university. He had left Lodz the first time a raw, ignorant youth, and he had returned an enlightened, educated man. Now he wanted to commence his postgraduate studies. He would study and make his own comments and notations in the margins of the Marxist books, just as his father did in the margins of his holy volumes.

What disturbed him now wasn't the prospect of prison, but the presence of workers from Lodz who had been convicted of assaulting and robbing Jews during the riots. Perversely, they reserved their fiercest hate not for the authorities who had tried and convicted them, but for the very victims of their violence—the Jews.

"Wait till we get back," they vowed with clenched fists. "We'll fix their wagons!"

The attitudes in Lodz had changed. No longer did workers rail against the bosses, but they stood now with caps in hand, humbly begging to be taken back. In Balut the people trembled at the very mention of May 1—originally a date celebrating freedom and independence, but now the symbol of violence and plunder. The song commemorating the pogrom had penetrated even to the prisoners' wagons, where the Jewish thieves chanted it over their eternal card games.

Yet for all that, Nissan wasn't despondent. He knew that in every war there were temporary defeats and setbacks. The path to truth wasn't smooth and easy, but strewn with obstacles and diversions. He had no doubt of the ultimate triumph. It would sprout from the soil as a seed sprouts out of mud and manure, like a creature born of a drop of semen in a mother's womb.

Not that he believed in a swift redemption. History had to pass through its inevitable stages, but in the end its inflexible laws had to prevail. There would no longer be the oppressors and the oppressed, distinct classes or nations, hatred and envy. All men would be free. All worldly goods would be equally apportioned. And the happiness would be universal since all of man's troubles, all worldly evil derived from unjust economic conditions.

This was as clear to him as the sky peering in through the bars of the convict wagon. He saw it as vividly as his father saw the Promised Land following the coming of the Messiah. But for the present the people in the car devoured one another the way the lice devoured their flesh. They bullied, taunted, tormented each other. Every few moments the word *sheeny* was heard. The soldiers said it, the workers and the criminals.

The older prisoners decided to have a little fun. They found a young peasant lad with a head of flaxen hair falling over his blue eyes. It was his first brush with the law, and the older men decided to initiate him. "What's your name, boy?" they asked.

"Antek," he said.

"Why are you here, Antek?"

"For buying a stolen horse."

"In that case, you'll have to be sworn in just like we were," they told him with mock solemnity.

"Sworn in?" he asked in puzzlement. "What for?"

"That you'll be a good comrade and won't rat on your brothers," they said piously. "Do you believe in the Lord Jesus?"

"Of course!" the lad said.

"Then you'll swear on the holy Bible. But first, you'll have to be blindfolded."

The boy's eyes were tightly bound with a dirty rag; then the eldest convict quietly dropped his pants and presented his bare rump to the blindfolded youth's lips.

One of the shackled prisoners recited a holy oath in priestly tones and made the blindfolded youth repeat it, word for word.

"Now, my son, kiss the good book," the ministrant ordered.

The lad bent forward and kissed the bare behind. The crowd broke out in a wild laughter.

The men pressed the boy's hand and laughingly asked, "How was the smell?"

The youth cowered in a corner, heaving in shame.

There were other perversities in the filthy car: thefts, abnormal couplings. Older prisoners forced themselves on boys and beat those that were weaker.

The old doubts concerning man's essential depravity began to replace the bright visions of redeemed humanity in Nissan's brain. Just as in his youth, he tried closing his eyes so that he would lose himself in his fantasies and drive reality away. Just as his father had done when doubts and questions assailed him, he began to repeat to himself the credos of his beliefs, the verbatim contents of Marxist theory that he recalled from books. This helped restore his faith and allowed him to forget the brutality and depravity that seethed all around him.

What concern did he have with people and all their petty, vicious weaknesses and egomania, with all these worms devouring one another just as the vermin devoured them? He wouldn't even look at them. He had given his life to an ideal, a dazzling ideal for which no effort or sacrifice was too great, and it was to that ideal, not to people, that he would dedicate himself.

In the stifling, stinking wagon the men played Blind Cow. With each round of the game, a new victim would lie down with his head between his knees while the others beat him until he identified the one responsible.

To Nissan, the men's coarse voices and raw laughter were like the roars of savage beasts.

THIRTY-SIX

———◆———

At the Austrian resort Carlsbad, the cream of Lodz society gathered to take the waters. The crush this season wasn't as intense as in past years. Many of the regulars had been ruined by the crisis, and those who had been able to make it strutted with particular pride and hauteur. The women trailed trains over the paved sidewalks, displaying gowns that couldn't be worn in Lodz because of the filth and grime. The men, in their short jackets and tight trousers or in light, vented frock coats with high collars and pointed-toed patent-leather shoes, bowed and waved their handkerchiefs with disdain.

"For the first time it's possible to enjoy yourself in Carlsbad," they observed. "So many upstarts gone, don't you know?"

"Yes, what a pleasure to be rid of the seamstresses and store clerks. . . ."

They felt particularly gratified that Flederbaum himself along with his family deigned to visit Carlsbad this year. Even his daughters, who had previously avoided the resort because it had become too Jewish, were present.

Among the others here was Dinele, the wife of Max Ashkenazi, accompanied by her mother. Haim Alter hadn't been able to make it. Things were going especially badly for him following the crisis, and for the first time he had been forced to let his Priveh go abroad without him. She had grown even more alluring over the years, and he had been forced to go into debt to send her since she had emphatically told him that she simply wouldn't have endured missing a season at Carlsbad.

Dinele, too, was without her husband, although he could easily have accompanied her. His mounting prosperity was the talk of Lodz. It was said that he held the Barons Huntze in the palm of his hand.

Still, he had elected to go to Russia on business. He couldn't afford to waste time on idle pleasure. He begrudged every minute away from business. Even though Lodz gossiped that he controlled the Huntzes, the barons were still his employers, and his goal of being the actual master of Lodz was as distant as ever. He wasn't content with half victories—it had to be everything or nothing, and he wouldn't rest until he got what he wanted.

He was busier than ever these days. Director Albrecht had never been the same since the workers had wheeled him around in a wheelbarrow with a broom in his hand. He had fallen as if into a stupor. He still came to the factory each day and sat in the huge chair that groaned beneath his bulk, but he no longer ran the factory. He didn't hear what was said to him, he misplaced papers, and he often forgot to pull up the socks drooping down on his legs or to button his fly.

The German secretaries with their smooth blond upsweeps chortled into their papers to keep from laughing out loud at his erratic behavior.

"The old fart is through," the barons agreed. And although they allowed him to come to the factory, they took away all his duties and assigned them to Ashkenazi.

Albrecht made no objections. He found solace in the young girls Melchior provided him in ever-fresh supply. Ashkenazi knew that the old man's end was near—his corpulence, his gargantuan appetites all pointed to an early collapse. But it was all academic in any case. He, Ashkenazi, was the actual, if unofficial, director of the factory. Not a single move was made without his knowledge and approval. He worked as hard as ever, kept a million details in his head, and wouldn't allow himself the pleasure of dropping everything and going off with his wife to Carlsbad. He didn't need resorts. He flourished in an atmosphere of dust, smoke, and tumult. It was only in times of idleness and quiet that he experienced pain and discomfort.

He was back on top now, having long surpassed his brother. His importance and influence grew daily. He kept secretly buying up Huntze stock, which he piled in the vault until it resembled a flight of stairs that would lead him to his goal— to the very tops of the factory stacks. . . .

But he often fretted during his numerous business trips. Dinele never came to see him off or met him when he returned. She saw to it only that he had sufficient underwear and other requisites for the journey. This disturbed him. He envied the couples who displayed so much love at their meetings at the station, kissing and whispering secrets. He was uneasy about his beautiful wife alone among the wanton playboys and gigolos who frequented the fashionable resorts. It wasn't for nothing that his father-in-law fretted so about letting his own frisky wife go there alone and—until this year—had always made it a point to accompany her.

He, Max, couldn't take the time for such things, but his brother, Yakub, did. Not that he could afford to do so. Despite the crisis, he had continued his spendthrift ways; he had issued credit to one and all and had squandered money without a thought for the future. The crisis had dealt him some severe financial blows—a number of his debtors had gone bankrupt, and he was close to losing the tens of thousands of rubles he had deposited as a bond with Flederbaum. But at the last minute his wife had bailed him out, as usual.

So long as he had been secure, she had stayed away from him. She refused to join him in Lodz and brooded in Warsaw with her pills and medicines. She knew about the dissolute life he was leading, but she refused to come to him.

But the moment she heard that he was in financial difficulties, she responded promptly. She sold one of the buildings she had inherited from her mother and presented the proceeds of the sale to him. She joined him in Lodz, gave him the benefit of her business acumen, and helped him in every way until he was once more on his feet. They rented a magnificent apartment, furnished it luxuriously, entertained lavishly, and maintained a gracious existence.

More than with anyone else, Perele established close relations with Priveh and even more so with her sister-in-law, Dinele. Their husbands didn't speak, but the wives became close friends and visited each other often.

But as soon as Yakub resumed his normal ways, Perele again began nagging him about the way he ate, slept, and relished all of life's pleasures. She disliked his companions and was jealous of every woman he came near, from his sister-in-law to the lowliest housemaid.

Again she fled back to Warsaw, and again Yakub drove his carriage through the streets of Lodz, tipping his hat to ladies. And even though his financial affairs were still shaky, he placed them in the hands of underlings and left the broiling city to go abroad for a few weeks.

Not that he needed resorts since he had the constitution of a peasant. He merely wanted to enjoy the activities in Carlsbad. It was a good place to relax for a while, particularly when one was unencumbered by a wife's company. So he packed his valises, booked a first-class compartment, and set out with his usual light heart.

With customary aplomb he strolled through the long train, greeting acquaintances, treating the men to cigarettes and the ladies to chocolate, kissing hands, laughing, complimenting. He lingered longest in the compartment where Dinele and Priveh sat, surrounded by a mound of valises, hatboxes, traveling cases, cushions, and satchels. When the train stopped, he sprang down to the platform to buy fresh fruit for the ladies. He helped them get through customs at the borders.

Priveh couldn't stop praising him. She had been entranced with him ever since he had moved back to Lodz and had become one of the town's leading playboys. Although she was already a woman of advanced years, she could still appreciate a dashing man's attentions. More than once she inwardly deplored the fact that she hadn't betrothed Dinele to him instead of to his brother. The more she came to despise her son-in-law, the more she grew to adore his twin brother.

While Perele was still living in Lodz, Priveh would frequently bring Dinele to his, Yakub's, house. Now that they were traveling together to Carlsbad, she appreciated his doing what she was accustomed to having her Haim do for her. She was grateful that he was around to take care of all those bothersome little details for which men were so much better suited.

"Yakub," she gushed, "if I wasn't such an old lady, I'd kiss you!"

Yakub drew back her glove, and her daughter's, then kissed their hands several times. "What a delightful surprise it was to run into you two," he beamed.

All three knew that the encounter had been no surprise. Just as he had waited for Dinele to show up as a boy, he had again made sure to check out which train she would be taking. But no one made reference to the subterfuge.

Wherever Dinele went in Carlsbad he materialized as if out of the shadows. Dinele clung to her mother, afraid to be left alone with him, but Priveh did everything to throw them together. She wasn't driven so much by a concern for her daughter's happiness as by a feeling of revenge against her son-in-law.

"Diana," she said to her, "why don't you take a ride with Yakub? It'll cheer you up. I'll stay here and listen to the music in the park."

By the glow of the milky moon shining down on placid fields, Dinele and Yakub held hands. "No, Yakub." She resisted each time he tried to kiss her. "No!"

Yakub took her hand and draped it around his neck. "Then

let's sit as we did when we were children," he said. "Do you remember, Dinele?"

"I remember," she said, her heart beating faster. But she could go no further. She, too, was afraid of God and, even more, of her own passions that she had subdued for so many years, and she ran back to the safety of her mother's arms.

THIRTY-SEVEN

———————◆———————

THROUGHOUT THE HUGE RUSSIAN EMPIRE from the Vistula in the west to the Amur in the east, men from the ages of twenty-one to the mid-forties were taken from fields, factories, and workshops and pressed into uniform. On walls, village fences, and city gates huge placards appeared displaying the two-headed eagle and proclaiming that the tsar Nikolai II, Autocrat of All the Russias, King of Poland, and Archduke of Finland, called upon his loyal subjects to defend the sacred Russian soil against the slant-eyed heathens who dared challenge the right of the empire to its Far Eastern territories. Whoever neglected to respond punctually to this call would be summarily court-martialed.

Alongside these grand royal proclamations sprang up small, poorly printed ones put out by the various revolutionary parties. They called upon the peasants and workers to disobey the official decrees, to avoid the war that only concerned imperialists of different nationality but similarly corrupt motive.

The more the police and the gendarmes tore down these notices, the more they proliferated. The people gathered before them and read their seditious comments. In cities and towns men of draft age raided government liquor stores, attacked soldiers, and avoided conscription.

In Poland and Lithuania, in White Russia, and in the Baltic lands, revolutionary circles harangued soldiers with antiwar propaganda.

The police and gendarmes countered by dispatching agents to agitate against the Jews, the enemies of Christ and of the motherland, and urged the loyal citizens to avenge themselves against the unbelievers. The patriotic call didn't go unanswered as men launched bloody pogroms.

The tattoo of drums and the priestly chants drowned out the laments of conscripts' wives left behind and the cries of the

Jewish victims. In working quarters, the flames of resentment, class hatred, and revolution blazed high. Strike followed strike. Trains and boats were jammed with men, horses, and arms bound for distant Amur.

Along roads and tracks leading from Russia to Lodz, which despite the war remained tightly linked with the markets of the Far East, two men raced to get back home.

Occupying his own first-class compartment on the Trans-Siberian Express sat Max Ashkenazi, sales representative of the Huntze Corporation. Huddled in his broad sable coat and caracul hat, his pockets stuffed with cash, IOUs, and contracts, he leaned against the plush seat, gazing out glumly at the desolate steppes and forests stretching for mile after mile, day in, day out, seemingly without end.

The train was off schedule as it puffed its way over tracks piled high with drifts. "When will we be arriving?" Ashkenazi kept asking the conductor.

"Hard to say, sir," the conductor said defensively. "The snow is blocking all the roadbeds."

The outbreak of war had caught Max Ashkenazi thousands of miles from home. Frantic telegrams kept arriving from the mill. The Far East, in which Lodz had a fortune in goods invested and which represented one of its most lucrative markets, had been cut off by the war. The trains were now reserved exclusively for military purposes. Traveling salesmen had been stranded without money or orders. Factories had ground to a halt. Notes were being called in. Bankruptcies mounted. Lodz was in a flux, its course uncertain.

As usual, the Barons Huntze weren't there when they were most needed. They were vacationing on the Riviera and wiring requests for money. His underlings urged Max Ashkenazi to get back as quickly as possible. Vital decisions had to be made.

He was by now official director of the factory, Albrecht having long since gone to his reward just as Max had predicted. He had suffered a series of heart attacks, culminating one evening as Melchior brought him a particularly fetching spinner. When Albrecht tried to service the fresh young thing, his legs collapsed under him, and he fell, lifeless.

The factory gave him an elaborate funeral. Several pastors sang his praises, and Max Ashkenazi personally laid a wreath of white roses upon his grave. The very next day he took over the late director's office. Melchior, who still recalled Ashkenazi from the days when he was a boy in his father's warehouse, drew himself up erect before him and reported in a thunderous tone, "At your service, Mr. Director!"

Along with Albrecht's position, Max inherited his splendid carriage. Neither Melchior nor the coachman was overjoyed with his new master. Melchior tactfully dropped a hint about the young ladies who had attended the late director and inquired if the new director might be interested in the same service. Max fixed him with an ironic glance and remarked, "Spinners should do their spinning in the factory."

Melchior accepted the decision with bad grace. "Cheap sheeny swine," he grumbled to the coachman, who concurred: "They're all tightwads. A man can't earn a decent tip anymore. . . ."

The other factory employees shared these negative views, but no one dared voice his complaint. Max assumed his task with his usual energy, perception, and zeal. He was familiar with every aspect of the operation, with every machine, every worker, every bolt of goods. He introduced a sense of urgency and purpose into the mill. The managers despised him, but they acknowledged his competence. And as one gear drove the other, the plant began to hum with renewed vigor so that its every component—metal and human—danced to the new director's tune.

Despite all this activity, Max found time for extended sales trips to Russia, during which he concluded enormous transactions. But wherever he might be, he knew exactly what was happening at the mill. He received daily wires and sent daily wires detailing his precise instructions. Now that the war had erupted in the Far East, he squirmed restlessly in his compartment, which for all its spaciousness was too small for him in his eagerness to be back at work.

It was largely so because he had a spectacular idea. At the very time when the rest of Lodz was slowing down production as a result of the loss of the Far East markets, he had found a way to pull off an enormous coup. He had concluded that a fortune could be made by turning out goods for the armed services. The military quartermasters made excellent customers. They were willing to let others earn a few rubles so long as they lined their own pockets. The factory was currently geared toward civilian goods, but the conversion could be easily accomplished. The only urgency was to beat the other manufacturers to the punch.

The one he feared most was Flederbaum. He, Flederbaum, had already demonstrated his influence with the governor in the railroad coup. Max couldn't afford another such setback. The matter had to be expedited forthwith, and the only way to do this was to circumvent all underlings, go straight to the top man in charge of military procurement, and dangle a carrot before him. Then, while all Lodz stood idle, he would be operating double shifts!

The very notion set Ashkenazi twitching. It was as if he were back in his factory now, listening to the hum of its machinery in an otherwise-stilled Lodz. At that moment the locomotive whistle blew in startling imitation of a Huntze factory whistle.

Max's carriage took him directly from the depot to the factory. He didn't even stop at home to clean up after the long journey. He couldn't afford the time.

With remarkably disciplined urgency, he began to pull all available strings to get to the man in charge of procurement. He could have used his bosses' help now since they had access to the highest places, but they were away as usual and the whole burden fell upon him. This didn't concern him. Actually whatever he managed on his own was all the more gratifying. Besides, he had something better than social position; he had that great equalizer—cash.

He began with a quiet trip to Warsaw. Once there he arranged through a go-between to meet with a certain operetta singer who was the mistress of an adjutant of the commandant. He went to see the lady and made his overtures.

Revolted to the point of nausea by his own extravagant compliments, he placed a diamond ring on one of the singer's plump fingers, which barely had room for any more rings. "May this be but a token of my deep admiration for your great art," he said in his broken Polish. "It would give me the greatest pleasure once again to enjoy your divine company."

"I'm deeply touched," she said with her most seductive smile. "I would be delighted to receive the gentleman in my modest little apartment in the company of my close friends."

Through the blond lady, he was drawn into a very odd circle that included dissolute officers, elderly wealthy admirers of the lady's talents, and the usual coterie of sots, gamblers, black sheep aristocrats, and roués.

Barely keeping from retching, he spent several days cavorting with his new friends, who shattered crockery and mirrors in cabarets and restaurants and forever drew their revolvers in response to real or imagined insults. But he managed to get to the commandant.

He came back to Lodz with heartburn and a headache, but in his pocket reposed an order for military goods which would bring enormous profits. And even as the rest of Lodz lay idle, the Huntze mill went on a round-the-clock schedule. Its stacks belched arrogant smoke; its red-brick walls vibrated with feverish impetus.

Again Max Ashkenazi was the talk of Lodz. Again people gazed at him as he rode through the poorly paved streets in his carriage.

"A regular ball of fire!" they exulted. "He could turn snow into cheese. . . ."

"He's found himself the right little war all right," others said in envy. "A sweet little war of pure gold. . . ."

Max didn't mind sending his barons all the money they asked for now. With his own huge profits, he bought additional Huntze stock, which had dropped to a new low, thanks to the war.

Down highways and byways, on sleighs and on trains, afoot and hidden under straw in peasant carts, another citizen of Lodz raced back from far-off Siberia to the city of his birth. He, too, had an important task to accomplish there.

The time had never been more propitious. There were frequent strikes. Demonstrations erupted in the streets. Because of the war, there was serious unemployment—the workers were resentful and ripe for rebellion. The revolutionary cells that he, Nissan, and Tevye had sown had proliferated. The May Day debacle that had ended in such ugly fashion hadn't eradicated the workers' urge for unity, as had been assumed at that time. They frequently demonstrated now, singing revolutionary songs and displaying open resentment against the manufacturers and the police.

Tevye had dispatched letter after veiled letter from which Nissan had gathered that his presence in Lodz was desperately needed. His comrades had even provided the money for his escape. And although his period of exile was nearly at an end, Nissan left before it was up.

He had grown tired of Siberia. There was absolutely nothing to do in the godforsaken place. Whole days were squandered on fruitless debates and wrangling. The variety of political factions was unbelievable. There were narodniks and Polish socialists, Social Revolutionaries, Jewish Bundists, and anarchists, along with various offshoots of every party, each full of scorn, sarcasm, rage, and derision toward the others.

Wretched, miserable, isolated from everything and everyone, they turned on one another with cannibalistic fury fed by enforced indolence. Each new arrival brought news of new parties, subparties, factions, and groups mushrooming in the nation—each complete with its own detailed and irreconcilable programs for Russia's salvation.

Along with the others, Nissan had given his tongue full rein. As an ex-yeshiva student he was inherently steeped in polemic and dialectic. For every occasion or reference, he had an apt quote, a flood of logic and documentation to douse anyone who dared question the absolutism of Marxist dogma.

"Only the straight path—no deviations!" he lectured the quibblers and nitpickers, just as his father had admonished those who dared stray even a hair from the Torah.

Black of eye, swarthy, with a small black beard and curly sideburns which brought to mind the traditional earlocks, he had retained the yeshiva student's habit of twirling his thumb in the air in the heat of debate.

He wasn't popular with the gentile exiles, who couldn't match his intellect and debating skills. They scorned his fanatic devotion to books, his refusal to take an occasional drink or join them on a hunting expedition.

The only one with whom he was close was the Social Democrat Szczinski. Although a Pole and an ex-seminarian, he shared Nissan's devotion to study and his aversion to all revisionists, particularly the Polish socialists, who sought to introduce nationalistic aspirations into pure Marxism. Like Nissan, he abjured the hunts and the drinking parties and elected the life of the ascetic. Even his blond beard took on the appearance of a Jewish Torah scholar's.

He enjoyed nothing more than studying with Nissan. He retained the zeal that had been instilled in him by the Jesuits and the conviction that the end justified the means. He sneered when discussing the enemies of the proletariat. He believed in the inexorable collapse of capitalism, but he lacked the patience to sit idly by while history dawdled toward this goal. He was determined, instead, to serve as the instrument of the cataclysm. Without the consent of his party, he had instituted a reign of terror in Lodz. Following his capture and imprisonment, he had been exiled to Siberia.

"Root them out, root them out!" he kept muttering on his strolls with Nissan.

It was in the company of this Szczinski that Nissan fled from Siberia. The moment he stepped off the train in Lodz, he could smell revolution in the air. It exuded from the walls of every building, hovered in the frosty air enveloping the sooty streets. The deeper he penetrated the poorer quarters, the more seditious the posters that greeted him from fences and walls. Two-man police teams, each accompanied by an armed soldier, patrolled the street corners.

Nissan went looking for the forger who would provide him the false passport he would need. He gingerly made his way through the neighborhood until he came to the right address. The flower pot stood in the window, as it was supposed to, indicating that it was safe to enter.

"How is Uncle?" he inquired of the young red-cheeked matron who answered his knock.

"He is well, and he sends his regards," she replied, flushing even deeper.

Nissan stepped inside and exchanged kisses with the woman, who was a total stranger to him. "At last," she said. "We were already worried about you. Are you hungry, Comrade?"

"Before anything else, some hot water please! It's been weeks already since I've had a bath."

That same evening a reception for Nissan was held at the young woman's house, complete with whiskey, cake, sausage, beer, and all the trimmings. A young man dressed in his Sabbath best sat next to a girl in her best dress. They posed as an alleged bride and groom. This was to allay the suspicions of the janitor, who, like all of his kind, was a police informer.

Tevye described the conditions in the city. "Lodz is ours!" he exulted. "You'll rest up a few weeks; then we'll put you to work. We need you here, Nissan."

"I don't need a rest," Nissan said. "I'm ready to start right in. I've idled away too many years already."

Within a few days he joined the revolutionary committee. His first appearance was in the Balut house of worship. An odd group had assembled for the combined afternoon-evening services. Most of them were young and dressed in modern style, the kinds of Jews rarely seen in a synagogue. The beadle, who was already familiar with the tricks of those who pushed solidarity, tried to thwart their efforts. The moment the cantor had recited the final words of the mourner's prayer, he slammed his fist on the lectern and announced that the preacher would promptly commence his sermon, but the radicals had anticipated him.

"Don't make a move!" a broad-shouldered worker exclaimed, blocking the door. "The one to talk won't be the preacher, but our representative. Comrade Nissan, the floor is yours!"

Nissan mounted the pulpit and looked around. For a moment he had difficulty launching his speech. He had already grown unaccustomed to speaking Yiddish. But the large crowd, the boldness of his comrades, who no longer feared arrest, filled him with a sense of warmth and with confidence, and he exulted that his years of effort had not been in vain. The words came with a passion that aroused his audience as well as himself.

The candles before the lectern dripped and melted from the heat generated by so many bodies inside the jammed room.

The streets of Balut didn't seem the same to Nissan. All the walls were plastered with revolutionary proclamations that the police no longer bothered to tear down. On every corner men openly talked sedition without gazing fearfully over their shoulders. The labor exchanges seethed with activity. Weavers, spinners, hosiers, seamstresses, tailors, cobblers in modern garb and in long gabardines milled about while union representatives held meetings, planned strikes, distributed literature, collected dues, and from time to time mounted some elevation to launch fiery speeches.

The common people of Lodz, from housemaids to indigent street vendors, came here to verbalize their complaints and seek redress. A huckster cited a landlord who had evicted him for nonpayment of rent; a housemaid had not been paid her wages; coachmen's wives bewailed their husbands' drinking up their pay; apprentices lodged complaints against masters who beat and starved them. Even couples who hadn't been able to solve their marital problems at rabbis' appealed to the unionists for assistance.

The exchanges kept an eye on working conditions, agitated for reform, and acted against those who flouted their directives. Here delegates were elected to visit shops and factories and check that the workers' hours and wages were being adhered to. From here goons were sent to discipline intransigent landlords and employers. Here lists were assembled of affluent citizens on whom levies would be imposed to support soup kitchens for the poor and to pay for the printing of revolutionary literature.

Such was the strength of the workers that the orders of the exchanges were observed more carefully than those of the police. The union organizers couldn't be bribed or taken to court for arbitration. They had their ways of punishing those who defied their directives.

And the stern king and inflexible tsar of the exchanges was Tevye the World Isn't Lawless. Urgent, inexhaustible, he was everywhere at once, his nose in every corner, his eye on everything. And constantly by his side ready to offer comfort and assistance was his daughter Bashke.

By now a fully grown woman, good-looking and capable, she could have long since married and been a mother, but she wouldn't leave her father, to whom she had been so closely attached since her childhood years. Her mother cursed her, predicted that she would end up in shackles, but Bashke lived only for her father even as she worshiped Nissan from afar.

Just as in the old days, when she had come to his room to collect the illicit literature, she still gazed at him with adoration. She didn't address a word to him, merely blushed when he came near her.

Nissan strode through the streets of Balut with a triumphant Tevye. "As you see," Tevye said, looking around the cramped streets, "it's ours, all ours now. . . ."

THIRTY-EIGHT

———◆———

THE GOVERNOR OF THE PROVINCE, von Müller, summoned the chief rabbi of Lodz along with the leaders of the community to his headquarters in Piotrkow. The community leaders donned black suits and top hats, the rabbi put on his silk gabardine with the medal he had received from the imperial court, and they went to Piotrkow. But the governor wasn't impressed with the finery or the medal, and he laid down law.

"You Jews are revolting against me in Lodz!" he roared. "If you don't discipline those hooligans of yours, I won't be responsible when the people turn on them!"

The leaders bowed their heads. "You must make the same distinction between us as you would between Germans and Poles, Excellency," they said humbly. "We're powerless against those elements among us that disobey the law."

"That's your problem!" the governor shouted, pounding the table.

The chief rabbi, who was a shrewd and pragmatic man, came up, as usual, with an inspired solution. "Would His Excellency be willing to inquire of his subordinates if even one of the rebels taken into custody wore ritual garments?"

The governor looked puzzled.

In his excellent Russian the rabbi explained that only those Jews who were true to their faith would wear a ritual garment, and therefore, those that did were uniformly loyal to the tsar.

The governor took note of this information, and soon after, the police began to check the attire of arrested Jews. Those who wore ritual garments were immediately released, while the others were detained.

News of the rabbi's brilliant inspiration quickly spread through the city, and even his opponents lauded his wisdom, but the ploy was short-lived since the rebellious Jews quickly took to wearing ritual garments, too.

In the meantime, the community leaders resolved to do something themselves about the radical element in their midst. They sent preachers to every house of worship to inveigh against rebellion and to promote Jewishness and submission to lawful authority. On the Sabbaths they sent teachers into the poorer synagogues to sway the young workers away from radical notions.

When this, too, made no impact, the leaders turned to the underworld to discipline the rebels. Ill feeling between the two factions had already been brewing for a long time. Prior to the birth of the radical movement, the criminals had been the masters of Balut. They extorted money from servant girls for the privilege of strolling through the woods on the Sabbaths. If a worker tried to walk with a girl, he would be approached by a tough claiming that the girl was his fiancée and demanding payment of a ruble under threat of a beating.

On Passover, when the workers showed up in their holiday best, they had to pay up, lest their new suits be doused with ink or slit with a knife.

But since the unions had been formed, the workers refused to pay tribute and had even beaten several of the toughs. And the toughs couldn't afford to lose face this way.

Besides, the unionists had begun to foil them in other areas. They persuaded the servant girls to avoid the company of toughs and to attend union meetings instead. They dissuaded the men from patronizing brothels, thus diminishing the pimps' income. Some of the whores had even been induced to leave the brothels and take up honest work.

Another thorn in the side of the criminals was that it used to be they to whom the poor Jews would come in times of trouble. For a fee of a few guldens, the toughs would "persuade" a husband to return to his deserted wife. For a few drinks and some stewed goose stomachs, they would crack a mean boss's ribs, slap around a straying wife, give a black eye to a girl who had dropped her fiancé for another man.

But now the Jews of Balut turned to the exchanges for redress of their grievances, and the toughs were left with no outlet for their muscle and their authority. Even worse, some of the toughest among them, who with their strength and daring had brought honor to the fraternity, went over to the side of the unionists and refused to have anything to do with their former cohorts.

All this rankled the criminal element of Balut and fired their rage against the unionists.

The merchants and magnates of Lodz, who had endured

so much grief from the unionists and had then been humiliated into contributing toward their support, were much happier to pay off the toughs to teach the radicals a lesson they would never forget. The toughs got together, armed themselves, and prepared for the showdown. They were joined by master teamsters, who held a similar grudge against the unionists for inciting their employees, the hired draymen, to demand shorter hours and higher wages. Besides, they, the unionists, denied the existence of God, mocked the rabbis, the saints, the synagogue, and the other pillars of Judaism.

The incident that brought things to a head was the matter of the "electricity."

A young worker of Balut had died of tuberculosis, and the members of the Burial Society promptly came to prepare his body for interment. They even brought along a ritual garment for the corpse because even if he had neglected to wear such a garment in life, it was only right that he go properly attired into the other world.

But the unionists claimed the body first and wouldn't allow it to be washed, clad in shrouds or the ritual garment. Instead, they wrapped it in a red flag and escorted it to the cemetery, singing revolutionary songs along the way.

At the cemetery a female unionist in a red dress proclaimed that when a person died, it wasn't his soul that departed his body, but his "electricity." The members of the Burial Society and the gravediggers swiftly spread this choice morsel of news throughout the city, and things began to hum.

"It's the end of the world!" Traditional Jews sighed. "Even gentiles believe in a soul. . . ."

"They'll bring a misfortune down upon the city—a plague or what not, may it not happen. . . ."

"They should be rooted out without mercy!"

"They should be denounced to the police!"

"They should rot in chains!"

All the preachers and teachers spoke of the "electricity" in the prayerhouses. The chief rabbi himself proclaimed that according to Jewish law, the unionists had forfeited their right to life since the holy books stated that those who drown themselves deserve not to be rescued, but to be held underwater.

Those who took the matter hardest were the master teamsters and the toughs of Feiffer Lane. The moment they caught a unionist alone, they beat him savagely. The unionists countered by striking back at the criminals. The police sided with the toughs. Tempers flared, and one night the war erupted.

On Prevet Street, "Uncle" Zachariah Poontz, a keeper of

several brothels, married off an orphan to a cobbler. Uncle
Zachariah had no children of his own, and he had taken in
the orphan girl, reared her, and married her off to a cobbler, not
to one of his criminal cronies, so that she would remain a
decent Jewish daughter.

The wedding was a lavish one. Several bands played. Many
guests gathered from both sides. The bride's side was represented by the pimps and thieves; the groom's, by cobblers,
tanners, and saddlemakers, healthy and robust youths and
unionists to the core.

At the canopy, when the rabbi of the underworld synagogue
piously recited the blessing in a nasal, epicene voice, the unionists couldn't contain themselves and burst out laughing. Uncle
Zachariah's bull-like neck flushed a deep crimson. "Don't
laugh at a rabbi, you scum!" he growled. "I won't stand for it!"

"Shut your yaps, Electricity!" his cohorts chimed in.

The tough young shoemakers thrust out their chests. "We'd
like to see who'll shut us up," they challenged.

Fists clenched on both sides. In the midst of his blessing, the
rabbi thrust himself between both factions. "Well, now, it's a
wedding, after all . . . it's a disgrace to fight on such an occasion. . . ."

Another quarrel erupted during the distribution of the
wedding presents. The guests from the bride's side were free
with their money and gave gifts of three, five, even ten rubles.
The crippled beadle of the underworld synagogue, a former
pickpocket, very ceremoniously stacked the banknotes on the
table. The unionists from the groom's side gave half rubles and
a rare whole ruble. The toughs started to heckle the workers.

"Hey, unionist, dole something out already!" they jeered at
those groping in their meager purses.

"Hey there, 'Lectricity, no slugs now. . . ."

The workers wouldn't take this lying down. "We've got
to *work* for our money," they said, "not like some others we
know. . . ."

The toughs bristled at the insinuation. "Who you trying to
needle?" they growled.

"If the shoe fits, wear it," the workers countered.

Just then a mug of beer hurled from the bride's side caught
a tanner full in the face. Blood and beer spurted together from
the youth's face onto the white paper dickey he had bought
specially for the occasion.

His comrades let go with several mugs at the bride's side.
Within seconds, the tablecloths, glasses, plates, and wedding
gifts lay smashed all over the floor. The men shucked their

jackets and grabbed chairs, candlesticks, knives—whatever could be used for a weapon. The women shrieked and shouted. The workers suffered a total rout—they were badly outnumbered.

The next day all the cobblers, saddlemakers, harnessmakers, and tanners walked off their jobs, to be joined by the organized draymen and butchers. With clubs in hand and knives in pockets, they descended upon Prevet Street and wreaked systematic havoc upon the brothels. They hurled beds and bedding through windows, slashed the whores' dresses, smashed the pianos, and tore the suggestive pictures off the walls.

"Go to work!" they shouted. "No more whorehouses and easy money!"

The girls screamed hysterically, and there was uproar in the street. Uncle Zachariah's wife tore the black, wavy wig from her head.

"Zachariah, save the girls!" she shrieked. "They're destroying our livelihood!"

But Zachariah was afraid to resist—there were too many of the workers. He ran for his cohorts, but by the time they arrived the workers had wrecked every brothel on the street. Feathers and down filled the air like snowflakes. Glass crunched beneath feet. The toughs, accompanied by the boss teamsters, advanced with knives drawn, but the workers formed a solid wall, and their cobblers' knives sliced flesh as easily as leather. This time it was the toughs who were routed and humiliated.

News of the unionists' victory carried through the city. The toughs were now too intimidated to come near the labor exchanges. A fear fell over the city's employers. Even the police were afraid to stand up to the unionists, the conquerors of Feiffer Lane. No one dared say a word when the unionists came to speak at a synagogue or to walk the workers off the job precisely at 7:00 P.M. No one haggled when their representatives came to demand a donation for their soup kitchens. Even the restaurateurs served a free lunch when a union representative brought in an unemployed worker to be fed. Manufacturers refused to show themselves in their carriages. They quietly went abroad, leaving their businesses in the hands of their managers until the troubles subsided.

From the Far Eastern fronts came even worse tidings. The slant-eyed heathens were clobbering the God-fearing Russians on land and at sea. The blind beggars who sang in the courtyards made veiled reference in their ditties to the Russian defeats. Cossacks spilled into every corner of the city.

THIRTY-NINE

———◆———

THE HUNTZE PLANT GROUND TO A HALT. The workers had walked off the job again. The factory director, Max Ashkenazi, didn't leave the grounds. He was afraid to show himself in the streets. Melchior made up the bed for him in the late Albrecht's huge office and stood guard ouside his door all night with a loaded revolver.

Max slept fitfully in the huge bed where Albrecht had been so lavishly pleasured by the young spinners.

Every minute the plant stood idle was like a thrust into Ashkenazi's heart. According to his contract with the quartermaster general, he had a huge shipment of military goods to deliver by a specified date. If this contract were violated, the factory would be severely indemnified, and he personally would be out a fortune. He had kept the plant running at full capacity, two shifts around the clock. Everything had been carefully planned and arranged. The factory had been running like a fine-tuned watch. Suddenly it had all come to a stop.

One detail Director Ashkenazi hadn't taken into account was the workers. He had planned everything down to the last screw and bolt, but he hadn't considered the human factor. And why should he have? Ever since he was little, he had known that there was never a shortage of hands in Lodz; there were always more than were needed. He also knew that hands needed work, all the work they could get. But suddenly the world turned upside down. One day, as he sat in his office, overburdened as usual with work, Melchior came in to announce that a delegation of workers from the factory wanted to speak with him.

Max looked up in amazement. "A delegation? I have no time for that now. Tell them to come back some other time."

Melchior went out to pass the director's answer on to the workers. He assumed that they would now withdraw, as they always did in such cases, but they didn't budge. "Tell the director that we, too, don't have the time and that if he doesn't see us this minute, we'll close down the factory," their spokesman said.

When Melchior reported the workers' response to Max Ashkenazi, he plucked his wisp of a beard again and again. His soft easy chair grew suddenly hard as stone. He adjusted his tie, which as usual was twisted to one side, brushed the ashes off his lapel, leaned back in his chair, and lit a large aromatic cigar. He assumed his sternest expression, then scribbled some meaningless words on a scrap of paper to show the workers that he indeed was busy.

They came in with their caps in hand, but exuding an air of complete confidence and assurance. Some even neglected to wipe their muddied shoes first.

Max Ashkenazi greeted them with an insolent puff of smoke. "Well?" he asked.

"We represent all the workers of the factory," the spokesman said. He proceeded to read a list of demands from a sheet of paper.

Max had the impulse to seize the paper, crumple it, and throw it to the ground just as he had that Saturday night when the workers had presented their demands in his father-in-law's factory, but he restrained himself. These were not Jews, but gentiles and prone to violence. They hadn't hesitated to shove Albrecht into a barrow and wheel him around with a broom in hand. Life to them wasn't worth a groschen, not their own or that of others, so he tugged at the ends of his vest as if it were too short for him and listened.

The demands were outrageous. They actually insisted on an eight-hour day—three shifts instead of two! Forgetting his resolve to remain cool and contemptuous, Max sprang from his chair.

"How long ago was it you worked sixteen hours a day?" he shouted. "And now twelve is already too much, too?"

"We can work twelve hours," the spokesman said, "but for the extra four hours we want overtime pay."

"Out of the question!" Ashkenazi snapped.

" 'For night work, time and a half,' " the delegate read from the paper.

"Nonsense," Ashkenazi said with a wave of the hand.

" 'A twenty-five percent increase in base pay,' " the man continued.

"Is that all?" Ashkenazi asked in a sarcastic tone.

"For now, yes," the spokesman replied passively.

Max Ashkenazi plucked at the tip of his beard. "I assume

that even though you are only workers, you are able to add and subtract?" he asked.

The men didn't know what he was leading up to, and they merely waited in silence.

Max quickly scribbled a set of figures. "If I were to give in to even half your demands, the factory would have to operate at a loss, and that's something no factory can afford to do."

"We have our own needs to think of," the spokesman said. "The factory's profits and losses aren't our concern."

Max flicked his cigar so violently that the ashes sprayed the lapels of his expensive English suit. "On the contrary, the factory's profits and losses are very much your concern. You're just as much part of this factory as I am. If it closes down, we all stand to lose."

"That's up to you," the men said.

"It's one thing to shut down a factory. It's quite another to get it running again," Max said with a rusty smile. "Times are hard. Thousands of people are out of work. They would consider it a blessing to get your jobs. I didn't close down our factory like the other manufacturers did. I searched out orders so that you could keep on working. Is this the way you want to repay me?"

"The director wasn't thinking of us, but of himself," the spokesman said. "If the director won't meet our demands, we strike."

Max tried another tack. "I'm only an employee here, just as you are. As you well know, the Barons Huntze are the owners of the factory. They're abroad right now. Only they can make such a major decision. The moment they're back, I'll present your demands to them. In the meantime, let's get back to work."

He was stalling for time. He couldn't afford to have the factory stand idle for even an hour at this time. But the workers wouldn't grant him the reprieve.

"We'll give you an extra few days to contact the barons," the spokesman said after conferring briefly with the others. "But that's all. We want your answer by then."

During his few days of grace Ashkenazi tried every ploy he knew to avert a strike. First, he turned to the method that had served him so well in the past. He no longer sent for Lippe Halfon but invited the police chief himself for lunch. He made it a point to relay the fact that the factory was engaged in war production in behalf of the brave lads at the front. By shutting down the mill, the workers would be hampering a patriotic effort. The authorities were obliged to exercise all the power at their command to prevent this. If they sent Cossacks to teach the traitors a lesson, things would return to normal.

The police chief licked his whiskers after the lavish meal but shook his head. He wasn't about to confront the workers at this time. He had enough troubles besides this. His men were frightened. Each day another policeman was shot. Nor would the governor become involved either. Times were no longer the same. The only thing left for him, Ashkenazi, was to deal with the workers in his own way.

Max tried other ploys. He called in each of the delegates separately and let each one know that if he would abandon the group and consider his own interests, he would be handsomely rewarded. But they wouldn't go along. Some took it as an affront; some became alarmed.

Max then ordered his foremen to recruit unemployed men and women in the streets to replace the regular workers and thus break the strike, but people were too afraid to scab. Many of them sided with the workers.

When all other means had been exhausted, Ashkenazi used his trump card. He shut down the factory himself in an effort to starve the workers into coming back. He knew that this would cut deeply into his production schedule, but he felt certain that such a bold move would assure him ultimate victory.

After locking the factory securely, Max barricaded himself inside and waited for the workers to capitulate. He was too clever to show himself outside the factory gates, while thousands of his men milled through the streets roused to a fever pitch by the agitators, and he had his meals brought in from home.

No one was allowed inside the factory. Melchior sat at the front door with a loaded revolver. Out of sheer boredom, Max even began to read the trashy novels his predecessor had been so fond of. He couldn't sleep through the long, languid night without the roar of the machinery to lull him.

But the workers didn't come crawling back, as he had expected.

For Nissan, these were days of furious activity. He collected funds for the strike, made speeches, wrote proclamations. This wasn't anything like that pathetic first effort years ago in Balut. This was a full-fledged strike involving thousands of true proletarians against a giant capitalistic enterprise. This was a struggle deserving his, Nissan's, most intense effort.

The time for which he had been waiting so long had finally come. The spark of discontent had leaped across the walls of the huge factories, and Nissan worked day and night to keep it glowing until it erupted into the blazing flame of revolution.

In his secret hideaway within the factory walls, Max Ashkenazi seethed when he heard that Jewish agitators from Balut were keeping his workers off their jobs. What right had they to mix into matters that didn't concern them? They didn't work for him now, nor would they ever. So why did they tear out their guts in behalf of gentile workers who despised them?

Most of his rage was directed against that rabbi's whelp, who was responsible for all his troubles. Hadn't the years of prison and exile taught him anything? The only thing gentiles required was the chance to work. They were strong, and they cared little whether they worked a few hours more or less. All they wanted was the few rubles so that they could get drunk on Saturdays. All those other notions stemmed from Jews. Being physically inferior, they couldn't put in a day's work themselves, and all they were good for was to turn the gentiles' heads with talk of socialism, solidarity, and other such twaddle. They would keep it up until they aroused the savage blood of the gentiles, and the result would be the same as usual—Jewish blood being shed.

Max bit his lips out of rage and frustration. Had the times been less touchy, he would have taught those Jewish trouble-makers a lesson. It was considered a good deed to punish Jews who turned gentiles against their own brothers.

But his hands were tied. Even the police were afraid to buck the rebels. And what would it lead to? How much provocation would the gentiles require to shoot or stab him, Ashkenazi, whom Nissan and his gang constantly denounced as a blood-sucker and an exploiter?

True, he was safe in his hideout for now, but how long could this go on? Every minute the factory stood idle cost him a fortune. There were millions waiting to be made and here he was, stuck away like some mouse in a hole. . . .

One sleepless night, as Max Ashkenazi's brain seethed with thousands of ideas and notions, it suddenly struck him that it might be beneficial to have Nissan in for a private discussion. True, he was an infidel and worse than any gentile; still, it wouldn't hurt to talk. He, Max, had always held great faith in his powers of persuasion. Not that Nissan was a fool. Far from it. They had already locked horns years back in his father's schoolroom and again that Saturday night in Balut. Nissan couldn't possibly know that Max had had anything to do with his first arrest. Besides, that was already ancient history. He had been exiled again after that, and he had undoubtedly forgotten all about the earlier incident.

In the event that Nissan still nursed a grudge against him, Max would prove to him that he was completely innocent. It had all been the doing of the police. In fact, he, Max, had pleaded in Nissan's behalf, even though it had been to no avail. If only Nissan agreed to talk things over with him, he would realize that Max was right. Max had been blessed with the power to reason with people, to speak straight from the heart.

He sat down and wrote a letter to his former classmate. In the erudite Hebrew employed by one scholar to another, replete with apt parables and quotes from the Gemara, he requested Nissan's presence at the factory in order to discuss a matter of the gravest importance. He added that it wasn't out of any self-pride or haughtiness that he invited the other to come to him, but merely as a matter of expediency since he, Max, found it impolitic to show himself outside the factory these days.

He signed the letter with a number of additional flourishes, read it over with satisfaction, and dispatched it with a trusted messenger, whom he admonished to deliver it into the right hands.

For several hours the committee debated how to respond to the message from the enemy camp. Ignore it? Refuse it? Accept it?

Tevye was against accepting—he suspected some sort of trick. There might be police waiting there to nab Nissan. But Nissan was of another opinion. Ashkenazi wouldn't be so stupid as to pull such a crude stunt at this time. He was too pragmatic for that. It might prove worthwhile to hear what he had to say. It never hurt to learn all one could about the enemy. But to allay any suspicion, he, Nissan, wouldn't go there alone.

One evening, accompanied by two companions, he made his way to the factory. The gate opened, then slammed shut heavily, just as it had in the prisons he had known so well. Max Ashkenazi was waiting at his office door. When he saw three people instead of one, he grew momentarily disappointed —he preferred one-to-one confrontations. But he quickly recovered and assumed a friendly, hospitable expression. He shook the hands of all three visitors and said in an affable German, "I'm very delighted to see you gentlemen. Do please sit down."

He decided to begin in a scholarly tone. He gazed searchingly at Nissan. "Recognized you at once. There's no mistaking the face of a scholar."

He didn't quite know how to address Nissan—whether to use the first person singular—and he solved the problem by mumbling the word inaudibly. But Nissan maintained a cool reserve, and Max decided on the more formal salutation instead of the familiar "thou."

"Albeit much time has already gone by since we studied together in your father's classroom, I can still recall the last lesson we studied together, the one dealing with the laws concerning the color blue. I still remember it by heart. . . ."

He glanced at the visitors and launched into the passage, twirling his thumb in the air as he did so.

"Do you remember, Nissan?" he asked nostalgically.

"I no longer devote myself to such things," Nissan replied coldly.

"What a pity" Ashkenazi clucked. "And I, despite my busy schedule, still like to glance into a holy book now and then. Why be ashamed to admit it? I even enjoy writing commentaries and innovations. Whenever I get a free moment, I jot down one or two. After all, man does not live by bread alone. . . ."

He glanced at the visitors, hoping for a glimpse of admiration for a director of the city's largest factory who still found time to write commentaries, but there was none apparent.

He turned to Nissan's companions. "You two gentlemen obviously aren't familiar with the holy books. You must excuse the depth of my feeling. . . ."

"We don't feel at all offended," the men replied airily.

"But you, Nissan—once a scholar, always a scholar," Ashkenazi said with conviction. "Whoever has once tasted the flavor of halakic controversy remains forever devoted to the Gemara, no matter how much he may resist. That's something that's rooted in the blood already."

He even related the amusing little anecdote of how he had responded to the barons' query with the reply that he had attended the Academy of Talmud under the Professors Abbayeh and Raba.

This put him into such a good mood that he went so far as familiarly to touch Nissan's knee, but Nissan withdrew coldly. At this, Ashkenazi abruptly dropped his jolly pose and reverted to his position as director of the Huntze mill.

"Well, to business," he said in the German he had temporarily abandoned for the more homey Yiddish. "As you gentlemen well know, the factory is on strike."

"We know," they said.

"The demands the workers have presented are surely not to

be taken seriously," he went on. "These, we both know, are negotiating tactics. After all, an eight-hour day?"

"That's long enough for a person to work," Nissan countered.

Ashkenazi regarded him with a smile for a few moments. "Will the agreement apply to me as well? Everyone knows that I work twice that, and longer."

"But you work for yourself, Mr. Ashkenazi."

"No, I work for the factory, for all its employees. If I didn't put in so many hours, this factory would have closed down, along with all the others, and thousands of people would be out of work. But thanks to the fact I'm not a clock watcher, thousands are being kept working not one shift, but two. We're all merely cogs in one great machine."

"But you earn more in one day than a worker does in six months, Mr. Ashkenazi."

"Each according to his worth—based on what he brings in. I'm not here because of my looks, gentlemen. Not on account of my Jewishness either."

He bent closer to the men and said in an intimate Lodz Yiddish, "It wasn't for nothing that I, a Jew, became director of a huge plant, overseeing thousands of gentiles. Do you think they love me here? They hate the sight of me, but they need me. Without me, the whole place would go to pieces. That's why they pay me what they do. Each according to his worth. Whoever turns out a yard of goods gets paid for a yard of goods. Whoever brings in millions gets compensated accordingly."

"That's exactly what we're fighting against," Nissan said.

Ashkenazi grasped the tip of his beard and plucked several hairs from it. "If gentiles utter such foolishness, I accept it," he observed in a singsong. "I showed them the facts and figures. I proved to them in black and white that if we acceded to even half their demands, the factory would have to shut down. Everything has its limitations. Even if a machine is worked beyond its capacity, it breaks down. But you are Jews. You are able to add and subtract. I am told some of your people have even studied economics. Look at this account I've prepared. It's correct down to the very last groschen. So tell me, how can we agree to such preposterous demands?"

"We have a different way of reckoning," Nissan said. "We eliminate the huge dividends paid the owners and the huge salaries paid the director and the managers."

Ashkenazi rose from his chair. "Hear me out, gentlemen," he said. "We don't operate a business for the fun of it. If no profits accrued, we would shut down the plant. That would put thousands of people out into the street. Is this what you want?"

"Is that all you had to say to us?" Nissan asked. "You didn't have to call us in for that."

Ashkenazi began to pace through his office. "I didn't send for you to discuss the factory," he said with some heat. "Because, let's not fool ourselves, you have no say when it comes to this plant. Your domain is Balut and the handworkers, while we operate on steam with exclusive gentile help. But even a mouse can make trouble, and you've been stirring up plenty of trouble. You're inciting the gentiles and—"

"We know nothing of gentiles and Jews, only of workers and exploiters," Nissan interrupted.

"But the Christians know of gentiles and Jews," Ashkenazi replied mockingly. "You talk of solidarity, unity, but try to put just one Jew in this factory, and the gentiles would carry him out on three stretchers!"

Nissan flushed. This was the weakest point of his argument, and he knew it. "That's your fault," he mumbled. "It was you and your kind that confined the Jewish workers to Balut—"

This time Ashkenazi interrupted him. "We're not talking like a director and workers now. We're talking like fellow Jews. Danger lurks over the city—terrible danger! Jewish blood will flow!"

"We have a defense corps organized, and we also have the goodwill of the working class. You can't scare us with such bugaboos, Mr. Ashkenazi."

Ashkenazi struck the table in anger. "Bugaboos, are they? At the meetings your gang organizes, the gentiles make threats against me not as Ashkenazi the director of the factory, but as Ashkenazi the Jew. The gentile speakers mock my broken Polish, my Jewish accent, and the workers laugh. The little Jewish shopkeepers shiver in their boots. The gentiles come in and tell them that when things get bad, they'll come back and rob them. It always ends up with Jewish heads being cracked. Do you remember the last time you called a workers' demonstration? What happened? Jews died! And now you Jews are again feeding the fires!"

The three men rose simultaneously.

"We didn't come here to listen to chauvinistic sermons," Nissan said.

"Bourgeois gall!" one of his companions erupted. "I didn't want to come here in the first place. Let's go, Comrade Nissan."

Nissan and the others left and took a droshky. The night was windy, rainy, chilly. The grimy city lay soaked under mud.

The few scattered trees resembled so many worn brooms. The driver didn't cease whipping his decrepit nag and abusing him for making such poor time. "Gee up, you carcass! Move it, you mangy nag!" he croaked.

The same gloom and misery filled Nissan's heart. Ashkenazi's bitter but accurate conclusion cut into him like a knife.

"We'll have to organize a defense corps immediately," he observed to his companions. "Tomorrow the question must be placed on the agenda."

"First thing tomorrow," the others mumbled, drawing their overcoats closer around them to guard against the cold and dampness.

FORTY

EVEN BEFORE THE STRIKE Max had been coming home less and less and spending more nights in the bachelor quarters of the late director Albrecht. At the same time he cut his wife's allowance for the household expenses.

Dinele felt deeply mortified. She was no longer a young woman. Even though, like her mother, she maintained the illusion of youth, her copper hair was now sprinkled with gray. The skin around her eyes had loosened and erupted into networks of fine, minute wrinkles. From carrying and delivering, she developed folds in her abdomen and broken blood vessels in her legs. She began to suffer all kinds of ailments, particularly female troubles. Men still looked at her in the streets since she was very skilled at disguising her defects, but when she came home and shed her corsets and stays, the first symptoms of age were unmistakably there, and she gazed anxiously at her husband's bed, which now stood empty more often than not.

The children were no longer with her. The elder, Ignatz, lived abroad. Introspective, moody, estranged, he had been a source of much grief to his mother. Just as the father was a bundle of energy and zeal, the son was a lazy, unambitious lout. He did badly at school and was forever at odds with his contemporaries. He couldn't maintain friendships since he always insisted on being the leader and bossed the others around. But where his father displayed the Ashkenazi will and energy, he was an Alter through and through. His was an unfortunate combination of genes, and it led to eternal family conflict. The result was that Ignatz went about in a constant sulk, seething with an anger and malice he himself couldn't define. He hated everything and everyone, but, most of all, his father, whom he considered his worst enemy. In his father's success he saw a reflection of his own inadequacies. He also sensed his father's derision when he examined his notebooks and report cards.

"Remarkable how the boy has inherited nothing from me," Max remarked on each such occasion.

The son would have been overjoyed to see his father a bleeding mess.

He did love his mother, but with a perverse, insalubrious kind of love. From earliest childhood he enjoyed tormenting her, being spiteful, refusing to obey. She was too wishy-washy to take stern measures with him—this was a job she felt belonged to a father. But Max was rarely home, and when he did show up, she couldn't bring herself to inform on the boy. Of the two, she much preferred her son. The only thing she could do when the boy pushed her over the brink was to cry, and this promptly made him contrite. He would kiss and fondle his mother and beg her forgiveness for being naughty.

But the moment she stopped crying, he reverted to his bullying ways. He played hooky, avoided people, hung around the house all day, half dressed, reading detective stories.

Bitter quarrels erupted when the father came home from business trips. Max Ashkenazi yearned for a son who would be a prodigy, a youth people would envy. But he didn't know how to communicate his feelings to his son in a diplomatic fashion; all he could do was shout and bark orders. But the louder he yelled, the more obstinate the boy grew, and it always ended with the father's wondering aloud how he could have sired such a dunce and the son's mimicking his father's general untidiness, his Jewish accent, and his pretensions.

One time, when Max left the house with his fly unbuttoned, the boy didn't alert him, only chortled with spiteful glee.

As soon as Ignatz managed somehow to get through the *Gymnasium,* he refused to stay in Lodz another second and promptly left for Paris, allegedly to pursue his studies, but he never even stuck his nose inside the university. Instead, he took up the life of a Left Bank bohemian, consorted with all kinds of depraved people, and constantly wrote home for money. The mother took out what she could from her household expenses or had the maid pawn some of her jewelry so that she could send Ignatz money without her husband's knowledge. Max seldom asked about their son.

"Write him to study hard, Diana," he would instruct his wife, and hand her the small check for the youth's monthly expenses.

"Why don't you add a few words of your own?" she castigated him. "You're his father, after all."

"Frightfully busy," he answered, and bustled out.

If it happened that his mother didn't send him what he con-

sidered was enough money, Ignatz threatened to kill himself.
She, therefore, went about constantly short of cash and couldn't
even tell her husband of her problem.

Nor was her daughter, Gertrud, at home much. Slim and
blue-eyed like her mother, she, too, was drawn to wealth and
gentility. Unlike her mother, though, she wasn't content to
live in that world vicariously but elected instead to realize her
fantasies.

She despised Lodz, the city of smoke, grime, and noise, and
hated her home, which was lonely and desolate despite the
elaborate decor. The furniture was heavy and ponderous, long
outmoded. The illumination was dim, gloomy. Rarely were
there any visitors. Her father was always preoccupied, seldom
home. He would bolt his meals and dash out again. Her
mother was totally absorbed in her novels. The Sabbaths and
holidays were drab, lacking all joy and festivity. And there was
that eternal void between her parents, an angry silence that cast
a pall over the household.

When she was a little girl, she used to love going to her
grandfather Haim's. There it was jolly. Her grandfather would
dandle her on his knee, tickle her cheeks with his beard, and
play so nicely with her. "Say the blessing, Gitele," he urged her
each time anew as he stuffed her with chocolate.

Even though he addressed her by that strange name, she preferred being there to home. There were all kinds of pretty
things—candlesticks, candelabra, snuffboxes. It was always gay
there, especially on Sabbaths and holidays. Haim Alter still celebrated the holy days, as he had in the good old days. He still
drew out the benedictions, sang the chants, invited paupers to
share his table.

Little Gertrud waited impatiently each year for Hanukah to
come around when her grandfather lit the candles; for Simhat
Torah, when the Hasidim gathered at his house to dance and
skip so comically; for the Days of Awe, when Grandfather
Haim donned a white linen robe and a silver-embroidered
skullcap and prayed with his hands held aloft. She even preferred to celebrate the Passover Seder away from the home in
which her father raced through quickly so that he could get
back to his papers. At her grandfather's house the Seder
dragged on for hours. The candles flickered merrily on the
table, Grandfather Haim sprawled expansively against his cush-
ion, and all the rites, chants, and prayers enraptured the little
girl.

"Grandpa," she cooed as she kissed him, "I love you so. . . ."

Because of her grandfather, she even grew temporarily pious

and recited her prayers and blessings, greatly irking her father. "He'll make a *rebbetzin* out of her yet!" he complained to his wife. "Why is she always there?"

When she grew older, she stopped going to her grandfather's so often; still, she couldn't bring herself to stay at home. She yearned for company, parties, balls, salons, games, and dances—the things her girlfriends enjoyed in their homes.

She felt estranged from her father and pitied her mother. She saw that her mother didn't love her father, and this fact both disturbed and puzzled her. She couldn't conceive how her mother could live with a man she didn't love for so many years. Why hadn't she left him? More important, why had she married him in the first place?

"Mama, did you ever love Father?" she asked her often.

"Do your homework," was her mother's response.

"Oh, how strange people used to be!" the girl said with feeling. "I would never marry a man I didn't love, not even if they tore pieces from me. . . ."

When Gertrud was graduated from boarding school, her mother began to think of the girl's future. She wanted to refurnish the house, invite company, get Gertrud involved with young people of proper breeding and background. Dinele knew that her own life was just about over. Although she had retained her good looks, she had missed the boat, and her life was slipping rapidly downward. She often decried her lost youth and wept into her pillow, but like any devoted mother, she wanted to assure a better life for her daughter.

Besides, the years had transformed her feelings toward her husband. She still didn't love him, but she had come to respect his strength, his energy, his leadership. This little man walked with the stride of a giant. During the years that she had estranged herself from him, with her children and her books, he had evolved into a man of knowledge and sophistication.

"Max," she implored him, "Gertrud is all grown up. We must think of her future. We must make a home for her."

She no longer resisted calling him by his adopted name. She only wanted to restore a state of harmony between them. But now it was Max who didn't respond to her overtures. He spent more nights away from home than not. Even on Sundays, when the factory was closed, he didn't show his face at home. "Frightfully busy," he told Dinele on the phone.

For the first time in their marriage, Dinele grew uneasy. She became convinced that her husband was having an affair.

At first, the notion of Simha Meir's running around with

women struck her as ludicrous. But on thinking it over, it no longer seemed so funny. Why not, indeed? She knew that he wouldn't take up with cheap streetwalkers. It would have to be one of his office girls or some dancer or actress, of whom there were hundreds in Lodz. Or maybe it was a real love affair and not a financial arrangement? Everything was possible now that women had grown as wanton as men. . . .

Dinele went to the mirror and studied herself with critical objectivity. The wrinkles around her eyes and the slackness of her skin stared back at her from the mirror. The gray in her hair was unmistakable. She felt unwanted and unattractive. During the time that she had been aging, Max had grown, if not handsome, at least distinguished. Strangest of all, he had retained his youthful appearance. He hadn't a wrinkle, a single strand of gray hair. If he were a touch more careful with his appearance, he wouldn't have been considered at all unattractive. His eyes in particular had remained bright and alert, burning with the fire of youth. Her friends had commented on it, but she had always scoffed at it, dismissed it. The truth of their observation came back now with particular sharpness.

Certainly, he was capable of a love affair. Women weren't all that choosy—especially when it came to a wealthy and important man.

The more she brooded about it, the more she grew convinced that her suspicions were correct. The same husband to whom she hadn't devoted a moment of thought in years now consumed all her waking hours. He suddenly acquired a vast importance in her eyes. And the larger he grew in her estimation, the lower her own self-esteem fell.

What need did he have of her, an aged, withered woman, when he could have all the fresh young girls he wanted? No wonder he didn't come home. Maybe they even joined him in mocking and laughing at her, his wife? . . .

She felt a stabbing in her breast. It was her first experience with jealousy. This was no longer a novel, but real life, and the pain was keen and urgent.

For a while she tried to persuade herself that he wasn't deceiving her but that something had happened to him to keep him away from home. She got out of bed and sat up listening for every sound. She peered through the windows into the dark night, starting at every ring of the gate bell, every knock on the door, every footstep in the courtyard. She even telephoned the factory, but no one answered. She let the phone ring many times, then hung up in despair.

She went into her daughter's bedroom to seek a little comfort, but Gertrud, too, wasn't home. She was out seeking gaiety and laughter wherever it could be found in the dank, smoky city. Dinele went back to her bed and lay awake until the first factory whistles pierced the foredawn air.

FORTY-ONE

———◆———

IT WAS INDEED A WOMAN who had estranged Max
Ashkenazi from his home, but not the young beauty Dinele
envisioned—rather a homely, hardly alluring elderly widow.

Following the fiasco with the army contract, Max felt a sense
of terrible failure and dejection. He had planned to use the
profits from the deal to buy up all the available Huntze stock
in one shot, thus giving him the majority of the shares and
making him the chief officer of the firm, the culmination of
his childhood goal. Now he was right back where he had
started. And what was particularly galling was the fact that
the opportunity had been so timely. The barons had, if anything, grown even more profligate, and they flooded their director with stock to be disposed of on the open market.

Max didn't release the stock into the open market but bought
it himself and stacked it in his safe, row upon row. He totaled
the certificates again and again with a deep sense of frustration.
If not for the unionists and their "revolution," he would be
King of Lodz now. He had been forced to pay enormous in-
demnities for his failure to meet the army contract. That and
lawyers' fees, court costs, and bribes had put a large dent in the
firm's assets, and his enemies in the plant gloated over his
setback and denounced him in letters to the barons.

The fiasco had set his timetable back considerably. It would
take years to undo the damage, and time, Max knew, was his
worst enemy. The years flew by, and the prize still eluded him.
He could wait no longer. He had to show Lodz, especially now
that his brother had once more bested him in such spectacular
fashion.

It started with a divorce. His sickly, bitter wife could no
longer go on living with Yakub. Each time her relatives tried
to restore peace and to reunite her with her husband in Lodz,
she ran back to Warsaw after only a couple of weeks, corroded
with jealousy and resentment toward his women, his robust

appetite, his roaring good health. She was barren, besides, and even though he never reproached her for this failure, he fondled every child he met, much to Perele's discomfiture, for she was even jealous of children.

What irked her most was when he played with his little niece, Gertrud. Although the brothers were estranged, their wives had remained friends. Even before they had become sisters-in-law, Perele and Dinele had been distantly related, and each time Perele came back to Lodz, Dinele, her mother, and her daughter came to visit her often.

Gertrud clung to her uncle Yakub. He provided her with the affection she should have gotten from her father. He bought her the prettiest dolls and toys. He drove her in his carriage, made the horses gallop, even let her hold the reins.

Slim, blue-eyed, with copper ringlets that trembled with her every move, with warm, plump, smooth arms and hands, she was the carbon copy of her mother from the time she and Yakub had played in the Ashkenazi courtyard. In Gertrud Yakub saw the girl everyone predicted would become his bride, and he carried her piggyback, as he had carried her mother so many years ago.

Dinele and Perele looked on with apprehension. Intuitively they sensed that there was something more to the game than was apparent between the uncle and niece. She was already thirteen, but she kissed and fondled him like a hysterical child and passionately cried, "Uncle, I love you so!" Whenever she saw him, she threw herself in his lap and embraced him, and he responded with hot, juicy kisses.

Dinele understood that in effect it was she Yakub was kissing, that in his love for the daughter he expressed his feelings toward the mother, not as she was now, but as she once was, and this both pleased and distressed her.

"Gertrud, you should be ashamed!" she admonished the girl. "At your age I was already engaged, and here you are acting like a child. . . ."

"Yakub, maybe you'd stop already!" Perele suggested bitterly. "I can't stand the hullabaloo. . . ."

After the others left, she berated him viciously. "What you do behind my back is one thing. But when we're together, act like a husband."

Yakub was puzzled. "Can't I even play with a child? With my own niece?"

"We know these nieces already," Perele grunted, and retired to her bed fully dressed.

After years of such a relationship they divorced. Max gloated.

Yakub wouldn't be getting even a groschen of the huge Eisen fortune. No one would come to his aid now when he again brought his sales agency to the brink of ruin. His seven years of plenty had ended. All he would be left with after the years of debauchery and carousal would be his carriage whip.

But it didn't happen quite this way.

Maximilian Flederbaum's notoriously wild daughter, Crazy Yanka, who had already gone through three husbands, suddenly fixed her eyes on Yakub and launched another of her reckless, impetuous affairs.

Lodz chortled over the madcap heiress's latest escapade. The whole town knew of her insatiable appetite for new lovers, but this time people questioned her choice. Although she herself hadn't converted like her sisters, she was as close as one could come to being gentile with her snobbish, aristocratic ways, and people wondered why she had taken up with Yakub, who not too long ago had still worn the long gabardine of the orthodox Jew.

"It'll last from Monday to Thursday," the Lodz wiseacres said. "Another of Crazy Yanka's flings. . . ."

But while it lasted, she rode with her new flame boldly through Lodz. Yakub whipped the horses into a gallop, while the heiress clung to him with a great show of affection and even kissed him brazenly, as only someone of her reputation could do.

Lodz relished this latest bit of scandal. It was bandied about in homes, cafés, stores, and factories. Even the seamstresses talked of it at their machines. A wedding was imminent, people said. And the news was brought to Max Ashkenazi by gleeful merchants who knew of the brothers' feud.

"He's a real go-getter, Mr. Director," they unctuously reported. "He's fallen into a fat bowl of gravy this time, your brother has. . . ."

Max stopped up his ears. "I haven't the slightest interest in it," he lied. "Shall we get back to business, gentlemen?"

Inside, he churned. The news of his brother's latest triumph wouldn't let him eat or sleep. He didn't know if the affair would end in marriage—he wouldn't even allow himself to consider such a possibility—but Yanka had installed Yakub as director of her father's factory and even moved him into the palace.

Old Flederbaum was seriously incapacitated. A disgruntled worker had stabbed him in the head, and by the time they pulled him away the damage had already been inflicted. Half of the old man's body was paralyzed, and he was confined to a wheelchair. Naturally he could no longer run the factory.

The responsibility fell to his children, but they weren't up to it. The daughters had converted and moved to Warsaw, and their husbands wouldn't consider coming back to Lodz, that filthy center of Jewishness, which they had managed to escape. The sons, on the other hand, were borderline lunatics steeped in occultism, mysticism, and sorcery and surrounded by priests, monks, and fanatics of every persuasion.

The only one with any sense was Yanka, but her sexual adventures left her no time for anything else, least of all business. Nor was it the custom in Lodz for women to run large commercial enterprises. She, therefore, entrusted the entire operation to Yakub Ashkenazi in order to spite her relatives and friends for whose refined tastes Yakub was too much the Jew.

Yanka always relished doing the unusual, something that would set people's tongues to wagging and shock them. But beyond that, she wanted Yakub to be always available when she wanted him, whether on the factory office couch or in her palace bedroom.

Yakub turned over his sales duties to subordinates and took over the operation of the Flederbaum mill.

Max Ashkenazi turned a poisonous green when he heard the news. How many more times would his lazy lout of a brother show him up? What had Yakub ever done to deserve such luck? Was being a human stud sufficient reason for such ample rewards?

Logic couldn't explain it. Was it some sort of black magic? There was even talk of a marriage. Flederbaum's entire fortune would fall into Yakub's lap. What other heights might his brother not attain? He was the only sane person in a palace full of lunatics, the only one with any sense of business, meager as it was. He was yet liable, God forbid, to become King of Lodz!

A sense of dread came over Max. For all his assimilation, he clung to a belief in a Providence. Was it Yakub's destiny always to get the best of him? If only *he* had gotten such a chance! He would have sent all those crackpots abroad to play with their ghosts and spirits. He would have seized the whole ball of wax for himself and become King of Lodz. . . .

No, this was too much to bear. To have the wine spill just as the cup reached his lips? . . . He could wait no longer. He needed a lump sum with which to buy up the controlling share in the firm, and he would get it.

A plan was hatching in his mind. It too involved a woman, but far from one like Crazy Yanka. In the course of his travels through Russia, he had had occasion to do business with a woman in Kharkov. She was a widow, no longer young, but a millionairess and childless, living all alone. She was big, lumpy, coldly rational, as tough and hard as any man. Her employees at her sugar works trembled at the sight of her.

Whenever Max came to see her, she received him very warmly and hinted that if she were married to a man of his acumen, she would entrust all her holdings to him. He had never taken these veiled invitations seriously, but her words made a deep stir within him now. With a fortune of this size, he could achieve his goal immediately. He would become King of Lodz. . . .

At first, the notion seemed bizarre, outlandish. But the more he mulled it over, the less ludicrous it appeared. His married life had been a farce. Dinele never so much as offered him a kind word, much less a trace of respect or recognition. To Lodz he was a giant; to her he was a nothing, a gnat. Was this the life he was so terrified of giving up?

And what did he have from his children? Their mother had reared them to despise him. She had planted the seeds of rebellion within them. His son was an idler, a wastrel. He took completely after his lazy grandfather, that dunce of a Haim Alter. Getrud was no better—a runaround who only followed her wildest impulses. What pleasure had he, their father, ever garnered from either of them?

True, he was already along in age, and people would talk, but what did he care about others? A person was obliged only to do what was best for him. Once he was master of the factory, King of Lodz, people would grovel and fawn before him like dogs. . . .

As for Dinele, he would settle a sum on her—a much more generous sum than she had brought with her as her dowry. He would either give her a lump settlement or pay her alimony, and he would see to the children's needs as well. He would pay his son's tuition as long as he remained in school, and he would marry off his daughter and once and for all get her out of his hair. They were no longer youngsters. They had to make their own way. When he was their age, he was leading his own life.

Still, it wasn't so easy for him to make up his mind about his wife. He had no inkling how to begin, what steps to undertake toward a divorce. Had she been unfaithful or lax in other ways, it would have been easy. But she was as inoffensive and dutiful as ever. Lately she had displayed more devotion toward him than ever before in their marriage. And if truth be told, he was still in love with her, even though not as desperately as before.

But soon he pushed aside all doubts and hesitations. He re-examined his life from the day he had moved into Haim Alter's house until the present. He summed up all the pluses and minuses, and it came out wholly one-sided. He had never enjoyed any kind of family life. He was like a stranger in his own house. Like a mendicant, he had to beg his wife for every crumb of happiness or take it by force. Now that she was older, she had suddenly decided to be nice to him, to call him by his chosen name, to play up to him and ask that they conduct a normal household with friends, company, and the like.

But it was too late for that. Now the advantage was his. A man in his forties was in his prime; a woman in her forties was over the hill. No, she hadn't done anything to earn his goodwill. It would have been different if she had provided him happiness until now. Then it would have been incumbent upon him to stick with her for the rest of her life. Marriage was like any other enterprise; there had to be equitable behavior from both partners. But to be made a fool of all these years and repay it with kindness and consideration? This wasn't Max Ashkenazi's way.

He gave himself up to self-pity. For years he, the yeshiva student, hadn't been good enough for her. Now she, the old bag, wasn't good enough for him. He could get the prettiest, the fanciest women. Lodz was his for the taking. Not that he would become a libertine like his swine of a brother. He, Max, would follow a respectable course and take a wife who didn't waste her life on stupid novels but who respected his business acumen, who understood the ways of the world, who was herself a woman of means. And he would attain the goal he had striven for from childhood—he would become King of Lodz.

As always, once he had made his decision, he didn't waste a moment but launched a furious effort to get things moving. He began by deliberately staying away from home and sleeping night after night at his apartment. This, he knew, was the right step. It was better to establish distance between himself and his wife. A woman made a man weak and a slave to his foolish desires. By maintaining a distance, the brain functioned with greater clarity and efficiency.

"Frightfully busy!" he replied each time Dinele phoned him at the factory.

Her calling and his indifference provided him enormous satisfaction. It was sweet revenge for all the years of neglect and deprivation to which she had subjected him.

Soon he began making frequent trips to Kharkov to court the Widow Margulit. Max's fingers already itched for her mil-

lions, but she was in no hurry to open her groaning strongbox
to him. Tough and as resolute as any man he had encountered,
she insisted on proceeding in businesslike fashion. Yes, she
esteemed him greatly, she had the highest respect for him, but
she had to look out for her own interests. She could have married any number of men, but she needed a husband who was
dependable, solid, with an excellent business sense, a man of
impeccable reputation, to whom she could entrust her entire
fortune without a qualm. Ashkenazi met all these qualifications
but one—he was married, and until he was free, there was no
point in pursuing the matter.

Max took apparent offense. "Don't you trust me, my dear
Madam Margulit?" he asked with a show of deep hurt.

Mrs. Margulit tried to express all the tenderness she could
summon on her coarse, mannish face. "I trust you implicitly, but
you of all people know that everything in this world must be
done in correct fashion. Business and friendship don't mix. We
are no longer children. We can wait. First the divorce, then—"

"I'll do it!" Ashkenazi cried, rising up on tiptoe, as he always
did when making a big decision.

Coming back to Lodz, he went straight to the mill. That
same evening, after he had caught up with his work, he called
in the company lawyer and consulted him about obtaining a
divorce.

"Did you ever sign a community property agreement?" the
lawyer asked.

"Fortunately, no."

"That simplifies matters," the lawyer said, and instructed
Max on how to proceed.

Max wrote his wife a letter in which he very matter-of-factly
summed up the facts. Their marriage of some twenty-odd years
had obviously been a failure, and he hoped it could now be
terminated on friendly terms. He was ready to provide for her
and for the children. All she had to do to expedite the matter
was inform him as to what arrangements she wanted.

He reread the letter several times, signed it, and gave it to
Melchior to deliver.

That night he went to bed pleased with himself and filled
with anticipation for the future. He dreamed that he was King
of Lodz and that the whirling smoke from the chimneys formed
a crown for his head.

FORTY-TWO

RAGE, HUMILIATION, AND WOUNDED PRIDE exploded within Dinele Ashkenazi upon reading her husband's letter. "Gertrud!" she shrieked at her daughter, who was sleeping off a late-night party. "Get up and come in here—now!"

Gertrud staggered in in her nightgown, her eyes heavy with sleep. She found her mother in a half faint, the letter at her feet. "What is it?" she asked in fear.

Her mother pressed her temples where the blue veins bulged beneath the skin. "Read it!" she said, indicating the letter.

Gertrud read and burst into laughter. "That's the funniest thing I've ever seen!"

The mother gaped. "You're laughing?"

"What shall I do—cry? You should have done it years ago. But better late than never."

"Get out!" the mother shrieked. "Out!"

She reread the letter, and its every sentence made the blood rush to her head anew. That this snot of a Simha Meir, this crass yeshiva boy whose every touch repelled her, should dare jilt *her*—the only daughter of Haim Alter!

At first, the sense of outrage was so intense that her only wish was to run to the rabbi and grant Max the divorce. She wouldn't carry the filthy little Hasid's name another minute. All she wanted from him was the dowry her father had laid out, and she would never look at his filthy face again. She would leave the house and everything in it. It was not a home, but a grave where she had buried her youth. She would go back to her parents.

But soon the feeling of hurt pride disappeared to be replaced by a sense of deep humiliation.

Damn his soul, the boor! . . . But in a way he was right. If she could live with him so many years and not leave him while she was still young, then it served her right that he was discarding her now that she was past her prime. He would remarry, build himself a handsome new house, and travel with his new bride, while she, Dinele, wasted away in her parents' home. He had used her up, drained her, exploited her beauty, and now he was tossing her aside like some old shoe in exchange for a young bride. He had suddenly decided that it would be better if they parted. . . .

Better, perhaps, but for whom? Certainly not for her. She had always been a slave. First to her parents, then to her children. It was because of them that she had failed to consider her own needs, her happiness. But what did she have to gain from a divorce now?

No, she wouldn't give him the satisfaction! Even though she despised him, she wouldn't let him go. Why make things easy for him?

This mood in turn was followed by a feeling of helplessness, of remorse and conscience. It was all her own fault. She had been too haughty, too disdainful. She had driven her husband from her side, scorned him, treated him with shabby contempt. She never gave him a kind word, a smile. True, she didn't love him. She had been forced into the marriage against her will, but she should have made the best of it. Most of the women she knew had done this. Her concept of life came only from books. She hadn't bothered to make friends. And now she was getting just what she deserved.

It had been her, a mother's, responsibility to make a home for the family, to assure her daughter a good match. But she had failed in this as well, and Gertrud sought her happiness outside, mostly with her uncle Yakub at the Flederbaum palace, where things were always bright and gay.

Dinele felt a stab in her breast, thinking about it. She knew that it wasn't so much the merriment that drew Gertrud to the Flederbaum palace as her attraction to her uncle. And this wasn't an attraction between an uncle and a niece, but one between a man and a woman. A woman, especially a mother, wasn't deceived in such things. That which she, Dinele, had lost in her life was now falling into her daughter's lap.

How unfair life could be. She, who was Yakub's age, was old and withered, while he had remained youthful, vigorous, filled with a lust for life. And Gertrud simply swooned over him. Who knew to what it might lead? . . .

And it was all her, Dinele's, fault. She had substituted a fantasy life for the real one. But real life was not a romantic novel.

She sent the maid for her mother. Priveh came—an elderly, imposing matron exuding the authority and dignity of age. She still wore the same wavy blond wig that she had worn all her life. Behind her trailed her husband—white-haired, aged, but with eyes still glistening youthfully. Priveh bristled when Dinele told her the news, grimaced with malice toward the whole male gender.

"He's lucky I didn't catch him here, that prodigy!" she screamed. "Else I would have poked his eyes out with my umbrella. . . . He dares to do this to my daughter? I'm off this minute to the factory! I'll slap him in front of everybody!"

They barely managed to restrain her.

"Priveshe, Priveh love!" Haim soothed her. "Don't get yourself so worked up! Leave this to me. It's a man's job, after all."

"A man?" Priveh sneered. "You're a dishrag, not a man!"

She knew that he had neglected to include a community property agreement in the articles of engagement, as other fathers did. Had such a clause existed, Simha Meir would be in a fine pickle now. But when it came to such things, Haim was a complete fool, and Priveh fixed him with cold blue eyes. "Pipsqueak! Dishrag! Milksop! First he lets himself be jobbed by that Simha Meir; then his own daughter."

Haim stood there shamefaced and distressed. "Well, now, enough, Priveshe," he bleated. "There is yet such a thing as justice in the world. I won't keep silent. I'll go to rabbis! I'll talk to people!"

"Run, old lady!" she mocked him, and went to the telephone. She called the Flederbaum mill, and in her best Polish that she still retained from her days at boarding school, she asked to be connected with the director.

"Yakub dearest," she cooed, "darling son of mine. Come over to Dinele's right away. Simha Meir isn't here, so you can come at once, my golden sun, my treasure. Hurry, won't you?"

Yakub came right over. "What's wrong?" he asked.

Priveh stuck his brother's letter into his hand. "Here, read!" she said.

Yakub scanned the letter rapidly. "Scum! Lowlife! Skunk!" he grunted at every sentence. When he finished, he flung the letter on the floor and dropped into an easy chair.

"Dinele," he said, "I'll stick by you if it takes my entire fortune. I'll turn it right over to my lawyer. Leave it all to me."

Priveh jumped to her feet and kissed Yakub on each cheek. "I knew it!" she exulted.

She shook her head several times and observed sharply, "I could slap myself for not having listened to you, daughter. Remember when you told me you wanted Yakub instead?"

Dinele blushed deeply, and Haim Alter bristled. "It was a

fated thing, after all. A marriage is decided in heaven. . . ."

The feud between the brothers Ashkenazi erupted anew, like a smoldering fire fanned high.

On one side stood Max with his obstinacy, single-mindedness, and energy; on the other, Yakub—daring, reckless, ready to take any risk and spend his last groschen for a friend.

Between them stood Dinele, her children and parents. They promptly moved in with her. They couldn't bear to leave her alone in such a trying time.

Max burned when the manager of his apartment house, little Shlomele Knaster, brought him the news. "Idiot, why didn't you stop them?" he demanded.

"What could I do?" Shlomele whined, his head nearly disappearing into his neck like a hen cornered by a feisty rooster.

Max turned near apoplectic when his manager relayed the news about his brother's frequent visits to his apartment. "Filthy seducer!" he hissed.

He did everything to coerce his wife into a divorce. He stopped sending her money for the household expenses and for the children's upkeep, but she never even felt the pinch.

"Nothing but the best in the household," Shlomele Knaster reported with some satisfaction. "I've looked, and I've seen."

Max's usual tactic of starving out an opponent, which had served him so well in the past, was useless here. His brother saw to that. Nor could his lawyers accomplish anything since Yakub's lawyers countered their every move.

Max decided to call his wife to a rabbinical trial. This was where he shone. He was an expert in the casuistic polemics so beloved by the rabbis. But Yakub wouldn't let Dinele answer the summons.

"I don't ever want to see your face here again," he warned the beadle who had come from the rabbi.

Max tried other tacks. He instituted eviction proceedings. Dinele grew alarmed when the bailiff served her with a summons to appear in court, but Yakub had his lawyer quash the proceedings.

When Max realized that he couldn't get satisfaction from either the Jewish or the gentile courts, he ordered his manager to commence a campaign of harassment. They began by shutting off the water and the gas.

Yakub sent for Shlomele Knaster and shook him by his lapels. "If you pull any more tricks, I'll beat you with a crop!" he threatened.

Shlomele's tiny head retreated within his collar. "Is it my

fault?" he squeaked. "I only do what I'm told. . . . I've got a wife and children to think of. . . ."

He reported every detail to his employer when he brought him the rent. Max thoughtfully scratched the top of his head.

"Tell me, Shlomele," he asked, "what shape are the floors in on the second floor above my apartment?"

"In very good shape," Shlomele replied.

"No, you idiot, they're in terrible shape. Barely holding up."

"In terrible shape. Barely holding up," Shlomele repeated obediently.

"First thing tomorrow, they've got to be ripped out."

"First thing tomorrow," Shlomele agreed.

"Once they're ripped out, you'll find other work for the men."

"I'll find other work," Shlomele echoed.

"And you won't say a word in the meantime. You won't repeat what I'm telling you even to your wife."

"Not a word," Shlomele promised, and hurried home to tell his wife everything his boss had just told him.

The very next morning the workers began ripping out the floors above Dinele's apartment. The noise was beyond endurance.

Priveh cornered the tiny manager and slapped him soundly. The little man rubbed his cheek and whined, "Is it my fault? I do what I'm told. I got a wife and children to think of. . . ."

A few days later workmen showed up at the apartment door to remove the ovens and replaster the walls. Priveh wouldn't let them in, but they wouldn't be dissuaded. They pounded on the door, demanding to be allowed inside.

Next, Shlomele rented the apartment next door to a turner, where the sounds of the lathes went on from dawn to midnight.

Priveh threatened to go to the factory and claw out Simha Meir's eyes. Despite all the provocations, Yakub wouldn't let Dinele move out.

"I'll squash you like a bedbug!" he threatened Shlomele Knaster.

The campaign went on. Dinele lay awake nights, weeping into her pillow. She dozed off only with the first factory whistles at dawn.

FORTY-THREE

AMONG THE STORE SHINGLES depicting yellow lions looking more like tomcats, rigid dandies with orange faces, slim canes in hand and corpulent brides with bouquets in their swollen red paws, hung huge posters proclaiming martial law in the city of Lodz.

The orders, signed by Brigadier General Konitzin, forbade citizens to congregate in the street, to hold meetings, to violate curfew, to disseminate malicious rumors. Anyone disobeying the law was subject to harsh punishment, including execution.

Next to these notices—often obliterating them—hung proclamations calling on the inhabitants to demonstrate in the streets, to strike and protest. Armed soldiers, directed by the police commissaries and their assistants, roamed the streets, driving, beating, arresting people at random. Cossacks stood in police station courtyards, flogging those forced to run the gauntlet.

The most vicious of the lot was one Yurgoff, a rangy assistant commissary with a cap pulled down low over his eyes and a retinue of bullies and bodyguards. From beneath his lowered visor he sniffed out revolutionaries like a bloodhound.

Those arrested were no longer taken to the Dluga Street jail, which was filled to overflowing, but housed in the military chapel that had been transformed into a temporary prison. But before the prisoners made it there, Assistant Commissary Yurgoff beat them until they were half dead. When Yurgoff and his Cossacks patrolled the streets, people rushed to get inside.

The unionist Samson, a house painter whom people had nicknamed Prince Samson for his opulent wardrobe and curled black mustache, decided that Yurgoff had to go and asked his representative to talk to the committee for permission to proceed. The representative met with the committee, but when they dawdled, Prince Samson grew impatient and decided to go ahead on his own.

He had a friend who was a chemistry student make him a bomb. He dressed in his most elaborate outfit, waxed his mustache, packed the bomb in a box which might have contained bonbons, and tied it with a red ribbon. Carrying the box in one hand and a bouquet in the other, he strolled along the street apparently on his way to visit a lady. Women gazed at him enviously; soldiers and policemen smiled indulgently.

When he reached the corner where Assistant Commissary Yurgoff lounged with his gang, Prince Samson carefully calculated the distance, then flung the package at the assistant commissary's feet.

Yurgoff was blown to bits. One of his legs still encased in its patent-leather boot was later found on the roof of a nearby building.

In response, units of soldiers sprayed the streets with bullets. When they finished, they raised their rifles and systematically shot up all the windows.

The hospitals were filled with the wounded, who had to be bedded down on floors and in corridors. The dead were laid out in rows at the morgue. The police didn't allow anyone inside to identify close ones and remove them for burial.

Inside the barracks, the soldiers cleaned their rifles and polished their boots for the funeral of Assistant Commissary Yurgoff. Members of the military band shined their instruments and practiced the funeral dirge. When the sun set, the people were confined to their homes.

But Lodz didn't sleep. In Balut the women and children dragged their pallets out into the courtyards to escape the vermin and stretched out on any available space—on stoops, wagons, drays, barrows.

The revolutionaries quickly prepared proclamations summoning the people to the morgue to claim the bodies of their comrades so that they might be buried with honor and dignity.

The agitators were everywhere, calling for strikes and solidarity. When the factory whistles sounded the following morning, no one heeded their call. By the tens of thousands, men, women and children streamed through the streets, shouting, milling, marching. All the stores were shuttered; all the workshops were idle; all traffic was halted.

Row by row, stride by stride, they marched. Like a spring torrent overflowing its banks and inundating everything around it, they poured through the narrow city streets with slow, deliberate stride, red banners fluttering, on their lips a song:

> The butchers shed the workers' blood,
> The people suffers endless pain.
> But judgment day is not far off,
> And we will be the judges then—

From every gate and door, hordes of people raced to join the ever-widening stream that now reached Piotrkow Street, the symbol of Lodz's wealth and authority.

"Close the stores! Off with the hats!" the marchers cried.

At the next corner the mob encountered a mounted officer with a drawn sword. Behind him stood a solid wall of soldiers, bayonets gleaming in the sun and playfully reflecting brilliant particles of light.

"Back!" the officer roared.

No one moved.

"Back, or we fire!"

Still, no one stirred.

"Fire!" the officer cried.

A volley of gunfire shattered the air.

The mass swayed momentarily like a field of grain under swinging scythes, but soon a hail of rocks and bullets began to rain upon the soldiers. The officer pointed his sword, but at that moment a rock struck him in the head and unhorsed him. The soldiers fell back, and the human wave pushed forward.

"Barricades! Set up barricades!" voices cried.

The workers toppled lampposts, loosened cobblestones, pulled signs and doors from shops. They stopped wagons and carriages, unhitched the horses, overturned the vehicles, and used them to fortify the barricades. The teamsters protested loudly, but no one listened.

Men and boys raced inside courtyards and commandeered boards, iron bars, tables, benches. A wagon carrying flour came by. The people seized the sacks of flour and used them to plug up holes in the barricades.

Like ants around a hill, they scampered about building, molding, reinforcing. Even streetcars were overturned, and rails were torn loose. The sound of heavy metal crashing muffled the groans of the wounded and the wails of those mourning the dead.

Lodz was paralyzed. All doors and gates were locked. The affluent people got out of town or took cover, and the city was left to the poor and the deprived.

They took up positions behind the barricades. Girls brought food from home to their fathers and brothers; boys collected rocks and boards. It was deathly still in the city but for an occasional shot. Night fell, but no fires were lit.

Along with thousands of others, Tevye, Nissan, and Bashke waited. The lovely June night hovered so bright and clear that no smoke or fire could dim its splendor. A pale moon cast a milky light. Stars winked, twinkled, played tag and hide-and-seek. A gentle breeze carried the scents of grass, acacia blossoms, and pine sap. It ruffled the people's hair and clothing.

Bashke looked up at the sky, which she seldom saw through the polluted mist that covered Lodz, and she inhaled the heavenly scents. "Ah, to die like this," she breathed, and closed her eyes.

"No, Bashke, we must live," Nissan said, and took her hand.

She returned his grip and felt currents stream from his hand into hers and all through her body. "Comrade Nissan, why must we deny ourselves happiness? Are we not entitled to it, too?" she asked.

"Yes, Bashke, but only after our struggle is won. Only then can we enjoy personal happiness."

"Will we live to see it?"

"We must have faith," he said solemnly.

Simultaneously with the morning star the Cossacks came. Orders echoed through the predawn air.

"Fix bayonets—Charge!"

The soldiers advanced with bayonets fixed.

"Comrades, let them have it!" voices cried behind the barricades.

A hail of rocks poured down on the advancing troops, and they wavered.

An officer rallied the troops. "Fire at will!" he cried.

The struggle raged a full day. The barricades held fast against the bullets. By afternoon the soldiers had taken up positions on adjoining rooftops and balconies and sprayed the workers from above. The workers scattered in panic.

"Comrades, stand fast!" their leaders implored.

The stampede halted, but as the rain of bullets resumed from above, the mass broke once more. Bashke sprang on top of a barrel and sang:

> Sing out, sing out our anthem high,
> Our flag flutters above the thrones!

And as she sang, she waved the red banner to and fro.

The men grew ashamed, and with resounding voices they picked up the song.

Two soldiers lounged on a rooftop looking down on the girl wrapped in the red flag.

"Bet you can't pop her," the taller one said.

"A cinch," the other said.

"What'll you bet?"

"A butt?"

"You've got it."

The short soldier sighted carefully and gently squeezed the trigger.

His companion grimaced, took a cigarette from his cap and passed it over.

Nissan and Tevye held the girl aloft on their shoulders. Her blood deepened the red of the flag.

FORTY-FOUR

———◆———

OUTSIDE FLEDERBAUM HOSPITAL, a bowed, brooding Tevye paced frantically, periodically pulling his skinny neck away from the sweaty paper collar. His bloodshot, febrile eyes kept straying toward the massive hospital gates and probed the draped upstairs windows.

They wouldn't let him inside to see his Bashke. Two orderlies in white smocks had carried her inside, then slammed the door in his face. "Saturday is visiting day. No visits on weekdays," they snapped.

Like a dog banished from the house, he scratched and clawed to get back in. "Let me in!" he whined unreasonably like a child unable to make sense of things. "She's my daughter, after all!"

He walked all around the building, seeking some means of entry. Finding none, he came back to the gate, waiting for it to open in order to launch a fresh assault upon it. But the beet-faced, droopy-mustached guard blocked his way. "Stay out!" he growled.

Tevye thrust a coin into his hand. "Let me in, my friend," he pleaded in uncharacteristic fashion. "That's my daughter in there."

The Pole kept the coin, but he wouldn't relent. "It's too hectic inside," he explained. "I got strict orders to let no one in."

The hospital gate opened frequently as the ambulances kept arriving with blasts of the horn and orderlies in bloodstained smocks brought in the fresh wounded. At the same time black-clad Burial Society members kept taking out corpses in hearses drawn by equally black-clad horses. Clusters of people rushed the hearses with shrieks and laments, but the Burial Society men wouldn't stop for the mourners, who were mostly paupers and not apt to hand out decent tips.

Keening women with wigs askew and with swollen eyes raced after the hearses that bounced and rattled over the cobblestones. The wounded were brought to the hospital on foot, in droshkies, or assisted by armed policemen. Anxious men, women, and children milled around the hospital gates, wringing their hands and lamenting.

Tevye didn't leave the hospital grounds to eat or sleep. His wife, Keila, cursed at him to come home, but he wouldn't. He tried to bribe hospital workers to check on his daughter's condition. He buttonholed arriving and departing physicians for some news. They repulsed him brusquely, but he wouldn't give up. The stalwart revolutionary had suddenly been transformed into a distraught Jewish father.

Finally, a doctor took pity on him. "It looks bad," he said. "The bullet pierced a lung."

Tevye felt his heart lurch. He approached every hospital employee he could find. He trailed after the guard. He followed the doctors, pleading, urging, begging until they finally relented, and flouting the rules, they let him in.

Inside the dim ward veiled in nocturnal shadows, the beds stood tightly wedged together. Screams of pain and anguish issued from all over. The nurses and orderlies kept out of sight as the sick and wounded cried for help.

"Quiet!" the attendants admonished them. "You're not the only one sick here. . . ."

Elderly women sighed. "Do they care about the patients then? They're too busy playing around with the interns. Oy, it's bitter to be a pauper!"

Bashke lay in bed gasping for breath. "Air!" she cried. "A little air!"

Tevye took her hand. "Bashke, child. . . . Tell me what I can do for you!"

"Air," she panted. "I can't breathe. . . ."

Tevye ran to the nurses and orderlies. "Do something, dear people," he begged.

"Talk to the doctor," they replied, looking bored.

When the doctor finally showed up, he wasn't of any more help. He felt the patient's pulse, grimaced, and walked away as surly as before.

"Open the window," he said to no one in particular. "And you," he said, turning to Tevye, "get out of here! This is a hospital. We don't need outsiders to tell us our business. . . ."

Tevye knelt at Bashke's bed. If it were possible, he would have expelled the air from his own lungs to let her breathe.

"Daughter," he moaned. "Tell me—what can I do for you!"

She stroked his hand feebly and whispered, "Daddy. . . ."

But soon she began gasping again like a fish out of water.

"I'm choking! Help me!"

She clawed at her bedding, tore her gown, pulled the hair from her head. Tevye shrieked until the attendants came running. They gave Bashke an injection and threw Tevye out of the hospital.

The whole night he milled about outside. By dawn an orderly came to fetch him. Bashke lay bathed in sweat. Tevye touched her hand. It was cold and limp. The orderly took her pulse and shook his head. She no longer screamed, merely breathed shallowly. Her teeth began to chatter; her eyes glazed and rolled upward. She took a last look at her father and lay still.

Tevye sent up a shriek. "People, help!"

The orderly strolled over and took his arm. "It's all over, mister."

Tevye collapsed on the bed and wouldn't let anyone come near his daughter's body. They dragged him away by force. By the time he tore loose the bed was already empty with merely an indentation to indicate that a person had just lain there.

Bent almost double, Tevye went to the hospital morgue, resisting all efforts of the guards to eject him. He spent the night sitting over his daughter's corpse. In the morning friends came to comfort him, but he didn't even hear them.

The funeral was lavish. The committee ordered the factories to close, and thousands of workers marched in the cortege. The body was draped in a red banner, and workers carried elaborate wreaths. Stores along the funeral route were closed. Passersby bared their heads. Spectators crowded sidewalks and balconies.

Tevye walked as if in a daze. He felt remote and hostile to everything and everyone. He sensed nothing but his personal loss. Bashke's dying glance darkened his memory.

Speeches were held at the cemetery, and songs were sung. Tevye couldn't bear any of it, not the choir, not the oratory. What did all this have to do with his Bashke? . . . He was furious when a member of the committee who had never met Bashke rose to deliver the eulogy.

Imposing with his snapping curls, black eyes, and trim beard, the speaker used his voice like a trained instrument, now raising it dramatically, now lowering it so that everyone was forced to lean forward. His tone ranged from bathos to biting sarcasm as he expertly manipulated his audience. At the same time he studied the faces intently to ascertain what impression his words were evoking.

As a final theatrical gesture, he took the girl's bloodstained blouse and raised it high. "On the blood of our martyred comrade, we vow our revenge!" he thundered.

This was too much for Tevye. He pushed his way forward, seized the blouse, and tucked it beneath his jacket. "Leave me alone!" he shrieked at the people who tried to restrain him.

The crowd was disappointed. The mood had been shattered. Tevye squatted on the freshly filled grave and gazed about him with the eyes of a madman. Standing next to him, silent and subdued, was Nissan.

Birds twittered, hopped, sang. From afar a factory whistle blew insistently.

FORTY-FIVE

━━━━━◆━━━━━

LODZ REVIVED. The war in the Far East had ended, and the far-flung markets of Russia had opened again. Orders came pouring in, and the factories worked feverishly to catch up.

All strikes and protests had ended as well. Soldiers who had been so thoroughly trounced by the slant-eyed heathens turned their attention to easier adversaries, the true enemies of the tsar—Jews, students, and revolutionaries. Authority was stripped from the police and turned over to military commanders who had done such an outstanding job at the front. In the cities the police assembled the cream of the underworld in teahouses, where, beneath idealized portraits of Nikolai and Aleksandra, commissaries and priests exhorted thugs, drunks, and rapists to rob, maim, and kill for Christ. Bearded monks with crosses and nuns with candles, tough barkeepers and hardened prostitutes, drunks and lunatics and assorted riffraff paraded through streets, bellowing hymns and assaulting the residents of Jewish quarters.

In Lithuania and in White Russia, armed troops assisted the rioters in their pogroms. With overwhelming force, they routed the members of the Jewish self-defense corps. Loyal Russians were transported to Poland to build railroads and to incite local residents (who needed little encouragement) against the enemies of the church and of the Little Father, Nikolai II. The prisons spilled over with rebels and malcontents. The courts-martial worked day and night to keep up. Gallows were erected overnight in prison courtyards. Each passenger train included its share of barred convict cars filled to capacity with exiles to Siberia.

In cities and towns, Jews fasted, recited special prayers, collected funds for the newly widowed and orphaned. Rabbis and preachers regained the pulpits from the unionists. They exhorted Jews to walk in the path of righteousness, to perform good deeds and submit to lawful authority.

Parents, too, regained authority over their offspring. Diehard unionists still put up occasional proclamations, but these no longer created a stir. Young people from affluent homes cast aside childish fantasies of a better world and focused their energies on obtaining an education and building careers. Others married and set up businesses. Girls found husbands or set up house with ex-revolutionaries. Many emigrated to America and Argentina. The revolutionary leaders went into exile in Switzerland, where they waged heated debates in coffeehouses. Others languished in prisons and in Siberia.

Lodz was back in full swing. The demand for goods in Russia was insatiable. Lodz industrialists held balls for military commanders during which they managed to lose money to them at cards. They collected enormous tributes for the city commandant, General Konitzin, and made him a present of a magnificent carriage and team so that he could maintain law and order in the city and keep the factories running. The workers no longer dared utter a word in protest. Nightclubs and cabarets did sensational business as the city's elite gambled, caroused, and enjoyed life to the hilt.

Among those who emerged from the crisis unscathed was Max Ashkenazi. Despite everything Yakub did to help Dinele, Max triumphed in the end. As usual, he had been the more persistent and persevering, while Yakub, just as typically, lost interest after the initial skirmishes.

As Max had anticipated right along, Dinele was too jejune to hold out for long, and she agreed to the divorce. But part of her condition was that Max pay her the sum of 100,000 rubles. He did so with a heavy heart and, in return, obtained her written promise to make no additional financial demands upon him.

With heads bowed, the husband and wife waited for the rabbi to conclude the ceremony.

"Will this never end already, dear God?" Dinele whispered to her mother as the repeated questions and answers constituting the ritual continued.

"A divorce is no trifle," the rabbi admonished her. "The holy Torah itself says so."

In the cab she sobbed in her mother's arms. "What did I do to deserve such a life? For what sins do I suffer so?"

Priveh consoled her. "You'll marry again, daughter, and you'll live a happy life. With the fortune you've got, you can do very well, the evil eye spare you. You're still pretty as a picture . . . a blooming rose. . . ."

The whole time at the rabbi's Dinele never glanced at Max once, but he kept looking at her. Without meaning to, he com-

pared her delicate pale skin, sad blue eyes, and shapely figure
with Widow Margulit's ungainly bulk and pebbly complexion,
and he felt a terrible sense of loss. But as usual, he found com-
pensations. He pictured the millions that would come his way
and allow him to buy control of the Huntze firm, and this
helped assuage some of his sorrow.

Lodz had been right in its prediction that the affair between
Crazy Yanka and Yakub Ashkenazi would last from Monday
to Thursday. It ended as quickly as it had begun. Nevertheless,
Yakub stayed on in the palace and retained his position at the
mill. In fact, he and Yanka remained good friends, even though
the relationship was no longer erotic. Her new flame was a
tenor who had appeared briefly with the Warsaw Opera and
whose career Yanka had decided to sponsor. It was the swarthy
Italian with whom she necked openly in public now.

Yakub, too, found a new playmate to while away his time—
his brother's daughter, Gertrud. She no longer felt obliged to
hide her love for her uncle. Following her parents' divorce, she
declared her total independence and snuggled up to Yakub in
his carriage, shrieking with a laughter that rang somewhat
hysterically.

Her grandparents were busy trying to marry her off, just as
they were their daughter. They had already found a very respectable man for Dinele, a widower with a successful business,
but she wouldn't hear of it. She was determined to live out her
life alone. For all her reluctance, her parents felt that with
time she would change her mind. They were riddled with guilt
and anxious to rectify the wrong they had done her. The only
drawback was Gertrud. It wouldn't do for a mother to marry
first, and Haim Alter kept talking to matchmakers about finding a fine young business prospect for his granddaughter.

As usual, Priveh scoffed at him. "With the kind of taste you
have, you must think we're back in the Middle Ages. Leave
this to me. I'll find her a modern type of fellow she could respond to. With ten thousand rubles' dowry, I might even get
her a doctor."

But Gertrud wouldn't hear of her grandfather's businessmen
or her grandmother's doctors. "How archaic!" she shrieked
with laughter.

"Do you already have someone?" Priveh asked slyly. "Are
you in love, you little *shiksa?*"

"I'll say!" the girl cried, whirling her grandmother around
the house.

No less willful than her father, she would let nothing stand in her way, and she put all her energy into breaking down her uncle's defenses. His feelings for his niece were ambivalent.

When she first stopped playing the role of the affectionate niece and declared herself openly, he grew somewhat afraid of her. She bore a striking resemblance to the young Dinele, except for her lips, which were redder, thicker, and somewhat petulant. Her teeth showed in a perpetual half smirk which captured her father's greed and need to dominate. Men found these lips a huge attraction. But Yakub was taken aback by her aggressiveness.

"Stop it, Gertrud!" he said, pushing her away. "Little girls mustn't act so silly. . . ."

"I'm not a little girl!" she protested. "And I know that you love me, too!"

Yakub tried to make a joke of the whole thing, but this served only to arouse her all the more.

"I won't be patronized! Treat me like a woman!" she exclaimed, stamping her foot in anger.

A half-mad passion reflected from her blazing eyes, and Yakub grew alarmed. He knew raw lust when he saw it. This was no infatuated child, but a yearning, ripe woman demanding her due, and he wavered. He was drawn to her—no doubt about it—but he didn't dare consider the consequences. How would he ever face Dinele again? And he began avoiding Gertrud, who pursued him with a persistence that was frightening.

"I love you, Kubush." She sighed, employing her favorite pet name for him. "Marry me!"

Yakub pushed her away. "Don't talk nonsense, child. Someone might hear."

"Who cares?"

"I could be your father."

"You can be my husband!"

"You're crazy! You must marry someone your own age!"

"I'm a woman, and I know what I want!" she insisted.

When Yakub saw that he was getting nowhere, he tried appealing to her filial sensibilities. "We couldn't do this to your mother. It would be a terrible blow to her. Especially now."

"Whose fault is it that she messed up her own life?"

"That's no way to talk about your mother," he reprimanded her. "You're your father all over. Simha Meir to a T. . . ."

Gertrud burst out crying. "Why do you torture me so? Is it my fault I love you and want your love? Don't I have the right to this?"

She fell to her knees before him and kissed his hands. "Hold me!" she pleaded ardently. "Kiss me! Love me!"

She sank her teeth into his neck, and her sharp nails dug into his skin. "Do with me what you will!" she moaned. "Forget who I am, what I am. . . . See me only as a woman who loves you and whom you love . . . my lover, my master, my king!"

She appealed directly to her mother. "Mommy, I know that I haven't been good to you, but give me your consent. Do it for me, for your little Gertrud. I can't live without him!"

Dinele was shocked, horrified. Not that it was totally unexpected. She had watched it coming for a long time with a mixture of wonder and apprehension. Now that it was out in the open, she sat as if petrified while her daughter kissed her, hugged her, urged her.

"Don't put it all on me," Dinele said. "Do as you see right."

The girl leaped to her feet and rose up on tiptoe just as her father did when he came to a decision. The mother saw it and shuddered.

Gertrud ran to tell Yakub the good news.

FORTY-SIX

———◆———

IT WAS JUST AFTER NEW YEAR. The great conference room at the Huntze mill was set up for the annual stockholders' meeting. The huge tables were covered with green cloths and surrounded with deep leather chairs. Boxes of Havana cigars were laid out for the gentlemen's pleasure. Assistant directors and managers shuffled around, looking for something to do to be helpful. Melchior, his muttonchops already gray, but his face as ruddy and vital as ever, stood erect by the door in his forest green livery, his hamlike hands along the seams of his breeches.

The board of directors represented the elite of Lodz—several German industrialists, a Jewish banker or two, a stray Polish aristocrat, a wizened dowager in incredibly old-fashioned attire, and, naturally, the Barons Huntze, trying to look bored and blasé, superior to the entire proceedings. Despite all their airs, they looked like horse grooms in monocles.

The mill director, Max Ashkenazi, was in a very jovial mood. His English suit bagged a bit, as usual, but his face was clean-shaven except for the wisp of beard which had been neatly brushed for the occasion. Each dot in his velvet vest seemed to protrude individually. Unfortunately he had no potbelly, as would have befitted a man of importance, and he compensated by walking with the abdomen thrust out. He also rose on tiptoe whenever he addressed someone taller than he.

The meeting hadn't yet been called, and those assembled milled through the large conference room, blowing clouds of cigar smoke at the royal portraits that still hung from the days when old Heinz Huntze had been in charge. They studied the various medals, blueprints, diagrams, photographs, plans, drawings, and charts displayed on the walls. Director Ashkenazi pointed to a chart which revealed that since his sinecure, the factory work force had grown from 3,000 to 8,000 men and women. The number of looms had increased accordingly.

"Be kind enough to glance at this, madam and gentlemen," he said, pointing to another chart. "As you see, the line representing the rate of production has mounted annually, except in one place, which represents that one flighty year when Lodz was busier striking than working. But soon, as you will notice, the rate of increase started climbing again, and we made up all the losses in a jiffy."

"Excellent," the board members agreed. "Very, very fine."

"Parallel to that, as you can see, is the rate of growth of our sales. Observe this map, if you will. The little flags represent the new markets we have opened up."

Ashkenazi's finger traveled the length and breadth of the Russian Empire, from the Vistula to the Amur, from China to Persia.

"Lately we've even gone beyond the borders," he added slyly. He compared the current map with previous ones predating his association with the firm.

"Since I was honored with the title of sales representative, we've managed to capture all these territories," he said with the air of a Genghis Khan.

"Very, very nice!" the directors chimed.

"And finally, all this has been accompanied by a corresponding rise in the value of Huntze stock."

Afterward, disdaining the assistance of the engineers and without consulting notes, Ashkenazi led the group on a tour of the huge factory, which was separated from the rest of the world by a high brick wall topped with sharp pickets.

The huge courtyard was crowded with sheds and storehouses, but few workers were in evidence. The heart of the operation lay underground.

"Madam and gentlemen, you will observe in sequence how the raw goods come in by train and emerge as the finished product baled and ready for shipment."

Through subterranean passages illuminated by red electric lamps, Ashkenazi led his little group to the railroad tracks that ran inside the factory itself. Cranes with huge metal jaws lifted incoming bales of cotton, barrels of dye, and crates of machinery and gracefully lowered them to waiting workers, who loaded them onto carts and wheeled them off to their place of storage.

"Mind the chains and hooks, madam and gentlemen," Ashkenazi warned. "And now, let us proceed."

He led them inside the boiler rooms, where the heat was a solid presence. Stokers shoveled coal into open, fiery yaws. Foremen fussed with gauges and thermostats. The stokers, stripped to the waist, their bodies covered with grime and soot, spit out their hand-rolled cigarettes and gazed with dulled eyes at the elegant, soft-bellied spectators. The stockholders recoiled from the blistering heat.

"More coal," the head stoker shouted at the younger men busy grabbing a quick snack of bread washed down by mugs of chicory.

From the boiler rooms, Ashkenazi led the group to the weaving rooms. Across huge halls stretched seemingly endless rows of looms. Women, mostly young, stood knotting threads that the machine had snipped, removing and replacing bobbins.

"How do you manage to hear in all this racket, Herr Director?" the visitors asked above the roar of machinery.

"It's merely a matter of getting used to it," Ashkenazi replied, and pointed out the course of the thread as it wound its way through the various wheels, arms, and rollers.

From here they proceeded to the washing, dyeing, and bleaching areas.

"Careful, madam and gentlemen, mind the wet floor."

A giant cloud of steam, moisture, and stench hovered over the dyeing rooms. The directors grimaced at the half-naked workers clattering in wooden clogs over the slippery stone floors. They laundered the goods, rinsed and dried them before huge ovens, steamed them, threw them into bins, and passed them through the press.

By now the visitors had had enough, but Ashkenazi wouldn't let them go. He made sure to stop to talk with every foreman, chemist, and designer. He even escorted his group into the shipping rooms, where the girls packed the goods for shipment.

The only ones not taking the tour were the Barons Huntze. They despised the sight, sound, and smell of their factory. They wouldn't dirty their boots in such a pigsty or rub elbows with the rabble in their employ. Instead, they waited in their palace, consuming cocktails until the meeting was called.

They deeply resented having been called away from their winter sports in the Tyrol Mountains to come to stinking Lodz. Besides, they were a bit apprehensive. Although they hadn't kept accurate count, they sensed that they had sold off too much of their stock. And as if out of spite, their luck had been running particularly bad lately. They therefore threw down drink after drink, waiting for the meeting to be called.

When they finally deigned to make their appearance, everyone breathed a sigh of relief. Everyone waited for the eldest Huntze brother to take his customary place at the head of the table and conduct the meeting, but at that moment Director

Ashkenazi rang a little bell and made an announcement.

"Madam and gentlemen, I have the honor to report that at this time sixty percent of the firm's shares are registered in the name of Max Ashkenazi. According to the by-laws of the corporation, it therefore falls upon me to chair this meeting."

A deadly silence fell over the room. All eyes turned to the barons, then to Ashkenazi, then back to the barons, who exchanged glances but kept silent. A strained, pregnant pause followed, to be broken by Board Chairman Ashkenazi.

"Madam and gentlemen, this meeting is hereby called to order," he announced, and took his place at the head of the table. His every word and gesture expressed the pomp and authority of the King of Lodz.

The factory officials approached with the same deference they had previously accorded the Barons Huntze. "All is in readiness, Mr. President," they announced, placing their reports before him. The barons didn't stay through the meeting but dashed back to their palace.

"Faster, you swine!" they bullied the servants packing their belongings. "We want out of this Jewish pesthole before night!"

By the time their train left that evening they were blind drunk.

All night the Lodz newspapers hustled to prepare news of the startling development for the morning editions, but it was a waste of time since within hours, all Lodz knew about it. In palaces and in restaurants, in stores and in theaters, in studyhouses and in marketplaces, in workshops and in cafés; in every den, rathole, and cubicle, people talked of nothing else but the new King of Lodz.

FORTY-SEVEN

————◆————

THE LUSH SLEEPING CAR COMPARTMENT of the Petersburg–Warsaw–Paris Express carried the director of the Flederbaum mill and his young bride to their honeymoon in Nice.

Before their eyes stretched miles of fields heavy with snow. Frozen telegraph wires bowed beneath their burden, and peasant shacks were buried to their roofs. The powerful locomotive sliced joyously through drifts cleared by peasants, who lined the rails waiting for the train to pass so that they could begin anew. Snowcapped Jesuses on wayside crosses were tilted, and icy black crows soared against reddish skies, presaging more cold and snow.

"Gertrud, did you remember to pack our bathing suits?" Yakub asked, running his fingers through his bride's copper curls.

"Bathing suits?" she repeated, looking at him.

"Of course! In two days we'll be bathing in the Mediterranean."

"Oh, what a wonderful world this is, Yakub," Gertrud exulted. "What fun it will be to spend a winter month amid sunshine and palm trees. I'd like to see the border already. It'll be the first time I've been out of the country. . . . Are you happy, Yakub?"

"Delirious, my child."

"But not as happy as I," she said, snuggling up to him. "A man is simply incapable of being as happy as a woman. He doesn't have it in him."

She covered his eyes, lips, and hands with kisses. "Bear, great big fuzzy bear," she purred. "I want you to devour me!"

She wouldn't leave their compartment or let him out even to buy a cigar or exchange a few words with a fellow passenger. Even during meals she clung to him, whispering endearments in his ear.

"Gertrud, behave," he admonished her as if she were a child. "People are staring."

"I don't want to behave." She pouted. "Let them stare all they want. As long as I have you . . . you. . . ."

In the crack express racing past frontiers and countries, they drained their cup of happiness. Caught up in her ecstasy, Gertrud sank to her knees before her husband and kissed his feet with slavish devotion.

"My lord, my master, my prince, my king!" she panted.

Across frozen streams, snowy fields, and forests, weighed down by a heavy valise, escorted by a pair of hard-bitten thugs with murderous eyes, Nissan Eibeshutz made his way toward the German border.

He had risen high in his party's central executive committee, the *Tsay-ee-kah,* and he was headed for the party's international conclave abroad. He tumbled into snowbanks; he forded icy streams; he fell to the ground and held his breath each time he heard a suspicious sound. But he continued to push closer to his goal. Finally, one of the brutes grunted, "Kraut territory just across the river. Let's push on!"

Nissan stepped out onto the ice, his brain overflowing with notions, plans, ideas.

The former palace of the late Baron Heinz Huntze was now occupied by one of much higher rank—the new King of Lodz. Following the takeover of their firm by the little Jew who had come to them so fawningly years ago, the Barons Huntze had severed all connections with the city they had always despised. Having no further reason to come there now, they offered to sell their palace along with the remaining stock they still held for a song, and Max Ashkenazi bought both.

Not that he had any more use for a palace than he did for carriages or servants. But being King of Lodz, he wanted all the trappings that went with the office. It wouldn't do for anyone else to live there. Besides, all the industrialists in Lodz occupied palaces next to their factories, and he didn't want to buck tradition. The barons were anxious for the cash, and he took the place over—lock, stock, and barrel, the Huntze coat of arms included.

Inside the huge high-ceilinged rooms, Max Ashkenazi seemed even smaller than he was. He and his second wife took their meals in the immense dining hall, the table of which could have seated thirty-six diners. The brown paneled walls, the massive carved buffets; the many-antlered chandeliers; the paintings of gory, shot ridden fowl oppressed the couple and rendered them silent. If they spoke at all, it was in whispers.

The liveried butler and footmen served exotic dishes with glacial disdain. The husband and wife barely touched the gentile dishes or the rare wines brought up from the cellar. The enormous wolfhound that had come with the palace lay on the rug, watching his new master and mistress suspiciously. He knew that they were terrified of him. When the mistress offered him a plateful of scraps, he didn't even bother to get up. He was eating too well to bother with scraps.

"Stuck-up beast!" she remarked to her husband. "What do we need him for around here anyway?"

If anything, Max was even more afraid of the dog than she was, but he was a part of the palace, part of his realm, and he would do nothing to diminish that realm.

"Let him be," he said.

The meals were interminable. The servants moved at their own pace. Long minutes passed between courses. Ashkenazi was on pins and needles, anxious to get back to the factory, but he didn't dare leave the table until the butler brought the box of Havana cigars signifying the end of the meal. Only then did he bolt like a boy let out of heder.

Even more unendurable were Max's nights.

For hours on end the maid primped and prepared Madam Ashkenazi for bed. She braided her sparse, grizzled, wiry hair. She rubbed creams and lotions into her rough skin. She dressed her in the costliest gowns of lace, silk, and tulle. The broad Louis XV bed with its blue satin canopy and profusion of silk pillows, cushions, and blankets was soft and inviting.

But all the salves, lotions, perfumes, and soaps; all the lace, silk, and tulle; all the soft lights couldn't conceal the shapeless form, the gravelly complexion, the sparse, wiry hair done up in girlish bows. An iciness exuded from the massive body, freed of its corsets, stays, and bands. Each leg was like a tree stump. Each chin quivered like jellied fish broth. The bed creaked beneath Madam Ashkenazi's bulk.

"Max!" she trilled flirtatiously. "Why aren't you coming to bed?"

Although she tried to invest her voice with tenderness, it emerged a hoarse bass, and a chill gripped Max Ashkenazi's heart. Like a man walking to the gallows, he strode heavily toward his bride.

A painting of a satyr pursuing a nude maiden loomed above

the bed. The girl suddenly reminded Max of Dinele—the same
slim, shapely form; the brown ringlets cascading down the
shoulders.

He slept fitfully amid the down, silk, and lace. The palace
clocks chimed mournfully. They reminded him of church bells
as he counted off hour after hour through the long winter night.
No matter how he twisted or turned, he couldn't get comfortable. The pillow suddenly seemed as though it were made of
stone.

He put on a robe, and quietly, so as not to disturb his wife,
he got out of bed. With a candle in hand he walked through
the maze of rooms and halls, many of which he had never seen
before. He was revolted by it all—the animal heads with the
horns and glass eyes; the swords, spears, axes, and daggers
glinting with un-Jewish ferocity. Strange visions flashed before
him: of riots, pogroms, Chmielnicki's massacres, of autos-da-fé,
Jews choosing the stake to conversion. . . .

Pagan statuary and paintings were everywhere. Hunters held
birds dripping blood; hounds battled bears; knights thrust
lances into men and into real and fanciful beasts; satyrs, fauns,
centaurs, nymphs, and bacchantes cavorted lasciviously.

Max looked up. They all were his, but they seemed to mock
him, the little Jew wandering like a frightened child through
the gentile palace on a winter's night.

He went into the dining hall. The brown walls and high
carved ceilings were veiled in nightly shadows. There was wine
on the credenza, but he didn't drink, even though he was depressed. The dog awoke, glanced at his master through slitted
eyes, opened his huge jaw in a yawn, then sank back into the
soft rug.

Dinele's image flashed before Max's eyes. Where was she?
What was she doing? Did she plan to remarry or remain
single?

What did it matter? They were no longer together. He had
to think about practical matters. Still, her image wouldn't
leave him. From Dinele his thoughts drifted to his children.
Ignatz was in Paris. It would be interesting to see how he
looked. He was probably tall, taller than his father. After all,
he took completely after his mother.

As for Gertrud, she had treated him, her father, abominably.
Without even consulting him she had rushed into an incestuous
marriage. She could have had anybody and had chosen that
pervert, that reprobate.

Max envisioned his beautiful young daughter with his
brother, and his flesh crawled. He had seduced the gullible

child just to spite him, Max. He could imagine Yakub laughing at him, savoring his revenge. . . .

What had that lout done to deserve this? First it was Kalman Eisen's granddaughter, then Flederbaum's daughter, and now— What did they see in him anyway? He was an empty-headed fool, an irresponsible dunce, who at the height of the season dropped everything to run off to the Riviera. Oh, yes, he knew all about his movements. Shlomele Knaster kept him informed.

Max pulled the robe tighter around him. His resentment of Yakub set his teeth to chattering. There he was with his fresh young bride, while he, Max, had to go to—

He shrank and grew dwarfed inside the high-ceilinged hall. The clocks tolled away the hours. He went to the window and parted the venetian blind. The factory loomed oppressively, its stacks thrust upward as if the walls had stuck out their tongues. He felt a chill and padded back to bed. The bronze Mephistopheles on a corner stand bared his teeth in a mocking grin at the King of Lodz.

III

COBWEBS

FORTY-EIGHT

———◆———

ACROSS THE POCKED, muddy roads of Poland; through towns and villages laid waste by war, slogged the men, horses, wagons, and fieldpieces of the imperial German forces. Peasants shielded pale eyes to gaze silently at the invaders. Their women clung with fear and curiosity to thatched fences and crossed themselves. Children screamed, and dogs barked. In town, Jews came out in front of their squat houses, while their young sons and daughters sang out greetings in Yiddish to the strangers. German colonists joyfully greeted their conquering compatriots.

Young and old, schoolboys and grandfathers, these were conscripts from Prussia, Saxony, Bavaria, and the Rhineland sent by their kaiser to occupy Poland and strip it of its raw materials for the war effort. They weren't the crack troops sent to the western front, but members of the home guard considered good enough to fight the Russian. Many wore eyeglasses held together with string. They tore the Polish earth with their hobnailed boots; their belt buckles carried the legend "God is with us"; their bayonets were double-edged—one edge to cut wire; the other, flesh.

They were followed by chaplains who exhorted them to kill for God, to impose the Protestant faith upon the heathen papists and turn them into obedient servants of the kaiser. And as they stumbled over the ruts in their yellow jackboots, they sang:

> The kaiser has a gun so wide,
> A sleeping man can fit inside.
> With each crack,
> A dead Cossack.
> With each blast,
> A frog less.
> And Krupp he sends them all to hell. . . .

Every acre of occupied territory was promptly restored by their military engineers. Telegraph wires were restrung; roads were repaved; bridges were rebuilt; abandoned railroad cars were collected and set back on the tracks. Tree limbs were cleared of dangling corpses of Jews the Russians had hanged in revenge for their defeats at the front. Walls were stripped of tsarist proclamations, to be replaced with neat German placards urging the surrender of all arms and a full inventory of all goods possessed in every household under the threat of death.

The greatest source of raw material and the industrial center the loss of which would most hurt the enemy was Lodz, and the kaiser's troops moved ever closer to that important prize. As they conquered territory, they appointed commandants, most of whom were East Prussian landowners who had lived for centuries among the Poles and who had kept them firmly under their Junker heels. Thus, it happened that the commandant of Lodz turned out to be the same impoverished aristocrat who had married Heinz Huntze's daughter, the honorable Baron Konrad Wolfgang von Heidel-Heidellau.

The war had been an absolute godsend to the baron. He had made a rapid advance owing to his impeccable bloodline and to his intimacy with officers of the general staff, and from captain of reserves he had risen to full colonel. He had also distinguished himself by displaying an iron hand in cowing the citizenry into meek acceptance of the occupation.

In the early days of the war, many Poles had retained sympathy for their Russian rulers. On city buildings and rural fences hung great placards signed by the Grand Duke Nikolai Nikolaievich promising the Poles that once the enemy was defeated, the land would once more be reunited.

The peasants believed the promise, and Polish nationalists urged the population to join in the fight against the invader. At the same time they condemned the Jews as spies, traitors, and German allies. In their newspapers and patriotic pamphlets, they told of Jews smuggling out diamonds in their beards and revealed that Jewish funerals contained not corpses, but gold for the enemy's coffers. Christian storekeepers, trying to rid themselves of the Jewish competitors who undersold them, denounced Jews to the Russians. Jews by the thousands were hanged, shot, imprisoned, and exiled to Siberia.

In the villages, Polish peasants, jealous of German colonists whose efficient use of the land brought them greater yields, denounced them to Russians, claiming that they sent secret messages to the German troops, using the blades of their windmills.

The Russian military commanders, who suffered defeat after defeat at the front, needed victims upon whom to vent their frustration. They bullied the townspeople to such a degree that they were terrified to leave their houses when the Germans marched in and too frightened even to give them directions. An occasional shot was fired from a house at the passing Germans.

Colonel von Heidel-Heidellau resolved to teach the inhabitants of Polish towns the meaning of German authority. As an object lesson, he had several villages set on fire, then had the town of Kalisz razed to the ground. It happened that a deaf-mute water carrier in Kalisz failed to stop at a German soldier's command and was promptly shot to death. Several passersby tried to tell the soldier that the man was deaf, but the soldier didn't understand them and shot them as well.

A young coachman responded by throwing a stone. The soldier staggered back to the command post with a bleeding head. Colonel von Heidel-Heidellau happened to be eating lunch. He wiped his lips, drank the last sip of beer, and ordered a roll call. When the soldiers were assembled, he ordered a Major Prausker to devastate the town with artillery. Houses came crashing down; people scurried like mice through the streets. The town elders came to plead for mercy, but to no avail. The artillerymen worked with precision, systematically razing block after block. By night the whole town was ablaze, and hundreds of corpses lay buried beneath the debris. The flames served to demonstrate the measure of German retribution for miles around.

The general staff commended Colonel von Heidel-Heidellau for his efficiency, and he was awarded the Iron Cross for valor. Because of this and because of his knowledge of the city where he had taken a wife, he was made military commandant of Lodz.

Accompanied by his orderlies, adjutants, dogs, and luggage, he entered Lodz on the heels of the occupation army, which had paved the way for him. The military engineers prepared the police chief's mansion for the colonel. His head adjutant, a young lieutenant with a girl's cream-and-peaches complexion, reported that the house had been thoroughly searched and cleaned and was now available for habitation. The baron looked around with a scornful gaze and slapped his gloves against the table.

"I will not stay in this pigsty!" he said, wrinkling his nose in distaste. He unrolled a map of the city and ran his finger over it.

"You see this street? There is a mill there with a palace alongside occupied by a Jew. That's where I will be staying."

"Yes, sir, Colonel!" the lieutenant barked.

"As you know, it's a bit touchy to requisition private residences in the first days of an occupation unless shots have been fired from inside. Isn't that so, Lieutenant?" the baron went on.

"Yes, sir, Colonel," the adjutant agreed.

"So how do you reckon to manage it?" the baron asked, looking searchingly at his adjutant.

"I'll take a squad and conduct a strict search, and if I find any evidence of shots having been fired, I'll confront the resident—"

"Thus proving that you're a champion idiot," the baron interrupted. "I couldn't care less whether shots were fired or not, God damn it! If there were no shots, there should have been. Do you get my meaning?"

"Yes, sir, Colonel!" the youth barked, blushing like a country maiden.

"All right. I want it taken care of at once. I don't want even a trace of Jewish garlic left. I'll be sleeping in the palace tonight, isn't that so, Lieutenant?"

"That is so, Colonel!"

Madam Ashkenazi grew very alarmed when a German officer and a squad of armed men appeared at the palace. Her husband was away. At the last minute he had been detained in Russia, where he had gone on business. Now he was stuck there, unable to return, to write, or even to send a telegram, and she was left to run things on her own in a strange city where she had neither friends nor relatives.

She had pleaded with Max not to dally in Russia and to hurry back since the enemy was approaching, but he had postponed his departure from day to day. "Frightfully busy," he had wired in answer to her urgent pleas.

She felt terribly vulnerable and distressed when the German officer pushed his way inside. "What's wrong, sir?" she asked.

"You are the mistress of the house? Consider yourself under arrest."

The officer stationed a soldier to guard the frightened woman while he and the rest of the men conducted a thorough search of the premises. Although nothing was found but some rusty swords and an old hunting rifle left over from the former occupants of the palace, the officer wrote a strongly worded report to the effect that shots had been fired from the house at German troops.

Madam Ashkenazi was subjected to a stern interrogation, and her face broke out in red blotches as she heatedly denied the accusation.

"Do you dare call German soldiers liars?" the lieutenant asked with assumed rage, a trick he had borrowed from his superior.

He released her from custody, pending a full investigation, and ordered the palace immediately vacated. Nothing was to be removed except her clothing.

Madam Ashkenazi wrung her hands. "But you're putting me out into the street. . . . That's inconceivable. . . ."

The lieutenant ordered his squad to take possession of the palace. A sentry was posted at the front gate, and a second soldier climbed the gate and unrolled a German flag to hang over the Huntze coat of arms. He also posted a plaque bearing the legend "Requisitioned" on the gate.

Madam Ashkenazi powdered her cheeks, donned her fanciest costume, and, clutching her umbrella as if it were a sword, raced to the headquarters of the city's commandant. She was ready to beard the kaiser himself to demand redress. But she wasn't allowed inside.

The same evening Baron von Heidel-Heidellau took possession of his late father-in-law's palace. "Very fine," he said upon hearing his adjutant's report. "Well done."

With deep pride he mounted the wide marble steps, strode through the halls, then dropped expansively into a soft easy chair, stretching out his long legs in their high-topped boots.

He stopped before the huge built-in mirror over the fireplace and studied himself in all his magnificence. In his gleaming helmet pulled down over the eyes, gray military cape, high-topped spurred boots, tightly girdled waist, and dangling sword, he looked and felt like a Roman proconsul, an impression he did everything to promote.

The table in the dining hall was set with all the delicacies the cook could scavenge. The butler wiped the neck of a cobwebby bottle and poured out some wine for the baron.

"Still left over from the old masters, Their Excellencies the barons," he said in his anxiety to please.

"Help me off with the sword. The boots, too!" the baron barked.

The butler promptly unbuckled the sword, but he had some trouble with the boots, and the baron kicked him hard. "Clumsy dolt! Make it snappy!"

The butler beamed. After the years of humiliation of serving a Jew who didn't know the first thing about servants, it felt grand to be properly chastised again, to submit to the authority of a strong master.

The baron ate the dinner and drank the wine with relish.

He took special pleasure in dining on purloined food, as a predatory beast enjoys the taste of prey it has personally killed. His veins stirred with the blood of ancestors who for centuries had lived off rape and pillage.

When the valet undressed him for the night, the baron shrank to a shadow of himself. Stripped of his belts, medals, and epaulets, he turned into a withered old man with blue varicose veins crisscrossing his skinny legs, a protruding pot-belly, and flabby, trembling buttocks. He looked exactly like a plucked rooster.

"Faster, faster!" he urged the valet, who rubbed him down with a sponge. He despised being seen in the nude.

Lying in the wide Louis XV bed amid all the lace, silk, and tulle, he called for his adjutant with the peaches-and-cream complexion and ordered him to read him the most pressing reports. The lieutenant handed him a list of persons sentenced to execution, and the colonel signed it without even a glance.

Afterward he told the adjutant to sit down on the edge of the bed and began to stroke his rosy cheeks. "You pretty boy," he lisped with his toothless mouth.

The lieutenant flushed deeply as the baron pulled him close with his scrawny arms. Again the baron felt himself the Roman patrician.

FORTY-NINE

———————◆———————

LONG BEFORE THE GERMANS occupied Lodz for the first time (they subsequently retreated), Max Ashkenazi had decided to shift his operations to Petersburg, now renamed Petrograd for patriotic reasons.

His reasons were several.

First, all the government banks had been closed in Poland, and depositors couldn't withdraw either paper money or gold. Ashkenazi had a fortune invested in these banks, including bonds and debentures from which he clipped lucrative coupons, and this money would be lost to him if the Germans occupied the city.

Secondly, cut off from its markets in Russia, Lodz would be like a severed limb. Trying to sell goods to the Germans would be an exercise in futility. For all the Germanic airs he put on, Ashkenazi knew that to get a pfennig out of a German was like pulling teeth. Besides, Germany had its own textile industry, and once the Germans entered Lodz, they would do everything in their power to destroy it as a competitor.

Russia, on the other hand, was both enormous in area and primitive in industrial know-how. It was made to order for a man, of his, Ashkenazi's, acumen.

On the basis of these conclusions, with the very outbreak of war, long before the Germans even neared Lodz, Max began to empty his warehouses and ship his goods to Russia. He also made the decision to dismantle his plant and transfer it lock, stock, and barrel to Petrograd.

It was an epic undertaking. The trains gave first priority to military transports, but Max managed to wangle a paper attesting that his goods were vital to the war effort, and he proceeded to expedite his plan.

Thus, it happened that by the time the Germans entered the city for the last time half his plant remained in Lodz, while the other half was somewhere in transit in Russian-controlled territory.

In far-flung sidings, depots, terminals, and whistle-stops, machinery, not only from Max's mill but also from the factories of Lodz industrialists who had thrown in with him, rusted in sheds, in warehouses, and under the open sky. No one knew where anything was. In the throes of the hasty retreat, Russia's railway system was in absolute chaos. As the Germans seized city after city, the entire Russian bureaucracy, which had flourished in Poland for a century, was in desperate flight. Governors, archimandrites, judges, gendarmes, nuns, file clerks, censors, executioners, monks, custodians, along with their families and possessions, joined in the panic.

By the tens of thousands the wounded filled the hospital wagons. Jammed in like chickens in a cage, Austrian prisoners of war headed for detention in Siberia were crowded together with criminal and political prisoners, including even peasants whose only crime was showing directions to the advancing Germans, and shepherds accused of sending secret messages to the enemies with cracks of their whips.

There were deserters and Ruthenian peasants, German colonists and rabbis, Catholic priests and common thieves. Most of the convicts didn't know why they had been imprisoned, when they would be tried, where they were going and for how long. All records had been lost in the confusion attending the withdrawal.

And there were the Jews—Jews by the thousands and tens of thousands—whole towns driven from their homes by the edict of Grand Duke Nikolai Nikolaievich, who needed such a diversion to cover his disastrous leadership of the Russian military effort. Old and young, healthy and invalid, pregnant and senile, they rattled along in freight cars meant for forty men or eight horses but now carrying more than 100 persons each. The guards bullied and abused them. They wouldn't allow them to get out for a glass of water, for medical assistance, not even to answer calls of nature.

At every stop with a Jewish population, the local Jews brought food for the refugees and removed corpses for burial. And amid all this tangle, turmoil, tragedy, and pandemonium, which not even the train officials could hope to unravel, Max Ashkenazi and his agents scurried from station to station, searching, probing, sniffing out the missing chunks of his plant.

Through sheer force of will, he salvaged them literally out of the ground. He wouldn't let the officials rest. He pleaded, demanded, bribed. Huddled within his broad sable coat and hat, his portfolio filled with documents and cash, he persevered and transferred Lodz to Petrograd. He reassembled the machinery, overhauled it, borrowed or purloined spare parts, cannibalized existing machines, fashioned order out of chaos, erected mills, which promptly proceeded to belch out smoke and steam as they worked full shifts to supply the army with canvas, burlap, and wool.

The elderly quartermaster general who bought his goods shook his head in admiration. "How did you manage it, Max Abramovich, something our smartest generals couldn't do?"

"With will and effort, Excellency," Ashkenazi replied.

"Maybe we should make you head of the general staff," the old general joked, and sighed deeply. "Ah, Russia, Russia, the devil take you! . . ."

Max organized a combine of all the émigré manufacturers, formed them into a united firm located on Vyborg Island with him as king once more. He controlled the production, set the prices, took the orders.

He even went to Turkestan to buy up bales of domestic cotton to keep the shifts working around the clock, seven days a week, Sundays and holidays. He sent agents throughout Russia to raid old factories for available parts. The orders rolled in, and New Lodz grew from day to day.

The Lodz refugees kept closer together here than they had back home. They socialized in the evenings, talked of home, traded news of Lodz. An occasional letter got through with the aid of the Red Cross via Switzerland, taking months to arrive. They formed their own association and rented space, where they prayed on the Sabbaths, observed the death anniversaries of loved ones, held masquerades.

They collected funds for poor refugees from Lodz and held meetings presided over by Max Ashkenazi, who was ever ready with a clever word, an apt suggestion, a brilliant innovation.

He rarely thought about Lodz. Here he had everything he wanted—money, power, respect. As far as he was concerned, Lodz—all Poland—was a closed phase in his life.

FIFTY

————◆————

WITH A VENGEANCE bordering on the fanatic, Baron
Colonel von Heidel-Heidellau undertook the task of purging
the Polish-Jewish pesthole he had loathed ever since he first
came there to marry the daughter of that upstart Heinz Huntze.

As befitted a German colony, he ordered the streets cleansed
of all animate and inanimate filth. Polish militiamen, entrusted
only with truncheons, carried out his commands with great
glee. They chased the Jews off the sidewalks where people had
always gathered to gossip, socialize, and do business. When the
crowds didn't disperse quickly enough, they were clubbed and
doused with fire hoses. The new laws also made it a crime to
throw a cigarette butt or paper on the street and to spit. The
gutters had to be doused with lime, and the garbage bins in
the courtyard smeared with tar and kept free of all obnoxious
waste.

Militiamen seized bearded men and bewigged women in
Balut and dragged them forcibly to the municipal baths, where
the men's beards and the women's skulls were shaved. Their
clothes were boiled in disinfecting vats, and their flesh was
scoured till it bled. But the more the baron's myrmidons
scrubbed and scoured, the more the epidemics flourished.

Baron Colonel von Heidel-Heidellau not only cleansed the
city of filth and grime but also purged it of food, employment,
and everything else of value. The factories stood idle; the
chimneys no longer polluted the clear blue skies; the sirens and
whistles no longer roused people but let them sleep as long as
they wanted.

Immediately after assuming command of the city, the baron
sent his men to strip all the factories of their thick leather transmission belts. The manufacturers elected a delegation to petition
the colonel to spare these belts, without which the factories
couldn't operate. Dressed in their snowiest linen and gleaming
frock coats, the members of the delegation called at the palace.

Among them was Yakub Ashkenazi, his gray beard now dyed an ebony black. It was the first time he had glimpsed his brother's new home.

The baron received the delegation sprawled in an easy chair. "The answer is no," he said, his monocle glinting.

The men appealed to the commandant's conscience. If the workers were deprived of their jobs, thousands of men, women, and children would starve. When the men's tone turned slightly insistent, the baron slammed his fist against the table.

"Who gives a damn about your workers?" he snarled. "I have my own people to think of!"

The thick belts made of the finest leather would make excellent soles for German soldiers' boots, and the baron had them shipped to Germany.

The next commodity to be appropriated was copper. It was collected from vats and boilers, from church steeples and door-post amulets, from door latches and frying pans.

Each day thereafter the baron thought up new ways to plunder the Lodz economy. He began, naturally enough, with the Ashkenazi plant. Down the subterranean passages leading directly to the railway line flowed an endless stream of metal, leather, raw cotton, silk, wool, and finished goods.

Madam Ashkenazi raised a protest each time. Brandishing her rolled umbrella as if it were a sword, she stormed the doors of her palace, only to be repulsed.

For every item requisitioned, the punctilious Germans issued vouchers which would be redeemable once glorious victory was achieved.

Madam Ashkenazi sat all day in her husband's large office, even though there was nothing to do there. She guarded the mill and agitated over every appropriated article. She locked the German vouchers away in the safe, hung the key around her neck, perused old ledgers. When night came, she retired to Albrecht's old bachelor quarters. She lay in his wide bed unable to sleep and waited for morning and another empty day. Of all her staff, she had kept only one maid, who cooked her meals and arranged her sparse gray hair into short braids tied with silk ribbons as before.

In Balut the handlooms were silent now, too. They stood draped in white sheets like so many corpses in shrouds.

The city, which had always thrived on turmoil, movement, and clutter, had become a ghost town. Its spotless streets brought to mind the paths of a cemetery. The Polish workers went back to their farms; the Jews walked around dazed and demoralized. German sentries at every corner kept the people confined to their own streets. The Germans searched every cart, every person, for contraband food. They didn't hesitate to lift women's dresses or tap their bosoms and crotches, searching for smuggled items.

Every stalk of wheat, every potato in the cellar, every newborn chick, calf, and piglet had to be reported. The fruit was plucked from orchards, the grass from pastures, the fleece from sheep. Hunters were stripped of guns, and fishermen of nets, so that all the game and catch were left for the victors. Even stray dogs and cats were rounded up and rendered for their fat. Their flesh would feed the animals in German zoos.

Along with the military spoilers came a horde of stout civilians in forest green mountaineer costumes with feathers in their hats. Wearing yellow gaiters to protect their boots from Polish mud, they swept through the countryside like a swarm of locust, ravaging the land.

Bakers, millers, butchers, grocers, street vendors, and artisans were placed under strict surveillance. The population was issued ration cards for bread that wasn't made of flour but from an abomination of chestnuts and potato peelings. It stuck to the gums and ruined the digestion. The rich bought food from the army of smugglers that had proliferated since the occupation, but the poor dropped like flies from malnutrition and disease.

Baron Colonel von Heidel-Heidellau had the Polish militiamen seal off the houses of the sick and spray Balut down with carbolic acid. Hordes of paupers were hauled off to disinfecting stations to be doused, scrubbed, and shaved. The gentile soldiers were amused by the elderly Jews' desperate efforts to avoid the razor. They leered at their daughters' effort to conceal their nakedness and jeered at their wives' sagging breasts, flabby bellies, and spindly legs.

But the epidemics raged on. The hearses couldn't keep up with the demand, and the corpses, minus even shrouds, were taken to their rest in handcarts.

To keep the population docile, the baron ordered military bands to entertain them with German victory marches. He stood on the balcony of his palace, contemplating the city lying submissive at his feet, and mumbled to himself, "That's what the scum need—baths and entertainment. . . ."

FIFTY-ONE

———◆———

NEVER HAD KEILA, the wife of Tevye the World Isn't Lawless, had it so good as she did under the German occupation. In these, her elder years, she was being compensated for a lifetime of toil, deprivation, and worry. She cooked huge pots of meat even on weekdays so that the savory aroma of fried livers, sautéed onions, and stews permeated all Feiffer Lane. The neighbors came to "borrow" a pinch of flour, a potato, a crust of bread, and she turned no one away.

It wasn't Tevye who was rewarding her for her years of privation. He hadn't changed a bit and still sought to save the world while neglecting his own family. Even in good times they had lived on the brink of starvation because he wouldn't listen to her, open his own shop, and hire a few employees. "I wouldn't become an exploiter even if you tore pieces from me!" he raged.

Keila had flayed him with scalding curses, but he wouldn't give in. He hired himself out to subcontractors, who often as not went bankrupt and didn't pay him. He raced around with unionists and stayed away whole nights at a time. Keila had to endure deep shame and humiliation during his periods of incarceration. Along with the wives of common thieves, she had to stand at the prison gates, waiting to deliver food packages to her husband. She had never enjoyed a moment of happiness with him. When all Lodz was swimming in money, her children went about ragged and hungry.

When Lodz was occupied and Tevye no longer even brought in the little that he used to, Keila was left with two choices— starve to death or suffer the humiliation of begging in the streets.

But someone in heaven had interceded in her behalf. Even though her madman of a husband had assured her that there was no God, she had never doubted. She had never stopped keeping a kosher household, lighting the Sabbath candles, heed-ing the rabbi's advice to discard a dish if some milk accidentally spilled into chicken soup. Tevye raged, snickered, vilified the rabbi for wasting their money, but Keila poured the tainted food into the garbage.

True, she couldn't make him say the benediction and had to spend Sabbaths at a neighbor's like some widow, but the kitchen was her domain, and she trained her daughters to be good Jewish daughters. Bashke hadn't listened to her and had come to a bad end, but the other children had been guarded from their father's crazy ways. Some had emigrated to America, but the youngest ones had remained in Lodz. They had nothing to do with their father, whom they considered a lunatic and an irresponsible idler with time for everything but his own family.

Now, during Lodz's darkest hour, Tevye's daughters were doing extremely well. They had become smugglers, and good children that they were, they brought all their earnings home. They bought their mother a fashionable wavy wig, which sat very incongruously on her lumpy gray head, and a new wardrobe of weekday and Sabbath dresses. They brought home all kinds of good things from the road—flour, groats, meat, butter, cheese, eggs.

They took a new flat on Feiffer Lane with gas illumination and indoor plumbing, bought new beds, nailed shelves to the walls to hold their photographs, and hung pictures of Nubian eunuchs bringing a nude blond slave girl to a swarthy sultan and of King Solomon settling the question of a child's parentage by ordering it cut in half.

Yes, God had taken pity on Keila for her devotion to Him over the years and for defending Him before her corrupt husband, and she praised the Lord, even though she didn't know how to pray properly; was generous to her neighbors; and dropped coins into the collection box hanging next to the greasy doorpost amulet. As often as Tevye tore down the collection box, so often she replaced it, fed it, and through her thick lips prayed to God to continue lavishing His favors upon her house, to guard her daughters from harm in their dangerous work, and to soften the heart of her husband and drive out the madness that had blinded him for so long and had forfeited him both this world and the world to come.

She had good reason to pray. The Germans conducted frequent searches for illicit goods. The first time they only commandeered the contraband, but if the offense was repeated, they jailed the perpetrators, and Keila's house was full of contraband. It reposed in her high beds under green blankets embroidered with lions, tigers, parrots, and flowers. Whole slabs of meat packed in straw lay between pillows. Sacks of potatoes, heads of cabbage, and beets were stored under the beds. In the old wardrobe, hidden away among the dresses, there was flour in small sacks and all kinds of grain. Inside the pillowcases, sugar was stored in little pouches. Even behind the picture frames—at the very foot of King Solomon's throne guarded by two lions—lay packages of saccharin used in indigent houses in place of sugar.

And even though everything was carefully hidden, there was no assurance that it wouldn't be found. The German home guards were good at unearthing hidden goods. Even better were the military police, who used bayonets to pierce pillows and who didn't hesitate to make people strip to their skin in their zeal to find contraband.

And Keila kept dropping coins in the collection box and praying that she and hers be kept from all harm.

During the week her daughters were away. With kerchiefs over their heads, in stout boots that could stand up to any terrain, with sacks draped over their shoulders, they slogged through the villages, buying up from the peasants a bit of flour, a chunk of butter wrapped in linen, a half gross of eggs, a cheese—whatever was available.

They kept off the highways, which were patrolled by the Germans, and stuck to back roads and paths that sometimes led through ditches and bogs. From village to village they slunk, bent under the weight of their sacks, eager to please their mother.

They endured all kinds of hardships along the way. They had to sleep in barns or under the open sky. Gentile youths harassed them. Sometimes the Germans caught them and had to be paid off with a few marks or with other means adversity had taught the girls.

But their compensation for this difficult, often debasing grind was the Sabbaths and holidays at home. Keila prepared trays of Sabbath loaves and cakes and fat stews. The girls swept and dusted the house, scrubbed the floors and sprinkled them with yellow sand, buffed the iron hoops of the buckets, and polished the tin candlesticks that replaced the brass ones the Germans had requisitioned.

All the pots, pans, and kettles were scoured until they gleamed. The finest glassware was put out. Flowers and laces cut out of paper were affixed to curtains, cupboards, and shelves. The pictures on the walls glistened; the blue-flowered plates gleamed. A velvet cloth embroidered with gilt letters and a

Star of David was laid over the twisted loaves. Tevye refused
to make the benediction or to slice the Sabbath loaves, but
Keila did what she could to set a proper Jewish table. She even
managed to strain out some wine from cooked raisins through
a cloth. The girls bathed, washed their hair, perfumed themselves, put on filmy underwear and dresses of the latest style.

Keila thanked God that she no longer had to go to strangers'
houses to celebrate the Sabbaths. Her home was now filled
with men—her daughters' fiancés, who spent their Sabbaths
and other free days in the house, eating, drinking, singing.

These were no pale, undernourished weavers in greasy ill-
fitting suits, but lusty, broad-shouldered youths in high-topped
boots and short jackets—smugglers one and all, good earners,
free with their money and perfectly content with their lives.

Although far from saintly—they were clean-shaven and not
averse to a quick smoke on the holy days—still, they didn't
refuse when Keila asked them to make the benediction over a
beaker of raisin wine or to start off the Sabbath loaf with a
blessing. Their simplistic attitude was that God earned His due
just as man earned his.

The candles flickered; the tablecloth gleamed; the girls
smiled radiantly; the youths laughed and told funny stories
about the road and the smuggling game. There was much
boasting and tales of bravado.

In her high-riding Sabbath wig and a wide apron, Keila
bustled happily in the kitchen. She served heaping portions to
one and all, took pride in her daughters' beauty and talents,
cast maternal glances at their fiancés, and through her thick
lips prayed to God for successful marriages for her girls and
many grandchildren and a serene old age for herself.

Even merrier than the Friday evenings were the Sabbath
days. Friends of the girls and of their young men came to
visit, and there was dancing, singing, and games of fantan.
Sometimes there would be a German present, a soldier who
worked hand-in-hand with the youths. He would sing German
songs, vilify his officers, and let his friends try on his uniform.

Keila knew that it would be best if she left the house on such
occasions, and she visited with a neighbor to listen to the
reading of the Pentateuch that she herself couldn't read or to
gossip about the shortage of potatoes.

Wandering all by himself through the house as if he were
a stranger was Tevye. His wife and daughters gazed at him
with contempt. He was of no further use to them, and all they
demanded of him was that he conduct himself as a human
being, join the family at the Sabbath table, make the benedic-

tion, slice the Sabbath loaf, and act like a proper father to his daughters since young men respected their fiancées more when their father behaved like the head of the household.

But Tevye wouldn't cooperate. He wouldn't even attend his own daughters' engagement parties owing to the presence of a rabbi. His daughters pleaded, Keila wept, but he wouldn't yield. "I won't share a table with a cleric!" he raged.

He seldom came home except for a few hours' sleep. He couldn't stand his bourgeois house with the pictures, the doorpost amulets, the coin box, the visitors, the German soldiers, and the sacks of contraband.

He despised the tasty dishes Keila served him out of pity. The only thing in the house he treasured was the yellowed photograph of his beloved Bashke. He was ashamed to invite his companions to his house. He would sneak in like a pauper, doze off for a few hours in a corner room since his daughters occupied the bedrooms, and rise with the dawn to get back to his labor exchanges and soup kitchens.

Following the Sabbaths, the house was in a shambles. Nut shells, apple cores, cigarette butts, half-filled glasses lay scattered amid stockings, underwear, dresses. Sometimes a youth who had stayed late would be sleeping on an improvised bed in the parlor.

The girls sprawled in their beds, all disheveled, legs and arms akimbo. With their hairpins, combs, camisoles, and various female paraphernalia, they seemed strange to their own father, and he was ashamed to glance at his own offspring.

He dressed quickly, stuffed his pockets with the books and pamphlets he was forever carrying, washed his face, and left.

"Lunatic, where are you off to now?" Keila called out to him with a blend of pity and mockery. "Wait up, and I'll get you at least a sip of coffee for your empty stomach."

"I'll eat at the soup kitchen already," he grunted, and ran out.

Keila gazed after him, watching his spare, bowed form and shook her head with its white nightcap and red ribbons. "God Almighty," she pleaded. "Why don't you fix his brain already? Sweet Father in heaven, do something for the poor madman. . . ."

She walked barefoot on her heavy legs into the kitchen to scatter the cockroaches which had occupied the empty pots during the night, and she mumbled her morning prayers, making all kinds of errors and transposing words and phrases.

A rooster crowed, his hoarse cry echoing across the silent city, where factory whistles no longer roused people to work.

FIFTY-TWO

———◆———

THE ONLY ONE IN LODZ who wouldn't yield to the commandant was Tevye, the leader of the unionists and chairman of their executive committee. Each order the baron issued, Tevye countermanded. In the middle of the night his cohorts fanned out with buckets of paste and rolls of proclamations, which they proceeded to glue over those signed by the baron.

Baron Colonel von Heidel-Heidellau flushed an apoplectic scarlet when he learned of the nocturnal depredations. "Wipe them out without a trace!" he frothed at Police Commissioner Schwanecke. "Crush the Jewish vermin responsible for this!"

The lame commissioner marshaled all his men to lie in ambush for the perpetrators. He also sent out spies and agents to trap them. A few were collared, and he personally kicked them in the belly, venting all the rage and humiliation he had been forced to endure from the baron.

He used all his policeman's wiles to learn the names of the group's leaders, but the prisoners wouldn't talk even when he starved them. Schwanecke then proposed they spy for him, but they wouldn't go along. Finally, he sent them into forced labor in Germany.

He had proclamations posted explicitly defining the punishment meted out for covering or defacing official German orders, but the same night the executive committee managed to cover all these proclamations with their own calling for an ongoing struggle against the army of the occupation and its lackeys the police.

The war between the baron and Tevye had been triggered by food. As one way to supply more food for the fatherland, the baron had turned to the workers' soup kitchens. A committee of Lodz's elite, including Yakub Ashkenazi, had maintained these soup kitchens, where the workers could get a bowl of thin gruel and a crust of bread. But even though the support for this effort came from the Lodz citizens themselves, the baron cast a covetous eye upon the enterprise.

They consumed a lot of staples, these soup kitchens—mounds of potatoes, flour, and groats that might have better gone to Germany—and the baron summoned the leaders of the citizens' committee to his palace and ordered them to add more chaff to the flour used for the bread.

"Excellency, the bread is already falling apart from all the adulterants in it," the leaders protested.

"Add the ingredients my senior medical officer suggests, and the bread won't fall apart," the baron said. "I'm not allocating any more flour for your rabble, and that's that."

When the men tried to explain that the substitute bread was making the population sick and spreading epidemics, the baron lost his temper. "There is plenty of ground to bury all the people of Lodz!" he roared. "Get out!"

The men left humiliated and cowed, and the bread in the soup kitchens was baked according to the commandant's orders. Once the baron got his way with the bread, he began to consider ways to conserve grain, potatoes, and fat. He ordered oil substituted for the fat in soups. The fat would be collected and shipped to Germany. Next, he cut down on the rations of groats. Finally, he came up with the brilliant idea of using potato peelings for the soup.

The baron's chief medical officer, who had discovered a substance to substitute for flour in bread, came up with the notion that potato peelings were healthful, appetizing, and nourishing. The baron called a press conference at which he ordered the newspapers to print this theory. The medical officer elaborated his findings with all kinds of scientific proofs. The baron listened approvingly and urged the editors to give the theory wide currency.

The press wrote the stories, and the kitchens used the peelings. But Tevye and his crew wouldn't take this lying down. He was now the leader of the city's revolutionary circles. Nissan was in Russia, the other comrades were exiled or at the front, and the responsibility for sustaining the rebellion had fallen upon his bowed shoulders. He alone organized committees, recruited new members, supervised the soup kitchens, and kept the whole movement alive.

Therefore, when the commandant's latest edict came out, Tevye felt it incumbent upon him to issue a fiery proclamation against the military oppressors, who first deprived the workers of jobs, then forced them to eat potato peelings like swine. Tevye's proclamations were posted right over the commandant's and called for protests and resistance.

The baron circumvented Schwanecke and personally took charge of disciplining the rebels. His men raided the soup kitchens, arrested the youngest and strongest among the workers, and shipped them off to forced labor in Germany, where the shortage of able-bodied men had grown acute.

Orders had come down from the general staff that more civilians be drafted for work in Germany, but the Polish men refused to report as directed. They knew from those who had gone there before them that forced laborers weren't fed, were domiciled in wet, unheated barracks, were guarded day and night, made to work without a break, and generally treated like convicts. Those who had gone there voluntarily weren't permitted to return, and for all these reasons, the Polish civilian men didn't respond to the conscription.

Alongside the baron's proclamations hung those of Tevye describing the conditions of forced laborers in Germany, and the people were more inclined to believe Tevye than the baron.

The baron responded by arresting workers and sending them forcibly to Germany. German military police, militiamen, and home guards were everywhere, collaring able-bodied men in the streets for the slightest offense. For congregating, for lining up at the soup kitchens or for bread rations, men were rounded up, confronted with trumped-up charges, packed into freight cars, and shipped off to Germany.

Polish militiamen arrested people who were less than clean or barefoot and took them to disinfecting stations. The elderly were allowed to go home, but the young were sent to Germany.

The more people were arrested, the more the proclamations against the commandant proliferated. They spoke of his illegal acts, his cruelties. They included protests from families of the detained, condemning the baron for conscripting civilians, which defied international law.

Tevye didn't rest, even though he was barely keeping body and soul together in such trying days. He spent each night in a different hiding place and never ceased inciting against the baron. He even sent accusations against him to socialist deputies in Germany, which brought inquiries from Berlin.

With the visor of his cracked cap pulled up onto his forehead, his bony Adam's apple bobbing under the paper collar, his tattered jacket stuffed with newspapers, books, pamphlets, and brochures, his eyes angry and slightly insane behind the lenses of his wire-framed glasses, he was everywhere at once like a punishing wraith.

It disturbed him that workers had been transformed into smugglers, beggars, vendors. He encountered them in the streets with their pails of pickles, baskets of candy, all kinds of junk that they were hawking, and they were ashamed to look him in the eye. Others went from courtyard to courtyard with sacks on their shoulders, buying up old clothes, even though no one was selling. Those less resolute gave up and turned to begging. The female workers sold themselves to German soldiers for a piece of bread. Others who had once worked for the party turned smuggler, opened illicit coffeehouses, conducted black-market transactions, and forgot their ideals. Many died, victims of starvation, exposure, consumption, and epidemics.

Tevye agonized that proletarians had been forced into such physical and moral degradation. Everything he had been striving for now turned to dust, scattered like chaff in the wind.

But his own faith held steadfast. He was firm in his conviction that a socialist world was inevitable. Out of blood and suffering and pain it would emerge like grain out of manure. But for now there was only darkness and despair. The whole world was drenched in blood; the workers and peasants were lulled by patriotism; the bourgeoisie incited brother against brother and nation against nation in order to turn the anger of the masses away from their true enemy. The climate was such that formerly class-conscious workers in the Western lands rushed into uniform to kill fellow workers of other lands. Even the socialist leaders defended the war budgets in their native lands, joined hands with the bourgeoisie, donned officers' epaulets, assumed ministerial rank. Some even fawned at the feet of bloody tyrants.

All this was a terrible burden on the bowed shoulders of the old weaver. If at least he had Nissan to commiserate with or to explain it all to him. . . .

The responsibility of redeeming the city was entirely his, and he avidly consumed the Marxist newspapers and brochures for guidance, but there was little he could do. He was too ignorant, too unprepared to show the way through the prevailing gloom.

But for all his dejection, sparks of hope glowed here and there like fireflies in the dark. Young male and female workers gathered around him, hungry for his guidance and leadership. They had remained true to him and to the party. Even though they starved, they refused to compromise their ideals with bourgeois activities.

They helped Tevye in his campaign, posted his proclamations, attended his meetings, recruited new adherents. They helped him set up a workers' soup kitchen which served as a club in the evenings.

In a brick building that a Lodz magnate had started to build for himself but that had never been finished as a result of the war, the kitchen was set up. There were no windows or doors installed yet, nor were the walls plastered, but the moment the Russians evacuated the city, the workers had commenced to make the place habitable. They whitewashed the bare bricks, hung portraits of Marx, Engels, and Lassalle. The girls enlivened the black ceiling with paper lanterns and decorations. Several of the youths who were carpenters nailed together benches and built a small stage draped with a red flag.

Hundreds of unemployed workers, including those who now hawked sticky candy in the streets, gathered in the soup kitchen for a bowl of thin gruel, a slice of gummy bread and for meetings, lectures, and discussions held there in the evenings.

Despite the bitter times, the youths and girls put on amateur plays, organized choirs, even had their own orchestra. And from this half-finished ruin, Tevye conducted his war against the commandant ensconced in his magnificent palace. Here he held secret meetings with committee members. Here he composed his proclamations. Here he planned his strategy.

The commandant had the building watched and frequently sent his agents there, but Tevye's people were on the alert, and the moment a suspicious person appeared, all he found were people eating soup. And even though soldiers often raided the kitchen, arrested some people, and drove others away, many came back in the evenings until the building was jammed wall to wall to hear the speeches and lectures.

Tevye faced them from the wooden stage, and the words shot like poisoned arrows from his lips. "Your time will come!" he cried, pointing a gnarled finger like a biblical prophet. "For that is the inexorable law laid down by our mighty teachers!"

And he gazed reverently up at the three faces hanging behind him.

FIFTY-THREE

———◆———

THE ASHKENAZI MILLS on Vyborg Island ground to a halt. Along with the other workers in the city, the thousands of men and women employed in the textile plants were striking. Troops guarded all the factory entrances.

Ashkenazi was livid with outrage and indignation.

The Russian general staff was planning a new spring offensive calculated to strike a finishing blow at the German and Austrian forces occupying holy Russian soil. Reserves of the last age-group had been called up, millions of new soldiers would be mobilized, and uniforms, gauze, and blankets would be needed.

Max Ashkenazi had worked like a slave to keep up his end of the effort, and business had been excellent. The bills were paid even before the goods were delivered. All payments were in cash, and the profits accumulated. Rather than deposit his money in banks, which he no longer trusted, Ashkenazi invested it in estates, buildings, factories, apartment houses. He had come to the realization that paper could become worthless, but buildings and land would always retain their value.

All kinds of brokers and agents dogged his footsteps now, offering him choice parcels of real estate, lucrative business ventures. Again he rode in a coach drawn by a team of handsome horses and driven by a stout black-bearded coachman.

In his broad sable coat and hat, carrying a portfolio stuffed with papers, he rode through the city, dashed in and out of banks, ministries, government bureaus, military offices. He also went out to check the buildings he had purchased or the factories into which he had bought.

His plants worked around the clock, getting the goods ready for the military. But suddenly the workers shut off the machines and walked out.

It started with bread. The local population wasn't getting enough to eat. The railroads gave priority to munitions and other military supplies, and no food was being transported into the city. The grocers in their white aprons over sheepskins hoarded the remaining foodstuffs and sold them at black-market prices. The grocers swore before the Holy Mother that they had no food in stock.

The poor housewives went home unable to feed their families. They gathered outside the municipal stores, stamped their feet on the frozen pavements, and cried to be served, but the stores remained closed. They, too, were out of bread. Elderly workers in sheepskins and fur hats joined the women. They grumbled, cursed, spit.

"Some life, eh? Work a whole week, then come home to nothing to eat. . . ."

"The stores should be torn down for hoarding food!"

"What we ought to do is stop working. No food, no work."

"We want bread!"

"Bread!"

The sergeants sent out squads of police to disperse the angry people lined up in breadlines. "Break it up. Go home!" the policemen cried. "When there'll be bread, you'll be notified. Don't congregate in the streets."

But the people wouldn't disperse.

"Give us bread now, you swine!" the women shrieked. "We can't go home to our children empty-handed!"

"Don't push us around, you parasites!" the men growled. "You're getting bread, but we ain't, and we ain't leaving!"

The police began to lay about with scabbards, but the people resisted. Youths seized cobblestones, chunks of ice, and snowballs and threw them at the police. Others shattered the windows of the stores. At first, the police fired into the air, and then—directly into the crowds.

A woman in a man's sheepskin and boots fell to the ground and stained the snow crimson. The police assumed that this would suffice to scatter the crowd, but the sight of blood only served to inflame them.

"Get the murderers! Tear off their heads!" people cried, and surged at the policemen. "Give us bread!"

Instead of bread, Minister of the Interior Protopopov sent the people the crack Vohlynsky Regiment, which had already proved its loyalty to the tsar by suppressing the revolutionaries in Poland in 1905. Troops were stationed by every factory, office, and bridge with orders to shoot the rebels.

Himself a craven toady and slightly deranged, Protopopov held the coward's view that the only response to opposition was force. With the tsar away at army headquarters in Mogilev,

Protopopov's only wish was to serve the German-born empress at a time when all Russia despised her.

He had always been fanatical about defending the honor of God's Anointed. When people had seen photographs of her husband awarding the Order of St. George to the wounded, they joked that while the tsar was with George, his wife was with Gregory—which was to say, the monk Rasputin, who was rumored to be Aleksandra's lover.

Protopopov had issued strict orders to the gendarmerie to quell such blasphemy. It was she, the tsarina, who had been responsible for his appointment, and out of gratitude he spent his days at her feet, talking of saints, sorcerers, and miracles and escorting her to the grave of the martyred Little Father, Rasputin.

He knew nothing of the situation in the land or in the city, nor did he care to know. His response to unrest was to call out the troops and order them to fire at will.

But the workers defied the patrols and filled the streets and squares of Petrograd, particularly the Nevsky Prospekt. Protopopov tried to close off the bridges to keep the workers from entering the city from the Vyborg Island side, but the workers made their way across the frozen Neva River and gathered by the thousands, demanding bread and freedom. Each time a new red flag rose above a cluster of people, and a speaker climbed to the shoulders of others to address the crowd.

Someone draped a red flag over the statue of Alexander III, and voices cried hoarsely, "Long live the republic! Down with the monarchy!"

Mounted officers with swords drawn lined up their men to face the mob. "Disperse, or we'll fire!" they cried.

The mob didn't stir.

The officers turned to the soldiers. "Ready!"

The soldiers raised their rifles.

The women thrust their breasts forward. "Lads, you wouldn't shed the blood of mothers who only want bread for their children. . . . You wouldn't shoot your mothers and sisters whose men are asked to die for their country while their children are being starved. . . ."

The officers sensed hesitation in their troops and issued the order to fire, but the soldiers wavered, then lowered the rifles.

The people responded with thunderous cheers. "Long live our comrades the soldiers!" the men cried, tossing their caps in the air. Women rushed forward to kiss the soldiers in their long gray greatcoats.

From all gates, houses, factories, workshops, from every

corner and nook, people came pouring like a swollen stream. As if by mutual consent, they headed for the Tauride Palace, where the Imperial Duma met. The deputies arrived from all over in carriages, in cars, and on foot. The mob stormed the palace and threw open its doors and gates.

Students, workers, and women raced to the barracks of the Litovsky Regiment.

"Comrade soldiers!" they cried into the high windows. "Come out and join us!"

At some barracks the officers shut the gates, locking the soldiers inside, and stationed guards to keep everyone out; at others, they didn't interfere and merely looked on.

The soldiers went out and joined the rebels. They went to those barracks that had been shuttered and smashed down the doors. The trapped soldiers swept aside their guards and joined their comrades. The street filled with workers, women, soldiers.

"Beat the tsarist lackeys!" they cried, chasing the policemen off corners.

The police vanished from the city. Minister of the Interior Protopopov cowered inside Tsarkoye Selo beside his beloved tsarina. If only the Holy Father Rasputin were alive to advise him. . . . All he could do was send telegram after telegram to the tsar at Mogilev.

The telegraph wires, bowed under the weight of snow and ice, carried two kinds of telegrams to Mogilev. From the Imperial Duma came lengthy telegrams describing the chaos and pleading with the tsar to form a new ministry which would be responsible to the Duma. From Tsarkoye Selo came telegrams filled with passionate endearments and stubborn pride.

"Be firm. Don't give in, Nicky, for you are God's Anointed," the tsarina exhorted her husband. "I am with you, your loving wife, who beseeches you in memory of our savior, Father Gregory, to show your authority, your iron hand and send loyal troops against the rebels."

The tsar in his Cossack greatcoat and fur hat paced in his headquarters, as he always did when faced with a decision. Nothing distressed him so much as having to think. All he had ever wanted was to be left in peace. He loved it here at headquarters, where there were no ministers, no conferences, and, above all, no decisions to make. He took a daily walk with his adjutants, dined with them at the officers' mess, chatted about the weather. In the evenings he played a game or two of patience or dominoes, read a newspaper, glanced over his letters, listened to some reports from the front, read a French novel, wrote in his diary, sent a loving wire to his wife, prayed, and went to bed to sleep like a baby.

The entries in his diary were simple. He described the weather, marked down how long he had played dominoes, what he had had for dinner. Occasionally there was some unusual news about a hunt during which he had managed to pot a hare or a wild duck. His telegrams to his wife were more impassioned.

"Dear Wifey," he would wire her in the evenings, "Angel, little dove, I kiss you fervently. I hold you in my arms and pray to God for you. My most passionate kisses. Your Nicky."

All of a sudden this existence had been shattered. From all sides came telegrams which crisscrossed and contradicted one another. The politicians begged him to give in while there was still time, and his wife urged him not to yield to his enemies.

If Father Gregory were still alive, he would have asked his advice. The Little Father had helped him even from afar. He had advised him to hold the icon he, Rasputin, had given him and shake it seven times before he attended a staff conference. Another time, when he had sent him a new holy image, he had wired him not to forget to comb the pictured saint's hair before making any decisions.

Now there was no one to turn to, and he didn't know what to do. His adjutants were as indecisive as he was, the generals were strangers. He didn't even know which of them was a friend and which an enemy.

For a while he did nothing at all. He followed his usual routine—played patience and dominoes, noted down the weather in his diary, and dined with his retinue. When the telegrams grew too demanding, he behaved like any henpecked husband and took the advice of his wife, whom he considered his mental superior.

The time had come to prove to Aleksandra that he was a man of character. She constantly admonished him to be as strong as his predecessors, Peter the Great, Ivan the Terrible. Now he would do it. He wouldn't take a conciliatory stand but act from a position of strength.

He summoned General Ivanov and dispatched him to Petrograd to restore order. As usual, he couldn't have picked a worse man for the job.

Soon after, accompanied by his retinue, he took the imperial train to Tsarkoye Selo in order to make a triumphant entrance into the city after the general had put down the rebellion.

But at Likhoslavl the conductor received a wire, signed by a certain stationmaster Grekhov, directing him not to take the train to Tsarkoye Selo.

When the tsar heard that some stationmaster had dared countermand the order of the emperor of Russia, the shock left him in a daze. His aides gathered ashen-faced around their immobile monarch. One of them suggested Pskov as an alternate destination, and the tsar nodded his agreement. He was willing to go anywhere but face that impudent stationmaster Grekhov. He dispatched a telegram to his wife: "The weather is dry and frosty. I long to hold you in my arms. I kiss you fervently and pray to God for you. Your Nicky."

In vain he awaited a reply from her or from his minister Protopopov. Over the imperial residence as well as over all government buildings, offices, and barracks red flags now fluttered. The soldiers tore the epaulets from their officers' uniforms. Minister of the Interior Protopopov, in whose hands the tsar had left the fate of his family and of the empire, was confined to the Peter and Paul Fortress along with the other tsarist ministers and guarded by troops of the Provisional Government.

FIFTY-FOUR

THE PRISONER NISSAN EIBESHUTZ was overjoyed but not surprised when the call sounded in Petrograd's Kresty Prison: "Comrades, political prisoners, you are freed by the revolution!"

Just as his father, the rabbi, had spent his whole life awaiting the Messiah and his redemption, his son had spent his whole life awaiting the revolution and its redemption.

He hadn't been able to estimate its exact arrival, but he had never doubted that it would come—it was one of the inexorable laws of Marxism.

The war had only strengthened this conviction. Despite all the tragedy and resurgence of patriotism and nationalism it had brought, it had also signified the beginning of the end of the bourgeoisie, the demise of the old world.

At the secret party conference held in Petrograd during the first year of the war, Nissan had posited a very unfavorable prognosis for capitalism. The warring nations, which with their lust for new markets and greed for money had resorted to arming the proletariat, would be done in by that same proletariat.

The other delegates had scoffed at him as a simplistic visionary who counted his chickens before they were hatched, but he had clung to his position. The world war had revealed to him the contradictions of the corrupt middle class. Nissan had perceived the bourgeoisie as a body rotting from within, like an old corpse riddled by various ailments.

The secret conference had been broken up by the police, who encircled the building and burst in to arrest the participants.

"Here is your revolution!" his comrades had grumbled at Nissan with bitterness as they were herded into Kresty Prison.

"Time will prove me right," Nissan had responded with assurance.

During all the time in prison he had never allowed a shred of doubt to mar his faith. His comrades had made fun of him. Each time a key scraped against a lock, they had sent up a chorus: "Here comes the delegation to free you, Comrade Nissan!"

But one day in late February the doors to the cells *had* opened, and voices had called to the political prisoners to come out.

"Comrade Eibeshutz, forgive us," the others begged him. "You were the one with the foresight, not us."

"Comrades, let us embrace," Nissan said graciously as he kissed everyone, even the soldiers who had liberated him.

He climbed into the truck along with his comrades and rode through the streets of Petrograd which were jammed with workers and soldiers.

"Hurrah for our freed comrades!" the people cried.

"Long live the revolution!" the liberated prisoners responded.

Like a boy on his first day in the big city, Nissan didn't know where to look first. The atmosphere was festive, and everything filled him with joy. He kissed and embraced total strangers.

The city, which was saddled with the responsibility of determining the lives of the more than 150 million citizens of the land, was itself in a state of chaos and confusion. The factories were closed; the streetcars weren't running; the police were nonexistent. The soldiers strolled about aimlessly.

The Duma was in total disorder. People wandered in and out at will. Whoever felt like it issued orders and decrees. The Provisional Committee was composed of persons from various camps and parties—from monarchists, who wanted to restore the tsar to power, to wild-eyed radicals and anarchists.

They talked, debated, argued, caviled. Soldiers kept bringing in frightened gendarmes, policemen, and officials, but there was no one to question them or decide their fate. Troops congregated around the Duma, awaiting orders. They had driven off their officers and needed new leaders to tell them what to do, but no leaders had materialized, and they turned to the Duma.

A stout, bearded individual, whose deep voice and dignified appearance made him stand out from the crowd, greeted each arriving regiment and congratulated it on joining the revolution. The soldiers responded with hurrahs, but they were still uncertain about what to do next.

Just as befuddled were the armed guards at the railway depots, bridges, post offices, telegraph offices, and other important stations. Military units kept arriving, but no one knew whether they were for or against the revolution.

In the Duma all kinds of rumors and tidings kept going around. There were repeated reports of the arrival of troops loyal to the tsar, and in the midst of conferences, the representatives made mad dashes to the doors.

Within the crowded rooms and halls of the Duma, people bickered, trying to form a stable government and restore order. But the conflicting ideals, concepts, and beliefs blocked any agreement. There were Monarchists, and Cadets, Progessives and Social Revolutionaries, Mensheviks, Bolsheviks, and Social Democrats, each further splintered into leftists and rightists, moderates and centrists. Some wanted a monarchy; some wanted the royal family imprisoned. Some wanted a socialist republic, and some, a dictatorship of the workers and peasants. Some called for instant reapportionment of land and an end to the war. Others wanted the war continued before they instituted a socialist government. Some insisted that Marxists could work hand in hand with the bourgeoisie; others disagreed violently.

In side rooms, soviets of workers and soldiers were formed to protect the evolving Provisional Government. To do this, the workers had to elect representatives in their factories, and the soldiers theirs in the barracks. But since the factories were closed and the soldiers were out in the streets, it was difficult to hold such elections. Therefore, whoever felt like it appointed himself a delegate.

In the midst of all the conferences and debates, men and women burst into the building and waved fists. "All you do is gab and gab while the workers are starving! Open the stores, and issue bread!"

The city was vulnerable to attack by any vandal.

Nissan threw himself into the effort of restoring order to the chaotic city. He joined committees and commissions, helped establish soviets, probed means of feeding the people, joined heated theoretical discussions concerning the interpretation of Marxist doctrine, helped conduct negotiations with generals and admirals about turning over power to the new order.

Following days of frenzied activity he would remind himself that he hadn't eaten and look for a crust of dry bread or a glass of tea just to keep himself going. Nor did he have a roof over his head. After the days in magnificent palaces, he spent his nights on benches pushed together in sordid little rooms.

But this didn't douse his enthusiasm. Each time he looked up and saw the red flags, the soldiers with the red ribbons on their bayonets, the streets thronged with workers, the royal monuments with speakers addressing crowds, joy surged through him again.

"It's come," he mumbled to himself. "I've lived to see it!" In his excitement he almost added, "Thank God."

FIFTY-FIVE

New Lodz in Petrograd was back in full swing but with some exceptions. Instead of the two twelve-hour shifts, the workers put in three eight-hour shifts. For night work, they were now paid double time. The labor unions, now firmly established in the city, demanded higher wages for all workers and equal pay for women employees. Production was diminished, too, as more time was spent on meetings than on working. New holidays were celebrated every other day, and there were parades to which the factories had to send delegations. No employer dared deduct for such absences.

Delegates and speakers made frequent visits to the factories. Representatives of various parties came—Mensheviks and Bolsheviks, Social Revolutionaries of every shade from extreme left to extreme right. Each drew the workers away from their vats and looms and detained them for long speeches, to which the workers responded with equal applause regardless of what ideals the speakers espoused.

Max Ashkenazi was repulsed by such working schedules, but he kept silent. In the early days, when his factory had first shut down and the workers had poured out into the streets by the thousands, he had remained skeptical about the coming revolution. He well recalled the events in Old Lodz in '05, when the workers had also spilled out into the streets, demanding freedom and brotherhood. Many of the Lodz manufacturers at that time had panicked prematurely and fled abroad, but he, Ashkenazi, had kept a cool head then, and he did so again. He knew that ultimately the shoemaker must return to his last, the weaver to his loom, the manufacturer to his office. That was how it had finally turned out, and things had returned to more or less normal. Despite the coddling they now received, the workers had gone back to their jobs, as he had gone back to his.

He had been exposed to workers all his life. He knew that they were always rebelling against something since it was in their character to whine. But ultimately they had no recourse but to bow their heads and give in. This was the way things had always been; this was how they would be in the future. In this world there had to be the rich and the poor, the rulers and the ruled, the content and the frustrated. Whoever had the skills, brains, and guts emerged the winner. Were things otherwise, the world couldn't go on.

He, therefore, hadn't grown overly concerned when the workers had walked off their jobs. "Nonsense, foolishness," he told his associates from Lodz, who feared the imminent fall of the government. The moment the authorities resorted to stern measures and gave the rebels a taste of the bayonet, they would scatter like mice. His opinion of the Russian worker was—if possible—even lower than that of the worker of Lodz.

He rode through the streets in his carriage, observing the excitement, the scuffles between the people and the police, but he took little interest in it all. The moment the Cossacks showed up with their lances, it would all be over.

But when the Cossacks refused to fire at the rebels, the first stirrings of doubt set in. It was the first time the tsar's soldiers had disobeyed their superiors. Still, he retained his faith in the status quo. An isolated incident, he thought. Soon other troops would come to punish the rebels. God knew, there was no shortage of soldiers in Russia.

But when entire regiments began to tie red ribbons to their rifles and tear off the epaulets—along with the heads—of their officers, Max Ashkenazi lost his assurance and began gazing with apprehension at the mobs in the street. "Has the world come to an end?" he wondered.

Each successive day's events disillusioned him further. Ministers were being arrested and paraded through the streets like common criminals. When the imperial train was seized and the tsar forced to abdicate, Max's senses reeled.

Not that he had any love for the autocrat. He knew that the Little Father had pardoned those who had taken part in pogroms. In one city, when the Jews had come forward to welcome the tsar, he had ignored them and acknowledged only the Christian clergy.

All this hadn't filled Ashkenazi with any great love for the emperor, but he knew that the tsar was the most powerful individual in the land. After all, coins bore his image. And he couldn't conceive how such a personage could be deposed by common workers and peasants, the scum of the earth. . . .

For the first time in his life he was in fear of the workers. He suddenly perceived a great force in those faceless lumps whom he had always considered something less than human, something created merely to work his looms. They could barely sign their names, and now they represented a force that sent shivers up his spine. If they were able to depose the tsar with all his millions of troops and gendarmes, what couldn't they do to a mere manufacturer?

It was a meek and subservient Max Ashkenazi who opened the gates of his factory in the first weeks of the revolution. He didn't know how to address his workers, and he walked on tiptoe around them. Before the union representatives could even pose their demands, he agreed to each one. He eavesdropped on the orators, but he couldn't come to any conclusion since they were all of a different opinion. Some were for the war, and some against; some preached instant socialism, and others gradual socialism. And each spoke with the zeal of one who would not accept anyone's views but his own.

Otherwise, he didn't mix in, didn't discuss the turn of affairs with anyone in the factory. He sensed that it would be best for him to keep silent, to watch, listen, and hold his tongue. But mentally he allied himself with the moderates, those who preached restraint and the continuation of the war to its ultimate victory. Not that Ashkenazi was a superpatriot or a militarist. Far from it. But war represented profits, and he barely restrained himself from applauding speakers who urged its continuation.

Following the first few weeks of confusion and disorder, Ashkenazi relaxed somewhat. He adjusted to the new conditions just as he had always adjusted to change. He knew from experience that for every action there was a reaction, a period of adjustment. After all the speeches, slogans, parades, and demonstrations were over, things would return to normal. The workers would go back to their looms, and the bosses would continue to make profits.

He was practical enough to know that things would never again be as they once were. There were the unions to contend with; the workers had to be granted paid leave, sick pay, disability payments, and other such benefits for loafing. The boss no longer dared speak up in his own factory.

Ashkenazi didn't even resent these changes. He didn't blame the workers for trying to better their lot. Everybody was out for himself. To the victor went the spoils. In their place, he would have done the same.

What interested him most about the revolution was how he could turn it to his profit. He knew that for all of the workers' triumphs, they would need manufacturers like him, men of business acumen to run the plants. The problem was how to make money during the interim. After all, what was a revolution but another business problem such as a bad season, a shortage of raw goods or of markets?

He therefore ignored all the turmoil around him and kept up production. Not as intensively as before, but still at a respectable level, and he stocked his warehouses with goods. He never veered from his routine. He still raced from banks to government offices, conducted business with the new people in charge, delivered war goods, and made profits. He set higher prices to compensate himself for all the losses he had suffered as a result of the revolution, all the holidays, paid leaves, shorter working days, and time spent on speeches, parades, and other such childishness.

On the whole, the new people were easier to deal with since they didn't demand bribes as their predecessors had. The only changes Ashkenazi instituted were superficial ones. He no longer had himself driven to work in his carriage but walked or took a cab. He changed his sable coat for an old, ill-fitting sheepskin since he didn't want to draw attention to himself in the streets, which were filled with rowdy workers and idle soldiers and sailors. And he used his profits to buy up gold and diamonds, which would retain their value no matter who was in power.

One day a familiar face turned up at the factory. Even though the man wore cheap clothes and a workman's cap and his beard was already gray, Ashkenazi recognized his old schoolmate at once—Nissan, the rabbi's son, nicknamed Nissan the depraved.

For a moment Max's heart lurched. He was afraid to let Nissan see him lest he take revenge for their past differences. He was likely to denounce him, Max, as an enemy of the working classes. Anything was possible in these trying times. But Nissan proved far less militant than the other speakers. He called on the proletariat to practice solidarity and even to work diligently until order was restored and steps could be instituted to develop the socialist system.

Ashkenazi felt relieved, and his fears dissipated. He even decided to do the polite thing and court the goodwill of his former opponent. He walked up and held out his hand to Nissan. "Peace unto you, Nissan," he said in Yiddish, then quoted: "'Friends may meet, but mountains never.' Do you remember me at all?"

"Like a bad penny," Nissan countered with an icy smile.

For a while the two gazed at each other without speaking;

then Ashkenazi broke the silence. "You turned out to be right in the end," he said, then quoted again, " 'Who is wise? He who sees the future.' So you have triumphed over us. . . ."

"We are not yet finished with each other, Mr. Ashkenazi," Nissan replied in Russian so that the workers could understand. "Keep on producing, accumulating capital, developing the economy. We will presently take it over. . . ."

Ashkenazi bowed his head as fear of the man in the shabby clothes overcame him again. "If there were disagreements between us before, they weren't caused by any ill will on my part but rather by circumstances. Now we have both grown older and wiser. I hope you bear me no grudge."

"You behaved as your class must," Nissan said. "Personal matters don't concern me. As an enemy of your class I won't behave any worse than you did, Mr. Ashkenazi. Once we are in charge and have the people on our side, we will take what is rightfully ours and turn the factories over to the people, their true builders and creators."

The workers, who had gathered to observe the duel between the bourgeoisie and the proletariat, snickered.

"The workers will always need an astute businessman to guide them," Ashkenazi countered with a smile. "They won't be able to run the plant by themselves."

Nissan shook his head in hopelessness, huddled inside his threadbare coat, and left in the truck to address workers in other factories.

FIFTY-SIX

———◆———

THE HOME OF THE DIRECTOR of the Flederbaum
mill was dreary and sad. The factory, like all the others in the
city, had been standing idle since the German occupation.
Everything valuable within it had gone to Germany—transmission belts, boilers, all metal parts. But the worst loss of
all was that of the raw goods. The German Raw Material
Procurement Department, which the Lodz Jews had promptly
dubbed the Robbed Material Procurement Department, had
systematically siphoned every warehouse dry, issuing for every
item taken vouchers which would be redeemable after the war.

Occupied Poland was saturated with such vouchers. The
merchants and manufacturers stored them in their otherwise-
empty safes; the petty merchants, who had had even their door
latches removed, kept them inside their Passover Hagadahs or
their penitential prayer books; the peasants tucked them away
behind their pictures of the Holy Virgin.

For now the vouchers weren't worth a plug groschen, but
they would be once the lousy Russians, the syphilitic French-
men, and the damned English had been properly trounced.
For now the population had to make do with stirring marches
and portraits of the kaiser and of von Hindenburg, looking
like rosy village brides with spiky mustaches.

Director Ashkenazi's house, therefore, was steeped in despair
and gloom.

Flederbaum's sons didn't even know there was a war on.
As usual, they were absorbed in their séances, their divinations
and meditations. They spent their time trying to establish contact with their late parents. Crazy Yanka, although by now an
elderly woman, was still intent upon her affairs. The older she
grew, the younger were her lovers. She took no interest in
the factory, and all she and the other Flederbaum heirs did was
to press the director for money. Whatever he gave them wasn't
enough. The money dribbled through their fingers.

But there were no more reserves to be drawn on. The Russian banks in which the firm's funds were deposited, were out of reach. The Russian bonds and securities lining the factory vaults were now worthless pieces of parchment stamped with the two-faced eagle. The workers massed outside the factory with caps in hand. They gathered like starved wolves that had conquered their fear of man to seek a handout, and nothing the police did would disperse them.

"Bread!" they howled. "We're starving!"

The ersatz bread the Germans issued once a month lasted only through the first week. It looked like clay and tasted even worse. Those with money bought up additional ration cards, both real and counterfeit. The poor lacked even the few groschen with which to buy the bread. And they massed at the factory gates.

The manufacturers had no recourse but to distribute a little money among them now and then. The commandant himself had informed them that he wouldn't stand for any unrest in the city. He wanted total obedience, clean streets, and enthusiastic responses to the military marches so that he would get a good write-up from the Berlin war correspondents.

During the first days of the occupation, Yakub Ashkenazi took none of this to heart. From his remaining resources, he issued cash to the Flederbaums and to the workers and took whatever he wanted for himself.

His young wife, Gertrud, had inherited her grandmother Priveh's extravagant habits. Fortunes trickled between her bejeweled fingers. She would accept only imported gowns, the costliest furs, the finest jewelry, the fanciest carriages. She would not be outdone by anyone. Like her grandmother before her, she extended soft white fingers to her husband. "More, Yakub, more. . . ."

In the years following their wedding, she had proved to her husband that she was indeed Simha Meir's daughter—a willful, determined woman who insisted on having her way. At first, she had confined these traits to their lovemaking. Although she was desperately in love with her middle-aged husband, hers was a consuming, overpowering love, like that of a black widow spider that devours its mate. She demanded his exclusive devotion. She wouldn't let him talk to another person, look at another woman, even applaud actresses at the theater. He had to spend every moment with her, think about nothing else but her.

She estranged him from the people whose company he enjoyed, from all his friends and acquaintances. She was jealous of everyone—male and female alike. In every person she saw a competitor, a rival for his attentions. She considered him her property, and she wasn't about to share what was hers with another. She was her father's daughter to her fingertips. She knew of no half measure. With her, it was all or nothing.

A prisoner of her own passions, who could kneel at her husband's feet begging to be totally dominated, she still managed to emerge as the dominant force in their marriage. She wasn't concerned with his moods, his feelings, his needs. She swallowed him alive, drained and enslaved him.

But with the same zeal with which she had won him, she later discarded him like an orange that has yielded its juice and pulp. She couldn't focus her interest on anything for long. She required novelty, excitement, new thrills and experiences. Following the early months of physical fulfillment, she began to make impossible financial demands upon Yakub. Her ambition was to become the social leader of Lodz.

Yakub was himself a spendthrift by nature, but next to her, he seemed a miser. She refused to occupy the house provided for the director and found a palace with carved ceilings, columns, statuary, and a circular driveway. It had been put up for sale by a bankrupt manufacturer.

She spent all her time renovating and decorating the palace. She squabbled with masons, carpenters, upholsterers. She constantly demanded something new and different. Everything—no matter how sound—had to be remade, rebuilt, repainted. She crawled over scaffolds, raced from shop to shop, buying things, bringing them back, exchanging them, having second thoughts, buying again.

Yakub longed for her company, but she had no time for him. Her passions were now directed at the palace. When he tried to embrace her, she slid out of his grasp. "Frightfully busy," she said. "More money, Yakub, more money!"

Yakub doled out the cash without even counting it. When the palace was finally completed to her satisfaction, the balls, parties, and receptions commenced. There were always people in the house; there was constant music, dancing, drinking, carousal, with Gertrud at the center of it all. She supervised the guest lists, weeded out those of her husband's friends she considered not important or distinguished enough, and courted people he couldn't abide—counts, barons, and people of such ilk.

Now in his middle years, Yakub was ready to settle down. After a wild, tumultuous life he was tired of people, of parties.

Gertrud was forever either entertaining or out having a good time. And his money reserves had run dry. The large salary he drew didn't begin to cover her enormous expenses, and he signed more and more IOUs and ran up enormous debts.

He didn't speak of it, but it tormented him when he lay all night waiting for dawn and Gertrud to come home. For the first time in his life he wasn't able to sleep. He lost his appetite, and his normally jovial spirit grew heavy.

When she spent an occasional evening alone with him, he was pathetically grateful. Just as she had in the early days of their marriage, she threw herself at his feet and grunted her passion. "Great big hairy bear," she panted, "eat me up alive. . . ."

His masculine pride salved, he talked to her about having a child. "Think how happy we'd be with a little girl with golden curls just like yours," he urged her.

He had always yearned to be a father, but he had another, a more ulterior motive. He hoped that having a child would slow Gertrud down, give her a sense of responsibility. She was wild. A reckless passion reflected from her eyes, the same look he had seen in Simha Meir. He was a little afraid of her, and he wanted to subdue her somehow. There was no better way than with motherhood.

But she wouldn't hear of it. "You want to saddle me with diapers and swaddling clothes? There'll be plenty of time for children. . . ."

She examined herself in the mirror. The image of the supple, willowy figure brought a look of sly satisfaction to her slightly mad eyes. "Ruin all this with a belly? . . . Disgusting!"

Years later, when she was in her thirties, she did give birth to a child—a girl just as Yakub had hoped. By now in his late fifties, his beard more gray than black, he was like a child with a new toy as he played with his little daughter. He stretched out on the floor, barked like a dog, hopped, and danced with the baby, brimming over with paternal pride.

The mother ignored the child. She didn't nurse her herself but turned her over to a German nursemaid with breasts like watermelons, while she went back to her parties and balls.

Yakub was both father and mother to the child. He discussed her care with the nursemaid; he dandled her on his knee; he cooed at her and hugged her. He had lost all urge to socialize. He came straight home from the factory and raced to the nursery.

He loved his home. He was delighted to be settled, a husband and a father. He yearned for more children. He missed his Gertrud, who had grown even more attractive and womanly.

But she had no more time for him.

She had undergone a complete change of attitude. Even though she herself had pursued Yakub shamelessly, had literally forced him to marry her, she now felt that it had been a sacrifice to marry an older man who was too tired and set in his ways for such a young, fun-loving woman as she. To make up for it, she wanted complete freedom to spend as much money as she pleased, to enjoy the kind of luxury that was her due.

She held magnificent balls at their palace, high-spirited affairs attended by men and women her own age. Even haughty German lieutenants with dueling scars were invited. They behaved as if they were bestowing a favor upon their hosts by condescending to mingle with Polish and Jewish riffraff. They danced with their hostess and paid her suggestive compliments.

Yakub shook their hands and made polite small talk even as he seethed with jealousy and resentment. He vividly recalled when the shoe had been on the other foot—when he had been the young man scornful of elderly husbands as he flirted with their gay, lively wives. It had been so enormously amusing at the time; it wasn't half as funny now.

He knew women in all their artifice. He knew how much passion and allure they could put into a seemingly innocent dance. He recalled the half smiles, the touches, the winks, the double entendres. He remembered how gratful the young wives had been when he rescued them from their elderly husbands' company. He recalled the lame jokes the husbands had made in order to save face.

Now it was happening to him.

He went to the nursery, sat down in a small chair beside his child's crib, and listened to her even breathing. His mother-in-law, Dinele, came tiptoeing into the nursery.

Since her parents' death she had been left all alone. Her entire fortune lay on deposit in a Russian bank. She hadn't heard from her son, Ignatz, since the beginning of the war, when he had written that he had volunteered in a French regiment. Silent as a mouse, she lived now with her daughter and Yakub, the only man she had ever loved. As she had all her life, she lost herself in her books, in the lives of the dashing heroes and the gentle heroines. Her only consolation was the child. She fantasied that it was her child—not Gertrud's—hers and Yakub's. And she smothered the little girl with kisses.

"Privehshe, my treasure," she cooed to the little girl, who was named for her great-grandmother.

Now, even though it was late, she could not sleep. She couldn't stand the noise and music drifting in from the other rooms, and she went to check on the child. She stood for a moment in the doorway before she saw Yakub. He sat there hunched over, shoulders bent, head bowed, and she felt her heart lurch. She approached on tiptoe and put a hand on his shoulder.

"Yakub," she said soothingly, "go to sleep. I'll stay up with the child."

Yakub looked up at her with sad black eyes. "No," he said. "I can't sleep."

"I can't either, Jacob," she whispered sadly.

She had addressed him by his old name, which she remembered from when they had played together in Abraham Hersh's courtyard in Old City.

FIFTY-SEVEN

———◆———

ALONG WITH THE OTHER REVOLUTIONARIES flooding back from prisons and exile to liberated Russia, the Bolshevik leader too was welcomed with flowery speeches, bands, red banners, and embraces. But the squat man with the naked skull and Tatar features didn't wax sentimental upon the occasion. He didn't weep with joy; he didn't kiss or embrace his comrades. He gazed ironically at the forest of red flags, his bald pate reflecting the gleam of the military trumpets blaring the "Marseillaise" in his honor, and narrowed his slanted eyes at the horde of welcomers, each a distinguished personage of handsome garb and plumage.

Their speeches left him unmoved. A narrow smile played at the corners of his sly slit eyes as he patiently listened to their cultured voices and waited to douse their rhetoric with cold, sobering logic.

His voice was as dry as he himself. He spoke in blunt, pithy phrases that conveyed exactly what they were meant to convey. He quoted no poets or martyrs. But he had the one trump card that enraptured the soldiers crowding the speaker's platform more than all the high-flown oratory.

"Comrades," he began, "all the power to the soldiers and workers. I urge you to desert. Don't shed your blood for the imperialist powers. Point your rifles against your true enemy— the bourgeoisie. Seize the factories from the manufacturers, seize the land from the gentry, and distribute it among yourselves. Do this, and all the workers and peasants of the world will follow your lead. An end to the war!"

At first, his tough words were received with mockery and contempt by the other party leaders. The newspapers jumped in to defame him. What could you expect from a man who had returned to Russia by sufferance of the enemy? After all, he had come in a sealed German railroad car. He had been encouraged in this by the German high command in return for his promise to turn his countrymen against the war. If he, a Russian, could do such a thing, he was a pawn and a traitor who deserved whatever the liberated masses did to him.

At meetings, the leaders of other parties castigated him mercilessly. Only a fanatic, a doctrinaire without a grasp of reality, could propose that Russia abrogate her responsibility to her allies in such craven fashion and subject her to German reactionaries who would enslave her once again. The Russian people weren't such cowards. They had given their lives to defend their country, and they would go on doing so. Only after victory was theirs would they build a socialist system.

There was no place in revolutionary Russia for the policy he and his lackeys advocated. The best thing would be to let them dig their own graves with their words rather than punish them and make martyrs of them.

The humorists had a field day with the squat bald man whose physical appearance lent itself so well to burlesque and caricature.

The smear campaigns left him unmoved. He smiled at his distorted image in the cartoons. He didn't care what they said about him. He didn't bother to justify his arrival in a sealed German railroad car. He ignored the accusations that he had been paid off by the enemy. He didn't even bother to defend himself against charges of being a German spy.

"Comrade, you must counter these accusations," his associates advised. "Your name and honor are being besmirched."

He smiled at them mockingly. "What for? Soldiers and workers don't read newspapers, and peasants don't read at all. As for the intellectuals, I couldn't care less what they think of me. Russia needs two things only—peace and land. That's the only thing the soldiers and peasants understand. . . ."

"But it's a matter of morality," his colleagues argued.

"We're not middle-class brides who need to guard their good name. We have one concern—the revolution. . . ."

He knew what he was about, the squat man. He gauged the mood of the Russian people perfectly. The soldiers, who were tired of war and who longed for their homes and wives, didn't care how he had arrived from abroad. They cared even less about Russia's allies, or about the spring offensive their generals had promised to launch in order to draw Ludendorff's armies away from the western front. Their only concern—as the bald man kept reiterating—was peace and land.

With the speed of fire leaping from roof to roof, these two words carried through the streets, barracks, harbors, trenches, factories, squares, and plazas.

When the powers that be saw that matters were growing serious—even alarming—they stopped the smear campaigns against the squat man. To counter his influence, they sent out their most eloquent speakers accompanied by bands and singers to rekindle the patriotic spirit of the troops. They mobilized new units, furnished them with the finest equipment, and shipped them off to the front to the strains of the "Marseillaise" to launch the spring offensive. But the huge military body had already been infected with the tiny bacillus of "peace and land," which promptly proceeded to consume the body from within. The soldiers threw down their rifles and hurried home on trains and on foot to their wives and their land.

Following the first uprising instigated by the squat man in July, the government ceased the war of words it had launched against him and resorted to force. The uprising was put down, and the squat man along with his lieutenants was formally charged with treason and with conspiring with the German general staff. Some of his comrades surrendered voluntarily in order to stand trial and to prove their innocence, but he went underground among the sailors of Kronstadt. The notion of subjecting himself to a trial struck him as preposterous.

His colleagues tried to reason with thim. They pointed out the need to absolve himself of all charges as a matter of honor, but he waved their suggestions aside. "Honor is for dancing teachers," he sneered. "Our job is to get on with the revolution."

He pointed to his devoted disciple who had elected to join him in hiding. "He's the only one with any sense."

One of his associates tried to warn him about his disciple. "You can't trust him . . . he swings with the breeze. He isn't motivated by revolutionary principles, only by his own ambitions."

The squat man smiled caustically. "You know the old Russian proverb: 'On a well-run farm, every pile of dung comes in handy.' He does good work for the revolution."

At first, he was sure that his enemies would flush him out and execute him along with his confederates. That was what he would have done in their place. But to his relief, he realized that they were dedicated democrats who were afraid to act boldly and decisively, and he resumed his seditious activities, inundating the soldiers and sailors with propaganda to desert the front and strive for peace and land.

The government leaders sent out their spokesmen to cities, towns, and villages, to factories and clubs. Across the length and breath of Russia, skilled orators urged the citizens to choose delegates so that a parliament of deputies elected by the people could begin to govern the land according to its wishes.

The squat man knew that his party was too small to win control of the people of Russia, and he, therefore, concentrated all his efforts on the soldiers and sailors in order to recruit armed men to his side.

He conceded to his opponents the body; all he wanted was the head.

And by autumn he had got his way. One wintry night in October, his sailors took over the capital. Railway depots, telegraph stations, telephone exchanges, water works, garrisons —everything was seized simultaneously. The Winter Palace, where the government was conducting its endless conferences, was menaced by gaping cannon and fieldpieces.

In the first days, when the squat man hadn't felt secure enough to seize power, he had sent emissaries to his opponents, the Socialist Revolutionaries and Social Democrats to join him in forming a coalition government composed of the socialist parties. His comrades had been upset. "How can we work with them?" they lamented.

"Once we're strong enough, we'll send them to hell," he had explained to them, as if to naïve children.

The opposition parties had consoled themselves with their triumph. Of the 703 deputies gathered at the Tauride Palace for the opening session of the Constituent Assembly, a mere 160 had been Bolsheviks. But the squat man knew what he was about. His opponents had the votes, but he had the guns. All the streets, squares, telegraph stations, depots, fortresses, prisons, and trains were controlled by his soldiers and sailors, and he laughed at his skittish comrades. On the first day of the session he ordered his troops to cow and humiliate the deputies of the other parties. They were made to walk a gauntlet into the Tauride Palace while the soldiers and sailors cursed and spat upon them.

"Counterrevolutionaries! Sellouts! Capitalist lackeys! Warmongers!" they cried as the terrified deputies shuffled between them. "We'll string you up to every lamppost!"

Among the deputies were two old revolutionaries from Lodz —Nissan Eibeshutz and Pavel Szczinski, who had shared exile in Siberia, who had studied together, escaped together, worked in Lodz for the revolution, and later met in Kresty Prison again.

The revolution had freed them both, and now they were on their way to the Tauride Palace as delegates of the people, but there the similarity ended. Szczinski wore a uniform and a pistol strapped to his side. He was now a trusted follower of the squat bald man.

Nissan, on the other hand, wore a ragged, unbuttoned coat with the pockets stuffed with newspapers, brochures, theses, and resolutions. He still believed in the power of the word, not the gun, in justice and in the voice of the people, which was like the voice of God.

"Hang the traitors! Shoot them! Blast them to hell!" the sailors growled in their rage.

Nissan tugged at Szczinski's sleeve. "See what you have sowed?"

Szczinski started to mumble something, but Nissan cut him off. "Is it I who is being called the counterrevolutionary, the capitalist lackey, the sellout? . . . Tell me!"

His friend bowed his head. He didn't dare look Nissan in the eye.

The Tauride Palace resembled a huge barrack, rather than a house of parliament. Soldiers with rifles and hand grenades were everywhere. Steel bayonets glittered their icy rage. The gallery was filled with tattooed sailors. "We ought to clean out the whole counterrevolutionary nest with machine guns!" they cried, their fingers closing on the triggers of their Mausers and Nagants.

Foreign correspondents looked on in disbelief. Never had they witnessed such an opening of parliament.

The first to take the floor were the adherents of the squat man. They proposed that the Constituent Assembly acknowledge their party's authority to the world and ratify all its laws.

The deputies of the other parties took umbrage. "Down with dictators!" they cried. "The Constituent Assembly does not bow to you—you must bow to it, the will of the people!"

One of the Bolsheviks took out a resolution the squat man had prepared in advance and proceeded to read it: "Inasmuch as the Constituent Assembly is an obsolete form of representation by the people, a form unsuitable for a time when the proletariat is threatened by its enemy, the bourgeoisie, and the revolution is in danger—this assembly is hereby dissolved."

The deputies launched a storm of protest. They pounded on tables and waved their arms, but at that moment Pavel Szczinski gave a prearranged signal to the soldiers and sailors. With Mausers and Nagants held shoulder high, they cleared the hall of the people's deputies.

Their heads bowed, deeply humiliated, the deputies slunk out into the dark streets of Petrograd. No streetcars were running; no streetlights were lit; no buildings were open. uniformed men milled through the streets. Armed with rifles and grenades and behung with bandoliers, they swaggered along the Nevsky Prospekt, smoking, laughing, cursing.

At all squares and monuments stood artillery pieces, muzzles pointing high. Field kitchens sent sparks shooting all around. A sailor played a gay tune on a concertina.

Nissan stumbled along in a daze of despair and disappointment. How many years had he waited for the first meeting of the freely elected deputies of a liberated Russia? How much torture, starvation, confinement, and deprivation had he endured to attain this day? And now, to be kicked out like a leprous dog. . . . And by whom? Not by the tsar's bullyboys, not by bourgeois lackeys, but by his own kind! He felt as betrayed and degraded as he had that May Day long ago, when the gentiles had transformed the celebration of the workers' freedom into an assault upon the Jews.

He crawled into the narrow cot in his dingy room and heaved into the pillow, lamenting the glorious day of redemption from which he had been so unjustly excluded.

The sound of gunfire kept echoing into the night.

FIFTY-EIGHT

———◆———

BETWEEN THE TROOPS of the Polish Legion that Commander Marcin Kuczinski had sent to Lodz to recruit youth and the German soldiers occupying the city, a state of deep animosity prevailed.

Ever since they had been forced to go to war as allies, the Germans had had nothing but contempt for the Austrians and for all the nationalities under their command, which included the Polish legionnaires. A major problem was one of communication. The Austrian Army encompassed Hungarians, Czechs, Poles, Jews, Ruthenians, Bosnians, Rumanians, even gypsies, most of whom knew no German outside of the few military commands.

Besides, after a drop too much, soldiers of these nationalities were inclined to express their hatred of Germans, who, accustomed to a single land, a single language, and a single set of customs, didn't take kindly to such criticism and looked askance at the Austrians for failing to discipline their subject nations and turn them into proper Teutons.

"Hey, you *kitche, pitche, mitchel!*" the Germans mocked their allies' jargons.

Besides, the Austrians were such poor fighting men that they invariably retreated before the Russians, forcing them, the Germans, to pull their chestnuts out of the fire. And they, the kaiser's troops, were, therefore, repelled by the sight of their ineffectual allies in their puttees, their silly little caps, and profusion of chauvinistic insignia.

The German officers regarded their Austrian counterparts as scum often consisting of sons of shopkeepers, peasants, or even Jews from Tarnopol and other parts of Galicia. You never could tell what kind of lowlife you might encounter at the Officers' Club or at a ball. And the Germans made sure to commandeer the best living quarters for themselves, leaving the dregs to the Austrians, and to take over all the important commands.

German enlisted men pretended they didn't see Austrian officers and failed to salute them. Or if they saluted, they did it so sloppily that it seemed more contemptuous than not saluting at all. If the Austrian officers reported the oversight, the German officers made a show of dressing down their men, but they did it with such tongue in cheek, that the German soldiers knew it was all right to keep ignoring their allies.

Following the Austrians' most recent routs during the Russian spring offensive and their inevitable rescue by the Germans, the enmity between the two allies had grown even more intense. The Germans even made obscene allusions to the initials *K* and *K* which stood for *Kaiserlich* and *Königlich*—royal and imperial, the title by which the Hapsburg House was known —and this evoked added rage and humiliation among the Austrians.

But the Germans were even more scornful of the Polish Legion, which had been founded in Austria and which functioned as an autonomous force with its own officer corps and uniforms, and they made fun of the legionnaires' Polish speech, their drooping caps and stirring, patriotic hymns. The moment the Poles started singing about dear old Poland, the Germans retaliated with a ditty of their own:

> All their bombs and all their Cossacks,
> All their lice and all their Polacks,
> We don't begrudge the Russky sons of bitches
> 'Cause all they do is give you the itches!

Those Galician legionnaires who understood German seethed, but the German soldiers wouldn't let up. They completely ignored the legion's officers despite orders to treat officers of all allied nations with the same respect as their own. Baron Colonel von Heidel-Heidellau's nape flushed a deep burgundy when the legionnaires entered the city in peasant carts drawn by skinny little Polish horses to recruit the youth of Lodz into their ranks. "Just look at that scurvy crew, would you?" he growled to his adjutant.

He had loathed Poles and considered them on a par with cattle from the time he had employed them on his estates in East Prussia. They worked like slaves for the lowest wages and were content to bed down in barns or even on the bare ground. Like all East Prussian landowners, he had always cast a covetous eye eastward, where land was plentiful and labor cheap. Now that he had the chance to show the Polish

and Jewish scum what Germans were made of, the legion had
suddenly been thrust upon him to raise his hackles with their
blue uniforms straight out of an operetta and their repulsive
jargon.

He had no option but to tolerate them. Orders were orders.
But he was furious at his superiors in the general staff for
visiting this ragtag crew upon him. The Austrians were bad
enough, but never in Germany's glorious history had a foreign
legion been permitted to be formed in an occupied land, with
its own language, command, and all the other accoutrements
of an army within an army.

It was all the fault of the accursed Austrians with their babel
of nations, races, and jargons. They weren't soldiers, but a pack
of swineherds and politicians. Now they had duped the German
general staff into allowing a Polish Legion to recruit in the
cities.

Baron Colonel von Heidel-Heidellau gritted his aristocratic
false teeth. He had orders to provide the Polacks with living
quarters, but he saw to it that these were little better than
pigsties. He made sure they wouldn't enjoy themselves in Lodz.
He had enough trouble contending with patriotic organizations
in the city that nursed silly dreams of an independent Poland.
Now the legion would encourage these seditious elements to
emerge into the light of day.

Among the officers of the legion arriving in the city was
Felix Feldblum, an old friend and fellow conspirator of Marcin
Kuczinski's. After breaking with the Proletariat party, Feldblum had joined Kuczinski in the Polish Socialist party, which
combined its struggle for socialism with a quest for an independent Poland.

Just as he had before, Felix Feldblum again toiled selflessly
for his new party. He printed proclamations on secret printing
presses; he wrote and set the party newspaper; he organized
study groups among Polish workers; he translated socialist
books; he attended secret party conferences; he went to prison,
escaped, was jailed again.

During the 1905 troubles, Feldblum had operated in Lodz,
where his implacable enemy had been Pavel Szczinski, who
regarded the Polish Socialist party as a vehicle of chauvinism
and reaction. Himself a former seminarian, Szczinski detested
Polish socialists, who ignored the plight of the working classes
to dream of an independent Poland. He sneered at the Jew
Feldblum in his role as an alleged Polish patriot.

When the World War broke out, Feldblum was in Galicia,
hiding from the gendarmes in Poland. He was arrested in

Galicia as a Russian alien, but shortly after, his friend Kuczinski founded the Polish Legion, and Feldblum volunteered for it. Like most Polish socialists, he believed that the greatest obstacle to freedom was tsarist Russia. Along with his comrades he believed that a Poland freed from the Russian yoke would establish itself as a land of brotherhood and equality, and he had placed himself at the side of his friend Kuczinski, just as he always had in the past.

Lieutenant Felix Feldblum hardly cut a military figure. He was already along in years; his curly hair and beard were thickly threaded with gray; his pince-nez had a habit of slipping down on his nose.

He was gawky, slightly stooped, quick of movement, and ungainly. His uniform hung loosely upon him, and his cap seemed forever askew. For all that, he proved an excellent fighting man. He was brave and conscientious. He never shirked or complained. He volunteered for dangerous missions, and he was quickly promoted to the rank of officer.

Now, along with the others, he had come to Lodz to recruit men into the legion, and down the same streets where he had once set up barricades, marched in demonstrations, and run from the police, he now strode with his sword strapped to his side.

The German soldiers laughed out loud when they saw him. The mark of the Jewish intellectual peered out from behind all his straps, medals, and epaulets. Even his own men gazed at him with derision. He looked more like a rabbi than a Polish officer.

Nor did he feel easy with his fellow officers. Few of them were idealists. There were many among them who cared little about socialism and knew nothing of Felix Feldblum's contributions to the cause. Like military men from time immemorial, they gave themselves up to gambling, drinking, wenching, barracks humor, and striving for promotions. They looked upon Feldblum as an outcast. He didn't gamble, drink, swear, or tell dirty stories. He didn't even blink when German soldiers walked past him without a salute. He fraternized with the enlisted men and didn't swagger about in his uniform, jangling his sword and spurs. He spent all his free time in libraries or reading, writing, and translating party literature.

Felix Feldblum agonized as he observed his comrades—former idealists—seduced and brutalized by army life. The officers put on airs and treated the enlisted men like dirt. His old friend and present commander of the legion, Marcin, daily grew less the socialist and more the martinet. He surrounded himself with sycophants and estranged himself from his old comrades. He even recruited priests into the legion to serve as chaplains and foster Catholicism among the troops. The songs the legion sang were patriotic, but not at all socialistic. And Feldblum cringed, witnessing his friend and his party's defection from its original ideals.

To block out these disturbing factors, Feldblum organized literary evenings, during which he lectured his comrades on the special mission that was incumbent upon a Poland which had suffered so much in order that through her anguish she might redeem the world. He quoted from the works of Mickiewicz, Norwid, and Wyspianski and envisioned a Poland that would serve as a model of justice and righteousness to the world.

In such times, he again recaptured the optimism of his youth. He reminded himself that he was fighting for an ideal, for a cause for which he was ready to lay down his life. The men heard him out but with reservations. An invisible barrier seemed to separate the stooped dark-eyed man with the grizzled curls from the fair-haired, florid, snub-nosed Slavs who seemed as if born to the uniform.

"Queer, that Feldblum fellow," they mumbled to each other. "Something very odd and disturbing about him."

"A Jew." The others shrugged as if that would explain everything.

FIFTY-NINE

———◆———

DESPITE ASHKENAZI'S UNWAVERING FAITH in the world's immutability, the shoemaker didn't return to his last, or the weaver to his loom, or the industrialist to his office. The world had turned completely topsy-turvy.

In magnificent palaces, Red Guards warmed their feet over fires fueled with Louis XIV furniture. They stripped the rooms of the costliest mahogany and camwood pieces and hurled old masters into the flames to roast their potatoes. They slashed chunks of cordovan leather from chairs to patch their boots and used the velvet from draperies to fashion leggings. The finest silk tapestries were cut into handkerchiefs for their sweethearts.

All bank vaults were sealed; all shops, shuttered; all factories, nationalized. Walls carried proclamations reporting takeovers, arrests, and regulations ordered by City Commandant Pavel Szczinski. Huge red banners spanning the streets assigned all power to the soviets and condemned the exploiters of the people. Posters showed a Red Guard spearing a capitalist whose fat belly gushed a fountain of gore, a peasant doing a dance on the neck of a landowner, an impossibly muscled worker giving the heave-ho to a priest, a rabbi, and a mufti, each displaying the symbol of his faith.

And one day it was Max Ashkenazi's turn.

A group of men in unbuttoned greatcoats showing traces of torn epaulets, with rifles slung on strings instead of straps, with fur hats pushed far back over their hair, chewing sunflower seeds or homemade cigarettes strode boldly into the mill and announced, "No one is to leave. This factory is hereby taken over by the Workers' and Peasants' Government. A meeting of all the workers will be convened presently."

Their leader, a youth in a student's cap walked into the office and came up to the desk.

"How can I best serve you?" Max Ashkenazi asked pleasantly, as if totally unaware of what was going on. "Have a seat," he added, pointing to a chair facing him.

"I want your seat," the youth said.

Ashkenazi took out a key and began to unlock the large iron safe, but the youth gestured brusquely. "Leave the key where it is. Touch nothing."

"It's only some private papers," Ashkenazi explained with a smile.

"There are no more private things," the youth pointed out. "Everything belongs to the Workers' and Peasants' Government. Turn over all your keys, after which you are free to go."

Even though he had been expecting this for weeks, Max Ashkenazi was in a state of shock when he came out into the street and the factory door slammed shut behind him. He stood there a moment as if stunned.

"Thrown out!" he mumbled to himself as if unable to grasp the enormity of it all. "Tossed out like a stray dog!"

He didn't know where to turn. The youth had told him that he was free to go where he pleased, but he had no place to go. For the first time in his life he had nothing to occupy him. He was in the same position as his former workers in Lodz whom he had locked out without ceremony.

He felt desperately alone in the alien city. He had no one here. He had been stripped of all his goods and possessions. The entire fortune he had accumulated during the war had evaporated in a single day.

In the first weeks following the takeover of his factory, Max Ashkenazi wandered through the streets, reading the huge banners calling upon the oppressed to seize back the plunder from the exploiters. He couldn't understand what this meant. He didn't feel like an exploiter. He hadn't robbed anyone of anything. All he had done was bought, sold, produced, and earned his rightful profits. True, in his day he had pulled a trick or two, but that was business. Whoever was the shrewder skimmed the cream off the top. This wasn't robbery. This was the way of the world. As for the workers, he hadn't forced anyone to work for him. He paid wages like everyone else, based on a cost-profit system. He felt no more guilty than a lamb. He, a robber? Those who came with guns and took away everything for which a man had slaved for years were robbers. . . .

If Max Ashkenazi's days were empty and dark, the nights were even worse. In a frayed coat and a worker's cap calculated not to draw any undue attention to him, he aimlessly prowled the streets, squares, and avenues of the once-lively city, which had always blazed with lights, carriages, troikas, theaters, restaurants, and cabarets and which now resembled some huge military encampment.

Long lines of people stood before the cooperatives, waiting to buy a crust of bread or a herring. The price of food rose by the minute. The peasant women who brought jugs of milk to sell in the city couldn't reckon the value of the banknotes, which changed from one street to the next.

Ashkenazi used his dwindling cash to buy food in the streets, which he prepared for himself in his mansion on Kamenniy Ostrovsky Prospekt. There was no wood or coal for heat, and the pipes had frozen from the bitter cold so that the water had to be brought up from a well in the adjoining street. Ashkenazi's servants had gone back to their villages to eat homemade bread and potatoes and warm their feet by the huge farm stoves. Their places had been taken by workers, sailors, and Red Guards, who stole and smashed the furniture and installed pot belly stoves with flues extending through holes in the walls and through smashed windowpanes. Each day there were more of them, and they kept pushing Max from room to room.

"Hey there, Little Father, which bunch are you with?" they asked, gazing suspiciously at his workingman's guise, which didn't match the costly furniture in his rooms.

Ashkenazi cowered in a corner, terrified by the brawny sailors exuding joy, abandon, righteousness, and fierceness all at once. "I'm a war refugee from Poland," he piped in a pathetic tone.

"You'll have to pull in your wings, Little Father," they responded slyly. "You take up altogether too much room for one Polish refugee in times likes these. . . . And you've got too many things, too, a regular furniture store."

They pushed him from room to room until he was left with just one. In the adjoining rooms they smashed furniture to fuel their stoves. Each blow of the hatchet was like a stab in Ashkenazi's heart. They also brought in girls for orgies, got drunk on home-brewed whiskey, played concertinas, danced, laughed, sang.

Ashkenazi lay in his wide bed, covered by all the blankets he had and his sable coat on top, but he couldn't sleep. There was no light, no heat, no water. The uproar next door never ceased. He cocked his ears, wondering how people could enjoy themselves in the face of imminent death at the front, and he envied them.

All the aches, pains, cramps, and twinges that had lain dormant while he was occupied asserted themselves now with a fury. There wasn't even a little hot water to brew tea with. The room was stacked with all kinds of objects that were soaked and frozen over. There was no place even to relieve himself.

The man who had run an empire and transported a city nearly 1,000 miles in the midst of a nation's deepest crisis now found himself unable to care for his own body. The young men and women laughed at him when he left his room in the mornings carrying a Chinese porcelain vase to fetch some water from downstairs. He slipped on the icy bridge that other pedestrians negotiated with ease. He clumsily knotted the rope to the vase handle and nearly fell in the well as he drew the water that he spilled more than he collected. The hand which had so swiftly run pencil over paper calculating sums in the millions couldn't grasp a hatchet to chop a piece of wood. His room was a disaster, and he neglected his person.

The long winter nights dragged like eternities. He listened to every scream, every gunshot. There were frequent fires. Houses ignited from the many carelessly tended stoves. There was no water to douse them, and the firemen didn't even bother coming. The buildings blazed like huge haystacks in the nights, illuminating the otherwise-unlit streets. The cries of victims echoed in the nocturnal stillness.

More than anything, Ashkenazi kept his ears cocked for the sound of the gate bell. There were nightly raids as groups of undisciplined men invaded the domiciles of once-affluent persons, dragged them out of their beds, and searched their rooms. They used bayonets to tear open furniture, looking for weapons, illicit literature, hidden gold and diamonds, and other contraband.

Ashkenazi kept no weapons nor any forbidden printed matter, but he did have something to hide. During the troubled days he had spirited some goods out of his warehouses and laid them away against a rainy day. He had entrusted some to acquaintances and hidden the rest in his cellar, where they now reposed, rising in value from day to day. He was anxious to dispose of them, but this wasn't easy. Potential buyers were skittish, nor could goods be openly transported. Everything had to be done in stealth.

He had also set aside a small cache of gold and diamonds where no one would think of looking for them. He had personally and with great difficulty sewn them into the lining of his sable coat.

He was desperate to flee the chaotic city, which no longer

had anything to offer him, but for this, all kinds of permits were required, and he was reluctant to show himself in the Red offices, staffed by men who kept their caps on inside and by women in peasant headkerchiefs. He was afraid to mention the name Ashkenazi in a city commanded by Pavel Szczinski, whom he remembered from the 1905 troubles in Lodz. He could expect little good from this individual with whom he had crossed swords in the past and who now held the power of life and death over him.

Besides, it wasn't permitted to take cash out of the city, except some paper money which was worthless. His plan was to flee the country, go abroad, and, from there, reenter Lodz. But he wouldn't leave without his treasure. What would he do in the world without a kopeck to his name? As for trying to leave *with* the jewels—this was certainly fraught with danger. There were searches at every twist and turn. For such an offense these days, one could end up a head shorter.

He mulled over ways of smuggling himself out of the country. For this, one needed a shrewd person who knew the right parties to bribe, but it wasn't so easy to find such a person. It was hard to know whom to trust these days. Petrograd was rife with spies, counterspies, and informers.

He, therefore sat at home, as restless as a cat on hot coals. He lived on whatever he could scrape up from the objects he sold one by one in the street. He bought his food from peasant women and prepared it himself. And he kept his treasure hidden against the time when opportunity might present itself.

Every knock on a door, every ring of a bell, every rustle on the stairs left him shaking. He often saw trucks filled with arrested people. No one in the city dared speculate about the fate of these people, but rumors went around that they were never seen again. Allegedly they were driven outside town, shot, and buried in secret plots. This, people whispered, was the source of the gunfire and the rumble of trucks in the nights.

Ashkenazi squirmed restlessly under his pile of covers. He couldn't even be sure of his neighbors. Once they had doffed their caps to him; now they might decide to denounce him. He had even less faith in the soldiers and sailors occupying his house. They could dispose of him without anyone's being the wiser and bury him somewhere like a dog among paupers and gentiles.

He was filled with self-pity. Why had he come here in the first place? His wife had pleaded with him not to go, but he had lost faith in a Lodz cut off from Russia. And what had become of all the millions he had acquired? They were in the hands of ignorant brutes who in their whole lives hadn't earned what he had in one day. He was broke, alone, sickly, feeling each of his years. It was all due to that brain of his, that overactive brain that never ceased scheming, plotting, conniving. A man had to take life as it came, just the way that brother of his did, Jacob Bunem.

He thought about his brother, whom he had loathed so fervently all these years. He felt no anger toward him now, only envy. *He*, at least, had had the sense to remain in Lodz, where he was probably living a safe, comfortable existence. *He* hadn't been driven by devils to leave home and family and run off to some godforsaken place in search of God knew what. He had stayed where he belonged and gone about his normal life with his wife.

For the first time, Max thought of his daugher, Gertrud, in positive terms. She was a fine girl, pretty and with a man's intelligence. Jacob Bunem was lucky to have her. He, Max, hadn't even gone to the wedding. He hadn't ever visited his daughter; he had remained a stranger to her.

His thoughts drifted to Ignatz. He tried to picture him as a grown man, but he couldn't. The image melted away. How he would have enjoyed seeing him now. . . . True, Ignatz had been a ne'er-do-well and had behaved badly toward his own father. Still, Max would have liked to see how his son had turned out. Possibly he had a family by now—a wife and children. Or maybe something bad had happened to him, God forbid. He had heard that Ignatz had volunteered for the French Army. He had always had a weakness for reckless, empty gentile pursuits. . . .

Ashkenazi trembled at the notion that some harm had befallen his son.

From Ignatz his thoughts strayed to his ex-wife. She suddenly appeared before him, looking as she had when she was young, tender, alluring. The memory of their life together returned with painful nostalgia. She had been cold to him, but the fault hadn't been entirely hers. He had always been too preoccupied with business to enjoy a normal life with her. Divorcing her had been an act of madness. He had humiliated her, demeaned her before the world. She hadn't done anything to deserve this. She had always behaved circumspectly, never caused him a moment of shame, as some other men's wives did. Just when she was about to mend her ways and spoke of making a new start and reviving their marriage, he had come up with his insane notion. . . .

He had never stopped loving her, yet he had exchanged her for another. His present wife was a shrewd woman, and she respected him, but she had brought him no happiness. She was more a companion than a wife. The nights with her were empty, meaningless. And why had he done it? For money, money that he no longer even had. Everything could have turned out so differently. He might now be enjoying a home, a wife, children, gratification.

He took some comfort in thinking about what he had left behind in Lodz. He was lucky not to have burned all his bridges. Now he would know what to do with his life. He would reconcile with his children, with his brother. He would even make up with Dinele and help her out in every way he could. God alone knew how things were going for her. . . .

He would become more tolerant of people in general. There was no reason to sacrifice oneself for material gains. Man proposed, but God disposed. One had no right to turn one's back on the world. He would help people, give to charity. If only he managed to escape from this hellhole and reach home, he would yet accomplish great things. Max Ashkenazi was still somebody. He wasn't one of your run-of-the-mill clods. He had made fortunes once; he would do it again. But he could do nothing in a land gone mad, a place where a man of means had to chop his own wood, draw his own water, haggle with peasants over every crust of bread, every bottle of milk. Once he reached the real world, the normal world, where brains, guts, and logic still counted, he would be back on top in no time. If it meant doing business with the Germans, so be it. He no longer even mourned the losses he had suffered at the hands of the Reds. The devil take them! They would shortly drag the country down and themselves with it. He would think of the revolution as just another business setback, like a shortage of raw materials or a recession. Apparently it had been a fated thing. All he cared about now was getting out of the country. And he was ready to pay plenty for this privilege.

There was talk in the street of members of the new regime who were only too happy to trade in goods they requisitioned in the name of the revolution. Ashkenazi had never doubted that it would be so. The only trouble was locating the shrewd man who appreciated the value of the ruble as opposed to the fool who believed all the slogans and propaganda. And being Jewish no longer mattered either—the Jewish Reds were worse than the gentile. Religion meant nothing to them, only who was bourgeois and who proletarian.

Max Ashkenazi huddled in his bed and asked God to help him. Lately he had found God again. He even went to the synagogue for evening services and convinced himself that his devotion would earn him deliverance from a lonely death among strangers. He pulled the covers over his head like a frightened child and listened to the cracking of frozen pipes, to mice scurrying in search of food, to the grunts and groans of the lovers next door, to the rumble of trucks in the street which made the remaining windowpanes rattle.

SIXTY

THE PERSON MAX ASHKENAZI had been seeking showed up at the House of God like the Redeemer. As Max was leaving the little synagogue where Jews gathered to pray, deplore the falling rate of currency, the shortages, and the demise of Jewishness, a round little man with a smiling face, a curly black mustache, and black eyes that were both sly and ingenuous came up and made a deep, ingratiating bow. He wore a derby, something seen rarely those days in the proletarian city.

"Delighted to see you again, Mr. Ashkenazi!" he said with the deference Max had been accustomed to in prerevolutionary days, when a man's wealth entitled him to certain considerations.

Ashkenazi glanced at the fellow and tried to recall who he was. The round little man didn't stop beaming, revealing pearly teeth beneath a coal black mustache. At the same time he tried to prod Max's memory. "Well, now, take a long look," he urged. "You couldn't have forgotten me already. . . ."

Had this been before the upheaval, Ashkenazi wouldn't have wasted even a second on such a pipsqueak. He was forever being pestered by all kinds of petty hustlers, small-time operators, go-betweens, and sundry opportunists, and he gave them all short shrift. But now that he was alone and desperate, anyone's attention was welcome, and he racked his brain, trying to identify the queer little man.

Finally, the fellow came to his rescue. "Miron Markovich Gorodetzky, *commis voyageur* at your service," he announced grandly. "I should have but a part now of what I've bought from you over the years. . . . But no use crying over spilled milk. . . ."

Something about the little man's costume and manner alerted Ashkenazi that here was someone who might be of use to him, and he decided to encourage the relationship. "You're from around here?" he asked.

"Oh, no, from Odessa. Actually I'm from no one place—I've lived all over Russia—but you might call me a fellow townsman since Lodz has been my base ever since I've been this high." And he held his palm some three feet off the ground. "I came there as a boy and worked for the biggest firms. Ah, a lovely little place, Lodz! Had myself a devil of a time there. The Lodz women—simply exquisite—a beauty each and every one. . . ."

Gorodetzky stuck out the tip of a rosy tongue and licked his lips lasciviously in memory of the Lodz beauties. He began elaborating on his experiences, but Ashkenazi cut him off. He had never been one to appreciate accounts of traveling salesmen's amatory conquests. He was eager to talk about practical matters, to sound the man out and determine if he could be of use to him.

"The seven years of great plenty are over, Mr. Gorodetzky," he said, choosing his words carefully. "No more traveling salesmen. No more business. . . ."

Gorodetzky stopped, gazed carefully at Ashkenazi as if making a decision, then put his lips to his ear. "Pavel Szczinski should have as many boils on his neck as Miron Markovich Gorodetzky has irons in the fire," he whispered conspiratorially, his mustache tickling Ashkenazi's cheek.

"And what does Szczinski say to that?" Ashkenazi asked, pointing to one of the commandant's orders, which covered every wall of Petrograd.

The little man looked at Ashkenazi with the pity reserved for the village idiot. "Szczinski gives orders, and Gorodetzky listens like that lamppost there," he said, first making sure to look to all sides. "Only yesterday I disposed of a shipment of goods for a nice piece of change, the devil take him. . . ."

Ashkenazi felt a shiver of excitement course through him. Providence itself had sent him the very person he had been waiting for. He pondered how best to express his urgency, but the little man didn't give him time to think.

"It was a delight to meet you again, Mr. Ashkenazi. I must confide that I'm not much for praying, but I do manage to squeeze in the mourner's prayer despite my busy schedule. That's one thing that must be observed no matter what. . . ."

"Of a certainty, of a certainty," Ashkenazi agreed, comforted by the importance the fellow ascribed to the mourner's prayer. He went so far as to take his arm, as he had once done with important Russian merchants.

"You're the real goods, all right," he assured the other. "You've got your head screwed on tight. . . ."

Gorodetzky took this as a compliment. "All my life I've thumbed my nose at laws," he confided. "For years they had regulations forbidding Jews to live or travel wherever they wanted, but I've been all over Russia. There isn't a corner of the land that hasn't seen Miron Markovich Gorodetzky. And I slept right in the police stations. That's the best way, the surest way. Now you can live anywhere you want, but you can't do business. So I thumb my nose at them again, and I do just as I please. And right under their very noses too. That's the best way, believe me. . . ."

He stopped again, gazed at Ashkenazi as if seeing him for the first time, then traced a wide arc with his fat little hand. "I've got them all in the palm of my hand, yes sir. Live and let live. . . ."

With each minute, Ashkenazi's hopes soared higher. This was the answer to his dreams. He deliberated for a moment, calculating how best to make his approach. He could have used this fellow from the very start. He seemed one of those people to whom nothing in the world was impossible.

He remembered this opportunistic breed from the old days. With their energy and drive, they could move mountains. They carried the goods of Lodz to the farthest reaches of the empire, and in the process they made the city wealthy. They were loved by everyone, especially the lusty Russians, who appreciated their gaiety, their endless font of jokes, their ability to get the job done. All these fellows needed was one whiff to sniff out the one person in authority who was corrupt and who would help them pull off whatever sleazy transaction was required.

Ashkenazi thought and thought how to make the approach, but the other beat him to the punch. "How did you come out of the catastrophe?" he asked abruptly with a rather devious glance.

Ashkenazi remained noncommittal. "So-so," he said, keeping his tone neutral.

Gorodetzki caught right on and became all business. "It seems to me we might do a little business, Mr. Ashkenazi," he said. "Frankly, you don't strike me as the kind who would surrender everything to those gangsters. Shrewd businessmen usually manage to put something aside. Goods are like gold these days. I can get all the buyers one could want. As for delivery, that needn't concern you either. Just leave everything to Miron Markovich Gorodetzky. As for my commission, we won't have to call in a rabbi to arbitrate. . . ."

Ashkenazi didn't bite immediately. He preferred not to rush into things, but the fellow wouldn't give him time to consider. "If you're worried about the money, I can give you a deposit in any amount and in any currency you want—tsarist, Kerensky, whatever. . . . Or maybe you'd prefer foreign currency? That wouldn't be a problem either. Miron Markovich Gorodetzky has it all. I know that when one is going abroad, it's best to have some foreign currency in your pocket."

Ashkenazi moved a few steps away. "Who said anything about going abroad?" he asked with suspicion.

Gorodetzky grew suddenly very serious. "Listen here, my friend," he said in untypically brusque fashion. "Let's stop beating around the bush. I know who you were, and I know who you are. Me, I've always been a nobody, and I always will be. I have nowhere to go. I'll have to make my way here already. I'll keep going as long as I can. And if I can't, there'll be one Gorodetzky less in this world and one more in the next. But you are another kettle of fish altogether. You've got something to go back to. Leave it to me, and I'll arrange it all for you. I've already brought more than one person out of here through my people. I can show you letters I've received from those I've helped escape—"

Before Ashkenazi could ge a word out, he drew a large stack of papers from a breast pocket and began to riffle through them. He selected one and began to read aloud: "My dear Miron Markovich—"

Ashkenazi held up a trembling hand. "Stop, God save you!" he pleaded. "Why are you reading this to me right here in the street?"

Gorodezky replaced the papers and raced after Ashkenazi on his fat little legs. "Mr. Ashkenazi, God Himself brought us together. We'll do something yet! And if you want my deposit, you've got it. . . . As much as you want and in good Kerensky money, not that Soviet trash. . . ."

Ashkenazi didn't want a deposit, and he held out his hand. "Good day to you. We'll talk again."

"In the synagogue where I say the mourner's prayer," Gorodetzky suggested. "I'm there every day."

He tipped his derby, waved a plump hand, and threw in a phrase in Lodz German. "An honor and a privilege, Mr. Director!"

Ashkenazi parted from him, feeling hopeful and uneasy at the same time. For some reason, Petrograd seemed more alien than ever. The cobblestones burned his feet like hot coals.

SIXTY-ONE

IT ALL HAPPENED EVEN FASTER than Ashkenazi had hoped for. Apparently there wasn't an obstacle in the Red capital the round little man couldn't surmount and Ashkenazi grew simply enthralled by his resourcefulness.

First, he bought the goods Max had hoarded in his cellar. Amazingly enough, it was the men in the leather coats themselves who came to take the goods away in their trucks. Ashkenazi was delighted, and he paid Miron Markovich a handsome commission, which the latter tucked away in his pocket without even bothering to count it. Next, he arranged for Ashkenazi to leave the country.

It all went off without a hitch. He introduced him to a pair of hulking, weather-beaten men, who merely puffed their pipes as he chattered away, then nodded to indicate their agreement. Ashkenazi felt uneasy around the taciturn gentiles, but Miron Markovich reassured him. They had already spirited more than one person across the Gulf of Finland. He, Gorodetzky, had the letters to prove it anytime Ashkenazi cared to read them. The men smuggled food and goods into Russia and went back with an empty boat. They were excellent seamen, and they had never yet failed him. What's more, they were in cahoots with the commissars, with whom they split their take, and he, Ashkenazi, couldn't have been in better hands if his own mother were taking him out of the country.

Afterward Gorodetzky performed a number of other services for Ashkenazi. He exchanged his rubles for foreign currency at the best possible rates; he helped him pack and secrete his valuables in plain gunnysacks.

On the day of departure Gorodetzky and Ashkenazi stopped at the little synagogue for a final prayer. Max Ashkenazi prayed with particular fervor, repeating the eighteen benedictions word by word. He raised his eyes piously heavenward as he recited the passage concerning the evildoers from whom he asked God's protection.

Everything went off on schedule. Gorodetzky had a droshky waiting to take them to the Finland Station, from which the train left for the seashore. It took a long time for the train to be hooked up, and its departure was delayed for hours.

Ashkenazi was on pins and needles the whole time. Each minute was for him an eternity, but Miron Markovich was as calm and cheerful as ever. "It's an old story already," he confided. "Don't fret. It'll all go as smooth as butter."

When the train doors were finally thrown open, a rush ensued. Despite the cold weather, many people lived in the summer bungalows at the seashore, and men, women, and children dressed in sundry cold-weather gear stormed the train, boarding it through doors and windows. Ashkenazi was like a man lost. Never in his life had he been forced to fight for a seat or to carry his own baggage. But Miron Markovich artfully wormed his way through the throng and found a place for them and the packages in the car. Within moments, he made friends with all the passengers, parried witticisms with one and all, and made himself perfectly at home.

"A bit more room there, Comrades. . . . That's it, Comrades, thank you!" he urged and cajoled as he arranged himself and his companion, rolling his *R*s extravagantly in his Odessa accent.

The train panted, whistled, and jerked as it chugged along with surly sluggishness. Like an incontinent dotard, it stopped for long rests at every tiny station.

Ashkenazi huddled within his coat to make himself as inconspicuous as possible. The seemingly endless journey gnawed at his nerve ends. He was deeply apprehensive about the jewels sewn inside his elegant sable coat. Miron Markovich comforted him and even found him a seat.

"Hey there, beauty," he said to a red-cheeked, snub-nosed girl. "How about being a good child and giving my father your seat? You have young, strong legs, and he's a sick old man. . . ."

The girl blushed at the compliment and started to get up, but Ashkenazi wouldn't take her place. He was doing his best to blend into the crowd, but that fool of a Miron Markovich simply wouldn't stop calling attention to them. He repeated anecdotes and told suggestive salesmen's jokes that sent the passengers into gales of laughter.

By evening they had come to the end of the line. Ashkenazi reached for his bundles, but Miron Markovich wouldn't allow it. He picked them up and escorted Ashkenazi to the very edge of the sea. A gust of wind nearly bowled Max over. The air was raw, acrid, salty. The trees bowed as if straining to uproot themselves and flee the desolation. The waves pounded the beach and rinsed the dark shore. Somewhere dogs barked.

Out of the darkness, a figure materialized. Ashkenazi cringed, but Miron Markovich touched his shoulder lightly. "One of ours," he whispered.

The dark figure took the bundles and moved ahead with giant strides. Gorodetzky started to say something, but Ashkenazi clamped his lips. "For God's sake, Miron Markovich!"

Soon they came to a small shack. Their escort knocked, the door opened, and they stepped inside a room illuminated by a dim lamp. Sacks, hides, barrels, and crates stood and lay on the floor. Sheepskins hung from hooks on walls. The two smugglers didn't exchange a word, merely puffed their pipes in silence. One fussed with a broken lantern, trying to repair it with huge, awkward fingers.

Gorodetzky promptly stretched out on one of the sacks and closed his eyes. He slept the way he did everything else— with sound and gusto. Ashkenazi tried closing his eyes, but his excitement wouldn't let him sleep.

For hours he lay awake, awaiting the hour of sailing. The wind howled; the waves pounded against the shore. He kept glancing at the gold watch given him as a wedding present by his father-in-law. The hours crawled like worms. The night was endless. Finally, after many hours weariness overcame him, and he dozed off. The dingy room was suddenly transformed into the bright dining hall in his palace. All the lights were lit, and the table was lavishly set. He sat at the head of the table with his wife beside him, not his present wife, but his first, Dinele. She was as young and beautiful as at their wedding. But even though she was young, their children were already full-grown. They sat at the table with beaming, glowing faces. Gertrud on one side, Ignatz on the other. Haim Alter and Priveh were there, too. Jacob Bunem sat next to him, Max. Everyone ate, drank, and celebrated his return. He told them of his travails, of the hardships he had endured to get home. He opened his valise and gave everyone a present. Soon they vanished, leaving him alone with his wife. She donned a silk nightgown and called him to their pink-lit bedroom.

"I'm coming, Dinele," he whispered. "Wait for me, my love. . . ."

He reached out his hand to douse the night-light, but as if out of spite, it grew brighter and glared into his eyes. He opened his eyes a slit. Two men in leather coats were shaking him roughly by the shoulder. "Enough sleep! On your feet!"

He rubbed his eyes and dazedly stood up. The men wore holstered pistols around their waists.

"Miron Markovich!" Ashkenazi bleated. "Miron Markovich!"

The men laughed. "Miron Markovich was suddenly called away to a wedding, but he sends his regards," one of the men taunted. "Well, get a move on! The truck is waiting."

With sudden, terrible insight Ashkenazi gathered what had happened—Gorodetzky had sold him out! He wanted to scream, to protest the injustice of it all, to decry the wickedness of man and deride his own naïveté, but no sound would issue from his lips. His tongue felt like a slab of leather glued to his palate.

His legs buckled and he fell. The men picked him up and tossed him in the truck like a trussed-up steer, his bundles on top of him.

"Floor it, Vanya!" they urged the driver. "It's getting late, and we've got lots to do yet this night."

The truck lumbered along the shore. The waves charged, then retreated as they had been doing for millions of years under all regimes and governments. The wind forced the trees to bow to its authority and whistled through their branches.

SIXTY-TWO

———

Tᴇᴠʏᴇ ᴛʜᴇ Wᴏʀʟᴅ Iꜱɴ'ᴛ Lᴀᴡʟᴇꜱꜱ lived to see his prophecy come true as Baron Colonel von Heidel-Heidellau was forced to slink from Lodz with his tail between his legs.

When the baron received the news of the collapse of the Hindenburg Line, the uprisings in Berlin and the kaiser's flight to Holland, he first flushed, then blanched, then finally turned yellow as a corpse.

"*Quatsch!*" he roared at his rosy-cheeked adjutant. "Read it again, Lieutenant, I can't see a thing anymore!"

When the lieutenant reread the telegram in an exceptionally firm voice, the baron began to slobber like a hysterical old woman and pound his temples with his fists. "No! No! No!" he wailed. "I won't have it!"

He suddenly resembled an old rooster who had lost his feathers to a younger challenger. Age and infirmity marked his sallow, deeply creased face. His adjutant tried to comfort him, but to no avail. Tears ran from all of the baron's orifices at once —the eyes, the nose, the mouth.

The adjutant dabbed at his superior's flecked uniform. "Colonel, you must pull yourself together. This is the time to be strong. . . ."

"All that's left is a bullet in the temple, Lieutenant." The baron sighed. "It's the only honorable way. . . ."

But instead of harming himself, he turned his rage against the world. After all, it wasn't his fault. He had carried out his assignment with honor, glory, courage. As yet no orders had come down from the general staff, and the baron decided to keep the news secret for as long as possible. No one, not even the officers, was to be told a thing. The press was to be closely censored. Life in the city would proceed in normal fashion.

"Absolute discipline is to be maintained," the baron warned sternly. "If any new reports come in, I'm to be informed directly."

The lieutenant followed the orders to the letter, yet rumors began to circulate through the city. The Polish legionnaires stopped saluting German officers. Students donned legionnaire caps and marched through the streets, singing patriotic songs and carrying flags displaying the white Polish eagle. Despite the stringent regulations, people converged in the streets, talking, arguing, exchanging rumors, and the Polish militiamen no longer made any effort to disperse them. Polish proclamations suddenly sprouted everywhere, reporting the German collapse and calling for an independent Poland.

The Polish soldiers from Posen who had been drafted into the Austrian Army read these proclamations with pride. "We'll be joining the Polish Army now. . . . We'll be fighting for our own country."

The German soldiers' authority evaporated completely. They were no longer conquerors, but a bunch of weary, confused peasants. They loosened their belts, unbuttoned their collars, and abandoned the erect posture into which they had been pounded and prodded. They began carrying their rifles butt up and milled about like a mob, ignoring their officers. "We'll be going home at last," they said with yearning.

Baron Colonel von Heidel-Heidellau's decision to maintain the status quo became a joke. Armed Poles stopped German soldiers in the street and demanded their weapons. The officers resisted, but the enlisted men had no such compunctions. The same home guards who had evoked such terror that one soldier was able to cow an entire village now surrendered their rifles to any schoolboy who demanded them.

Alongside the patriotic proclamations other placards appeared. They began with the phrase "Proletarians of the world, unite!" and called for solidarity among the workers and for a continuing struggle for justice and freedom.

Tevye swept like a wraith through the feverish city, watching the old order crumbling before his eyes. First it was Russia; now it was Germany and Austria. The other nations would shortly fall in line as well. The disillusioned masses whom the capitalists had so thoughtlessly armed would turn their guns against their true enemies. The old world was reeling under all the assaults upon it. The crowned heads were being deposed; history was following its inevitable course. Germany, the epitome of capitalistic power, was falling to the Reds. The whole globe was ablaze. Like fire on a hot day, the flames of revolution would sweep the world. Soon the backward nations—India, China—would rise up as well, all the colonies ruled and exploited by the imperialists. . . .

No, he hadn't been deceiving himself, even though he had been jeered at, mocked, considered a madman. His own faith had already wavered. In the bitter days of the war he had nearly given in to doubt and despair, but he had always revived his courage and maintained his resolve. Now he saw that he had been right all along.

But the old world wasn't going to yield gracefully. Like a wounded beast, it still snarled, bit, and showed its claws. In Poland the reactionaries crawled out of their holes. Church bells rang, and synagogues offered up blessings to the new rulers just as they had to the old.

From his command post in the soup kitchen, Tevye inveighed against the rising surge of Polish chauvinism. The Zionists, on their part, did their best to influence the Jewish masses. Under the Germans they had been afraid to proclaim the Balfour Declaration openly, but their newspapers now carried detailed accounts of the land the English had promised to the Jews, and in synagogues, prayers were offered to that English lord. There was even a demonstration planned, complete with scrolls of Law, Jewish flags, and Zionist hymns.

Tevye knew and feared the power of such propaganda; he knew how easily the masses could be bedazzled by nationalistic songs and pageantry. He no longer bothered to go home but slept on a bench in the soup kitchen and grabbed a bite whenever he could. He used all his waking hours to counter the appeal of the Polish patriots and the Zionists. Besides, it was still necessary to work on the German soldiers before they left the city for good—to urge them to form soldiers' councils and ignore the orders of their officers.

Alongside their Iron Crosses, German soldiers' breasts began to sprout red ribbons. From the commandant's palace, a red flag suddenly began to flutter in place of the imperial standard. German soldiers tore off their epaulets and held speeches, reporting to their comrades the latest developments in Berlin.

One day Tevye himself addressed the German soldiers' council. In the broken German he had picked up from German weavers in Lodz, he poured out his passionate appeal. The men didn't catch his every word, but his zeal and feeling struck a responsive chord and evoked a mighty cheer from them.

The baron rolled up his shade to see what had roused the men to such fervor. With complete incredulity he studied the figure spellbinding his troops. Apparently this was the king of the Socialists, who had given him so much trouble in the past. His first impulse was to draw his pistol and dispatch the Jewish swine, but he held back. In the prevailing mood his men might easily tear him to pieces. He rolled down the shade and surrendered himself to dark brooding. This kind of scum was ruling Germany now. Its regent was an ex-saddlemaker. And who knew what was happening to his, the baron's estate? The lousy serfs were probably stripping it acre by acre. East Prussia itself would possibly be absorbed into an independent Poland. . . .

He felt his eyes fill with tears, and the corners of his slack mouth quivered. Below, Tevye stood on top of a truck while hundreds of German soldiers cheered his every word.

His wife, Keila, looked on dumbfounded. She turned to her daughters and sighed. "If I wasn't seeing it with my own eyes, no power on earth could make me believe it. The world has gone stark raving mad!"

SIXTY-THREE

FELIX FELDBLUM, WHO HAD GIVEN his whole life for a free Poland which would serve as a model of justice and morality to the world, had lived to see part of his dream fulfilled. Poland was now an independent nation. The crown of thorns that fate had placed upon its head had been lifted. The royal castle on top of a mountain in Krakow, where the bones of Polish kings and poets were interred, no longer served as a barrack for Austrian cavalrymen and a stable for their mounts. The Polish flag fluttered over Krakow, as it did over all Poland.

The Krakow legionnaires, who had nicknamed themselves the Crocuses, were now headed for Lemberg with fire and sword to liberate that Galician city from the local Ukrainians, who had claimed it for themselves. Included among the regiments in this army was Feldblum's. He strode heroically forward, leading his men into battle as they bawled their regimental hymn:

> General Roja at our head,
> We Crocuses forge ahead.
> The Russkies we will slay,
> And celebrate all day,
> As the sheenies cry "*Oy-veh!*"

By the thousands and tens of thousands, demobilized soldiers of various armies now roamed the land. They clung to the sides and tops of trains in an effort to get back to their homes in the Ukraine, in Crimea, Podolia, Volhynia, and White Russia.

Chaos and confusion reigned among the troops of the shattered Austrian Army as that multinational, polyglot empire unraveled like a poorly patched garment. The wanton, undisciplined soldiers plundered their military stores, robbed their regimental paymasters, and ran wild through the towns and villages of Poland, killing, raping, plundering.

Ethnic and nationalistic urges, long stifled by dominating

masters, now surfaced. Poles, Czechs, Hungarians, Rumanians, Serbs, Croats, Bosnians, Slovenes, and Ruthenians suddenly discovered their national identities. Alsatians replaced German insignia with French. Poles from Austrian-occupied regions displayed the Polish eagle and bedazzled the Polish girls. Veterans with revolutionary sympathies affixed red ribbons to their breasts.

The only ones with no homeland to return to were the Jews. Hooligans of all persuasions daubed their homes and shops with obscene and threatening slogans. The sounds of nationalistic and religious songs were accompanied by the tinkle of shattered Jewish windowpanes.

The ones to suffer worst were the Jews of eastern Galicia. First, the Cossacks swept through the area, then the famines and epidemics. The younger Jewish soldiers returning to their homes pinned Stars of David to their uniforms. Their gentile comrades jeered them. "Why don't you go back to Palestine? . . ."

The older Jewish veterans were anxious to shed their uniforms and resume their lives. They let their beards and sidelocks grow and thought about rebuilding their homes, reopening their shops, marrying off single daughters. But the ancient feuds and rivalries that had ruled the region for centuries hadn't abated, and each group demanded the Jews' total loyalty and obeisance.

In Lemberg the warring factions took up positions and opened fire at each other, with the Jews in the middle, as usual. Jewish veterans organized a defense corps, and in order not to antagonize either side, they declared themselves neutral. The local Poles signed a pact with the Jews, but they seethed with resentment at what they considered an act of treason. "Just wait till our lads get here," they warned. "We'll teach you sheenies what it is to be neutral. . . ."

When the Crocuses arrived and drove off the Ukrainians, the Jewish quarter was offered to them as a prize. A mob of priests, clerks, streetwalkers, nuns, housewives, criminals, teachers, monks, nurses, and assorted civilians gathered to egg on the conquerors. "Get the sheenies!" they howled. "Hang them by their beards! Smoke them out like rats!"

The legionnaires formed into squads of ten men, each led by an officer and a noncommissioned officer. They quickly disarmed the outnumbered Jewish defense corpsmen and hanged their leaders. They surrounded the quarter and settled down for the night to launch the next phase of the exercise.

At precisely seven the next morning, machine guns were set

up at Krakow Square, Onion Street, Synagogue Street, Zhul-
kiew Street, and all strategic corners. Not even a worm could
escape the blockade. When all was in readiness, the order was
given to open fire. The machine guns commenced their deadly
rattle while infantrymen lobbed grenades into the houses.

Screams rent the crisp November air. After long minutes a
cease-fire was ordered, and patrols were sent out to conduct a
house-to-house assault. A command post was set up in the municipal theater, where messengers arrived with orders and
brought back reports from the field.

The legionnaires battered down doors and shutters and dealt
with the occupants as ordered, while their officers and noncoms
searched for valuables. They tucked the jewelry and money into
their field packs and rolled the less valuable items into blankets
that they stripped off the beds.

In some of the houses Jewish veterans of Polish regiments
put on their uniforms, hoping thus to blunt the fury of their
attackers, but this didn't impress the legionnaires. "A Jew is a
Jew!" they said. "No exceptions."

Young women were raped in front of their loved ones. Husbands were forced to watch as their wives were repeatedly
ravaged. Older women were beaten mercilessly, pregnant
women were trampled, and babies were bayoneted in their
cribs.

"Let no Jewish seed remain in Christian Poland!" the officers cried.

The booty was thrown into army trucks and carted off to
collection points, where it was sorted and distributed among the
civilians. Ladies in furs wrestled peasant women in babushkas
for trinkets. People came in cabs to haul away the loot.

On the second night of the exercise an order came down to
burn the Jewish quarter. Trucks brought barrels of kerosene
stolen from Jewish-owned stores. Straw mattresses and feather
beds were dragged outside and doused down. All exits to the
quarter were sealed off, and the torches were applied.

The screams of anguished men, women, and children rose up
to the heavens along with long tongues of fire and coils of
smoke. The eyes of the onlookers reflected the hungry flames.
"Fry in your own fat, Jews!" they shrieked.

Those who tried to escape from their houses were picked off
by sharpshooters.

Next, the soldiers turned their attention to the houses of
worship. First they stripped them of all their gold and silver
crowns, fescues, and handles, then tossed the scrolls of Law
outside. When two teenagers risked their lives to rescue the

sacred objects, they were shot down. Several of the officers fashioned turbans out of the velvet and satin mantles from holy arks and mimicked Jews swaying at prayer while their men trampled and urinated upon the scrolls. The synagogues were then set on fire.

Inside, a number of the Jews wrapped themselves in their prayer shawls and white linen robes and made their confessions, beating their breasts with their fists. An officer more sensitive than the rest had the doors opened so that the Jews could escape the inferno, but it was too late.

For three days and nights the carnage continued, while looters ran through the quarter, picking through the rubble. On the fourth day the survivors crept out of the smoldering ruins. They dragged away the charred corpses of their loved ones, whose remaining bones would be buried in earthen jars according to Jewish law. The remnants of the scrolls of Law were buried in the same fashion.

The bodies that were more or less whole were draped in prayer shawls and laid out in rows for idenification by relatives. The liberation of Lemberg was reported in all the Polish newspapers as a stunning victory against Bolshevik insurgents. The spirit of independence spread from Lemberg to the other cities of Poland. Jews were dismissed from all jobs even distantly related to governmental concern. Polish soldiers seized elderly Jews in the streets and tore out their beards, flesh and all. Jewish merchants were dragged out of shops and cafés and forced to sweep streets and dig ditches. In churches, priests offered prayers to God and His son who had redeemed the nation destined to serve as a model of morality and justice to the Christian world.

In Lemberg a mass funeral was held for the victims of the pogrom. Among the black-clad thousands, one figure stood out boldly in its light blue uniform of the Polish Legion—that of Felix Feldblum, socialist, champion of the oppressed, Polish patriot.

SIXTY-FOUR

———◆———

FROM ALL OVER RUSSIA people drifted back to Lodz, but Max Ashkenazi wasn't among them. Each day his elderly wife dragged herself to the railroad station on swollen, half-paralyzed legs to ask the arriving passengers if they had any word of her husband's whereabouts, but no one had seen him or heard of him.

Except for her maid, Madam Ashkenazi was alone. But she had never stopped fighting to protect her husband's interests. First it had been the Germans; now it was the Poles. With her rolled umbrella in hand, speaking in a broken Polish, she raced from office to office, demanding the return of her lawful property. The clerks laughed at her and ignored her, but she persisted. The workers, incited by anti-Semitic propaganda, demanded that she reopen the factory. They besieged her apartment and kept food from being brought to her, but she wouldn't give in. She no longer expected anything out of life, but she was determined to live long enough to finish the task she felt was incumbent upon her. When the keys to his home and factory were back in her husband's hands, she could die in peace.

All the letters and telegrams she sent to Max through the Red Cross were for naught. Finally, she decided to turn to the only person in Lodz who might help her, her husband's brother. She knew that he was on bad terms with Max. She knew that Max's first wife was living at the house and that the door might be slammed in her face, but she swallowed her pride and took the gamble. She would do anything to find her husband.

She rang the doorbell of the mansion, and when a maid opened the door, she took all her anxiety and embarrassment out on the girl. "Don't stand there like a ninny!" she boomed in her mannish voice. "Tell your master that Madam Ashkenazi wishes to see him! Do as I tell you, girl!"

From inside the house she heard a piano and a child's

laughter. These two sounds served only to dampen the old woman's spirits, and she gazed with impatience at the door leading off the foyer. After what seemed an excessive wait, the door opened, and Yakub Ashkenazi came out, smiling graciously. "It's a pleasure to have you visit my home," he said, pressing her hand warmly.

She was touched and taken aback by his attitude. She didn't know what to do with the umbrella that suddenly seemed so superfluous. Yakub resolved her indecision by taking it from her. He helped her off with her coat despite her reluctance.

"I don't wish to take up too much of your time, Mr. Ashkenazi," she mumbled. "I only want your advice. . . ."

Yakub pooh-poohed her. "What can you be thinking of, Sister-in-law?" he said, and taking her arm, he led her not into his office, but into his dining room. "You'll rest up a while and have some tea with us."

When she saw the two women approaching, Madam Ashkenazi froze in her tracks, but Yakub gently steered her forward. "This is Sister-in-law Ashkenazi," he announced.

The women came forward with hands extended. "Our pleasure," they said. They asked her to sit down and rang for the maid to bring tea.

In their rather insistent demand for the tea, they sought relief from the strained situation. For a moment the three women studied one another. Looking at the mother and daughter, Madam Ashkenazi felt her age and grossness as never before.

Dinele and Gertrud, in turn, gazed at the woman who had usurped their home and position. Dinele flushed and felt a sudden chill. Yakub sought to relieve the tension with small talk, but his words hung in the air.

It was the child who finally did what the adults couldn't. Little Priveh burst into the room and immediately ran up to the strange lady. Totally uninhibited, saucy, gay, she boasted about her new doll.

"This is my little Mimi," she lisped, showing off the doll in her blue silk dress and red hair ribbon. "And I have a new bear, too. He's very fierce, and his name is Boomboo. . . ."

Madam Ashkenazi hugged the little girl. "My angel," she crooned, kissing the child's plump hands. "You are gold, a treasure. . . . You light up the house. . . ."

The women commenced to fuss over the little girl as Yakub beamed proudly.

Madam Ashkenazi was no longer so anxious to leave. Her in-laws inquired about her well-being, invited her to visit them often. Gertrud went so far as to call her Auntie. Presently and without anyone's being aware of it, the conversation turned to the one who was on everyone's mind.

"God alone knows what's become of him," Madam Ashkenazi despaired as tears filled the eyes of the other women. By mutual agreement, they decided to launch a search for Max Ashkenazi.

First, Yakub would go to Berlin, the only city where Russia still maintained an embassy, to learn what he could about his brother.

It wasn't so easy to go to Berlin those days. The trains were packed with demobilized soldiers, and foreign passports were hard to obtain, but Yakub managed it. He had always known how to circumvent regulations, to cut through red tape. His erect, towering figure exuded such presence and assurance that the guards, flunkies, and underlings unlocked all doors for him.

He was received very graciously at the Soviet embassy in Berlin. They took down his brother's name and promised to let him know the moment an answer came back from Petrograd. But when after two weeks he still hadn't heard anything, Yakub decided to go back to Lodz, then proceed to Russia to pursue the search on his own.

People tried to dissuade him. They pointed out all the dangers associated with a country torn by unrest and civil war. But Yakub was determined. He packed his bags, sewed money into his clothes, took along all kinds of documents and certificates to prove that Simha Meir had been born in Lodz, and made ready to depart.

Madam Ashkenazi embraced her brother-in-law and kissed his hands out of gratitude. She stripped off her jewelry and stuffed it into his pocket.

"Take it, Brother-in-law. It might come in handy," she urged him. "Jewelry has value everywhere."

Yakub protested, but she insisted. She removed an amulet from around her neck and hung it around his.

"This comes from the Rabbi of Karlin himself," she said. "It will protect you from every harm. Wear it for me."

Gertrud and Dinele were as effusive in their farewells. "My hero, my knight," Gertrud whispered tenderly as she had on their honeymoon and kissed his face, lips, eyes, even his beard.

Dinele prepared all kinds of things for the journey—food, underwear for him and for Simha Meir. She blushed like a bride and looked up bashfully at her son-in-law. "Go in safety, and come back with Simha Meir," she murmured shyly. "Godspeed. . . ."

Equipped with valises, containers of food, addresses, currencies, jewelry, and the Rabbi of Karlin's amulet, Yakub left on his mission.

The trains resembled a multinational fair. Demobilized soldiers and civilian refugees clung to all the wagons. Hirsute, starved, pale from years of detention, wearing wooden clogs instead of shoes and leggings of rags tied with string or telegraph wire, with sacks and bags slung over their shoulders, they had to beg a little food to stay alive. There were White Russians, Caucasians, Chuvashes, Kalmucks, Yakuts, Uzbeks, Kirghiz, Jews and Ukrainians, Tatars, Circassians, Cossacks, Georgians, and Armenians.

Disillusioned by the patriotic slogans with which they had been lured into battle for tsar, God, and country, embittered by the years away from their homes and families, brutalized by the pain, the hunger, the bloodshed and degradation, duped, swindled, and deprived by their officers, they streamed aimlessly like stampeded cattle. And ever present among them were the human vermin, the scavengers who in every time and every place nourish themselves on their fellow man's misery.

"Now I'll have lots of land and life will be good," a peasant said to no one in particular.

"They say the Reds are starting a new war," a second veteran said. "This time we'll have to fight our own kind."

"The landowners are back in power in the Ukraine," a third reported. "They say the peasants are being flogged just like during the socage. . . ."

"Not true! The Ukrainians want the bread for themselves. They don't want to share with the White Russians, who want to grab everything for themselves. That's why they're being flogged. All the Ukrainians should get together," a fourth veteran commented sanctimoniously.

"I won't fight no more. Had enough. Now I'll do for myself and for the wife. So long since I've seen her! . . . I miss her so, such a young, fresh woman," a rangy youth said nostalgically.

"You fool, she's got someone else by now," an older man observed slyly.

"Shut up before I smash your jaw, son of a bitch! Don't talk about things you don't know," the youth cried, seizing the other by the throat.

"Easy, brother," a broad-shouldered, pockmarked ex-soldier intervened. "You ain't been standing by her bed either. Any woman would be a fool to wait so long. A woman is like a bitch in heat. If it ain't one dog, it's another."

"That's so. My folks wrote me the very thing about my old

lady," a bearded soldier interjected. "She tied up with another, and she's already got two bastards by him."

"What will you do when you get home?" the others wanted to know.

"I don't know," the bearded soldier said. "Maybe I'll forgive her, and maybe I'll kill her."

From personal matters the conversation drifted to more general topics.

"They're burning the churches," someone in the corner said abruptly. "They've outlawed praying, those Red devils."

"Yes, the Jews have all the power now. They say even the new tsar is a Jew. . . ."

"He's got horns like the devil," an elderly gentile said. "Someone told me the papers said so. . . ."

"Yes, true. It's all the Jews' fault. They started the war to make money. . . ."

"They ought to be beaten."

"We Ukrainians know how to handle Jews," a lame soldier interposed. "The rope is the only cure for a Jew."

The others nodded in solemn agreement.

The wagon seemed to throb with blind hatred, ignorance, animal passions. It choked Yakub like a poison gas, but it didn't deter him from his mission. The train crawled along like a snail. Whole days were lost standing on some forsaken siding. But gradually, circuitously, it neared the Red capital.

SIXTY-FIVE

———◆———

FROM THE DAY MAX ASHKENAZI had been snatched from the brink of salvation and flung into a dark dungeon, he had lost his will to live. His cellmates tried to draw him into a conversation, but he wouldn't answer. Out of sheer boredom the Red guards questioned him about his past, but he kept his lips sealed despite insults, beatings, and general abuse. Each night someone was taken from the cell, never to be seen again. Each time the lock creaked open, Max was sure his turn had come. He had made his confession to God, and he was ready to die.

The guards laughed at him. "Not yet, Little Father. Others got to take their turn first."

"No bullet for you," his cellmates assured him. "They don't shoot speculators, only politicals."

But he didn't believe them. He repeated the psalms he still recalled from his childhood and awaited his end. The other prisoners never shut up. They boasted of exploits, cursed, quarreled, fashioned dough into chess pieces. One elderly man in a tsarist uniform did calisthenics without a rest. Max only squatted on his cot with his feet drawn under him and waited.

The men in the leather coats told him nothing. *When* convicts were executed was not their concern. They only took him upstairs for interrogation, beat him when ordered, then brought him down again.

Max died not once but a thousand times. And being a corpse, he severed all connection with life. He didn't bother to comb his hair or beard; he didn't tend to the clothing which stuck to his body. The other prisoners waged an implacable war against mice and vermin. They squashed the bedbugs against the walls, but the bugs merely regrouped on the ceiling and dropped down onto their sleeping bodies.

Max didn't even bother to brush them away. The guards jeered at him. "That's what happens to them what no longer has servants to do their dirty work. . . . They end up like stinking garbage bins. . . ."

Max didn't respond.

Some of the men took pity on him and urged him to take himself in hand, but he no longer cared about anything. He was immune to pain, dirt, insults, sympathy. His only sense that remained acute was that of hearing. He was alert to every scrape and rustle, to the lightest step of the leather-clad men coming for him for the last time. And as the weeks and months went by, this sense grew ever keener. It reached such a degree that he could no longer sleep nights. The merest sound from the other side of the door roused him. He fell into a state of perpetual expectancy. He was bereft of all fear but filled with the anticipation of his end.

When a guard suddenly burst in on him after many months of waiting and told him to follow, Max sprang from his cot eagerly. That which he had been expecting for so long had finally come. He walked mechanically, not knowing or caring if it was day or night. When his escort led him inside a bright room and pointed to the person awaiting him, Max didn't understand the simple words spoken in a clear tone.

With glassy eyes unaccustomed to bright light he stared at the towering figure without recognition.

For a long while the two men confronted each other silently. Finally, the stranger came up and put his lips to Max's face. "Simha Meir," he whispered, pressing the bundle of rags to him.

The two all-but-forgotten names pierced like a knife through the prisoner's apathy and cleared his brain. At first, his arms drooped like frozen limbs seeking warmth and life; then they began to tremble violently within the other's crushing grip. The cracked, scaly lips opened slightly. "Jacob Bunem?"

He sank to his knees and commenced to kiss his brother's hands like a beggar acknowledging a generous benefactor.

Yakub recoiled: "Simha Meir, what are you doing? God in heaven!"

Max groveled at his brother's feet like an old dog allowed into the house on a rainy night. "You won't leave me here anymore," he sobbed like a child. "You'll take me home with you, won't you, Jacob Bunem? Tell me you will!"

Yakub caught the terrible stench rising up from his brother's body, the stupefying odor of mold and decay. Consumed by pity and revulsion, he grasped Max by his ragged jacket and lifted him to his feet as the tears ran down his cheeks and into the dyed beard.

SIXTY-SIX

———◆———

THE JOURNEY HOME WENT MORE SMOOTHLY than the brothers Ashkenazi might have expected. For a healthy bribe, Yakub obtained seats in the wagon. For a bottle of cognac that he gave the conductor, the latter even took the weakened Max into his cubicle and treated him to a glass of tea from his samovar. The train proceeded slowly. In Orsha, the border city between Russian and German territory, the men in the leather coats and red stars on their breasts passed the brothers through without a hitch. The only problem was that there would be a wait of several weeks before a new train was assembled to Minsk.

Max was afraid to linger in the rough border city, and Yakub asked to see the commissar in charge of evacuation. With his usual aplomb and brass he got past the guards, and in no time he was on a first-name basis with the commissar. Instead of weeks, the brothers had only a few days' wait till a military train was assembled.

Max plucked nervously at his beard when Yakub brought him the good news at the inn where they were staying. "Nothing seems too hard for you, Jacob Bunem," he said in admiration. "You make me feel so inadequate. . . ."

Max felt deeply ashamed. For years he had considered Jacob Bunem a worthless idler and a dunce when, in fact, he was a dynamic man of action. He saw now that blood was thicker than water. When he was in deepest trouble, who had risked his life to save him? . . . But things would be different from now on. He, Max, would know how to appreciate his only brother's love. They would be like one. They would live together, work together, help each other, go hand in hand in everything—in business, in joy, and, God forbid, in sorrow. He, Max, would make it up to Jacob Bunem for all his rancor and hate over the years.

He would also be a father to his children. The moment he

rested up and got back his strength, he would go to France and seek out his son. He would bring him home, take him into the business, and help him establish himself. This way there would be an heir, someone to perpetuate the House of Ashkenazi. Nor would he let Gertrud out of his sight again. She was a sweet child, a good daughter. Even though he had abandoned her, she hadn't forgotten her father. She had personally urged Yakub to come to his rescue. She had even sent him presents.

Now he would be a real father to her. He would rectify all his past sins. And the fact that she had married Jacob Bunem was all to the good. He saw for himself what a dear, sweet person his brother was, far superior to all the young men of Lodz. And he had a sweet little granddaughter now, too. Jacob Bunem had shown him her picture. A little treasure and with a good Jewish name—Priveh. . . .

Recalling his mother-in-law's name, he felt a pang of remorse. He hadn't been much of a son-in-law to her. Because of his greed for money, he had harmed her and everyone close to him. If only it were possible to undo all the wrongs he had committed against Priveh and Haim Alter. . . .

But Dinele, their daughter, was still alive. She had sent him her best wishes through Jacob Bunem; she had forgiven him everything.

How different things might have been if he had had the sense to understand what life was all about! But he had been blind, deluded. All he had ever wanted was money, power. Because of money, he had ruined his life and the lives of others. As ancient Jews had sacrificed their firstborn to Moloch, he had sacrificed himself on the altar of money, had worshiped the golden calf. . . .

Max felt a sense of gratitude toward his present wife, too. Yakub spoke of her with admiration. He praised her business sense, her devotion in guarding his, Max's, property in the face of fearful obstacles. But much as he appreciated his wife's qualities, Max was overcome with feelings of tenderness for Dinele, the first and only love of his life, the mother of his children. How good it would be to spend the last years of his life knowing that Dinele no longer resented him. . . . It would be impossible now, after all he had been through, to resume his empty life in the great palace with only the old woman for company. He would see to it that his loved ones never grew apart again.

A few times he started to discuss this with Yakub, but he held back. Yakub sensed his inner torment and tried to cheer him, but Max felt no joy inside—only vague misgiving and apprehensions.

The ride went faster now. In Minsk, which was still under German rule, the brothers spent only one night. They paid a bundle for a room in a hotel. For the first time in months Max reveled in a soft, comfortable bed. The train to Vilna was jammed, but again Yakub managed. As usual, gold opened all doors for him. From Vilna, the brothers sought permits to take them directly home, but the German officials stamped their travel cards only as far as Lapy.

"Lapy is Polish territory now," they said. "There you will be home already."

In the train heading for Poland, the brothers Ashkenazi detected their proximity to "home."

"Hey, quit pushing, you damned sheenies," the Polish passengers screamed at the Jews. "Get out of here. . . . Go to Palestine!"

Blind hate and animosity permeated the wagon.

"Just wait till we get you on Polish soil," young men in scouting attire threatened. "We'll do you just as we done Lemberg. . . ."

"Hey, give us a shears and we'll snip us a few beards!" a heavily mustached Pole laughed, ostensibly feeling around in his pockets.

The farther the train moved from Vilna and the closer it neared the Polish frontier, the bolder the gentiles grew. The Jews cowered in the corners. Max gazed with frightened eyes at his brother, who sat silent, his fierce black eyes glaring defiance.

The train stopped in mid-field. "Everybody out!" the German conductors cried. "It's only a few kilometers to Lapy. This is as far as we go."

Everyone got out. In front of a small sentry box stood a soldier with a Polish eagle fixed to his cap. A linen streamer strung between two trees bid the travelers welcome to free Polish soil. The gentile passengers broke into cheers. Women dropped to their knees and kissed the ground. One ran up to the sentry and slobbered over his red, chapped hands. "Jesus!" she cried, hugging the youth. "A Polish soldier at last!"

Just then an elderly Jew started screaming for help. From all sides youthful fists pounded his aged skull amid coarse laughter.

"We're home all right," Yakub observed dryly.

The brothers Ashkenazi walked the few kilometers across a sandy plain, their baggage carried by a peasant in a blue, drooping cap. At the station over which the red and white flag fluttered, armed gendarmes rattled the long swords they had only recently acquired and preened with pride.

"The Poles can go. Jews and Bolsheviks to one side!" a flaxen-mustached gendarme cried.

The station, with its huge Polish eagle, portraits of generals, small flags adorned with pine needle garlands, and the inevitable Jesus languishing on his cross, was jammed with passengers and soldiers. At a bare wooden table sat a distraught man in an unbuttoned shirt, pounding his fists against his hairy chest.

"Here, cut open my heart and look inside!" he cried. "I swear on our Lord Jesus and His sacred wounds that I'm no Bolshevik! I'm running away from them! I've escaped from Siberia but I lost my papers along the way. . . ."

"We know all about you, brother," a bowlegged gendarme with a rabid dog's face sneered. "We got information that you were a commissar under the Bolsheviks. We'll beat all that nonsense out of you. . . ." He raised his pistol and waved it over the other's head.

Max felt his heart sink. He glanced at Yakub, who sat pale but immobile, awaiting their turn. Presently a soldier escorted them to the table.

"Now we're going to have some fun," he confided to the other passengers along the way. "It's the Jews' turn now!"

The bowlegged gendarme turned to the brothers. "And where are you two Moshes coming from?" he asked, baring yellow fangs.

Yakub took out their papers and laid them out on the table. The gendarme didn't even glance at them. "Strip!" he barked.

The brothers looked at each other dumbfounded. They were in the middle of a crowd. Besides, there was a woman in uniform sitting at the table. The gendarme shrieked at a soldier, "Strip them down to their skin! Shake them down for anything at all!"

The soldier began to tear off the brothers' clothes as the people looked on expectantly. A pimpled stripling of a lieutenant, with skinny legs, a pointed nose, a pencil mustache, and a hussar jacket draped over one shoulder, sidled over to the table. Yakub pushed the soldier aside and turned to the officer. "Lieutenant, my brother and I are manufacturers and residents of Lodz. I beseech your protection!"

The lieutenant silently took off his hussar jacket and cap, revealing a bristly crew cut. He gazed up at the tall Jew through narrowed gray eyes. "So? Manufacturers and residents of Lodz?" he repeated. "Not Bolsheviks then?"

"God forbid, Lieutenant!" Max interjected. "I've just been saved from the hands of the Cheka. Here is proof. . . ."

"Well, we'll see," the lieutenant said. "Since you're no Bolshevik, you wouldn't mind shouting, 'Death to Leibush Trotsky.'"

"Death to him indeed," Max said with a smile.

"I said, 'Shout it!'" the lieutenant cried, pounding the table.

"Death to Trotsky!" Max croaked.

"Louder!" the officer insisted.

Max raised his voice, but the lieutenant still wasn't satisfied. "Louder, you damn Jew!" he seethed, turning purple. "Louder, or I'll give you something to shout about. . . ."

Max screamed at the top of his lungs.

"Now shout, 'Death to all the Leibushes!'" the lieutenant dictated.

Drenched in sweat, Max only panted heavily. The lieutenant struck him across the face with a riding crop. "Shout, before I skin you alive!"

Yakub strained toward the table, but several gendarmes restrained him.

"Shout!" the lieutenant bellowed.

Max looked around at the faces glaring hate all around him. "Death to all the Leibushes!" he cried, repeating it until he couldn't go on.

"Good," the officer said. "And now give us a dance, manufacturer and resident of Lodz. A nice little dance for our lads. Step lively now!"

Yakub strained to tear free. "No, Max!" he cried.

Max ignored him. He gazed at his tormentors as one might face a pack of mad dogs and began to whirl awkwardly in a circle.

"Faster! Livelier!" the gentiles cried, clapping their hands in accompaniment.

Max spun until his legs gave out and he collapsed.

"Leave him there, and bring the other one," the lieutenant ordered.

The gendarmes led Yakub to the table. He stood there pale but unflinching.

"Now it's your turn. Dance!" the officer ordered.

Yakub didn't move.

The lieutenant flushed. He was aware of his men watching the contest of wills. After a while he rose from place and seized Yakub by the beard. "Dance!" he shrieked. "Dance, you damn Jew!"

At that moment Yakub tore loose and slapped the gawky youth so hard that he fell back and struck his head against the wall.

For a moment no one moved. Then the uniformed woman ran up and helped the dazed officer to his feet. Max crawled toward his brother, standing alone in the center of the room. "Yakub!" he cried. "Yakub!"

The lieutenant wiped his flaming cheek and with a trembling hand began to grope at his holster. He had to tug the snap several times until he got the pistol free. "Stand aside!" he cried, then emptied the pistol into Yakub's body.

"My coat and cap!" the lieutenant screamed, trying to keep his voice from cracking.

Max clutched his brother's head with both hands. "Why did you do it?" he screamed, struggling to raise him from the ground. A trickle of warm blood ran down Yakub's face and into his dyed beard.

From his perch above, Jesus gazed down with a knowing, long-suffering expression.

SIXTY-SEVEN

———————◆———————

FOR THE ENTIRE SEVEN DAYS OF MOURNING that Max Ashkenazi observed for his brother, his brain never ceased churning. He had been taken directly from the funeral to Gertrud's house, where father and daughter now sat in the living room with mirrors draped and chandeliers covered with crepe and mourned their loss together.

On the first day of mourning Max Ashkenazi took no food or drink. Dinele brought him milk to keep up his strength, but he wouldn't accept it. He only drew on his cigars and dropped the ashes on his unshod feet. He spoke to no one and read from the Book of Job:

> Let the day perish wherein I was born,
> And the night wherein it was said:
> "A man-child is brought forth"
> . . . Let them curse it that curse the day,
> Who are ready to rouse up their mourning.

Gertrud leaned over the book and gazed at the Hebrew letters that she couldn't make out but that managed to reflect her sorrow. Max didn't comfort her. He had nothing to say to the daughter to whom he had brought only misery. The only time he had crossed her threshold was after a tragedy. He had brought only death to those who had forgiven him and sought to save him.

He buried his eyes in the book to avoid facing those he had wronged all his life. His present wife sat beside him and with her heavy, half-paralyzed hand tried to comfort him, but he ignored her as well.

"Is there not a time of service to man upon earth?" he read. "And are not his days like the days of a hireling? . . ."

On the second day of mourning people came to commiserate with Max Ashkenazi. They forgot whatever wrongs he had done them in the past and came to him, the former King of

Lodz, now demoted to a tiny bench instead of a throne. They
brought him news of the city, but he had no urge to listen.
What did he care about such things? His life was forfeit. He
was old, spent, broken. He had planned a new life in the
bosom of his family, but God had deemed it otherwise. At the
threshold of this new life He had driven him off like a leprous
dog trying to enter a house. . . .

Apparently he was fated to bring only grief to those he loved.
As one sowed, so did one reap. No, there was no place for him
in the world. His fate was sealed. Somehow he would live out
the few years left him. How much longer could he last, after
all? Why even think of starting anew? He had never had any
great needs. He certainly needed nothing now. A crust of bread,
clothes on his back, a place to lay his head. The sages were
right. There was no difference between man and beast. Each
bore his own burden. Man struggled and strained until he fell
in his tracks, whereupon the others trod over him, later to fall
themselves.

On the third day of mourning Max Ashkenazi ceased brooding on the folly of life and considered such things as duty,
obligation. He dared not renounce his responsibilities. Even if
he himself required nothing, there were others to consider—
Gertrud, Little Privehle, Dinele, Ignatz, his elderly wife. . . .
He couldn't leave them to fate. He had to be their protector,
their provider. He had to take himself in hand and use his
remaining powers to maintain them in comfort and security.
In olden days when a man died, it fell upon his brother to
care for his family. This was a good custom. It honored the
life of the deceased.

No, the House of Ashkenazi couldn't be permitted to topple.
He, Max, would see to that. He would restore it and correct
all his past wrongs . . . pay back his loved ones for all the
misfortunes he had heaped upon them.

He listened now to the visitors who came to pay condolence
calls and paid attention to their comments regarding the state
of business in the city. He still took no part in their discussions,
but he listened. Not that he had any more interest in a country
which had treated him so abominably and so viciously murdered his flesh and blood. No money on earth could tempt him
to remain in a place where a Jew was considered something
less than dirt, something to be squashed underfoot like vermin.
He would go to the Land of Israel, as his Zionist friends advised. He no longer considered them wild-eyed visionaries for
wanting to transform Jewish merchants into peasants. He
realized that it was he who had been wrong. Why build fac-

tories and mansions so that others could snatch them away at will? He would liquidate everything at whatever cost and take the entire family to the Jewish homeland. He would sit in his vineyard among his own kind and fear no one. His life would be secure, serene. He would eat the bread of his own fields, drink the milk of his own cows. The moment he concluded the period of mourning, he would flee from those who thirsted for Jewish blood.

His visitors praised his decision. "Words of wisdom," they said. "If you lead the way, Mr. Ashkenazi, half of Lodz will follow. . . ."

On the fourth day of mourning Max Ashkenazi abandoned his plan to plant vineyards and work the land. This was a task for young people who knew no other skills, but it hardly befitted a man his age to become a peasant. What good could come of it? The earnings were minimal. You needed the cooperation of heaven. You based your livelihood on the sun, the wind, the rain, every whim of nature. You also needed physical strength. Didn't God say, "In the sweat of thy face shalt thou eat thy bread"? He, Ashkenazi, no longer had the strength for this. . . .

Besides, it behooved every man to do what he knew best. No, tilling the soil in the Land of Israel wouldn't benefit him or the Jews. He could contribute more by creating something big there. He would transport his factories there. He had done it before; he could do it again. . . . A nation couldn't exist on only what it grew. The wealth of a nation lay in its industry, and he, Ashkenazi, would establish an industry there, just as he had in Lodz and later in Russia. He would put up factories in the Holy Land. He would provide jobs for thousands of Jews and sell the goods they produced throughout the world, thus bringing valuable capital into the country. Instead of being King of Lodz, he would be King of Israel. . . .

Such an effort was certainly worthwhile. He would show the gentiles what Jews were capable of. What had Lodz itself been but an empty village not too long ago? People with energy had transformed it into a world-renowned center of industry and trade. Now it was time to do something for Jews, as Jacob said to Laban: "And now when shall I provide for mine own house also?"

On the fifth day of mourning Max Ashkenazi's fervor to expedite his new plan cooled somewhat, to be replaced by calm, studied reflection. A man was a fool to fly off half-cocked, to act on the spur of the moment. A man of reason considered carefully before taking such an important step. Better to test the water ten times than plunge in recklessly once. To establish an industry in the Land of the Ancestors was surely a noble gesture, a boon for Jewishness, but to build castles in the air was plainly stupid. It wasn't that difficult to put up one factory or many. The main thing was to have an outlet for the goods these factories produced. Such markets had to be created. True, Lodz, too, had once been a sandy waste, but it had been part of a country that desperately needed goods. The Russian Empire had a population in the hundreds of millions. And what was Israel? A land of penniless Arabs who dressed in rags and didn't need textiles. Nor would it be easy to compete with the English. One Englishman could outsell ten Jews. As for the Jews who lived in the Land of Israel, they were few in number and scholars for the main part. With Jews, generally, it was good to enjoy a Sabbath meal, but not to do business.

And what about the water there? Was it the right kind for scouring the goods? There were all kinds of other obstacles, too. It was easy enough to launch an enterprise; it was quite a problem to sustain it. All in all, the effort presented enormous difficulties. Israel was a land that subsisted on charity, on donations from abroad. If things turned out badly there, the Jews themselves would turn on him.

On the sixth day of mourning Max Ashkenazi listened intently to the merchants and manufacturers who came to him. They all were eager to know if he would be reopening his factory, when he would be doing this and what kinds of goods he planned to produce. The world had begun to recover from the effects of the war. Along with the first swallows of spring the traveling salesmen, buyers, and commission agents had made their appearance in Lodz. New markets had opened up in the neighboring agrarian nations, and all eyes were on Max Ashkenazi, the former King of Lodz. Like children playing follow-the-leader, the merchants and manufacturers looked to him to show the way. "If you take the first step, we'll go along," they told him.

On the seventh and last day of mourning Max Ashkenazi rose from his bench and began to pace through his daughter's living room.

He'd be damned if he'd give in! Just because they, the Poles, wanted to push him out, he would spite them and stay. A plague take them! He had slaved to build his fortune while they caroused with their cards and their women. He had sacrificed his personal happiness, and now they thought they could simply walk in and gather the fruits of his labor? . . . He'd be damned if he'd hand it all over to them on a silver platter!

There was no such thing as getting something for nothing in this world. . . .

If only Jacob Bunem had understood. . . . They could now be working hand in hand to become the masters of Lodz. But Jacob Bunem had chosen the gentile way. For "honor" he had sacrificed his life. What nonsense! If a pack of mad dogs attacked a man, was there any reason for the victim to feel degraded? Dogs were stronger than man, but they remained dogs, and man remained a man. The Jews of old had had the right idea. They held the gentile in such deep contempt that his insults and derision meant less to them than the bite of a mosquito.

No, it didn't pay to give up one's life for such foolishness. The strength of Israel lay not in physical force, but in intellectual superiority, in reason. Since time immemorial, gentiles had persecuted, mocked, and oppressed the Jew, and he had been forced to keep silent because he was in exile, because he was a helpless minority, a lamb among wolves. Could the lamb then oppose the wolf? . . .

Had Jews adopted the gentile's ways, they would have already long since vanished from the face of the earth. But the Jews had perceived that theirs had to be a different course, and it was this perception that had lent them the moral strength to endure and to accumulate the only kind of force the gentiles respected—intellectual and economic power.

This was the strength of the Jew and his revenge against the gentile. Not with the sword, not with the gun, but with reason would the Jew overcome. It was written: "The voice is Jacob's voice, but the hands are the hands of Esau." The Jew lived by his reason; the gentile, by his fists. For hundreds of years Jews had danced to the gentiles' tune because they were too few to resist. In times of danger the Jew was obliged not to sacrifice his life, but to appease the wild beast in order to survive and persevere.

If only Jacob Bunem had realized this! The humiliation that the bully imposed upon his weaker victim dishonored not the victim, but the tormentor. How did the saying in the Ethics of the Fathers go? "Those that drown others shalt themselves be drowned."

He had begged Jacob Bunem not to resist since it was sheer folly to fight against hopeless odds. The wild beast had to be turned away with reason and cunning. But his brother had always been headstrong. He had let his blood, rather than his reason, guide him. And blood was the way of the gentile.

Ashkenazi's eyes misted over. It hadn't been fated that he

and his brother work together, but he would defend what was his with fang and claw. He would again be King of Lodz. Much as they loathed him, they would be forced to doff their caps to him and await his pleasure. He would show them who was master of Lodz. . . .

A Jew's weapon was money. Money was his sword, his shield. And he would use this weapon to pay his enemies back for his degradation and for his brother's murder. But to do this, he would have to keep his head. One rash, irrational act of temper, and the battle was lost, and he, Max Ashkenazi, wasn't about to give his enemies an advantage.

On the eighth day following the period of mourning Max Ashkenazi shaved, put on a fresh suit, and went out to reconquer the city that had once been his.

SIXTY-EIGHT

———

WITH THE ENERGY AND ZEST of a young man, Max Ashkenazi launched the campaign to regain his usurped kingdom. As always, he approached the task with purpose, single-mindedness, and unswerving tenacity.

He began with his palace, which had been assigned as the residence for the new magistrate of Lodz, Puncz Panczewski. A man of his standing could hardly occupy the official residence house, which was little more than a barrack and which had once been used by the Russian chief of police because even though the title was no longer used in republican Poland, Puncz Panczewski was a prince of the bluest blood.

Ashkenazi insisted on the return of his legal property, but the magistrate didn't respond to his letters, whereupon Ashkenazi engaged a team of Poland's finest lawyers and sued. The judges pulled every trick in the book to drag out the case and cause the Jew to grow so disgusted that he'd drop the suit, but the Jew wouldn't be put off that easily. He threw all his resources into the effort, bribed whomever necessary, and got the case heard before the highest court of the land. Eventually he won his suit and forced the Honorable Puncz Panczewski to vacate the palace.

The dour, heavy-mustached magistrate fumed over the fact that good Polish judges would find in favor of a Jew over a Christian. He offered to pay rent to stay on, but Ashkenazi wouldn't hear of it. If he was going to be King of Lodz, he needed the palace as a symbol of his royalty. Besides, it was a matter of pride and revenge. The gentiles had made him eat dirt, and now he would return the favor. This wasn't a railroad depot in some forsaken village. Here he had been king, and so long as laws still prevailed, no power on earth would rob him, Max Ashkenazi, of what was his.

Magistrate Panczewski made sure that the palace was thoroughly vandalized before turning it over to the Jew. His servants smashed furniture, defaced walls. What they didn't destroy, they stole. But Max Ashkenazi did get his palace back, and all Lodz buzzed about his triumph.

"He's the same feisty scoundrel as ever." People chortled. "You can't keep a good man down. . . ."

Next, Max turned his attentions to the factory, now shuttered and half dismantled. It was in even worse condition than the palace. The Germans had removed most of the machinery, all the transmission belts, and boilers. It would take a fortune to restore the plant to operating level, and Ashkenazi was short of capital. In fact, he was virtually broke.

First, he tried to obtain credit at the State Bank. Dressed in his most elegant outfit and smoking an expensive Havana so that he appeared to exude an air of affluence and total self-assurance, he approached the bank director. The latter, who had been a bank officer under the Russians and who knew Max Ashkenazi from the old days, received the request with a show of sincere sympathy.

It surely was a most praiseworthy, even a patriotic gesture to seek to rebuild the industry in New Poland. It would undoubtedly help assuage the problem of unemployment, which was unfortunately very troubling since idle workers tended to demonstrate and bait the police. Unfortunately, however, the director's hands were tied. All of the bank's assets had been allocated to the promotion of agricultural ventures. Perhaps when the nation got back on its feet—

Ashkenazi understood perfectly. The new masters of Poland had no intention of restoring a Jewish Lodz, a Jerusalem on Polish soil.

Magistrate Puncz Panczewski had special reason to despise the city. Even though he held a high rank in New Poland, leadership of its second largest city, he was disappointed. He would have preferred an ambassadorship to Paris or Rome, where he could have associated with persons of his own station rather than with a pack of garlic-eating sheenies. But in New Poland it wasn't the aristocrats who got the plum jobs, but all kinds of shysters, party hacks, and ex-convicts. Only a few members of the nobility had been appointed to high posts, and even they weren't permitted to use their titles on the official papers. His own superior, the minister of the interior, had been imprisoned under the Russians, and he, Panczewski, a scion of one of Poland's noblest families, had to take orders from a common jailbird.

But the worst affront of all had been his appointment to a filthy Jewish pigsty, where he had to mingle with all kinds of herring snappers, to treat them as equals, and even to invite some of them to his balls and receptions. He also had to be nice to correspondents from foreign newspapers, usually sheenies who questioned him closely about the lot of the Jews in his area of jurisdiction. He had to entertain these scribblers and convince them of his tolerance toward Jews.

Lately he had been assigned a particularly loathsome task. An important diplomat had arrived from abroad to investigate the persecution of the Jews in Poland, particularly at the hands of the army. The diplomat had been accompanied by several high-ranking officials from Warsaw, who ordered him, Panczewski, to give this diplomat, who also happened to be a Jew (he even went to a synagogue on the Sabbath), the red-carpet treatment. The newspapers didn't fail to mention that the diplomat was a native of Poland, a grandson of a Jewish tenant farmer. . . .

Not that Puncz Panczewski was any more anti-Semitic than the average Pole. But he preferred the Jews to behave as they had in his childhood, when they groveled before the squire and kissed the hem of his cloak. What he didn't like were Jews with the huge mustaches of the Polish gentry, Jewish bankers with their frock coats, Jewish intellectuals with all their pushy ways, Jewish magnates with their palaces and splendid carriages. So long as the Russians had ruled, he could do nothing about such upstarts. The Russian governor-general himself preferred their company to that of the impoverished Polish gentry. But now that Poland was independent, things had to be restored to normal—the squire had to return to his mansion, the peasant to his manure pile, the Jew to his long gabardine and peddler's sack.

Fortunately many of the ministers shared his views and vowed to turn Polish industry over to Christian hands, particularly in Lodz, the Jewish stronghold. And he, the magistrate, made it his business to expedite this effort in every possible way. He ordered the director of the State Bank to withhold credit from Jews and to issue loans at low interest and long terms to any Pole who opened a new factory or bought an established one from a Jew. He also supported the Polish Manufacturing Corporation founded by the Christian Unity Party for the purpose of developing its own textile factories and spinneries in the Judaic city. He brought down ministers from the capital to the opening of the first Unity factory, as well as bishops and priests, who sprinkled the new buildings with holy water. He called in the representatives of the National Christian Labor Union and persuaded them to grant a special con-

tract to the new factory in which its workers agreed to a
no-strike clause and to submit their grievances to arbitration.
He extended the Unity factories all kinds of credits and sub-
sidies. He himself, along with several ministers and leading
deputies, held large portions of the firm's stock, and they did
everything they could to make the venture grow and prosper.

The Jews sent delegations to Warsaw to point out that by
withholding credit from Jewish manufacturers, the government
was actually promoting unemployment, but Panczewski persuaded the prime minister that Poland's most valuable resource
and prime priority was its land—the vast estates, forests, and
farmlands. If Poland was to have industry, it should be one controlled by Christian gentry and capitalists. Naturally, none of
this policy was ever officially declared since the Poles knew
what an international fuss Jews could kick up when they felt
discriminated against.

The one Jew the magistrate really had it in for was Max
Ashkenazi. It wasn't only on account of the humiliating experience with the palace. It was mainly due to Ashkenazi's
gall in seeking to reestablish himself as King of Lodz. He
would let Ashkenazi squirm in vain, trying to raise credit for
rebuilding his factory. When it all came to naught, the Unity
Party would buy it up at auction for a song. And following
Ashkenazi's failure, the other Jews would vacate their palaces
and go back to their gabardines and their peddler's sacks.

For several weeks Ashkenazi made every effort to obtain
credit in Poland. He went to Warsaw, talked to various persons
of influence. Some promised to introduce him to private bankers; others suggested that he take in a Pole as a front man, as
other Jews were doing, and thus obtain a loan from the Polish
banks. The very editors of anti-Semitic newspapers which
piously deplored such marriages of convenience entered into
these secret arrangements with Jews.

Ashkenazi was offered a very distinguished Pole for a
"partner." The factory would be extended all the credit it
needed, and the magistrate would be brought down a peg or
two. But Max wouldn't go along with such a scheme. He had
always maintained that a man had to make his way alone in
the world, and he couldn't bring himself to surrender a fortune
to some idler just for his fancy name. He was quite proud of
his own name. The name of Ashkenazi represented achievement, intellect, authority. The name might be repugnant to
the Poles, but there was a big world out there where it was
known and respected. He would go to London and have a talk
with the English industrialists. He would convince them to

invest in the rebuilding of his factory, which would be a valuable market for their raw materials.

As always when in pursuit of a goal, he dressed impeccably, and without knowing more than a word or two of English, he set out for Manchester and London. At a meeting held in one of London's biggest hotels, Max Ashkenazi made his proposal. The English didn't care if his name was Jewish or Turkish. All they wanted to know was how they could profit from the deal. And Max Ashkenazi convinced them.

Following his triumph, Max went to a nearby synagogue to thank God for His grace, then enjoyed a delicious meal at one of the kosher restaurants of Whitechapel.

He came back from England accompanied by a specialist his backers had assigned to keep an eye on their investment. Max put the Englishman up in his palace and kept him out of everyone's sight like some precious gem. The red-haired Englishman had some trouble keeping up with Max's German, but he didn't miss a trick when it came to matters dealing with the factory. With the funds he obtained from his new associates, Max not only restored the factory but also imported from England the very latest machinery, which was many times more efficient than that known in Lodz. Everything was geared to the very latest techniques, which were so ingenious and innovative as to astound the local engineers.

Predictably the anti-Semitic press castigated the Jewish "king" for bringing foreign capital into the New Poland in order to enslave the nation to outsiders rather than developing its own industry. The caricaturists had a field day depicting Ashkenazi with crown askew over dangling earlocks. They drew his thin lips thick and pendulous and made a beak of his straight nose.

Ashkenazi relished it all. Nothing gave him more pleasure than spiting the people he despised. Again his name was on everyone's lips; again he was a force to reckon with. Again he sat in his office while a servant in uniform—no longer the aged Melchior—stood ready to fulfill his every wish. Polish engineers, managers, designers, and architects groveled before him, awaiting his pleasure. "Yes, Mr. President!" they chorused again and again.

All kinds of fallen princes, dukes, and barons waited outside his door with letters of recommendation hoping for a job, no matter how humble. Thousands of workers were lined up outside the factory gates with caps in hand. Many still wore their uniform jackets. Ashkenazi gazed out at them through the high windows of his office. For all he knew, they included the murderers of Jacob Bunem. . . . Now they stood for days, hoping and praying for work from a Jew.

Even as the subsidized Unity factories stood idle, Max's plant worked three shifts. Puncz Panczewski himself, wearing a stiff collar and a black tie with a gold cross pinned to it, came to the opening of the plant and lauded its owner for bringing jobs to the depressed city.

Afterward the two men shook hands. Each felt as if he were clasping a handful of thorns.

The towering stacks of the Ashkenazi mill, which for so long had seemed to gaze down upon the city with senile impotence, again spurted foul smoke into the sooty skies. Again the whistles blew, rousing the city's inhabitants from sleep. Again merchants, brokers, and agents crowded Ashkenazi's office. Again his salesmen fanned out across Eastern Europe, reestablishing old contacts, opening new markets, attending trade fairs, shows, and exhibitions.

Again Max Ashkenazi rode down Piotrkow Street, no longer in a carriage, but in a touring car driven by a uniformed chauffeur, who blew the car's distinctive horn to warn the other vehicles to make way for the King of Lodz.

The people followed the wispy figure huddled within the car and mumured in awe, "It's the same old Ashkenazi. Nothing can keep him down. . . ."

SIXTY-NINE

———◆———

LIKE A GLUTTON RELEASED from an enforced diet, the long-starved city went wild, trying to make up for its years of deprivation. Again the police chased pedestrians congregating on Piotrkow Street, and again they were ignored. The jobbers, brokers, and agents were back in their element—scribbling, bickering, haggling, gripping each other's lapels, testing thread over match flames, unraveling fabrics, shouting, jostling, gesticulating—as if nothing had intervened.

Lodz was Lodz again. The cafés and restaurants were crowded with patrons buying, selling, bragging, telling smutty jokes. Cabbies whipped starved nags to rush merchants to banks, stock exchanges, countinghouses. Newsboys screamed headlines. Loaded drays rumbled over cobblestoned streets. Chimneys draped a heavy veil of stinking smoke over every house and courtyard. The hobbled soles of workers' shoes echoed against the cracked sidewalks, and whistles and sirens rent the air with their deranged shrieks.

The poorly printed marks issued by the fledgling Polish treasury dropped in value from day to day, even from morning to evening of the same day. People couldn't wait to rid themselves of them as if they were tainted. Housewives tried to shop as early as possible before their money grew even more worthless. Merchants changed prices even as they weighed out the goods. Some closed altogether to open later when their goods brought higher prices. Peasants wouldn't sell the food they brought in from the country, preferring to let it rot before accepting worthless cash for products they had sweated to grow.

The factories worked around the clock, and everything they turned out was snatched up by merchants the moment it came off the line. The city and the nation were overcome by a fever of consumption. Manufacturers took loans from banks regardless of the rate of interest. By the time these loans fell due their actual value was a hundredth of what it had been at their inception. Customers lined up at stores to buy valuable goods for worthless money. Bank officials were on the phone all day, taking quotations. Curbstone brokers raced around, buying and selling money.

The newspapers put out edition after edition listing the latest currency rates. The treasury issued new money, simply tacking on new zeros to the banknotes. Beggars flung bills in denominations of hundreds of thousands into the faces of their benefactors. Professors and economists wrote doomsday articles predicting the coming crash. Anti-Semitic newspapers blamed the inflation on the Jews. On walls, in marketplaces and bazaars, placards sprang up depicting hook-nosed, blubber-lipped Jewish bankers trampling on Polish currency. Here and there a Jewish secondhand clothes dealer paid with a cracked skull for the perfidy of his co-religionists. Policemen did their bit for the economy by chasing money lenders, who tossed the worthless bills into the gutter to avoid arrest. The landed gentry, the ministers, and the deputies of the Polish parliament, the Sejm, took enormous loans from the State Bank to buy up land, tracts of forests and estates.

In the meantime, people went on with their lives. They married, had children, married off their offspring. Like flies caught in spider webs, the men, women, and children of Balut sat glued to their looms, working until they dropped. But all the millions they earned weren't enough to prepare for the Sabbath.

The chimneys of Ashkenazi's plant belched black smoke into the sky, and its whistles blew shriller than ever as the English machines spit out goods at a blinding rate. But none of this brought Max any satisfaction. He saw the direction in which Lodz and the nation were heading. He knew that the paper chain holding everything together must soon break. And who would suffer from the tragedy? Not the profiteers and speculators, but the innocent, the ethical. Soon the suppliers would demand payment for their raw materials not with the Polish mark, but with stable foreign currency. But there was no foreign currency available in Lodz.

His own position was precarious. He had gone into heavy debt on the basis of expectations fashioned of logic. But in a time of madness, logic became absurdity, and absurdity, logic.

He sat in his large office surrounded by turmoil and excitement but unable to shake off his melancholy. He knew that the best solution would be to withdraw from the collective madness and shut down the factory, which now drifted like a rudderless ship toward its own destruction.

The best course in such instance was to drop anchor and wait for the storm to subside, but this he could not do. If he threw his thousands of employees out of work now, they would blow up the factory with him in it. Nor would Panczewski do anything to protect him. He would catch it from all sides—from the unions, from the press, even from the Jewish revolutionaries, although he employed no Jews. The government might even decide to seize his factory on some pretext or other. There was no such thing as justice anymore under the new regime. A man was no more a master of his own property here than he was across the border under the Soviets. But rather than steal from *everybody,* as the Soviets did, the Poles stole only from the Jews. They only awaited the slightest excuse to rob him blind. Even though the law was on his side, by the time he was through with the lawyers and judges they would have picked his holdings to pieces.

No, he could do nothing to avert the coming calamity. He would let his ship drift until it struck a rock and sank.

The men with whom he did business tried to comfort him. "Let the madness go on, Mr. President. Maybe it will all turn out for the best. For now, things are booming, and everyone is getting by. Let tomorrow be God's sorrow. . . ."

But Ashkenazi wouldn't let himself be lulled by such easy optimism. That was what had brought down his father-in-law, Haim Alter. That was for idlers, dreamers, utopians. The catastrophe was coming, and no blind, silly faith would avert it. . . .

Just as in the past the clatter of machinery had represented cash falling into his pocket, now it symbolized yet another nail being hammered into his coffin.

Still, he rose each morning at dawn to go to his office, and he stayed there late into the nights. His sickly, half-paralyzed wife remonstrated with him: "Max, get more rest. The 'golden' business won't run away, God help us. Think of your health first."

"I can't stay in bed while the factory is operating," he explained, and dressed hurriedly to get to the plant in time with the first worker.

The servant brought him a magnificent breakfast on a silver platter, but all he could get down was a crust of bread and a half glass of milk, the meal of the lowliest beggar. The only things that kept him alive now were his work and his premonitions of the future.

SEVENTY

JUST AS HE HAD MISCALCULATED in business, Max Ashkenazi also miscarried in his effort to straighten out his personal life.

He did everything he could to begin a new existence, one that would make up for his previous mistakes. He had sworn to do this in Petrograd, then in the prison dungeon, and finally during the seven days of mourning for his brother. It was because of him, Max, that his daughter had been left a widow, and he resolved to pay her back for all the grief he had caused her both intentionally and unintentionally. He had also determined to bring back his son from abroad in order to be a father and a protector to him. And lastly, he was anxious to do right by Dinele, to make up for all his sins against her so that her final years, at least, would be serene and untroubled. But the house that he had so mercilessly destroyed would not let itself be put together again. The glue that would cement the broken shards simply didn't exist.

The moment the palace was his again, he insisted that his daughter move in with him. He didn't need such a huge place just for himself and his wife. More than ever he was appalled by the vastness of the rooms, the emptiness of the unused wings. Loneliest of all was the huge table in the dining hall where the couple dined in morose solitude.

Ashkenazi yearned for the warmth and friendliness his daughter and granddaughter would introduce to the glacial rooms. Priveshe's laughter rang like the bell of a merry sleigh when she raced through the spacious halls. But even though both Max and his wife begged her to move in with them, Gertrud declined.

Max suspected that her reason was that she didn't want to leave Dinele alone. He discussed the matter with his wife, and she agreed to apportion a separate wing of the palace to the two women. The present Madam Ashkenazi had nothing against her husband's first wife. They were all of an age when such things as jealousy were forgotten, and all that remained was the easy camaraderie of birds seeking to flock together. But Dinele, too, refused the offer.

Deeply disappointed, Max sent his ex-wife and daughter large amounts of money so that they would lack for nothing. He also saw to his brother's estate so that Gertrud would suffer no financial worries in the future. But for all that, she wouldn't move into his palace or get close to him.

She pitied her father now and sympathized with his loneliness, but she felt no love for him. The years of estrangement wouldn't allow themselves to be erased overnight. She even nursed hidden resentments against him. It was because of him that she had lost her husband. All her father had ever brought her had been anguish and misery. She wasn't religious, but she *was* superstitious, and she believed that her father had always been a jinx to her. She didn't reprove him, for she saw how miserable he was. Life had paid him back for all his sins. Apparently there was such a thing as justice and retribution in the world.

Her mother urged her to take little Priveh to visit her grandfather. "He is still your father," she reminded her. "He keeps calling. He even sent his car around for you."

When, on rare occasions, Gertrud did come to visit, her father put all his business affairs aside. He gave her presents and embraced her. He took little Priveh on his scrawny lap, crawled on all fours on the rug for her, and barked like a dog. That which he had neglected to give his own children, he now gave to his grandchild in excess. His elderly wife hugged the little girl in her half-paralyzed arms, kissed her plump little hands and every ringlet on her head.

After she and her mother left, the palace seemed lonelier than ever.

Next, Max launched a vigorous effort to bring his son home. He sent money, letters. After lengthy urging, Ignatz came. Max didn't recognize him. Before him stood a burly, mature man with nothing of the boy he remembered. His voice was grating and deep, coarsened by the years of military service. Max had to stand on tiptoe to kiss him. Ignatz barely responded to the greeting. He spoke mostly French, which his father didn't understand. He was the quintessential soldier. A deep scar ran down his face, emphasizing his tough, un-Jewish appearance. "Caught this at the front," he explained with a laugh, as if recalling some happy memory. "The bastard sliced me good and proper. . . ."

Ashkenazi recoiled from the brutal stranger. He felt even more alienated around the woman his son had brought with him. She was swarthy with high cheekbones and black eyes lacking even a trace of Jewish origin. She wore long earrings and lots of bracelets over her brown wrists and revealed thin, shapely legs beneath her short skirt. She understood nothing but French. Ashkenazi suspected that she was a native of one of the French African colonies. He flushed when she kissed his cheek with a passionate *"Mon père! Mon père!"*

She carried around a tiny dog, constantly kissed his black button nose, and addressed him in fervent endearments spoken in some strange tongue. She was totally without inhibition. She would rush up to Ignatz, shower him with kisses, whisper endearments, and generally carry on in an indecent manner. Knowing his son's violent temper, Max avoided asking Ignatz any questions about her.

After a few days Max began to discuss practical matters with his son. He offered to take him in, teach him the textile business so that there would be someone to carry on the House of Ashkenazi after he, Max, was gone. But Ignatz refused to set foot inside the factory. He spent his days fencing, swimming, playing with the dog, and squabbling with the woman. During their frequent, violent quarrels she screamed until the window-panes rattled. Max didn't understand a word of the flood of invective that escaped her, but he sensed the passion behind it. Normally Ignatz didn't answer. But when her voice grew too shrill and she flew at him with her nails, he knocked her down like any gentile laborer.

Max's blood ran cold. He felt deeply embarrassed before his wife and servants. But the dusky woman didn't seem to mind too much. The moment she finished sobbing, she powdered her face, applied lipstick and mascara, and began to kiss and fondle Ignatz with the same fervor with which she had attacked him minutes before.

At mealtimes she wolfed her food and drank glass after glass of wine. Ignatz often borrowed his father's car and raced it through the countryside, terrifying peasants and livestock alike. The police kept charging him, and whenever Max needed the car, it wasn't available.

Worst of all were Ignatz's insatiable demands for money. He consorted with all kinds of unsavory characters, gambled heavily, frequented cabarets, ran around with officers, and got drunk. Night after night he was brought home senseless. He also abused the servants and threw magnificent tantrums.

When Max tried to remonstrate with him, Ignatz threatened to leave for Paris.

"What will you do there?" his father asked.

"I'll join the Foreign Legion," Ignatz grunted, glaring with hate at his father. "I'm sick of everything anyhow. . . ."

But Max wouldn't let him go. Again and again he gave him money and bailed him out of trouble, hoping for some change in his son's attitude. But nothing pleased Ignatz. He detested the meals served him; he despised Lodz, its people, its language. He talked only of Paris. His woman skulked about even surlier than he. Once in a while a cloud seemed to lift from Ignatz's eyes. He was pleasant to his father and brought Dinele to the palace, where he clung to her like a child. Max looked on befuddled while Dinele blushed like a schoolgirl.

Ignatz shoved his parents together roughly. "Well, kiss and make up!" he growled, as if issuing an order to a corporal. "Enough feuding already!" And he beamed with pride over his accomplishment.

The swarthy woman clapped her hands. "Bravo! Bravo!" she cried, laughing insanely.

The parents assumed at those times that their son had changed, that he was now ready to settle down, take up a decent existence and provide them some pleasure for all the past grief he had brought them.

But he quickly reverted to his wild, sullen ways, went to Warsaw for days at a time without letting anyone know where he was, and returned in a foul mood. One day he announced that he could no longer remain in the city that stuck like a bone in his craw. He left with his woman and his things right then and there. A week later a curt telegram arrived, informing Max that he was back in Paris and requesting money to be forwarded to his hotel.

Max telephoned Dinele to tell her about the telegram, knowing how she worried about their son. "At least we know he's alive, the bargain . . ." he reassured her.

There was no hope for Ignatz, he knew. He would never amount to anything. He, Max, had wanted an heir to perpetuate the House of Ashkenazi, but this wasn't to be. His only fear now was that his son would convert, if he hadn't already done so, God forbid. . . .

"What did I do to deserve this?" Max wondered. He had worked like a horse all his life, abjured all pleasures. For whom had he worked, after all? Certainly not for himself. He had never needed anything then, and he didn't need anything now.

His entire daily food intake amounted to a few groschen. For whose sake had he begun everything anew? Only for them, his children. And what was the result? His daughter avoided him; his son was a wastrel who despised him. . . .

Following the days of worry and heartache at the factory, he had nothing to come home to but his gnawing loneliness and his sickly wife's groaning. At work he could still achieve a measure of forgetfulness, but the nights were long and unbearable. All kinds of brooding thoughts came to the surface. Hidden ailments of all sorts erupted. His bones ached; he suffered heartburn, stitches in the side. There was pressure on his heart. He had suffered these complaints even before the war, but he had never bothered to consult a doctor—there simply had been no time for it. His work had kept him too busy to think about such things. Doctors had warned him to guard his health, but he had ignored them. He had no patience with illness. He had even neglected his teeth, unwilling to spare the time for the dentist's chair. He would swallow bicarbonate of soda to still the burning in his chest and apply hot-water bottles to ease the pains in his sides and back. He had refused to go to the spas to which the doctors had directed him. Now the ailments came back all together. His wasted body was racked with cramps, aches, pains. His wife urged him to see doctors, brought in the biggest specialists to examine him, but he refused their services. He knew beforehand what they would tell him—to get plenty of rest, to go to resorts, to cease all worry, to get plenty of sleep, and generally to take care of himself.

He wasn't able to follow a single one of these advices. His plant was in terrible trouble. His wife was sick. His house was like a mausoleum. His daughter was estranged; Ignatz wrote or wired only when one of his checks was late. Nor could Max stop thinking about his brother. He still pictured him as he had seen him last—his body stretched out on the ground, with the trickle of blood running down into his beard and coagulating there. As much as he tried to chase this image, it wouldn't go away. He took all kinds of sleeping pills and potions, but to no avail. His system grew quickly accustomed to each one so that they had no effect upon him.

He had failed miserably in his attempt to rebuild the shattered House of Ashkenazi. The shards lay irrevocably scattered, and as he padded through the dark palace in his bathrobe and slippers, the bronze Mephistopheles bared his teeth at him in a malicious, sinister smile.

SEVENTY-ONE

———◆———

THE PAPER CHAIN holding Lodz together burst into a million pieces. The poorly printed marks were taken out of circulation to be replaced by silver guilders complete with the inevitable reliefs of Poland's saviors. Along with the worthless marks also vanished all the work in the city, all hustle and bustle, all trade, the whole paper existence.

The warehouses were saturated with goods for which there were no buyers. The stores no longer sold a groschen's worth of merchandise. The jammed sidewalks grew deserted. In the cafés and restaurants waiters stood around swatting idly at flies. The agents, brokers, moneychangers, commission men, and traveling salesmen sat at tables, scribbling away, but they didn't order so much as a cup of coffee. They only chain-smoked, lighting their cigarettes with million-mark notes.

Lodz had come full circle. The speculators, profiteers, idlers, and various dreamers and hangers-on had managed to land on their feet, while solid businessmen, shrewd investors, insiders, and so-called experts ended up stuck with mounds of the worthless marks.

Just as Max had predicted, representatives of foreign wool and cotton suppliers came to demand payment for their raw goods. But all their customers had to offer were excuses. A rash of bankruptcies erupted. The courts and lawyers worked overtime. The musty, dim offices of notaries filled with husbands putting all their worldly goods in their wives' names.

All factories stood idle. Not a wisp of smoke rose from the sooty chimneys. Workers by the thousands milled in the streets. Huge mobs lined up before labor exchanges, waiting for announcement of jobs that never materialized. Help was needed in France to dig coal, and the men surged forward to sign up. Agents of shipping lines tantalized the people with tales of life in the Americas and urged them to buy tickets and emigrate. Elegant flimflam artists posed as foreign consuls and issued counterfeit visas and passports on the spot. Anti-Semitic agitators vilified Jews for conspiring to ship good Christians out of the country in order to take over Poland for themselves. Priests and monks took up collections for the construction of a new church in the city. Revolutionaries issued proclamations urging a revolt of the oppressed. Secret agents, policemen, patriotic housewives, and students set upon these agitators and hustled them off, beaten and bloody, to the police stations.

"Hang the Trotskyites!" they bellowed. "Send them back to Palestine!"

In Balut, malnourished children peered out from behind grimy windows at the deserted streets. Secondhand clothes dealers walked about with empty sacks, their gloomy eyes cast heavenward but bereft of all hope. Real and pretend cripples crawled and slithered through courtyards, parroting beggars' laments.

The people of Balut had nothing more to hope for. The mills had already destroyed their livelihoods even before the collapse. The Polish and German workers wouldn't allow them into the factories, not even into those owned by Jews. They couldn't collect workmen's compensation since Magistrate Panczewski bent the law so that only employees of large factories were eligible for such payment.

Young and healthy Jewish youths applied at the labor exchanges for the filthiest jobs—digging sewers and building roads —but even this the gentiles denied them. "Beat it, Moshes!" they hooted. "Starve to death!"

All that was left them was charity and the soup kitchens set up by the Jewish community. The storekeepers dozed the days away without taking in so much as a groschen.

All the activity now centered on the railroad stations. Men, women, and children carrying bundles of bedding and Sabbath candelabra filled all the wagons as Jewish Lodz raced to escape. Wives went to their husbands in America, fathers to their children, children to their parents. Farmers anxious to go back to the land emigrated to Argentina.

Jewish boys and girls carrying military knapsacks and blue and white flags set out to colonize Palestine. They sang their Hebrew songs and danced their horas. Those who came to see them off shouted, "Next year in Jerusalem!"

Affluent Jews, accompanied by their bejeweled wives and daughters, took trains to Italian ports; from there they would sail on luxury liners to Palestine. They weren't going there to till the soil and dry the marshes like the pioneers, but to buy and develop real estate, build plants and factories, and restore their fortunes.

Lodz was in a crisis. You couldn't earn a groschen in a city glutted with goods for years to come. Like hyenas, tax collectors descended upon the city to grab what they could for the national treasury. The only people seen in the deserted streets were soldiers and civilian officials in gorgeous uniforms replete with braid and insignia. They confiscated machinery from cellars, stripped bedding from beds, removed food from shops, and took everything away to be sold for taxes. Jewish housewives trailed after the wagons, lamenting as if hearses were removing their loved ones to their final rest.

Business establishments were sealed; jewelry was plucked from women's necks and wrists; men's watches and wallets were seized. The wealthier Jews fled the city, salvaging whatever they could in order to resettle in the Land of Israel and build a new Poland, a new Piotrkow Street in the Land of the Ancestors, in North or South America.

The city gentiles stood before the gates of their houses, watching the exodus of Jews from the land their ancestors had occupied for a millennium. They didn't know whether to cheer or mourn.

Peasants shielded their eyes to watch the crowded trains rush by. Their wives listened to the exotic songs chanted by the Jewish pioneers, and their flaxen-haired children ran out from behind thatched fences with their dogs to scream and bark at the trains and hurl rocks at the windows.

Lodz was like a limb torn from a body that no longer sustained it. It quivered momentarily in its death throes as maggots crawled over it, draining its remaining juices.

And as the city succumbed, so did its king, Max Ashkenazi. Without the smoky air to breathe, without the hum of machinery to lull him, he languished. He lay awake nights, reviewing his life. The images of those he had known and wronged passed before his eyes—his parents, his in-laws, but especially Jacob Bunem. He could see the trickle of blood run down into the beard and congeal there, and his own blood chilled. He put on his robe and slippers and wandered through the palace. He went to the window and looked out at the deserted factory, at the stacks looking like huge extended tongues thrust into the sky.

He went to the bookcase and glanced over the books. He stopped where the Jewish holy volumes were kept somewhat out of sight and took down a worn copy of the Scriptures. He took it back to bed and switched on his night lamp. He leafed through the pages, scanning the moralistic exhortations in Ecclesiastes and Proverbs. They no longer struck him as preposterous ravings of fatuous dotards but as observations rife with truth and perception. He came to a folded page. It was the Book of Job, which he had been reading during the period of mourning for his brother. Eagerly he began to read half aloud:

So Satan went forth from the presence of the Lord, and smote Job with sore boils from the sole of his foot even unto his crown. And he took him a potsherd to scrape himself therewith; and he sat among the ashes. . . . Now when Job's three friends heard of all this evil that was come upon him, they came every one from his own place, Eliphaz the Temanite, and Bildad the Shuhite, and Zophar the Naamathite; and they made an appointment together to come to bemoan him and to comfort him. And when they lifted up their eyes afar off, and knew him not, they lifted up their voice, and wept; and they rent every one his mantle, and threw dust upon their heads toward heaven. So they sat down with him upon the ground seven days and seven nights, and none spoke a word unto him; for they saw that his grief was very great. After this opened Job his mouth and cursed his day—

From the adjoining rooms the clocks tolled the hour. Max Ashkenazi put down the book to listen. Just then he felt his chest tighten as if gripped by steel pincers. He cried and reached for the bellpull, but by the time the servant came his master was already dead. His head had fallen upon the opened Bible, and his fingers still clutched the cord.

SEVENTY-TWO

———◆———

ALL LODZ TURNED OUT for the funeral of Max Ashkenazi. Piotrkow Street was black with people, droshkies, carriages, and cars. Wild-bearded Hasidim walked next to top-hatted bankers, grimy vendors, clerks, brokers, heder students, beggars, thieves, workers. In Max Ashkenazi's passing they saw the demise of Lodz itself. His funeral was its funeral. And they trudged along, mourning not his passing, but that of their own existence.

Three women in black walked just behind the coffin, one widow supporting the other.

The gravediggers had already prepared a grave small enough for a child for the King of Lodz. A stranger recited the mourner's prayer. Men stooped to throw handfuls of dirt upon the coffin.

"Dust thou art and unto dust shalt thou return," they mumbled over their shoulders.

A dense cloud settled overhead. The wind blew dust into the people's faces. With feet as heavy as the leaden sky, they turned back to the sullen, desolate city.

"Sand," they complained, shielding their eyes from the pursuing dust. "Everything we built here we built on sand. . . ."

In the swiftly falling dusk, a flock of birds formed in the shape of a crescent and cawed against the ominous sky.

(Warsaw-New York, 1933–1935)

ABOUT THE AUTHOR

ISRAEL JOSHUA SINGER, the older brother of Nobel Prize-winner Isaac Bashevis Singer, was born in 1893 in Bilgoraji, Poland, the second of four children of a rabbi. At the age of two, he moved with his family to Leoncin, the scene of the memoir, *Of a World That Is No More*. In 1916, he contributed to Yiddish newspapers in Warsaw and then in Kiev, and in the latter city his short story, "Pearls," was published, which brought him immediate recognition.

In 1921, I. J. Singer was hired as a correspondent for the *Jewish Daily Forward*. This association lasted until the author's death, and his articles were compiled in the book *New Russia*. In 1927 he wrote his first novel, *Steel and Iron*, which was followed, five years later, by *Yoshe Kalb*. I. J. Singer came to the United States in 1934. He died in New York on February 10, 1944.

Distinguished works of fiction,
now in new editions from

BANTAM WINDSTONE BOOKS

THE CONFESSIONS OF NAT TURNER by *William Styron* (#14668-8 • $3.95)
This Pulitzer Prize-winning novel by the author of SOPHIE'S CHOICE is the brilliant story of an American slave revolt led by a remarkable preacher named Nat Turner. *The New York Times* called this novel "magnificent ... one of those rare books that shows us our American past, our present—ourselves—in a dazzling shaft of light."

GILES GOAT-BOY by *John Barth* (#14705-6 • $4.95)
This bawdy, wickedly funny novel by the author *The New York Times* calls "the best writer of fiction we have in America" features the incredible George Giles, conceived of by a computer, born of a virgin and reared on a goat farm among bucks and does.

NIGHT OF THE AUROCHS by *Dalton Trumbo* (#13919-3 • $3.95)
This gripping final masterpiece by the author of JOHNNY GOT HIS GUN examines the Holocaust from the point of view of the executioner and discovers "that dark yearning for power that lurks in all of us ... the exquisite perversion when power becomes absolute."

VISION QUEST by *Terry Davis* (#14815-X • $2.50)
This exciting novel by a major new voice in American fiction is at once exuberant and grave, funny and gentle. It has been called by John Irving "the truest novel about growing up since THE CATCHER IN THE RYE."

Read all of these Bantam Windstone Books, available where-paperbacks are sold.

Here are the Books that Explore the Jewish Heritage-Past and Present.

Fiction

☐	14867	**Exodus** Leon Uris	$3.95
☐	14701	**Mila 18** Leon Uris	$3.50
☐	13564	**Holocaust** Gerald Green	$2.50

Non-Fiction

☐	01265	**The Jewish Almanac** Siegel & Rheins, eds.	$9.95
☐	20153	**Children of the Holocaust** Helen Epstein	$3.25
☐	13810	**World of Our Fathers** Irving Howe	$3.95
☐	13807	**A Treasury of Jewish Folklore** Nathan Ausubel, Ed.	$3.95
☐	14420	**The New Bantam-Megiddo** **Hebrew & English Dictionary** Levenston & Sivan	$2.95
☐	14331	**Treasury of Jewish Quotations** Leo Rosten	$3.95
☐	11170	**Wake Up, Wake Up, To Do the** **Work of the Creator** William B. Helmreich	$2.25
☐	20530	**The War Against the Jews** Lucy S. Dawidowicz	$3.95